AS FATE WOULD HAVE IT

DAVID M. BROOKS

ILLUSTRATION BY VICTOR GUIZA

outskirts press

As Fate Would Have It

v2.0

This is a work of fiction. Names, characters, businesses, places, events, locales, and incidents are either the products of the author's imagination or used in a fictitious manner. Any resemblance to actual persons, living or dead, or actual events is purely coincidental.

The opinions expressed in this manuscript are solely the opinions of the author and do not represent the opinions or thoughts of the publisher. The author has represented and warranted full ownership and/or legal right to publish all the materials in this book.

Outskirts Press, Inc.
http://www.outskirtspress.com

ISBN:978-1-9772-3960-0

Cover illustrated by Victor Guiza

First Edition

PRINTED IN THE UNITED STATES OF AMERICA

Dedicated to
Faith Mackenzie Shaw
(2001-2019)

And all those who are born
To a fate that is not of their choosing,
Yet proudly create their own destiny.

Part One

"...What a long strange trip it's been."
---The Grateful Dead

1

It was always the same…to a point. Chris can see the small crowd of seven dressed in black, hooded robes gathered around the casket at the top of the hill. The features of their faces are indiscernible, deep in the shadows of their hoods. Their heads are bowed as if in silent prayer, their black-gloved hands clasped together before their waists.

The Priest standing at the head of the casket also wears a black, hooded robe with his face equally concealed. He is reading from a large, worn black book that he holds delicately in his two large hands. He wears the same robe as the mourners around the freshly dug grave but his long, white, bony fingers are free of gloves, perhaps to make it easier to turn the pages as he reads. The Priest also wears a red band tied around his waist, while the others wear a black one around theirs. The Priest towers over the others, standing tall at six and a half feet, while the rest of the mourners surrounding the gravesite are all no more than five feet in height.

The casket they are gathered around is suspended over an open hole in the ground awaiting the Priest's final words of comfort for the living before being lowered to its final resting place. Chris is still far enough down the hill that he can't make out the words the Priest is reciting from his Bible, but between the low breaking waves of the wind gently urging him on from his back, he is able to hear some of the chanting, yet doesn't believe they sound like any words he has ever heard before, let alone understood.

Chris slowly makes his way up the winding path between scattered tombstones on both sides. The faces of the old, gray markers seem to be watching Chris as he passes. Somewhere on a subconscious level he is asking himself if it is even possible, if the dead resting under these final acknowledgements of their lives could be watching him as he slowly ascends the hill. Subconsciously he feels as though he is interrupting a play in progress, as if he is walking across center stage as the actors in black on the hill remain in character, continuing their story, uninterested in his approach. Yet the audience, the gray and decaying faces etched with memories of better days, the tombstones, have shifted their attention to the newcomer, to himself. Subconsciously he feels many eyes upon him. But on a conscious level, his own eyes and mind are fully riveted on the approaching scene at the apex of the hill.

He is reluctant to go up the hill but he knows he cannot retreat. When he stops walking, he feels the wind pick up behind him as if laying a gentle but firm hand on his back to coax him along in the right direction. The sun is beginning to sink behind the hill. The sky directly above is still a cloudless, slowly darkening blue, but the sky peeking out from behind the burial mound is a combination of a deep red and a brilliant, fiery yellow, causing what appears to be a strange glowing aura around the silhouettes of the ominous looking group clad in black surrounding the casket.

The air around him feels heavier than normal and he seems to have to swallow each breath into his lungs and then let it out again slowly, cautiously. There is a scent of wet grass in the wind, sweet like a freshly mown lawn on a dewy spring morning, but its taste seems tainted with something less pleasant, something dead, as it wisps past his lips in its gentle gusts. He dreads reaching the top of the hill, but he also senses that he wants to get there, if he must, before the sun's light loses its hold on the day.

As Chris nears the site atop the hill, all the mourners in black, slowly, appearing as unsurprised as though it were called for in their previously read and well-rehearsed scripts, turn to face him and watch him approach. Even the Priest falls silent, closes his book, and shifts his attention from the Bible in his hands to the newcomer. Yet even as Chris approaches the site, their faces remain eerily just out of sight with the sun at their backs.

Chris stops walking, again wanting to turn and run in the opposite direction, but the wind behind him urges him forward with increased force. The day is still hot even as the sun sinks into the earth and his hands and face are drenched in sweat as he takes a few more steps toward the small crowd.

He can't take his eyes off the closed coffin, yet he can feel all the other eyes on himself. The coffin itself is a deep ebony, with elaborate carvings in its side in the same dark black, only revealing their presence as he approaches the fresh hole in the ground.

As Chris reaches the site, standing at the foot of the hole, he looks up at the Priest standing on the other side. The Priest says nothing but slowly bows his head again towards the coffin, willing Chris' eyes to follow. Again, the wind picks up, chilling the sweat on his face and raising goose bumps on his arms. He can still feel the watching eyes of the audience now behind and below him, senses an anticipation with their gaze causing more sweat to fill his pores and be chilled by his skin.

Chris opens his mouth to ask the Priest who is in the coffin but then thinks better of speaking to the Holy Man. Something about him scares Chris in a way he doesn't want to think about. He looks back at the coffin. He knows he will see who is in the coffin soon. He always does.

He watches helplessly as the coffin lid slowly opens on its own.

Chris woke up feeling a bit disoriented, lost and exhausted, the face in the coffin still lingering on the edges of his mind. It was a new face again, no one he knew or recognized. He had known none of them, in fact, since the first, but that didn't eliminate his ever-present fear that he would know the next one. And he usually knew when a new face was going to appear. No, he *always* knew when a new face was going to appear. That was part of the problem.

He drags himself out of bed and into the shower where he tries to wash away the remnants of this recurring dream each day upon awakening. The memories rarely fade, but the feel of the warm water running over his face, the enveloping and seemingly purifying heat that pounds against his skin, is needed. It makes him feel a bit cleaner just beneath his skin, nearer to the soul. The dream always makes him feel used and violated in a way he can't quite explain even to himself. It leaves him feeling as though he has done something wrong, trespassed where he shouldn't be trespassing, dabbled where he shouldn't be dabbling. But most of all, it leaves him feeling tired. So very, very tired.

The first time he had had this dream, he had seen the face of his girlfriend in the coffin, or his ex-girlfriend, as she had just become at the time. When the dreamland coffin had opened and he stood gazing at her face, her eyes had suddenly opened, seeing only him.

"YOU DID THIS TO ME!" she had yelled as she lay there. "THIS IS YOUR FAULT!"

Chris had bolted awake immediately, his pillow drenched in tears mixed with the sweat running down his face. The dream had been so vivid and seemed so real and had refused to fade from his consciousness the way most dreams do upon awakening.

As soon as he began to recognize the familiar surroundings of his bedroom and realized that it had been just a dream, he had raced to the hospital to see her, sure that she had died during the night.

She hadn't.

He ran down the hospital's corridor without stopping at the receptionist's desk on her floor to ask a nurse of her condition, despite the fact that Sherry, his (ex)girlfriend, had said she never wanted to see him again. Without thinking, he burst into her room sure that her bed was going to be empty.

It wasn't.

Sherry awoke with a start as the door to her room swung open and banged loudly against the wall.

"What the hell are you doing here?" she sneered at him as she realized who had wakened her. "I thought I told you I never wanted to see you again! Look what you've done to me!"

"I am so sorry," was all Chris could think to say as he lowered his head and turned back towards the door he had just bounded through. "I just needed to make sure you were okay."

"Oh, I'm okay, if you consider never being able to walk again as okay," she said sarcastically as tears began to well up in her eyes. "Now get out of here!" she screamed. "I meant it when I said I want you out of my life!"

Chris retreated back through the doorway, quietly closing the door behind him. He was glad she was okay, well…at least not dead like his dream had wanted him to believe. It was true that she was never going to walk again. And it was true that it was his fault, or at least he never argued with her that it hadn't been.

In fact, it had not been directly his fault, but he had been the one to talk her into bungee jumping with him. *If only she could have landed on top of me when the bungee cord had snapped instead of the other way around,* he wished silently. But that hadn't been his fate apparently. What had happened had simply happened, and he could never change that. There was no going back. Now, six months later, he was still trying to learn how to live with it.

It had been only their third date. A mutual friend had set them up on a blind date a week earlier and they had seemed to hit it off well right from the get-go.

Chris was 29 years old, a well-groomed, tall, and very shy desk clerk. Most women considered him a head-turner with his dark eyes, dark hair and dark complexion. He'd been thin and lanky most of his life, but over the last few years of his early adulthood, he had filled out his six-foot two-inch frame rather well. But his shyness had kept him humble…and single. He never complained of his single status. In fact, he often gloated playfully about his being "his own master" to the growing number of his friends getting married whenever they asked when he was going to get around to finding "the one." Despite his faithfulness and loyalty to singledom, his friends still enjoyed setting him up on the occasional blind date, which he allowed them to do more than he actually cared for, to humor them more than anything else.

Sherry was 24 years old and fresh out of college. She had no idea what to do next with her life but was ready to see what the world had to offer. Quite a looker herself with her long slender legs and long blond hair, the two looked very comfortable together and hadn't stopped smiling since they had been introduced. Chris was just beginning to feel that maybe his married friends could be on to something, and Sherry had been able to think of no complaints thus far either.

On their fateful third date, Chris and Sherry had gone to the State Fair to see *Classified Trash*, a new bluesy metal band they had both heard for the first time on the radio during their first date and had instantly liked. Having both liked the song they had heard from the new group, they had dutifully and romantically declared the song "*Baby Whatcha Gonna Do (For The Rest Of Your Life),*" by *Classified Trash* as "their song."

They arrived two hours before *Classified Trash* was scheduled to play and had walked the fairgrounds merrily chatting and people-watching, enjoying their new-found puppy-love. Chris had always loved roller coasters and thrill rides. He had never bungee-jumped before, but it had been high on his list of things to experience the moment the craze had become popular. They found themselves by the bungee cord apparatus and watched a few people jump off the metal tower and fly towards the ground, only to be snatched back up about twenty feet before hitting a giant air-mattress. After two or three bounces on the bungee cord, the thrill-seekers were slowly lowered to the mattress where they slid the remaining six feet down its side to solid ground.

Chris decided the time was right for him to try it himself. To fly, if only for a moment, without wings. Other thrills on his list of things to be experienced at least once in his life, things like hang gliding, parachuting, mountain climbing, pyramid exploring, were equally high priorities, if not more so, but bungee jumping was the only one before him at the moment, presenting him an opportunity to cross one off the list.

After purchasing a ticket from the grungy man in the tiny square hut beside the entrance for twenty-five bucks, the going rate for a few seconds of terror (not to mention a chance to impress his new girlfriend…a fair price, he figured), he passed along his ticket to an equally distracted and slightly grumpy looking man at the gate. Next, he proceeded to a third man who strapped him into a harness for the ride. Then he climbed the 100-foot tower and walked boldly out to the edge where a fourth man waited with the final safety instructions and told him he could jump whenever he was ready.

Chris had taken the next step without hesitation. He had heard of people dying doing this, but he figured just as many people drowned in their own bathtubs every year and that didn't stop him from taking a bath, so he wasn't particularly worried about the dangers in bungee-jumping. Besides, he and Sherry had just watched several jumpers take that leap of faith and every one of them came away saying, "Wow! That was great!" So, stepping off the tower had come easily for him, and his reaction, as he approached Sherry after sliding off the giant cushion, had been the same as the others he had witnessed returning from the thrill.

"Wow, Sherry. That was great!" he said, all smiles. "You have got to try it once."

"No way," Sherry had replied. "Flying isn't one of this featherless creature's ideas of fun," she added with a giggle.

"You've never flown?" he asked.

"No."

"What's your favorite food?" Chris asked, not willing to let her off the hook quite *that* easy.

"Pizza. But what's that got to do with the price of tombstones?" she quipped back.

"Say you'd never eaten or tasted a pizza before," he reasoned, "then you wouldn't know what you're missing. Same thing here. It's wonderful and you don't know what you are missing out on."

"People have died on that thing, Chris. You call that fun?" She pushed out a pouting lower lip as she said this, but the smile had not disappeared altogether.

"No one has died on *this* one," he replied with a wink. He wasn't positive whether that was true or not, but figured it probably was. "That was mostly when bungee-jumping was new. People didn't take the same precautions they do these days."

Chris had been steering them back towards the man in the hut as they talked. He pointed up at the pricing chart. "Look. You can even go two at a time. How about if we go together? I'll keep you company so you won't get too scared. Come on," he prodded, "it'll give us something to tell our kids."

He winked again at her and even though she knew he was just teasing her, it was his charming, confident wink that had weakened her resolve and caused her to agree to just one jump… on the grounds that he would never ask her to do something like this again.

Chris triumphantly agreed, paid the man at the counter another thirty-five bucks, the discounted price for two, and the two young lovers got harnessed up and climbed the tower.

Their cord had snapped on its way back up from its first extension and the two of them had fallen the remaining twenty feet to the air-mattress. They had gotten their legs tangled up together as their limbs flew everywhere, reaching for anything to grab, but of course nothing was there. They had bounced together off the mattress in a tangled human ball and rolled down its side to the hard earth awaiting gravity to enforce its law. Chris landed on Sherry's back, bending it in ways in which a back was not meant to bend.

They were both rushed off to the hospital. Chris had been knocked out cold and suffered a mild concussion while Sherry had broken her spine and was paralyzed from the waist down. Three days after the accident, Chris had been released. Sherry was still in critical, but stable condition.

He stayed with her in the hospital, along with Sherry's parents, until she awoke for the first time since the accident, almost a week and four extensive surgeries later. At first, she looked confused as she scanned the room with eyes squinting against the brightness.

As she began to regain her focus, she saw her parents standing over her with their *"my poor baby"* faces on. Next, she became aware of the fact that she was not at home in her soft and fluffy bed where her parents had last stood over her in this manner as she awoke from a long fever once when she had been sixteen. The bed was hard and cold, the sheets a spotless white that seemed to intensify the brightness that still slightly burned her tender eyes.

The last time had been bad enough. She had later discovered in talking with her parents that the doctor had actually assigned a percentage of a chance of survival to her condition. It had been an 80% chance, a very good chance indeed, but it is still a bit unsettling to know that your life has as good a chance to live as a sunny day sometimes has for an unexpected rain shower. Sometimes it can rain when you least expect it.

Sherry had gone with the odds on that occasion, remaining sunny and bright as the clouds blew innocently by. She had awakened as her fever returned to a manageable level to see her parents leaning over her, smiling and telling her that they loved her, but with very tired and sympathetic faces. This time, however, a visible sorrow remained in her parents' faces as she saw them lean in and over her. A sadness remained in their eyes where she had seen relief on the previous occasion. She instantly understood that this time might not be as good as the 80% chance she had had before. She struggled to mentally shake off the blankness in her mind that still concealed the events that had led her to her current situation.

Then she saw Chris. He was standing slightly back and to the right of her parents. Everything came back to her in a massive and cruel flood of understanding. The large steel frame, the harness, the cord, the last step off the platform; the fall, the helpless feeling as she grasped the air for purchase of anything, the feel of the plastic airbag as they first made contact. And then the crack. She remembered hearing the crack as she had felt the airbag's yielding contact replaced by the hard earth. That was the last thing she remembered…but it was enough.

Anger flared up inside her as her first reaction to seeing Chris. She remembered not wanting to do the bungee jump. She remembered trusting Chris. She remembered that awful *crack*. He was the one who had brought this misfortune upon her. It was his fault that she was in whatever kind of mess she was in.

Not having the strength to relay the message she desperately wanted to direct at Chris, she slowly shifted her gaze back to her mother and father and weakly said, "Will you ask him to leave? Tell him I never want to see him again." Then she calmly closed her eyes awaiting to hear her parents carry out her request.

They hadn't needed to say a word to Chris. As they turned and looked at him, prepared to carry out their daughter's instructions, he saw the hurt, and the hate that hadn't been there a little while earlier, in their eyes and simply turned and walked out of the room without another word.

It was that night that he had his first dream.

2

It was two a.m. Monday morning and Chris found the mountain of papers to be delivered in their usual spot on his half of the duplex's shared driveway outside his garage door. Ever since he and Sherry had taken their fateful plunge together six months earlier, Chris had become quite withdrawn from the rest of the world. He had quit his full-time job as a desk clerk for Holiday Inn shortly after the accident despite the manager's understanding and willingness to give Chris as much time off as he needed to recover. But he didn't want to be around people. At least not now. Not yet. Not for a while. He needed time.

Slowly he had acquired more and more paper routes for what had been his part-time job, turning it into full-time work. Delivering newspapers out of his car, he didn't need to deal with people. There were no questions to answer, no looks to ignore, no pity, no stress. Chris tooled along the streets of his neighborhood and surrounding areas, never traveling more than five miles per hour, driving down the wrong side of the streets from mailbox to mailbox during the wee hours of the morning when the night is at its darkest. Leaning out of his driver-side window, rain or snow or five-below, seven mornings per week, he stuffed the morning newspaper into plastic tubes attached to the sides of the mailbox posts.

The 'tool of his trade' was a brand new, dark purple Dodge

Caravan. He had traded in his ten-year-old Honda Civic with just over 150,000 miles on it. His Dad had gotten it for him as a graduation present. New way back then, it was the only car he had ever owned, but lately it had seemed to be spending more time in the shop than in his garage. His new mini-van with the sliding back doors on either side for easy loading and unloading of his paper routes was the only item he had purchased with the money from the insurance settlement. The rest he had tucked away into a savings account in case he hadn't found new work for a while after not returning to the Holiday Inn.

He hadn't planned on turning his part-time paper route into a full-time bacon basket; at first it had seemed only a means of keeping busy through the dark nights while at the same time not having to really concentrate on anything very hard. Working the early morning hours of two a.m. to seven a.m. felt serene and relaxing. He ignored most of the stop signs, the only light on the street coming from his own car's headlamps, the only lights on the houses from his orange flashers reflecting off the panes of glass in the dark windows. Occasionally he would run across another vehicle with its dome light bright, its driver under the yellowish glow inside the car thumbing through a list of addresses looking for his next stop to deliver a rival newspaper. The two vehicles would quickly flash their high-beam headlights at one another, a late night/early morning comrade's salute to each other in recognition of their common solitude and tasks, much the way passing motorcyclists on the freeway feel an obligation to wave at each other even from across the medians as they pass in opposite directions, or the way mailmen and bus drivers always wave at like vehicles passing them whether they can actually see the other driver or not. The few carriers out combing the neighborhoods while all their neighbors sleep feel a certain bond in sharing the darkness together in a much less populated world than those working by the sun's light. But the 'high-beam salute' was as close as they ever got to contact, their only form of communication, which was, in Chris' mind, just another benefit of the job.

Each morning as the darkness slowly began to give way to the light of a new day, Chris would empty his mini-van of his nightly papers and return home to crawl tiredly into bed. Sleeping during the morning daylight hours seemed to help his mental state a bit. When waking suddenly from his recurring dream, he would awaken with the sun filtering in through the slats of the blinds covering his bedroom windows. He discovered it was easier on his nerves waking in the dim light, being able to readily identify with his surroundings without waiting for his eyes to adjust to the blackness of the night.

Another benefit to his new career in the night.

He had grown to expect his daily trek through the graveyard, but he still felt uneasy each morning as he closed his eyes in search of the seemingly ever-needed rest.

He had seen Sherry again each night in his dreams. The second night he climbed the hill to her dreamland gravesite she had become calm. When the coffin opened and she looked at Chris through eyes that seemed to be missing the sparkle and life they had once held, she spoke softly,

"I'm sorry, Chris. I know I can't blame you. Not really."

"If I could trade places with you, Sherry, I would," Chris replied. "I'm so sorry I made you jump with me."

"It wasn't your fault," she repeated. "If it hadn't snapped on us, then it would have snapped on the next unfortunate pair. Bad luck is all it was. Very bad luck. And I was weak for giving in to you. I blame myself more than anything else."

"No, you shouldn't..." Chris began to respond, but then just couldn't think of anything he could say that could help her predicament.

She lay still in her coffin, devoid of emotion, her eyes seeming to focus somewhere behind him, through him. A few long, quiet seconds passed. Then Sherry almost whispered,

"This is my fate. I'll be okay. I'll be moving on soon."

Her skin, like her eyes, seemed to be lacking animation. Her color appeared dull and flat, almost fading. He wasn't sure, but he thought she even looked to be a bit more faded than in their first short encounter on the previous night.

Chris awoke once again with Sherry's voice still echoing in his ears. *Had we really spoken to each other somehow?*

A shiver coursed down his spine.

Ultimately, as he stood motionless in the shower with his eyes held tightly shut, his face directly under the warm, pulsating water, he decided it had just been his subconscious trying to relieve some of the guilt he was willingly burdening himself with. He certainly didn't want to mistakenly barge into Sherry's room again thinking she had forgiven him in a dream only to have her chase him out a second time with her rage and hate. But her voice, still in his head, seemed to have been so real. The repeated dream, in all its clarity in memory and detail, had seemed so real.

And she had been *fading*.

The next night, the third night in as many days, Chris found himself taking the now familiar climb to the top of the hill where the mourners and the Priest stood in their red-gold aura around Sherry's awaiting grave. Again, he could feel the eyes following his every step. Again, he felt the wind standing guard at his rear. Again, he wondered if maybe it was best that he couldn't see the features of the Priest's face. Again, he

had to await the opening of her coffin. And again, she appeared to be a bit more faded somehow, the eyes a bit more distant.

She had spoken emotionlessly the previous night and sounded even less caring, less hopeful, tonight. In a voice lacking any fluctuation, she told him that the doctor hadn't located all the internal bleeding. She said she was going to be leaving soon, "moving on" as she had put it for the second time now.

"Tell him about it," Chris pleaded. "They can still help."

"No, I can't. They won't hear me like you do. Maybe you could tell them. But it won't matter. This is my fate. I can see that now. I didn't know what to do with my life. It's because I wasn't going to be around to do anything with it. Deep down…maybe I knew that."

Chris awoke again on a wet pillow, Sherry's words still running freely inside his head, still challenging his fragile grasp on reality. Real or not, possible or not, he couldn't ignore the smallest of chances that there was still something he might be able to do to help her.

He shot out of bed and threw on the same clothes he had worn the day before, still on the floor where he had numbly shed them seemingly only moments ago. He skipped the shower and toast and juice with which he had begun each day for as long as he could remember and raced down to the hospital to pass along the information that Sherry had conveyed to him during the night.

As he drove into the hospital's parking lot, he stopped to wonder for the first time what the doctor might think as he tells him he missed something and that Sherry was still bleeding somewhere inside her body. And what would he say when they inevitably ask how he comes to know this? She told him last night in his dream?

He decided to go in and see Sherry first despite her adamant insistence that she never wanted to see him again. The dream had seemed to be more than a dream. Maybe they had been communicating somehow. Maybe she had experienced the same dream last night. Maybe she had forgiven him. Maybe she was reaching out for help in the only way she could. Maybe he could still help her.

He knew he was wrong about the 'maybes' the second he entered the room. Recognizing him instantly as he came in through the door, she said calmly and flatly to him, "You don't get it, do you?" Then with more energy than his dreamland Sherry looked capable of summoning, screaming with all the strength she could muster, the real Sherry shrieked, "GET OUT OF MY LIFE!"

A nurse had come running immediately at the sound of her screaming voice and saw Chris standing at the foot of her bed looking dazed and confused. All the nurses working the floor, as well as all the doctors, receptionists and Candy Stripers, not to mention a good number of the nearby patients, were quite aware of Sherry's request that Chris not be allowed to come near her again. Had he stopped to ask about her condition before entering her room, they would have turned him away assuring him that her request still stood.

"You are not supposed to be here," the nurse said to Chris. "Why don't you come with me," she said extending an arm to show him the way through the door. "I'll send the doctor in to see you, Sherry," then followed Chris into the hallway.

With Sherry's door closed behind them, the nurse faced Chris sympathetically. "She really, really doesn't want to see you, you know. I know you care about her," she added, trying to be firm and gentle at the same time, "but you really shouldn't come back."

"But she asked me to come," Chris said, wishing he hadn't as soon as the words spilled out of his mouth.

"That wasn't the way I heard it in there," she replied quickly. "Please don't try to see her again. She needs time to recover, psychologically as well as physically. We've still got your phone number," she bargained, "and I'll call you if anything changes. But you must not come back again like this. Okay?"

"But she's still bleeding inside," he said, beginning to feel a panic creeping up inside himself. Suppressing the attack from within, he swallowed hard and continued, "She told me to come tell you because she *can't* tell you."

And then of course, the question he had predicted and feared he would need to answer; the nurse asked, "And why can't she tell us if she can tell you?"

Chris bowed his head and looked at the floor, not wanting to see the nurse's reaction to his next statement, but he couldn't think of a lie that would get done what needed to be done. So, he spoke the truth, hoping the old adage was right, that the truth was indeed always the best policy.

"She told me in a dream last night. She told me that she was still bleeding inside and I had to tell someone because she couldn't. Won't you at least have the doctor check?" he pleaded.

"I will tell the doctor about your dream. He'll talk to her himself I am sure. She is in very competent hands. I'm sure she'll be okay. The doctor is keeping a close eye on her."

"But she *can't* tell him! She doesn't know! I mean, she does know, in my dream she told me, but she doesn't know when she's awake!" Chris was shaking his head as he spoke, as if he couldn't believe what he was saying himself. "I know it doesn't make sense, but I know I talked to her." Trying desperately to sound calm, sane, "It was real." And he discovered, as he said those last three words, that for the first time he himself truly believed that it *had* been real.

"Like I said, I'll let the doctor know. Now you must go and I promise to call you if anything changes."

"You're going to check?" He knew he was on his way back out the door in a matter of moments. He just wanted to know that they were going to check, whether they believed his story or not, just check!

"I will tell the doctor everything you told me. I will do it right away. That's all I can promise you, Chris. The doctor will do what needs to be done."

Chris didn't say another word. He glanced over his shoulder at Sherry's closed door and then slowly left the building. There was nothing else he could do here for her and he was clearly not wanted here.

That night, the fourth in four, Chris dreamt again.

Her eyes had lost all their original color now. Her black pupils were now a dull gray, favoring white. Her dark brown irises appeared to have been washed away through time to a light tan. He thought he could make out a wrinkle in the soft pinkish velvet that lay beneath her head. If not for the clothing covering all but her face and hands, he thought he'd be able to see right through her.

"Did you tell them?" she asked.

"I tried, but I don't think they believed me."

"I guess it was meant to be then," she whispered softly. She closed her eyes.

Chris awoke to the sound of his own quiet sobs. Light was filtering in through the slats in his window. He didn't feel as if he had slept at all. Sherry was all he could think of. Time was running out. He didn't have any idea why he knew that, but he knew it without a doubt as he sat up in bed. Time was running out. He couldn't let it rest.

This time he didn't head straight into Sherry's room. He knew, or thought he knew, that the Sherry in there was not of the same level of consciousness as the one communicating to him in his dream. He went instead to the nurse at the receptionist desk, a different woman than the one who had escorted him out of Sherry's room the morning before, and asked to speak directly to Sherry's doctor.

"We were just going to call you, Mr. Battles," the nurse said, studying Chris' face closely as she spoke. "Sherry passed away early this morning."

Chris felt his knees go weak beneath him and had to grab the counter to keep himself from collapsing. His face went pale and his dark eyes darted back and forth wildly in their sockets. He couldn't believe what he had just heard. But then, he could believe it. In fact, he understood far more than he felt anyone else in the world ever would. He understood far more than he wanted to. He understood that he had been too late.

"Are you okay?" the nurse asked as she started to rise out of her chair to round the counter and try to catch Chris, if need be. Chris did not collapse and the nurse stayed on her side of the counter, noticeably relieved.

Struggling to hold back the spectrum of emotions building inside his head at a run-away freight train's pace--guilt and shame and anger and denial and sorrow--Chris asked in a barely audible voice, afraid he already knew the answer, "Was it…internal bleeding?"

"Yes," the nurse confirmed. "She died in her sleep. She went peacefully."

At that point, no longer able to think about his grip on the counter that was assisting his knees in holding him upright, Chris did collapse to the floor.

3

Chris didn't sleep again for three nights. He was afraid of what he might see in the dream now if he did sleep. He didn't know how he could face Sherry again, even if only in a dream. He had failed her a second time, and this time she had died as a result.

Finally, on the fourth night since Sherry's passing, Chris did sleep for his body just couldn't stay awake any longer. He hadn't been back to work, he wasn't answering his phone, he hadn't been eating, and combined with the lack of sleep, he was quite a ragged sight. He hadn't shaved since the accident and his beard had begun to grow thick with black whiskers from the top of his cheek bones to the middle of his neck.

Mostly he sat with the dim light of the sun peeking through the drawn shades by day, by night the only illumination coming from a 40-watt bulb in a floor lamp in the corner of his bedroom and the glow from his computer screen.

He had just purchased the computer a few months earlier with a Christmas bonus from Holiday Inn. Until this point, he had used the computer sparingly, a weekly email to his parents to satisfy their never-ending obsessive curiosity about his life. He figured it must be a "parent" thing. He looked forward to being a dad someday himself, the key word being "someday." For now, he was in no hurry.

The first night after Sherry's death, Chris had spent most of the night pacing the floors of his small duplex. Bedroom to kitchen to living room and back down the five-foot hall past the bathroom and back into his bedroom. Fearing the idea of going to sleep, he had actually stood at the side of his bed, lifted up the mattress and leaned it against the wall so that he could not lie down on it. This left the room wide open and every time he entered it, he made a long slow loop and paced right back out the door without stopping.

As he walked, he tried not to think about Sherry. He tried not to think about the dream. He tried thinking of when he should go back to work. He tried thinking of what to have for breakfast. Despite the fact that he had always had the same thing for breakfast, it was still no simple task to think about it anymore. Four times during the first long and seemingly endless night, he thought maybe he could think better, or less, in the shower. He tried to think of things to think about. But nothing could seem to shake the unwanted thoughts that continued to press so hard against his tired brain. The hill, the tombstones, the eerie glow in the sinking sky, the Priest, the casket, the fading of Sherry.

Thinking back on it, he wasn't sure anymore if she had actually been fading or not. Maybe a trick of the eye or something. Maybe just being more aware of details the more often he visited the dreamland site. He managed to convince himself during his several mile trek from room to room that in dying, it made more sense (not that *any* of it truly made any sense at all, but…) that she would begin to solidify in her predestined coffin as opposed to fading out of it. If he were to go back to sleep now, he was sure she would be there again, more solid than ever, dead, but waiting for him, nonetheless. And because he felt responsible for her death, because he had failed her, he didn't think he could face her again. But he knew that if he slept, he would return once again to the hill, he would feel the eyes upon him, watching, anticipating, judging. If Chris had his way, he would never sleep again.

His parents called three times, all before noon, the day following Sherry's last. Chris let each one ring until the cheerful sounding answering machine fielded their concerns for him. He knew they would just keep calling all day until they heard from him, and his mother still left a message consuming the entire two-minute talk-time allotted on the machine for each call, so he decided to go to his computer and drop them a quick, and hopefully calming email to satisfy their persistence.

Apparently, his note worked. The calls stopped and he had received an email in response to his, restating their vows of unconditional love with a request to keep them up to date and to call sometime; they were thinking about him. He responded with another email, assuring them that he appreciated their concerns and that he would indeed let them know if there was anything they could do, but right now he just needed some quiet time to himself.

This method proved to work over the following few months. As long as he continued to get at least a couple of quick emails off to them in Seattle each week, they seemed content. They continued with the daily messages of encouragement and concern, but that beat the constant phone calls for now. It wasn't that he didn't want to talk to his parents, he loved them very much and had always kept in regular contact with them. But right now, he didn't want to talk to anyone. He didn't want to answer the questions about how he felt. He didn't *know* how he felt. He didn't have the answers. He needed time. He needed to be left alone for a while. He needed to stay awake.

He knew his parents would be quick to answer his initial email so he started idly browsing around the Internet while he waited for their letter. He looked at news pages, less interested in the news itself than in how easy it appeared to be to retrieve it. He found a few sports stories of mild interest, checked the weather conditions for his weekend paper route, just in case he actually felt up to doing it this weekend. He looked up Holiday Inn's corporate website which he had always meant to do since getting his computer but hadn't bothered yet.

When he heard the metallic "You've Got Mail!" it startled him while he was absently reading about the first Holiday Inn to be erected. It was boring, but it was mind-consuming boring. An hour had passed and he hadn't thought once about the casket atop the hill. His eyes were heavy and bloodshot and tired, since he had not slept the night before, but his second wind had kicked in once the sun had risen, along with another hot shower and two bowls of *Lucky Charms* cereal, the main staple in his diet the last few days.

Chris clicked on the icon of a mailbox and read his new email. It was his parents' response, as he had expected. They were the only ones he got any mail from anyway, but he managed to crack a small smile thinking how he would have lost in the office pool as to how long it would have taken for that response to come. His money would have been on ten minutes, fifteen tops. It had actually taken an hour. He loved his parents, loved the fact that they cared so much, but he also didn't want to worry them needlessly. There was nothing they could do that might help his current situation, at any rate.

Then recalling how he had just spent the last hour not thinking about the things he didn't want to be thinking about, over the next two days, until he just couldn't keep himself awake another minute, most of his time was spent exploring the Internet.

He was fully aware of the fact that he couldn't stay awake forever. He finally brought his mattress back down from the wall and straightened out the pile of sheets and blankets that had crumpled to the floor. He had begun nodding off in the chair in front of the computer every few minutes and his neck was stiff and tense and sore. He knew sleep was going to win the battle of wills soon, and decided he might as well get comfortable and prepare for the ride. Suddenly he didn't seem to care for thrill rides any more. Suddenly he thought the merry-go-round was looking pretty darn good again, its boring routine circles taking you nowhere--predictable and tame.

Sixty seconds after Chris laid his head down on his freshly fluffed pillow on that fourth night since Sherry had died, he was out like a light. And at some point, after he had fallen asleep, he found himself once again on the winding path between the old gray markers leading towards the hill where the Priest and his small band of mourners dressed in black stood around the open gravesite. He tried not to walk the path with which he had grown so familiar in his dream; tried to will himself awake; tried to defy the pull, to close his eyes, to not see, to wish the scene away. But the wind behind him continued to urge him forward. His eyes refused to close. His feet refused his command to stand fast, to turn and run. Reluctantly, he ascended the hill.

Nothing had changed. The Priest still held his same solemn, watchful post. He could still feel the faceless blank stares coming from the mourners surrounding the grave. The coffin sat closed, poised to be lowered into the freshly dug earth as it had each previous time he had approached. Everything was the same, yet he sensed that it wasn't. Chris knew that whatever was under the coffin's lid was not *going to be the same.*

For a moment Chris wondered, now that Sherry had died, why the coffin hadn't already been lowered. The funeral had been yesterday. He hadn't been invited to the funeral, of course, but he had seen her obituary and the funeral plans the night before while perusing the

Star Tribune newspaper online. She had been buried earlier yesterday afternoon, her coffin now six feet under the earth's surface. Yet here was her coffin in front of him, still above ground, still waiting for him.

The coffin began to open, just as it had every night that he had taken this unwanted trip to the edge of the hole. Panic began to creep under his skin as he felt a shiver run the length of his back. He couldn't face Sherry, or whatever might be left of Sherry in the coffin, even if this was just a dream. But Chris peered into the coffin as it opened despite his desperate wish to change the ever-recurring script.

His eyes widened and a wave of relief flowed through his body as he realized that Sherry was no longer in the coffin. There was still someone there, but it wasn't Sherry.

Of course, it isn't her, *he thought,* she's dead. *And then as an afterthought,* Why am I still having the dream?

Now laying in Sherry's coffin was an elderly man. His face was covered with the lines and crinkles and cracks of old age. His hair was thin and white. His eyes appeared dim and faded, like Sherry's had been, lifeless, but still seeing. Unlike Sherry, he wore a broad, genuine smile on his face, looking eerily out of place on an old man laying inside a casket. His skin was pale, but not as pale, or faded, as Sherry's had appeared on her final night. He was dressed in what looked to be his best Sunday suit, complete with a red carnation above the left breast pocket. He was quite noticeably very happy to see Chris.

"Hi there," the old man said after the lid to his coffin had completely raised. "Are you my angel? Can I go see Annie now?"

Chris was still getting over the fact that Sherry was no longer in the coffin and couldn't think of a response to the question. He knew he was no angel and he had no idea who this man was, let alone who Annie was. Chris looked up at the Priest, confused and feeling embarrassed for being assumed an angel while in the presence of a truly holy person. But the Priest didn't seem to mind, didn't even seem to have heard what the old man had said. He continued to stand silently at the head of the grave with his head bowed, holding his now closed Bible to his chest with both arms crossed over it.

"I'm sorry, sir, but I am no angel," Chris finally said in response to the old man. "And I don't know why I am here…wherever here is."

"You must be here for the transition then, until my angel comes for me. My angel is going to take me to my wife. She was called last year, and now I have finally gotten the call to join her," the man said, still smiling ear to ear. "God gave me cancer so that I can be with her again."

"You are dying?" Chris asked, though he knew the answer already.

"I am moving on,*" the old man explained. "Our spirit never really dies. Our bodies get old and tired, but our spirit, our soul, that which makes us who we are,* moves on.*"*

"How long have you been sick?" Chris asked.

"It's been three months," the old man replied. "It's been awfully lonely, the waiting, that is. I am glad you are here to keep me company until my angel comes. It mustn't be long now. I am looking forward to being with my Annie again soon."

"I don't know why I am here," Chris repeated. "I don't think I am supposed to be here. I don't even know where here is."

"Oh, you can't be here if you aren't supposed to be here, my friend," the old man said. "This is a place where our spirits await the angels to guide us to Heaven. This is where we shed our physical bodies and move on to a truer form of existence. This is where we come to be reunited with our loved ones who have moved on before us, and with God."

"But I am not moving on," Chris pointed out. "I am asleep. I am dreaming. And you are in my dream. Or maybe somehow, I am in your dream. I don't know. But I know it is just a dream, it just doesn't feel like a dream. But it is *just a dream," Chris added, trying to convince himself more than anyone else.*

"Not everyone knows they are moving on,*" the old man continued. "Some folks are taken from their bodies by God before they are finished with them. Only God knows why, but that is His will."*

"No," Chris said. "I am not here to be moving on. *I am not here as anyone's angel. This is a dream. This is just a dream! IT'S JUST A GODDAMN DREAM!!" he yelled, looking up at the Priest in defiance.*

As if provoked by his own admission of this fact, or his denial of any other possibilities, Chris suddenly woke up. He could still see the old man in his mind's eye quite clearly. He could still hear the raspy rhythm of his aged voice.

Chris looked sideways at the clock glowing in the dark on his bedside table. 4:30 a.m. He felt exhausted but knew there was no way he was going to get any more sleep, so he dragged himself out of bed and made his way to the shower.

It was then, standing under the warm and pulsating water, that he decided he couldn't go back to his desk clerk job. He had no idea at the time how he was going to pay the bills on his part-time weekend paper route, but he knew he couldn't face people right now, and being a desk clerk in a busy hotel in downtown Minneapolis meant facing people all day long. He couldn't face the questions and the sympathy and the generic words of encouragement. Nothing anyone could say could possibly make him feel better about being responsible for a young, vibrant woman's death. And then there was the dream. How could he explain that to anyone? Sherry was now gone. But the dream still remained.

Over the following few weeks, Chris began to alienate himself from his friends and the life he had known before the accident.

He had received a $150,000 settlement (plus related expenses) from the insurance company that covered the bungee operation, only a drop in the bucket compared to what Sherry's grieving parents had received, but still more than he felt he deserved for his role in the whole mess.

He picked up some additional paper routes for the Minneapolis Star Tribune to help make up for the loss of his full-time work at the Holiday Inn. He knew he'd need to replace the full-timer with a new one eventually, but for now he couldn't find the motivation to go out and hunt down a new source of income.

Instead, he began filling in for the Tribune, delivering routes for carriers on vacation or sick, or routes that didn't have a permanent carrier assigned to them for the time being. Before long, taking on the routes that he liked as his own whenever he could, he had accumulated enough permanent routes to keep himself busy throughout each night and he discovered he was making almost as much as he had as a desk clerk. And he was able to do it all from his own car, alone, without interaction with people.

Three months after Sherry's death, the only people Chris spoke to anymore were the faces in the coffin of his daily demented dream. His papers were always dropped off in his driveway sometime after midnight for him to have delivered by 7:00 a.m. each morning, seven days per week. His friends had by then given up on trying to bring him out of his funk. And his parents in Seattle, 1600 miles away, didn't even know yet that he had not returned to his job of the last six years at Holiday Inn. It would have just made them worry more.

Chris had come to accept and expect his daily trek through the graveyard. The old man that had been in Sherry's coffin after she had died had been there each night for almost a full month. They talked about the old man's life and his wife that he expected to be joining soon. Chris discovered his name was William Shavver and his wife's name had been Annabelle.

William and Annabelle had owned and managed their own little antique shop and had never had any children. The store had been their whole life. They had kept it open all the way up until Annie's death, but William had been unable to keep it going by himself. He had sold the store for much less than it was worth and had begun his wait to join his wife in Heaven from the day the sale was finalized, praying every night for God to take him that night in his sleep. But each morning he had awakened to discover he was still among the living.

Now God had given him cancer and he was very excited about being reunited with his wife. And, according to William, God had sent Chris to keep him company until his time to depart finally came.

Chris didn't say so, but he didn't believe that was why he was there. Being raised by atheistic parents, and steeped in logic and science, he had never believed in God. Though he had to admit, he hadn't yet come up with a better reason for his being there.

After two weeks of visiting and getting to know William, Chris began to see the change. The *fading* had begun. William's time was drawing near.

Chris genuinely liked William and his stories of how he and his wife had come upon this antique or that one. When he found the new face of a middle-aged, over-weight man who looked like a car dealer you wouldn't want to buy a car from, he had mixed emotions. He hoped that William was now in some way with his Annie once again…though he doubted it.

The new face, and the many faces that followed over the next few months in his dreams, never quite touched him the way William Shavver had. Some were happy to be *moving on,* as William had put it, and some were quite bitter about it. The ones that were tough were the few that didn't even know it was coming.

When William had given Sherry's coffin over to Barry "Trust Me" Johnson, who didn't stay long before his appendix burst, Chris had surfed the Internet seeking out the obituaries from newspapers around the country trying to confirm William Shavver's life…and death. Three days, hundreds of newspapers and thousands of deaths later, Chris decided the search was fruitless but that his not finding William's name neither proved nor disproved anything. He was a nice old man. Let him rest in peace.

Chris wished *he* could rest in peace.

Up to now, he mostly just listened to the inhabitants of Sherry's coffin as they talked of their lives or tried repenting their misdeeds in hopes of gaining favor into the heavens. A few of the faces were there for a week or two, but most came and went in a matter of two or three days. He never recognized any of the new faces and he was grateful for that. He often wondered when he went to bed if he might someday see one of his own aging parents in the coffin and how he would react. Or maybe even his own face. But so far Sherry's had been the only face he had known.

Chris fell into a routine. He delivered his papers by night to pay the bills and keep from going hungry, though his appetite had also dropped off quite a bit since the accident. During the morning daylight hours he slept, and dreamt. He usually spent the rest of his time sitting at his computer on the small desk in the corner of his bedroom backed against the newly, heavily draped window. He mindlessly surfed the web for nothing in particular and kept his parents' concerns at bay via timely emails. He kept the house dim to dark around the clock. Most light, Chris had ascertained, just tended to reflect obnoxiously off the computer screen, making it more difficult to read.

Chris no longer feared going to sleep. He never looked

forward to it, and there was still something very unsettling about the Priest that Chris continued to try *not* to think about. But sleep was a necessity, a fact of life, for now. The only options were not options.

Maybe this is my penitence, he thought, *my price to be paid for the bed that I made. Or maybe this is my fate, preordained by some greater being, by God. Sherry's life and death just another foothold or stepping stone to fulfill some twisted plan for my otherwise meaningless existence.* But usually what he fell back on was, *Or maybe it's just damn, shitty luck.*

He really couldn't bring himself to believe in any single supreme being, a God. At this point in his life, however, he wasn't going to say there wasn't one, either. But a God worthy of the praise He received world-wide, Chris figured, could never be so cruel as to dish out the pain and torture that exists on a daily basis among non-believers as well as believers. Or else He has a very sick sense of humor. And *fate*? The idea that he had no control over his life, that his script was already written, that *he-was-who-he-was-and-was-going-to-be-who-he-was-going-be-and-there-wasn't-a-damn-thing-he-could-do-about-it-like-it-or-not* philosophy never sat well with him at all. If nothing else he believed in this world were true, he wanted that one to be; there was no such thing as *fate*. He needed to know that mankind controls its own destiny. If mankind is destined to self-destruction with nuclear fall-out and genetic screw-ups in the name of science, so be it. But he wanted to be the one deciding what he did with his life as he lived it, who he'd call his friends during that life, and which flavor ice cream he had for dessert at his last meal. He wanted to be the one responsible for asking Sherry to jump with him. He wanted to believe that his life was and always had been his own--his own triumphs, his own choices, his own mistakes. The good and the bad, but his nonetheless. That was important to Chris. Maybe the last strand of reality holding his vulnerable state of mind together. So much of what he had always believed was being tried and tested right now.

But *fate*...only a true Devil would allow such a thing to exist.

4

Barry Johnson, the man who followed William Shavver in Sherry's coffin, hadn't known his death was just around the corner, but that was only because he hadn't been paying attention. A picture is worth a thousand words, or in Barry's case, a life story.

Barry was a good hundred pounds overweight. His hair was black and matted to his forehead in thick, small clumps. It didn't look like it had been washed in months. His face had a five-day growth of whiskers, salt and pepper in color, heavy on the salt. He probably dyed his hair to maintain its glossy black shine, Chris had assumed. His eyes were too close to his nose and too small for his round, fat face, making him look shifty and not very bright at the same time. And he smelled of alcohol.

Chris learned in Barry's brief stay that he hadn't been a car dealer, but rather a life insurance salesman. In the early days, having been blessed with the gift of gab in a small town on the rise, Barry's little one-man operation had done well, keeping him well fed and well liquored. But as Berry grew bigger, so did the town, along with the competition. As technology advanced and marketing and advertising strategies evolved beyond the neighborly door-to-door methods of the past, Barry got left behind and he didn't bother putting up a chase. In fact, about the only thing Barry chased any more was his beer with a scotch.

Just looking at Barry, one could guess the basics of his story.

Chris listened as Barry blamed his misfortunes on everything under the sun--progress, computers, cut-throats, big business and big bucks.

Chris said very little in response and obediently listened while wishing he would wake up. But the dreams actually seemed to be getting longer, consuming more and more of his sleep time. He wasn't sure; after all, he was supposedly asleep and time is hard to judge while in that state. Occasionally he had started taking *No-Doz* while delivering his routes at night, not always trusting his ability to stay awake in the quiet darkness on his own. Minnesota nights are generally cool to cold though, and the chill in the air as he leaned out his window shoving the papers into the tubes also helped keep him awake. But as the weeks dragged on and the dreams got seemingly longer, his tiredness became more and more an unending test of his endurance.

Barry had not returned on his fourth night. It wasn't until that fourth night when another elderly man appeared in Sherry's coffin that Chris realized that Barry had had no idea that his number had been called. He had been there talking about how he was going to get back at the companies that had driven him out of business one night and then he was gone the next. He had faded quickly, as had Sherry, since his time had been near, Chris assumed. After the third session with Barry, while in the shower recalling some of the paranoid statements Barry had made about Corporate America, Chris had decided Barry wasn't going to be around much longer. Then, the very next night, Chris' prediction had held true.

The new face, the new elderly man, like William Shavver, knew he was dying and was welcoming his upcoming death. Also, like William, he welcomed Chris' presence. Barry had never even questioned Chris' presence…or the surroundings in the dream. Barry had told his stories as though he were sitting on a bar stool in his neighborhood bar talking to the only person in the room too drunk to get up and walk away. But as the new elderly dream-guest once again questioned Chris's role in his life, or death as the case may be, he suddenly realized that Barry had been as clueless to his upcoming demise as he had been about the real reasons he was run out of business.

But if Barry hadn't known he was going to die, Chris wondered, *how the hell did* I *know*? *Someone* must know because they appear to him in a coffin. Sherry had known, William had known, now this new elderly man knew. Chris had assumed, since he was beginning to believe that this was something more than your average run-of-the-mill garden variety dream, that the dying people had somehow opened a psychic channel or some kind of direct line, linking their subconscious minds to his. But in any case, he suspected it had been *them* contacting him. Sherry had said she had tried to contact the doctors, but they couldn't hear her like he could. Naturally, he assumed *she* had contacted him.

But if Barry hadn't known…

It was time for a shower.

Under the warm, pulsating water once again, Chris felt better able to think.

Maybe the soul, one of the three major components of human life (the trio being the mind, the body and the soul, he concluded as he began to wash his hair for the second time), was the one dialing the number independently and without the knowledge of the conscious mind--a theory Sherry's split personality between the dream world and reality would support. Her anger was maybe too strong, he tried to reason, creating a wall of rage blocking the message her body had sent to her soul and was trying to send to her mind. Her soul had then reached out to another soul that would listen. His.

So why hadn't the dreamland Barry known of his predicament? Because Barry's soul hadn't known? His body and soul weren't communicating?

This only brought Chris back to the same two spine-tingling questions that had put him into the shower to begin with. *If Barry didn't know he was going to die, how the hell did* I? And, *Who's contacting whom?*

Too much for his tired and frazzled mind to do battle with, even in the shower. Chris turned off the water and tried to forget about the questions currently running circles around his logic. Nothing seemed to make sense. He felt numb in the brain. He felt like he was on a ride that had gone out of control and there was no getting off.

The next three hosts--or guests, he was no longer sure who played which role in this dream--were all people having led full lives and willing to shed their tired old bodies to allow their spirits the freedom to live anew. Chris was just beginning to disregard the all-important questions of who knows what and who's dialing up whom when a young boy appeared in the foreboding catafalque.

An elderly woman, another recipient of the modern-day plague, a cancer, had faded to the point that Chris had not expected her back. Before the coffin had opened, he had finally summoned the courage to speak to the Priest. He asked a single question, to which the Priest did not answer.

Tired of coming to this site day after day after day, tired of not having the answers to the hundreds of questions mounting in his brain, tired of being so damn tired, Chris looked up at the Priest and asked, "Why am I here?"

For just a moment, Chris thought his voice had gone unheard by the tall figure in black. Then slowly, the Priest's head rose, his face still hidden within the depths of his hood. Chris could almost feel the Priest's eyes needling his body. It made him feel invaded and somehow vulnerable and he wished he hadn't spoken to him at all. The Priest really, really scared him for reasons he couldn't quite grasp. It was one of the many things he tried not to think about when awake. But just when he thought the Priest might speak, the coffin's lid began to creak slowly open and both had returned their attention to center stage.

That was when he saw the boy, Benjamin.

Benjamin opened his eyes as if awakening from a nap as the coffin revealed its newest tenant.

"Who are you?" the boy asked as his gaze settled on Chris.

"My name is Chris. And who might you be?"

"Benjamin Christopher Worthington," the boy replied with a smile.

"Well, Mr. Benjamin Christopher Worthington, that name is longer than you are!" Chris said, trying to match the handsome young lad's blue-ribbon smile.

"Yeah," Benjamin giggled, "my Dad says I'll grow into it."

Chris' smile, fake as it had been to begin with, vanished completely with Benjamin's last words. Either his dad had a very cruel and sick sense of humor telling a dying boy that he would grow into anything, or Benjamin's dad didn't know his son was going to die soon. Nor, it seemed, did Benjamin himself know. How soon this untimely death was supposed to arrive was hard to tell. Benjamin was not in any noticeably advanced stages of fading. But the questions swarmed back with a force banging hard against his brain. Who was contacting whom here? And if Benjamin doesn't know that he is dying very soon, how could he himself possibly know?

Chris thought the Priest could probably answer both those questions, but he didn't dare ask…not because of the old adage that ignorance is bliss, but because of the other one, how curiosity had killed the cat.

Trying once again to push the Priest out of his mind, Chris asked Benjamin, "Do you know where we are?"

"You're in my dream," Benjamin exclaimed with innocent glee.

Benjamin looked to be no more than five years old. He had short dirty blond hair with bangs cut neatly across his forehead. His cheeks and nose were dotted with freckles and his blue eyes were still animated as he smiled, though the sparkle one would expect to accompany them on such a youthful face wasn't present. He was wearing Power Ranger *pajamas and held the action figure of the ranger in red close to his heart. Chris couldn't imagine why this healthy-looking young boy was going to be dying soon. And he certainly didn't want to turn Benjamin's dream into a nightmare by asking him about it if he didn't already know.*

But the questions would not rest in his mind.

Telling himself he would not have asked the question if he thought Benjamin knew the real answer, Chris asked, "So, Benjamin, what do you want to be when you grow up?"

"A police officer of the law," Benjamin replied without hesitation. "I am going to serve and protect my neighbors and friends just like my daddy does," he added with obvious pride in his father's work.

He really doesn't know, *Chris thought.* So how on earth could I possibly know?

Chris listened to Benjamin tell a heroic short tale of good defeating evil, his red Power Ranger *being the hero for the good side in this particular chapter, until Benjamin appeared to be getting tired.*

"I'm going to go back to sleep now," he said with a big yawn.

"Okay," Chris answered, feeling very tired himself. "Thanks for inviting me into your dream, and for the story."

"I didn't invite you," Benjamin said as his eyes started to drift closed. "You just came. But that's okay. You're a nice man."

"And you're a nice boy, Benjamin Christopher Worthington. I am very happy to meet you. Sweet dreams now." And then as an afterthought, Chris added, "Be careful, Benjamin."

What felt like just an instant later, Chris was in the shower standing under the pounding water trying to rekindle some energy from the wet heat and to wash away the memories from the night. This was the shower in which he decided to go see the district manager of his paper route job and see if he could add a Monday through Friday route or two or three to his docket. That eventually evolved into six weekday routes and three weekend routes, replacing Holiday Inn's income sufficiently enough that Chris quit thinking about looking for a new full-time day job.

Over the next two weeks, Chris and his body made the necessary adjustments to convert from life under the sun to life under the moon. He usually went to sleep as the sun was waking up, not waking up himself until noon or a little after, if his dream allowed him to sleep that long. His morning showers had become increasingly long, just as his dreams had seemed to become. Sometimes he stood under the running water motionless, eyes closed, for forty-five minutes, or until the hot water started to cool despite having been cranked as far to the left as it would go. His little five-by-five foot, undecorated, windowless, white tiled cubical with nowhere to sit, smaller than the closet in his bedroom, had become his own personal sanctuary.

He generally ate twice a day, once after waking up and showering in the early afternoon, and once around midnight before getting ready to deliver his papers. More and more, with each passing day, and with each passing new face in his recurring dream, the rest of his waking hours were being spent in front of his computer. Mostly he located and read obituaries from small and large newspapers around the country. He wasn't looking for anything in particular, he was just looking. So many deaths every single day. He felt a bittersweet luck that he only had to deal with a few per month.

Reading the obituaries also helped him deal with the apparent impending doom for all the people of his dream. Every day there are more people dying younger, more horribly, more suddenly. Tragedy is a daily event happening all around us at all times. Usually, probably for the sake of our own sanity as a society, we ignore as much of it as possible. We hide it in small print at the back of the daily newspapers. People generally don't appreciate being reminded of their life's true fragility, of their actual vulnerability. We read about the spectacular and unusual deaths, the ones that have touched the masses with their lives, and the ones closer to the heart, the ones we know. But for every one of those that appear in the headlines and front pages, for every death that we hear about on the news or from friends and family, there are thousands more tucked away and out of sight.

Out of sight, out of mind.

We're all going to die, that's a given. We all know it. We each deal with that fact in our own way. But when and how is what scares us. We keep ourselves busy building relationships, planting roots, pretending that it won't happen to us, at least not until we are ready. But if we open our eyes, we'll see that it is happening all around us all the time, and to people that weren't ready at all.

Benjamin appeared to be one that was not ready. The thought that something was going to happen to take this boy's life before he had the chance to live it was eating away at Chris. If Benjamin were healthy, as he indeed appeared to be, then, Chris reasoned, his death was going to be an accident. But isn't that the antithesis of the word 'accident'? Unless the accident was part of a pre-scripted fate, in which case it could not technically be called an accident, in which case, then technically speaking, there was no such thing as an 'accident'. But that would mean fate existed, which was something Chris just could not accept.

His head was spinning.

How can I know if an accident is going to happen if fate does not exist? he thought. *And if fate does not exist* (as he so avidly believed) *and Benjamin is going to die from an accident, then doesn't that mean he might also live? That the accident could be avoided?*

His mind now raced a mile a minute. The concept and related theories that he so enjoyed debating with friends in the past, about the possibilities of the existence of fate, now compared to a peewee league baseball coach suddenly getting a chance to coach in the majors. The basics were no longer enough. The ideals and old theories had to be tossed out the window. He was in over his head, in the big leagues without the skill, up shit creek without a paddle. Chris was beginning to think his mind was possibly not even equipped to handle the answers to the questions it was now beginning to raise, the most important one of which had now become, *Can I save Benjamin*?

5

From the instant Chris had come to accept the idea that his dream was, on some level anyway, indeed quite real, he also accepted the possibility that it was not limited to the Minneapolis/St. Paul area. He knew he had never left his bed. He hadn't been experiencing any of that out-of-body mumbo jumbo he had heard described by people on the Sci-Fi channel or on George Noory's all-night radio program that he often listened to while delivering his newspapers. They were dreams. He knew this. He slept. And he dreamt. The same dream. Every day. Involving real people. But it was still just a dream.

Somehow, however, he also knew it was more than just a dream. He had no idea what that 'more' entailed, nor any better idea on who was contacting whom after talking with Benjamin, let alone how. But he was convinced that somebody was definitely contacting somebody. And that it was real.

Now, what about Benjamin? How long would he have? How long has it been since he appeared? One week? Two? He knew he had to do something, he had to try.

Chris knew with a name like Worthington, finding the one he wanted would be no easier than the proverbial needle, but it was admittedly a lot less hopeless than a Johnson or Anderson would have been. He also realized that 'long distance calls' were probably as easy and likely as local ones on whatever channel he had been using for these prophetic dreams, but grabbed the White Pages for Minneapolis and for St. Paul first. That was as good as any place to start.

There were fifteen Worthingtons in the Minneapolis White Pages and another eight listed in the St. Paul offering. Yet another deterrent to Chris' search was that the name he knew was that of a child. His parents might be listed, but Benjamin certainly would not be. It was only two o'clock in the afternoon and most people would probably still be at work, but he opened up a Mountain Dew, settled in by the phone, and dialed the first number anyway.

At midnight Chris rubbed his tired, bloodshot eyes and pushed himself back from the computer. His sixth list of Worthingtons retrieved from the Internet White Pages, covering most of the major cities throughout the mid-western states, lay next to the computer on his desk. On each trip to the website, he had filled a page, front and back, with Worthington phone numbers and then signed off the Internet to make the phone calls. He had made hundreds of calls, many of them having to be repeated several times throughout the day before getting an answer. None had been the Worthingtons he was seeking. The last twenty Worthingtons reached had all made comments to Chris about the current time of night--some of them with understandable anger--so he decided it was time to stop for now and get ready for his routes. He hadn't stopped to eat all day. The lack of results had been expected, but was frustrating all the same. He headed for the shower.

For the first time since the accident, since this nightmare had begun, Chris was anxious to get to sleep.

Hope.

He had clung to that word all night while delivering his papers. *Fate* was still something Chris thought could simply not be a factor. Thus, seeing a face in the coffin, a young face, a healthy face, merely meant it was a *probable* outcome, not necessarily an absolute outcome. Even Nostradamus had said of all his prophecies that nothing was absolute, that man's destiny and fate lay solely, in the end, in his own hands. (His insight had also apparently reflected a personal lack of faith in mankind's collective common sense and human nature in general as contributing factors to his visions. They were generally not of the more optimistic variety of prognostications.)

But Chris wasn't worried about the destiny or fate of mankind right now. Just the fate of one small boy. Or the probability of one small boy's life, as he felt more comfortable wording it to himself.

The thought had first occurred to him in the shower before throwing a frozen pizza in the oven for dinner. He was feeling very frustrated about the wasted day, the hours upon hours spent fruitlessly on the phone. Then he was even more frustrated at the thought that the more he broadened his search, the less likely it became that he could do anything about it even if he did find Benjamin. But he felt if he could at least talk to him, the conscious Benjamin, or his parents, or the family dog or anyone in contact with the boy, he might be able to *change* something. That something might be just enough.

Then as he was working up a healthy lather of shampoo, trying to figure out the best way to figure out Benjamin's phone number, he suddenly thought, *Just ask him for his phone number when you see him again*! *YES*! It was that easy! He smiled widely--something he hadn't done in months. Could it be that simple? It seemed like such an easy solution to an impossible question after spending hours upon hours on the phone to Worthington households all over the Midwest to no avail. He was sure, especially if he thought hard about it all night while delivering his routes, that he could remember to ask Benjamin for his phone number in the morning when he fell asleep and met him at the top of the hill.

Hope. There was always hope.

The sun, along with a few cars, joggers, and dog walkers, was beginning to come out as Chris delivered his last paper and headed home. Despite the fact that this was just before he normally went to sleep every day, it was his favorite part of each day. He hated going to sleep anymore. He hated being forced against his will to return to the gravesite every night to stand among the Priest and his band of mourners and meet dying people. But this part of the day--watching the sky change colors, having the finish to a long night's work just minutes away, watching the houses and businesses and streets slowly come to life, listening to the quiet, still sounds of the night give way to the ever-increasing sounds of the coming day--this was his favorite time of day.

On a portion of his drive home after his final delivery each morning, across the median and traveling in the opposite direction, heading towards downtown Minneapolis, the rush hour is just beginning to mass. Chris' mini-van is usually still a lonely vehicle making use of the three lanes of highway traveling south bound. The analogy and the irony the scene portrayed in relation to the direction his life had taken since the accident did not go unnoticed by Chris.

Chris had never been much of a drinker. An occasional glass of wine during the evening. Two or three times a year, despite swearing "never again" after each time, a good drunk with a few friends had still been considered a good time. Lately, however, Chris had begun the habit of tipping back a shot (or two) of scotch each morning before bed to help him sleep. Despite how tired he was each morning when he lay down for sleep, he was tense, not wanting to go to sleep. The scotch seemed to help him take the edge off. It helped him go where he had to go with a tad less anguish and trepidation.

This morning, however, Chris didn't need the new crutch. He had hope. This morning he was simply going to ask Benjamin for his phone number and then give him a call after he awoke. He had never had any problem remembering conversations he had shared with William. He remembered verbatim the first words Sherry had screamed at him in his very first dream several months earlier. He was absolutely sure that, if Benjamin didn't consider Chris to still be a stranger after their two weeks of sharing a dream together and refused to give it out (his dad was a cop, after all), he would remember the boy's phone number when he awoke.

For the first time since the accident, Chris couldn't wait to get to sleep.

Chris could still feel the eyes that followed his progress up the hill each time he visited the dreamland gravesite and he tried to ignore them and focus on his task at hand.

The phone number.

The hill lay in front of him, the wind still pushing gently from behind. The Priest was just folding closed his precious book and He and the mourners, as they always do, turn their attention first to Chris as he approaches, and then to the coffin as it opens.

The phone number.

"Hi Chris!" Benjamin said cheerfully as the coffin had fully opened and his eyes had followed suit.

"Hello, Benjamin," Chris replied.

The phone number.

He was so focused on his mission he had all but forgotten the familiar watching audience.

Benjamin had been the dream's host now for fifteen days. Chris had been watching for any signs of fading, but before tonight, he didn't think there had been much, if any, change in Benjamin's appearance. Tonight, Chris saw the sands of time were indeed still in operational order. Benjamin's eyes seemed to be three shades of blue lighter than they had been twenty-four hours earlier. His skin seemed to take on a hint of the colors surrounding him, almost like a chameleon, as if blending in with the coffin's interior a bit more. He was definitely beginning to fade.

"Benjamin, I have a favor I need to ask you. I need to call you on the telephone," Chris started to explain. He took a nervous glance towards the Priest, half expecting him to try to stop the obvious next question, to claim it was 'breaking the rules', or worse, not in the script. But the Priest just stood there as silent and motionless as he always did after closing his book. Still, his mere presence bothered Chris. His silence, feeling he could speak if he chose to do so, made Chris very uneasy. But he wasn't going to ask permission to ask the question. He looked back at Benjamin laying in the coffin and continued his quest.

"I need your phone number, Benjamin, so I can talk to you and your parents. Will you tell me what your phone number is?"

For a moment, he thought maybe Benjamin hadn't memorized his phone number yet, or that his dad had warned him never to give it out. Benjamin looked thoughtfully at Chris and he realized that Benjamin was sizing him up, deciding if it was safe to reveal the secret numbers to the man he had only recently met in his dreams. He had obviously been told by his parents that this was privileged information and not to be handed out to strangers. He was a good kid, Chris thought, and tried not to look as desperate for the number as he felt.

"Why do you want to talk to my parents?" Benjamin asked.

A simple enough question, but one Chris had not prepared himself for. He couldn't just come out and tell Benjamin he might be in danger. He didn't want to scare the boy.

Thinking quickly, keeping one eye on the Priest, Chris said, "I just want to tell your parents what a wonderful job they are doing raising such a fine young lad as yourself. I have enjoyed visiting with you these last two weeks and I wanted to see if maybe I could take you and your parents out to dinner or something like that to say thanks." And then the clincher, "You like McDonald's?"

"Cool! Yeah!" Benjamin exclaimed. "I love McDonald's! Happy Meals rule!" he said, pumping his small fist into the air.

"Well, give me your phone number and I will give your mom and dad a call tomorrow and see if maybe we can't get something arranged. If that sounds good to you."

"You bet! It's 555-5647."

Chris smiled broadly and a bit smugly as he glanced at the Priest across the grave. Then he realized he still needed an area code.

"Do you know your area code, Benjamin? What city you live in?" Chris asked.

"Area code?" Benjamin asked in return.

Damn, almost there, *Chris thought. "The three numbers in front of the numbers you gave me," he explained. "The area code for what city you live in."*

"I don't know any codes," Benjamin said. "But the phone number is 555-5647."

"What city do you live in? I can find the code if I know your city," Chris continued. Come on, Benjamin. We're so close now!

"I live in Kansas," Benjamin said, a syllable at a time, making it sound more like 'Can-Says'.

"Is that Kansas City or Kansas State, Benjamin?" Chris asked patiently.

"It's Kansas," Benjamin stated firmly, sounding quite sure of himself. "Like where Dorothy lives."

"Do you live in a town?"

"Nope. We live in out-of-town."

"On a farm?"

"Yep. A BIG farm," Benjamin said with pride.

"Do you know what town your farm is near, Benjamin?"

Chris wasn't sure, but out of the corner of his eye, as he continued to drill Benjamin for the crucial information, he could have sworn he saw the Priest's shadowy lips turn up at the corners. He wasn't sure, but Chris thought maybe his frustration here was amusing the Priest, that he had smiled.

"Ummmmmmmm..." Benjamin was saying, trying to think of the answer Chris was fishing for. "Kansas."

"Okay, that's okay, Benjamin. I'll figure it out. I'll call you tomorrow, okay?"

"Okay!" Another small pump of the fist into the air.

The Priest was making Chris nervous. More so than usual. He couldn't explain it. But he had the phone number and he had the state. The number of possible area codes would be down to a manageable hit and miss quantity knowing the phone number was in Kansas. Mission accomplished.

But the smile Chris had sensed on the Priest did not sit well in his mind. I didn't *see* the smile so much as I *felt* it, *he admitted to himself, with no real proof to back up his thought. But he was convinced it had definitely been there.*

Another thing Chris seemed to realize was that the more he knew lately, the more he wished he didn't know.

6

Chris was on the phone five minutes after he woke up a little after one in the afternoon. Kansas has only three area codes covering the entire state. On the second one he tried, he got an answering machine featuring Benjamin's now familiar and cheerful young voice.

"Hi! Um, sorry you missed, um, missed us. Um. Please, um, leave a message after the beep and, um, we'll, um, call you back. Bye!"

Chris hung up without leaving a message. He decided he had better write out what he wanted to say on the answering machine to ensure their interest and a return call without alarming them or scaring them by saying anything at all about what was actually on his mind. He also didn't want to sound like a kook and lose all credibility in an already seemingly insane and unbelievable situation.

After thirty minutes of writing out dozens of potential messages to Benjamin's parents hoping to ensure a return call from them, he realized he was directing the message to the wrong people. If he directed the message to Benjamin, his parents are going to want to know who he is and talk to him immediately, regardless of what the message says, assuming that they will be the ones that first hear it.

Chris redialed the number without preparing his speech on

paper. The third ring was again answered with Benjamin's message. After the beep, Chris left his message to Benjamin.

"Hi, Benjamin. This is Chris Battles in Minneapolis. I liked your message on the phone. I'm not sure you remember me, Benjamin, but I wanted to talk to your parents about the things that we talked about before. My phone number is 651-555-6956. Please tell them to call me as soon as they can. Calling collect is fine, too." Then recalling a phrase Benjamin had recited in each of his *Power Ranger* stories, he added, "It's Morphin Time! Bye for now."

Chris hung up the phone and waited.

Usually in the afternoons while he was surfing the Internet, he had the after-school children's programs on the TV for background noise. The sounds coming from the cartoons and fantasy dramas were as colorful as the pictures that its young viewers were so attracted to. He never watched, just listened, as others might listen to the radio. He was familiar with the *Power Rangers*, the theme of the pajamas Benjamin wore and of the stories he liked to tell. "It's Morphin Time" was the phrase chanted by the Rangers before they *morphed*, or transformed, from average pimple-popping teenagers into galaxy-saving superheroes. Mentioning them would undoubtedly let Benjamin's parents know that he did indeed know their son. They'd most certainly now want to know who he was and how he knew their son.

Chris didn't believe that Benjamin would remember their shared dreams or who Chris was, the way that he did. Sherry hadn't. He assumed Benjamin's parents would drill their son about him before calling back to see what the two of them had supposedly talked about. His dad was a police officer, after all. He hoped that fact would work to his advantage.

Chris was feeling high with hope. Maybe, he even thought, he had already tipped the scales in Benjamin's favor by making contact and raising the guard of a cop-father protective of his son's well-being, thus preventing whatever was supposedly going to happen. He wouldn't know for sure until he found a new face in his dream before watching Benjamin fade too far. Benjamin hadn't yet faded to near the point the others had been before not returning the following night, but he *had* started to fade. Chris knew there wasn't a whole lot of time left, maybe a week, five days. But that was still enough time for hope.

Without the Internet to occupy his time, and having been regenerated with energy from his high hopes, Chris spent the afternoon giving his half of the duplex the most thorough cleaning it had seen in several years. He had decided to give Mr. Worthington at least until after the dinner discussion, if that's when they decided to bring it up, before he himself tried calling back. But he guessed he should be getting the call sometime around seven that evening. He had absolutely no idea how he was going to convince Benjamin's dad that what he had to say, as crazy at it may sound, might save Benjamin from some unknown and unexpected horror. He simply knew he had to try.

He had guessed wrong about the time, but not the caller. When the phone rang at five-fifteen, Chris was inside the tub scrubbing the tile walls. Banging his knee hard against the bathroom door frame as he ran, he made it to the phone by its second ring. Noticing the "Out-of-Area" reading on his caller ID, he knew at once it was his call from Kansas.

The third ring completed and Chris sat down next to the phone and picked it up.

"One moment, please," Chris said into the receiver and then placed it in his lap, took a deep, slow breath, then brought the receiver back to his ear. "Hello?"

"Is this Mr. Chris Battles?" a man asked.

"Yes, it is," Chris replied, content for now to let Officer

Worthington dictate the pace of this delicate and possibly all-important call.

"Good. I'm glad I got you direct. My name is Thomas Worthington. You left a message today for my son that sounded, well, mysterious, for lack of a better word. Needless to say, we asked him about you and he doesn't remember having ever met you. Also, needless to say, this concerned me greatly as he is only five years old and you are not. You said in the message that you wanted to talk to his parents. You have one now. Please explain."

"Thank you for calling back so quickly, Mr. Worthington. I do believe this is a fairly urgent matter, but I'm not quite sure how to begin," Chris said. It appeared that Mr. Worthington wanted to get right to the point, however Chris didn't think giving out too much info too quickly would help his cause. He proceeded slowly, "You're a policeman, right?"

"Yes, I am," Officer Worthington replied. He sounded less surprised and more aggravated by the fact that Chris knew this. "How is it you know so much?"

"Benjamin told me you are a policeman. He said he wanted to be one too when he grows up." Here was his last chance to find out different before making a complete fool of himself. If Benjamin's father knew Benjamin wasn't going to 'grow up' because of some unnoticeable disease or organ deformity, he would surely say so now.

"When did you talk to Benjamin? And where?" Mr. Worthington asked, beginning to sound a little impatient.

"This is not easy for me, sir. You'll understand here if you give me time, but please bear with me," Chris said, still trying to figure out how and where to begin. "I'm not quite sure where to start," he admitted honestly.

"Are you connected with the schools?"

"No."

"Well let's start there. Who do you work for?" asked the officer in Mr. Worthington.

"Well, that isn't really important in this, but I deliver newspapers for the Star Tribune here in the Minneapolis, Minnesota area," Chris replied, but offered no more information and waited for the officer's next question.

"So how did you meet my son?" Mr. Worthington asked, now also with a touch of frustration tainting his voice. An understandable and predictable question, to be sure, but equally understandably, not the question Chris wanted to answer next.

Taking another deep breath, Chris said, "Okay. First of all, I want you to understand that it is Benjamin's well-being that I am concerned with here. You must trust me on that. I am only trying to help. Okay?"

"What is this all about, Mr. Battles? I am not a patient man when it comes to my son's well-being, as you put it."

"I understand that completely and I apologize for the way this sounds," Chris said. The last thing he wanted to do was agitate Mr. Worthington. He needed him on his side. "Just hear me out completely and I will tell you everything I know. Is that a deal?"

"Deal," Mr. Worthington agreed with a loud sigh, noticeably straining to remain patient. "So talk."

Chris gave up on the idea that there was a way to make his story sound sane and hoped that Thomas Worthington was a man capable of keeping an open mind, a *very* open mind. He finally started at the beginning, with the accident he and Sherry had experienced together, and then with the dreams in which Sherry had informed him of her dilemma. He then carefully explained her *fading* and how she had died.

"Are you going to tell me that you met my son in a dream? Is that where you are going with this?" Mr. Worthington interrupted, his impatience proving true to his word.

"I am getting to that, but yes," Chris said. "But before you come to any premature conclusions from that thought, keep in mind that I am talking to you right now from Minnesota because of the phone number Benjamin gave to me last night in this dream." Chris knew this was probably the crucial point in determining the way the rest of this call was going to go. He paused for a moment to let that last bit of information sink in for Mr. Worthington. He hoped the next sound he heard would not be the phone at the other end being hung up.

Mr. Worthington finally broke the silence. "Are you trying to tell me that you think my son is in danger of dying?" he asked.

He still had an edge to his voice, a touch of sarcasm saying that he didn't believe a word Chris had said. But at least, Chris thought, he appeared willing to listen. He hadn't hung up on the craziness…at least not yet.

"Sir, I started seeing your son in my dream about two weeks ago. There have been quite a few others between him and the first one I told you about. One of them lasted a month before he faded and died. I am sorry to put it like this, but based on the people I have met in my dreams over the past few months, I don't believe Benjamin has two more weeks. I don't even think he has one week. He has begun fading." Speaking fast now, getting to the heart of the matter, not wanting to be interrupted, Chris continued. "I know this is the last thing in the world you want to hear and I wish I could be more specific, but I am hoping that just because I see him in my dream, it doesn't mean he has to die like the others have. They were all old or sick or injured. But Benjamin is healthy, is he not? I don't really understand any of this any better than you do."

"Benjamin is in excellent health," Mr. Worthington confirmed, his voice sounding a bit distant. Chris could tell Thomas Worthington was deep in thought, his brain, for the sake of his son, trying hard to grasp what his ears were relaying to it. But Chris wasn't sure acceptance had yet been achieved.

"Yes," Chris said, "that's what I thought. Then that would mean that there could be an accident that might happen sometime in the next few days, or week. I don't know. I just know that he is alive right now and healthy and there's no reason for him to be appearing in my dream. But if the patterns hold true, Mr. Worthington, I am sorry to say that Benjamin's life is indeed in great danger. I asked him for his phone number last night in the dream so that I could warn you. He told me you are a policeman. I hope this means you can give him even better protection. At least until I don't see him anymore in my dream. If someone new appears and Benjamin is still fine, then I'll know that whatever was supposed to happen, didn't, and the danger will have passed. Do you understand, Mr. Worthington? I know this sounds crazy. I also know that I can't be sure about anything, but I do truly believe that Benjamin's life is in danger. Please just tell me that at least over the next week or two, you won't let Benjamin out of your sight for an instant. I will call you again tomorrow, and every day, to tell you about the dream and whether or not I am still seeing Benjamin in it. Will you do that? Watch him around the clock right now? He needs you, Mr. Worthington. You must trust me on this, for his sake. I don't know how I know what I know beyond what I have told you, but I cannot ignore it. He's a wonderful boy, as I am sure you know, sir. Will you keep him with you?"

A very loud silence hung in the air. Chris wondered for a minute if maybe Mr. Worthington had heard enough of this hogwash and simply hung up the phone in disbelief during his last frantic pleas for help on Benjamin's behalf.

Finally, Mr. Worthington said, "You are asking me to put a lot of faith into something that sounds like total bullshit coming from someone over the phone who I have never met, Mr. Battles. How on earth do you expect me to believe any of this?"

"Your son wears Power Ranger pajamas to bed and sleeps with the red one. He likes to re-enact their stories in his imagination," Chris said calmly.

"All that proves is that you could be a peeping-tom pervert. You know I can have you picked up by the Minneapolis police in minutes if I have to. I have your phone number, too. I called up there to have a background check run on you right before I called you. I'm sure by now they have all the info they need and are just awaiting my word."

"I assure you that is not the case, Mr. Worthington. I am not liking this any more than you are. These dreams have been a curse for me. I wish I didn't have them. But I do." Now it was Chris' turn to express a little impatience. "I do have them and for the past two weeks, your son has been the featured guest star. You can ignore me and call me a kook and then feel like shit for the rest of your life if I am right. Or you can keep an extra close eye on Benjamin for the next few days and possibly prevent something bad from happening to him. It's just for a short time, Mr. Worthington. Maybe your knowledge of this alone will have already altered something and Benjamin will not return to my dream tonight and he'll be fine. Maybe there's nothing we can do at all about it. I just don't know. But I do believe, myself, that if Benjamin stands a chance, he's going to need your help. He's going to need you to believe."

"Why doesn't Benjamin remember you, as you do him?" Mr. Worthington asked.

"I don't know," Chris replied honestly. "As I said earlier, Sherry didn't remember talking to me in my dream either. But what she told me in my dream had been true. This is fact."

"If I heed your warning here," Benjamin's father said,

sounding nervous now, which was probably a good thing, "in the unlikelihood that this could be anything other than total bullshit, are you willing to let me send a couple of men down from the Minneapolis PD to talk with you in person about all this?"

"If I have to tell more people about this craziness in order to help save Benjamin's life, then yes, send whomever you like," Chris replied.

"I won't let him out of my sight, Mr. Battles. I can't say that I truly believe much of anything you have told me, but I do believe that you believe it. That's enough to cause me more concern than I am comfortable with. I am going to send a couple officers over to give you a little interview, though. Please try to cooperate with them. I'm sorry if it inconveniences your schedule, but I'm sure you must understand."

"I understand fully, Mr. Worthington. I'll call you tomorrow as soon as I wake up. Until then, promise me not to let Benjamin out of your sight. Okay? Promise me? For Benjamin."

"You can count on it, Mr. Battles. You have succeeded in making me sufficiently uneasy about all this. I will not let anything happen to my son. I'll be in touch. And I suppose you feel a 'thank you' is in order here, but I think I will reserve that comment until after this matter is resolved."

"I understand, sir."

The two men hung up and went about their respective tasks at hand--Thomas Worthington's task being to find out as much as possible about one Chris Battles of the Minneapolis area while at the same time not letting Benjamin out of his sight; and Chris' task being to pass the time until work so that he could get back to sleep and see if Benjamin was still hosting...and still fading.

7

After hanging up the phone, Chris returned to the Internet White Pages he had been using the day before to try to locate Worthington households around the neighboring states. Using Benjamin's phone number as his 'search' criterion, he was able to find the listing for Thomas Worthington, 619 County Rd. L, Mulvane, Kansas. Copying the address, he then visited *MapQuest*, a website that creates maps. By entering in his own address and the Worthington's address, the website put together not only a detailed, street by street, doorstep to doorstep list of written directions, but it also showed a map of the suggested route. By then highlighting any portion of the route map, one can zoom in on that particular area. After highlighting and zooming in four times, Chris had learned that Mulvane was a small town about ten miles south of Wichita, and the spot marked with the red 'X', 619 County Rd. L, was on a rural highway with no more than two lots per country block.

Chris felt a chill as he grasped the impact of what he was looking at on his computer screen, who he had just spoken to on the phone, and what it was he was trying to do. He was looking at the place where a boy he had only dreamt about was actually living, and was supposedly soon going to be dying. He had just spoken to the father of the boy in his dream thanks to the phone number obtained in the dream. And he was trying to work against whatever force was making these predictions come to him in his dreams. He no longer doubted for a second, however, that his dreams were anything but very, very real. The 'guilty conscience' theory for his dreams long since thrown out, Chris had come to accept as fact that he had entered a portion of reality that most humans were lucky enough to never discover.

Chris book-marked the map page with Benjamin's location and address and closed out his Internet service.

In almost three months since Sherry's death, since he had mentioned to the nurse how Sherry had contacted him about her dilemma, he had kept his daily nightmare to himself, telling no one else about his recurring dream. Now hearing the whole story out loud for the first time as he recounted the last three months for Thomas Worthington, he had to give Benjamin's dad credit for not hanging up on the outlandish tale half way through.

There was still hope.

Chris had agreed because there was no logical reason not to, but he was not looking forward to having to repeat his story yet again for whomever Mr. Worthington was going to have visit him. He thought there was a good chance, too, that it could have been a bluff, that Officer Worthington was just looking for a reaction. But it had been no bluff. Inside of ninety minutes from hanging up the phone, two plain-clothes detectives showed up at Chris' door.

Chris gave the detectives a shorter, more condensed version of the tale that he had told Mr. Worthington. But even the short version had given them enough to haul him down to the asylum if they chose. Their main purpose, Chris was told, had not been to judge his sanity, but rather to determine whether he might pose a threat to society, or more specifically, to Officer Worthington's son in Kansas.

They were apparently satisfied that Chris was not going to

be a threat to anyone. After listening to his tale and asking what sounded like a couple of token questions that had little to do with the matter at hand, the two detectives shook his hand, thanked him for his time, and asked him to stay in Minnesota for now.

He assured them that he had no plans to travel any time soon. He could tell they hadn't believed that his dream had any basis in reality, but it was his character they were primarily concerned with. But Chris didn't care if they had believed him or not. He hadn't tried to convince them as he had Thomas Worthington. They had nothing at stake, no reason to question reality as they knew it. He hadn't expected them to believe him. He was just doing as Benjamin's dad had asked, for Benjamin's sake.

Looking up from the bottom of the small hill, Chris watches the familiar scene play out. The Priest stops reading from his book, folds it closed and moves it to his chest. His attention, and that of the mourners at his side, turns toward Chris as he approaches his party. The coffin lay closed awaiting his arrival.

As Chris joins the others at the edge of the hole, he studies the Priest. Again, he wants to ask the Priest who is in the coffin. He knows the Priest knows. But it is what he doesn't know about the Priest that scares him enough to remain silent.

The coffin begins to creak, announcing that it is proceeding to open, and Chris holds his breath. He had worked very hard while delivering his papers not to build any false hopes for this moment. He wanted to see that Benjamin was no longer the coffin's resident, to call Mr. Worthington tomorrow and hear that Benjamin is still alive and healthy and fine. Then he would know, at that point, that Benjamin had escaped his untimely, premature death. But he hadn't allowed himself to believe that that had all been so easily accomplished with just one phone call.

Getting to know Benjamin over the last two weeks, Chris had learned that Benjamin lived in a large family. He had said that he lived on a big farm. The farm belonged to his father's brother, Uncle Patrick. Benjamin's family helped with the farm's chores in exchange for rent. He didn't have any brothers or sisters himself, but his aunt and uncle had provided him with four cousins close to his age who he'd grown up with just like any natural brother or sister. The household, in all, contained four adults and five energetic children under the age of ten. With so much family around and a dad who was a cop and trained to deal with unusual situations, not to mention the fact that they lived in a rural area eliminating hundreds of other variables present in a big city environment, Chris couldn't help but think that the scale must be tipping back in Benjamin's favor.

While delivering his papers all night, he continually assured himself that even if Benjamin was still his morning host when he returned, it didn't mean he had failed him yet. But when the lid to the coffin did finally come open and Benjamin peered out from within, Chris felt his heart sink with a heavy thud and realized he had not squelched his hopes as much as he thought he had.

"Hi, Chris!" Benjamin said.

"Hi, Benjamin."

"Are we going to McDonald's?" he asked with a smile. "Did you talk to my dad?"

Apparently, Chris figured, Benjamin forgot his dreams the way most people do upon awakening. This would be why he didn't recognize Chris' name when his dad asked him about it. Chris was probably part of just one of hundreds of dreams Benjamin forgot about once he awoke each morning.

Chris wished he could forget each morning.

"Yes, I did talk to your dad, Benjamin. Thanks for giving me

your number yesterday. We're trying to work it out," Chris said, and then added, "You have a great dad. He cares about you very much."

"Did you see the Power Rangers *yesterday? The* Power Rangers *rule!"*

"No. I missed them yesterday," Chris replied.

Benjamin then filled Chris in on all the action he had missed out on during yesterday's episode. This was the usual fare for their visits during the two previous weeks. Chris tried to listen attentively, as he always did, but while Benjamin described the deeds of the day by the Rangers, Chris couldn't help but notice that not only was Benjamin obviously still in Sherry's coffin, but his fading had gotten worse… much, much worse. His eyes had lost all but the faintest hint of color. His skin seemed to be growing thinner. His time was getting close. Too close. He knew he would have to be even more convincing when he called Mr. Worthington again. He knew that so far, despite his efforts, he had changed nothing yet. But he wasn't giving up.

Chris woke up a little after noon and went through his usual morning ritual of shower, toast and juice. He then called Thomas Worthington to inform him that the danger was still present, that Benjamin was still fading. No one answered the phone. The answering machine was also apparently turned off. He figured he would try again later in the afternoon when everyone started gathering for dinner. For now, he decided to try to take his mind off things he couldn't control and wrote his bi-weekly email to his own parents and surfed aimlessly around the Information Superhighway to pass the time.

At four o'clock there was still no answer.

At five o'clock there was still no answer.

Six o'clock, no answer.

Six thirty, seven o'clock, seven-fifteen, still no answer.

It wasn't until ten o'clock that night, and eight more phone calls with the same results, that Chris learned why the Worthingtons were not at home. Their home was no longer at home. Apparently, according to the lead story the anchor for the ten o'clock news was reading, a rare early March tornado had run through southern Kansas shortly before noon. Tornado season in Kansas usually didn't begin until late April. The news reported that the tornado had been responsible for eighteen deaths, at least seventy injuries and several billion dollars worth of damage in and around the small communities just south of the Wichita area. Pictures coming in from their news-copter showed several farm houses that had been leveled to the ground. Chris knew at that moment that Benjamin would not be returning to his dream the next morning.

8

Since Benjamin's departure as host, over the next three months Chris had developed certain coping mechanisms to help him deal with the dying faces that visited him each day. He tried not to get too personal with them, tried not to care.

After emotionally draining himself over Benjamin and failing to save the boy's life, he had convinced himself that he couldn't have made a difference anyway. He knew trouble and grief lay ahead for the healthy looking visitors of his nightmare, but he had no way of knowing what that trouble could possibly be. He could start asking them for their phone numbers as common practice, but he would never know what to be warning them of. He figured he would just end up needlessly scaring them, making their last days on earth more miserable than they may already be. He didn't see how telling someone there was a pretty good chance they were going to die in the next few days could be considered help…even if they did believe him.

He didn't blame himself for not coming through for Benjamin the way he did when failing to inform the doctor of Sherry's news from the other side of consciousness. But the loss was still something that had to be dealt with. It wasn't like the loss when someone close to you dies. Chris cared for Benjamin, had genuinely liked the boy, but had really only known him for a little over two weeks. He was now just another of the many, many names in the obituaries he spent an hour or two reading every day.

While still not willing to give in to the concept of fate, he had decided that changing the outcome of the premonitions he had been cursed with was simply beyond his ability. Or at least, as of yet, beyond his understanding. There was still so much he didn't understand.

Originally, he wanted to know things like: Why was he having this dream? Who was making the connection possible? Why can he remember the dreams but the others in his dreams cannot? And of course: Can he alter the predicted outcome? Anymore, however, Chris really only wanted to know the answer to two questions, and even one of those he would concede for the answer to the other.

One: he wanted to know if the Priest in his dream had a bigger role in what was going on than simply being a prop. If that were possible, Chris suspected he did. And two: he wanted more than anything just to know when and if this nightmare was ever going to stop. The first question he would gladly forget about as best he could if he had a satisfactory answer to the latter one.

But the dreams neither stopped, nor did he ask the Priest when, or even if, they ever would stop. Instead, he met Martha, a 54-year-old, never-married grade school teacher who was teaching her final classes. And John, who had been born just fifteen years earlier with a spinal disease that was now calling in its hand. He met Perry the plumber and Robert the bank executive whose hearts were simply getting tired of beating. And there were others, more than he tried to recall anymore. Most appeared in his dream with a certain degree of fading already present and their eyes almost white where color had once been prominent. But a few arrived as William and Benjamin had, looking pretty good for a week or two before the fading began.

Now, six months since the dreams had begun, Chris' life had been turned upside down. He worked by night instead of by light and avoided contact with the world outside his own lonely routine. His friends no longer called or checked in, not because of what had happened to Sherry, but because Chris had *moved on* himself, in a way, and left his friends behind. He had returned not one of their concerned calls, and their concerns eventually shifted to other things in their own busy lives.

His hair had gone uncut. He shaved, but only occasionally, and was currently sporting a ten-day growth. He had visible bags under his dark eyes, making them look sunken and sad. And the first few strands of premature gray lay amidst his thick black hair. He didn't own a bathroom scale, but guessed that he had lost at least twenty pounds. He was using a tighter notch on his belt.

The only thing that had improved over the last six months was that his house was a lot cleaner than it had ever been before. To help pass the time, to keep his mind occupied, usually in the last couple of hours before going out to deliver his routes, he dusted and vacuumed and picked up and wiped down. Chris' appearance had certainly seen better days before the accident, but his house had never been cleaner.

Although he tried not to think about it, the same questions he had no answers to continued to threaten his grasp on reality. During most of his waking hours, surfing the net, cleaning house, working, he was able to keep his mind on the tasks at hand--not completely, but sufficiently to push back the questions that truly haunted him. But every morning as he laid himself down to bed, these same questions would fight their way back to the front of his brain and go to work on him as he tried to fall asleep. Because he always felt in such need of sleep, the questions running amok in his head didn't keep him awake each morning as they otherwise might have, but they didn't dissipate as he drifted off, either. Often times, people with hectic, trying or emotionally draining lives find sanctuary in their sleep. For Chris it had become his own personal Hell.

Part Two

“Welcome to my nightmare.”
---Alice Cooper

9

Carly Brandt sat down at her desk in front of her computer with a cup of her favorite organic tea. Jerry wasn't due home from the bowling alley for at least two hours yet, giving her plenty of time to say 'hi' to a friend or two. Actually, he was probably done with his bowling already. The four-man league to which he had devoted every Friday night for the last who knows how many years (since before the two of them had met, anyway) started at 6:30 p.m. sharp with the final frames needing to be done and out of the way in order for the 9:00 p.m. leagues to begin on time.

It was 8:45 now and Carly could see her husband in her mind's eye, a big, cuddly, teddy-bear of a man when she was six months pregnant accepting his proposal, but having since evolved into just a mean spirited grizzly. He was probably at this moment drunk from the eight to ten beers consumed during the male bonding portion of the evening, red faced and grinning ear to ear as he loudly and obnoxiously recited to his buddies the wife-bashing lines he loved so much, just like the ones Norm always came up with on *Cheers*. She could see him, in her mind's eye, trying to put his personalized bowling ball away in his monogrammed bowling ball bag and sliding his new bowling shoes off his feet at the same time without losing his balance. In this version of her daydream, he never maintained the necessary balance needed to keep from falling on his smug face. Watching him bloody his nose on the ball return or dropping the ball on his foot as he lost his balance always gave her a secret, and only slightly guilty, smile.

In one more recent variation of her weekly daydream, Jerry falls down the single step to the settee area while trying to catch the ball as it rolled off the lip of his bowling bag, having missed the hole he was trying to drop it into. Then upon catching the ball with the grace of a drunken NHL'er trying his hand at ballet, he comically trips up the single step leading farther out onto the varnished wood approach to the lane and proceeds to fall forward, face smashing ball as ball smashes ground. The bowling ball rolls slowly down the gutter on its own. Jerry lays spread eagle on his large belly, half in the gutter himself. His buddies are standing around all bug-eyed and holding their guts as if they were about to split open if they laughed any harder. But then they all stop laughing and stare in silence with gaping, stupid mouths hanging open as a large pool of bright red blood rapidly spreads out from under Jerry's unmoving head…

…this version had caused a quick hand to rise up to stifle the cheer trying to escape her smiling lips the first time it had played itself out in her head a few weeks ago.

But Carly had never been so lucky. Tough as it may or may not have actually been for him at this particular time each week, he apparently always seemed to manage to get his ball and shoes back into his bag without hurting himself. Then he would manage to get across the street to the strip club with his buddies without getting hit by a car. Finally, somehow, he'd drive the five miles home after a few more drinks without getting killed, killing someone else, or even getting pulled over by the cops and hauled in for a DUI. The latter being the most likely of outcomes, the most realistic, she thought. And whenever it started getting much past 11:00 pm on Friday nights and Jerry hadn't squealed to a screeching stop inside the garage announcing his return home yet, that was the one she was secretly rooting for.

But putting that fantasy aside for now, Carly, or *LorettaC* as she was known in the cyber-world, was turning her attention to the chat room she frequently visited where she could try to forget about her alcoholic husband a short while.

After dutifully sending Jerry off to the bowling alley on a full stomach, she had raced to pick up the dishes and get them washed and set for drying. Jerry thought buying a dishwasher was a waste of hard-earned money when they already had a kitchen sink with perfectly good running water, not that he had ever washed a dish himself.

Next was the laundry, washed and dried, neatly folded and put away or hung. A bedtime story for the kids. Their toys picked up out of the living room, the kitchen, the hallway, and stored for tomorrow when they'll all be spread about the house once again. The kids themselves settled and quiet in their beds. Now it was finally her turn.

Friday nights, with the chores done, the kids in bed, and Jerry out, was her time. She looked forward to those two precious hours every single week. Two hours to get away and explore other worlds and other lives. Two hours in the cyber-world to escape her increasingly depressing and tension-filled existence in the real world. She usually logged onto the net for a few hours a week during the day while Jerry was at work too, but the kids were usually demanding her attention and most of her cyber-friends were at their own jobs during the day anyway, so the socializing was never very fruitful during those times. Friday night was the time she looked forward to.

In the real world, she worried. She worried about her two babies, Johnny and Sasha. Johnny, her first born, was now 4 years old and Sasha had just turned 2. Carly was 24 and Jerry, the king of the castle, as he often put it, was 27. Jerry had been the manager of the Texaco Food Mart when he had hired Carly to run the register. They still hadn't yet officially established between themselves that they were of boyfriend/girlfriend status about a year later when Carly discovered she was pregnant with Johnny. Jerry had decided to "do the right thing" --well actually, "might as well give the kid a name" was closer to the words spoken in his anticlimactic proposal, but she had tried not to sweat the details back then. She had the kid to think about, after all. But now she worried.

Jerry had quit the Texaco Food Mart job, after she had the baby, to try to make more money. He had gotten into construction, road work, saying the benefits were better even though the pay was about the same. She didn't necessarily blame the job, but that was about the time when the transformation from teddy-bear to grizzly bear had begun. But also, at that time came the new home, the new baby, the new wife, the new bills, the new responsibilities and demands, not to mention the new expectations. So, she didn't think it was fair to label any one event as the one that had triggered the transition. It had happened, and how or why or who was to blame had long since ceased to matter. Dealing with it was now the issue. Or to be more specific, getting through each evening without any raised voices, or worse.

So far, Jerry hadn't gotten much worse. He had slapped her once, hard, but had felt badly enough about it afterwards that she didn't think it would happen again. But things between them still seemed to have changed once that slap had been delivered. Another wall had been erected that was likely never going to come down. She didn't think Jerry would ever harm her or the kids, but lately she had begun to feel a little unsure about a lot of things, that being one of them.

But Friday nights she put her worries aside. He always came

home drunk and happy. He wasn't so bad when he was drunk. In fact, she always made it a point to offer him a drink after dinner each night during the rest of the week to loosen him up a bit, maybe get him a little tipsy. That seemed to be where a hint of the old teddy-bear still survived. Jerry usually turned down the after dinner drink anyway. He didn't like to drink a lot all the time, he just liked to drink a lot when he drank.

Turning on her computer, AOL dutifully announced, "You've Got Mail!", and her own weekly transformation from Carly to *LorettaC* was instantly completed. Carletta was her given name though no one had called her anything but Carly since the day she was born. If she hadn't seen the name Carletta on her birth certificate after her parents had passed away while she was in college, she could have gone through life never even knowing what her true birth name had been. When choosing a new name for the Internet, she had chosen a new form of her name, opening the door for a new personality.

Her buddy list sprang into view in the upper right-hand corner of her screen as it always did upon connection. She had seventy-four names on her list, most of which she had merely chatted with a time or two and popped onto the list in case they ever revisited. But at least twenty of the names on the list she considered to be her cyber-pals and talked with on a fairly regular basis. However, none of them knew of her worries and concerns and lost dreams from the real world. She cast them off like old skin, along with her name, whenever she entered cyber-land.

Tonight, she noticed that her best cyber-pal was online, *LadyAvec2*. She immediately double clicked over her pal's screen name on the buddy list and brought up the Instant Messaging feature which allowed her to communicate in real time with her friend.

LorettaC: evenin', Lady! Any nightlife out there tonight?
LadyAvec2: haven't been on too long but kinda quiet so far what are you up too this eve LC?
LorettaC: oh the usual…lookin' for trouble
LadyAvec2: you and me both kiddo
LorettaC: so how'd the f2f go last week? Was he a keeper?
LadyAvec2: nah, never happened
LorettaC: what happened, thought you two were stoked
LadyAvec2: he learned his French
LorettaC: and put 2 and 2 together, eh…hadn't you told him?
LadyAvec2: exactly—about two more than he had in mind it hadn't come up yet…thought it was obvious
LorettaC: well if it wasn't obvious, he was obviously the wrong one anyway, if you know what I mean
LadyAvec2: yeah…hee…don't need another egotistical air-head…but his pic was sooooo cute!
LorettaC: gotta make up your mind girl…can't often get everything in one neat package
LadyAvec2: well I'm still hoping
LorettaC: aren't we all, Lady
LadyAvec2: I thought you had yours already in captivity, LC
LorettaC: that I do, but a little tweaking here and there couldn't hurt
LadyAvec2: yeah, we tend to choose with our hearts instead of minds in the heat of the moment
LorettaC: actually the choice was kinda made for me by a little bundle of joy
LadyAvec2: shot-gunned it, eh?
LorettaC: that's another tale for another time. right now I'm ready to party

LadyAvec2: saw Stubabe7 on a little while ago but the room has been dead tonight
LorettaC: ok well I'll be around a little while here…drop you a pop if anything crops
LadyAvec2: I'll take the top
LorettaC: OH!! And I thought you were a LADY, Lady!
LadyAvec2: I like to be a lady in control
LorettaC: maybe you can come here and teach mine a thing or two
LadyAvec2: ahhh, I think we have discovered where the tweaking is needed
LorettaC: another tale for another time
LadyAvec2: sounds like a sore spot, too you ok LC? you can tell lady
LorettaC: I'm fine but thanks for asking
I wouldn't mind being on top for a change though I must admit…hee
LadyAvec2: lol…the only way to fly, love here if you need me k?
LorettaC: go get laid, Lady…then give me ALLLLL the details
LadyAvec2: a lady never kisses and tells!
LorettaC: lol…you'll break
LadyAvec2: oh god I hope…hee…we are toooo bad!
LorettaC: the only way to fly, love catch up with you later there be good :p
LadyAvec2: and be a party pooper?!?!…hee laters ;)

Carly had met *LadyAvec2* in a single parents' newsgroup on the Internet. Carly wasn't actually a single parent, but more often than not she felt like one. In the newsgroup, single parents from around the country, even occasionally from around the world, posted concerns and gripes and questions and plights about parenting solo. Members of the newsgroup could respond to the posting by others or post a fresh idea for all to read. Carly had posted a response to one of *LadyAvec2's* more humorous postings pertaining to the difficulties of finding a decent babysitter. *LadyAvec2* had sent an email back to Carly in response to her comments and then the IM's began and they'd been friends ever since, almost a year now.

LadyAvec2's real world name was Julie. She was a 28-year-old single mom of two, ages 3 and 5. Her husband, Brad, the father of her two children, had apparently been scared off by the prospect of three mouths to feed, four including his own. When Julie had returned home from the hospital with her second new addition to the family, curious as to why Brad hadn't picked her up, she found a note saying she'd find Eric, their first born, with Grandma, and probably wouldn't be able to find him for a while.

'For a while' had apparently turned into forever. It had been more than three years now and Julie hadn't seen or heard a word from him. No phone calls. No postcards. No child support. Even if he did find the balls to suddenly show up on her doorstep again, he wasn't going to get through the threshold, this she knew. By now she figured he was dead somewhere. Easier to put him behind her, thinking he was dead. Easier on the kids, too, in her mind, saving them from possibly hoping for the hopeless.

Lady was four years older than *LorettaC.* Both had two kids not yet old enough for school. One was single wishing she were married, the other married wishing she were single. The grass is always greener and all that. They enjoyed bantering back and forth about the pros and cons of married life, or lack thereof. They teased each other, encouraged each other, rooted for each other, but had never actually met each other. Carly lived in Minneapolis, Minnesota. Julie lived in Chapel Hill, North Carolina. But *LorettaC* and

LadyAvec2 both lived in cyber-land as neighbors who had drank together, laughed together, cried together, and partied together. Though they had never met face-to-face, f2f, as it is called in cyber-lingo, they had exchanged pictures via attachments to emails so they did know what each other looked like, as well as each other's kids, of course. They had become good friends. But even though Julie was one of the very few in cyber-land to know Carly was *LorettaC's* real name, and the *only* one that knew what she looked like, that was just about all she knew of the real-world Carly.

LorettaC was more fun than Carly, bolder, wittier, more spontaneous, happier--everything Carly wanted to be, but wasn't. No one in *LorettaC's* world, including her best cyber-pal, knew who Carly really was when not sitting in front of her computer screen.

After saying good-bye to *LadyAvec2, LorettaC* stopped in at their local gathering hole, a chat room called *SpouseBashing,* its main topic once inside being self-explanatory in its title. This is where she had met most of the screen names that appeared on her buddy list. Once entering the chat room, up to 25 people can communicate together at once, each typing messages onto their own screens that all present 'in the room' can read and respond to instantly. On a busy night, as Friday nights usually proved to be more often than not, the chat room would be full and more difficult to enter, but tonight was not one of those nights. Pulling the link to the chat room from her bookmark menu at the top of her screen, she clicked on the title *SpouseBashing* and instantly found herself 'in the room.'

Lady had said the room was dead tonight and she hadn't been wrong. Glancing at the list of the room's occupants, she didn't recognize any screen names as the regulars. *LadyAvec2* was a regular. *Stubabe7* was another regular. He was always good for a few laughs with his reverse spouse-bashing. *Stubabe7* claimed to be the one that all the rest of them were bashing. The one you love to hate. Of course, everyone truly loved *Stubabe7* in spite of this, or maybe it was because of this....no matter, the regulars all understood that this was the cyber-role he had assumed and he played it very well.

The dialogue running across Carly's computer screen from these names she didn't recognize couldn't hold her interest. She clicked on the 'exit' icon and left the room.

Another glance at her buddy list told her that *LadyAvec2* was still online, but she didn't feel like going there again tonight. She had come very close to spilling the beans. In all fairness, if she were to tell all with anyone online, Julie would be the one, but *LorettaC* really enjoyed her new online persona and made a conscious effort to keep Carly out.

Every now and then Carly thought she might want to find a true friend online, one to be honest with and more confiding in, and again had thought of Julie in those moments. The role *LorettaC* had adopted certainly had served its purpose, and part of its strength lay in its consistency. But to have someone to confide in, to trust the darker sides with as well as the lighter sides, to talk about the things that truly mattered--that was still missing.

There were six other names appearing on her buddy list as currently online, but none that sparked any particular memories. She ignored them and went to see what the cyber-mailman had stuffed in her cyber-mailbox this week.

Aside from the assorted invitations to porn sites that seemed to invade her mailbox each week, there were five more letters from unrecognizable sources and one from *LadyAvec2* dated from last Saturday. Carly deleted the invitations and unsolicited attention without opening them and double-clicked on the only entry left. It was entitled, "Duh!"

Hey there LC!

Parlez vous francais? Non? Me neither but some things you just know...no? The dude 'avec' the cute pic wasn't quite blessed 'avec' a quick wit. He asked if my last name was Avec while we were thinking about where we might meet this evening. After I told him it was French for 'with,' the light bulb finally went on in his head as he figured out the significance of the number 2 all on his own. That was when the stuttering began. What a loser. His Loss! I was even feeling horny tonight...hee! Oh well, back to the drawing board.

So how's it going over there on the other side? Been getting any lately. <slap, slap> HEE! Okay, so maybe I'm still a little horny. I didn't have a back-up plan tonight. Sitter's on her way already. I want to go out and do something tonight, and now I'm all dressed up and no where to go. So you want to meet me somewhere tonight? My treat! Catch the next flight down and the party's on me...sans men! See?! There goes that French again. What a dork. He don't know what he be missin'!

Snow melted away yet up there? I miss the snow. We get a dusting here and the schools close for the week. Don't miss the sub-zero, though...but then I guess I discovered tonight you just can't escape that no matter where you move to.

Okay, okay...done feeling sorry for myself here...hee! Gonna go out and get drunk tonight. Then I guess the 'back-up plan' will have to be the shoebox in the back of my closet

before bed tonight. I hope the batteries are more alive than the men around here!! <giggle>

Have a great week, LC! Talk to you soon!

Lady

Carly closed the email. *Lady*, like *Stubabe7,* always had a way of making her chuckle. She couldn't remember the last time Jerry had made her crack a smile…let alone chuckle. But for now, she was *LorettaC* and chased Jerry out of her head just as quickly as he had entered it. *LorettaC* had better things to think about.

She would normally have immediately whipped out a witty reply to her best cyber-friend, but she had just gotten done speaking to her a few minutes earlier and, truth be told, she was currently envying Julie's single status a little too much at the moment. Envy had always been a tough one for her to suppress. She knew life was no bed of roses, but she thought hers had a few more weeds in it than she had bargained for.

Bidding *LadyAvec2* a silent adieu (*There goes that French again*, she thought with a snicker) *LorettaC* moved on to her next favorite online activity, browsing profiles in the Twin Cities.

This pastime had originally spawned from a desire to meet a friend, a local friend. Someone to meet for coffee. Someone to shoot the shit with. Despite having a husband and two wonderful kids, she felt very lonely.

After clicking on the 'profile search' option from her Internet pull-down menu, she would type in her search preferences. For location she always typed in "Twin Cities or Minneapolis or St. Paul." Next, she would click on the box in the lower right-hand corner marked "return only names currently online." When she was still actively looking for a local friend, she would also click on the "female" square for a gender preference, but having long since given up on that mission, she usually now left that option open. She also used to type in "married" for the requested marital status, and "kids" in the hobbies space, hoping to find a friend with interests similar to her own. But after a few attempts at getting conversations started with her search's offerings of potential candidates, none had sparked any possibilities for growing into the type of friendship she was hoping to find. She eventually gave up on this method for finding a local friend online and had at that time given birth to *LorettaC*'s new persona who had come to acquire quite a few cyber-friends over the past year.

Tonight, allowing a little of Carly's despair from the real world to infiltrate into *LorettaC*'s world, along with the usual location and online status, she typed in the word 'fate' into the option "search profiles for the following word or phrase." Then moving her arrow on the screen down to the "search" command, she gave it a click while overdramatically chanting out loud to herself with a giggle, "Oh Great and Powerful Cyber-Lord, Destroyer of the Past, Destiny of the Future, Seer into all living rooms of this vast land, take me to my FATE!"

After a four or five second wait while the search engine churned and processed the preference information she submitted, the results appeared. Everyone living in the Minneapolis/St. Paul area who had included the word "fate" in their personal online profile and were currently sitting in front of their computers and signed on to the AOL Internet service was listed on her screen in front of her.

One screen name.

F8meNOT.

Never before had any of her searches produced only one name. Many had been so far-fetched or ridiculous, or, as was often the case, too picky, and would spit out the message "No profiles were found to match your request," but none had ever produced only one. Most, in fact, usually read "1-20 of more than 100 profiles found." But never only one. Ten a few times, five every now and then, three a time or two. But never one.

"Must be fate!" she said, feeling adventuresome as she eyed the screen name of the sole person in all the Twin Cities to answer her call.

Before just barging in on *F8meNOT, LorettaC* clicked on the button labeled "read profile." This would usually tell her enough to know whether or not she wanted to chance interrupting whatever the unsuspecting screen name was doing just because she was bored. She looked for things like age and hobbies and quotes. She loved to read all the quotes people came up with. Many were lines from movies or quotes from songs. Many were obviously inside scuttlebutt or gibberish that made no sense at all to a browsing outsider, but most were pieces of advice. Thousands of dime store philosophers out there in cyber-land giving their two cents worth of worldly knowledge or self-proclaimed ingenious insight. Giving credit where credit is due, many of the hundreds and hundreds of one- and two-line quips were indeed insightful or sound words to remember, advice to live by, or at least made sense enough to debate, but many were downright laughable. Her favorite so far, one she had IM'ed *Lady* about when she had stumbled onto it during one of her profile searches, had a toast for its quote. It read:

Personal Quote: **Here's to being Single**
Seeing Double
And sleeping Triple!!!

She hadn't IM'ed *mr69forU,* the author of this personal quote. She knew all she needed to know about him to know what he would undoubtedly want to talk about. She avoided those types. She wasn't always sure what she was looking for in all the profiles she liked to read, but she was quite sure of what she wasn't looking for. But all his 'definitely nots' aside, his toast had given her and *Lady* a good laugh. With that done, she had closed out the profile and moved on to the next one, looking for another laugh…or even a giggle was passing as good, these days.

F8meNOT's profile now appeared on *LorettaC's* screen.

Member Name:	**Chris**
Location:	**Twin Cities**
Birth Date:	**Aquarius**
Sex:	**Male**
Marital Status:	**Single**
Hobbies:	**Thrill Seeker**
Occupation:	**Customer Service**
Personal Quote:	**If fate is the excuse we use to cover our bad decisions, while God's Goodwill gets credit for the good ones, does that mean the Devil is in control of our fate except when God feels like changing it? Who has the final say? God? Satan? Me? You?**

Cool, Carly thought as she read the personal quote a second time, *one that requires thought. I like him.* She read it a third time. Thought about it some more. Reread the entire profile. Read the personal quote one more time. She thought about IM'ing Chris to start up a good old-fashioned debate on the subject of his quote, if he was game, but heard the screech of tires outside as they rounded the corner entering her street too fast and assumed, correctly, as she glanced up at the clock on the wall above the desk, that it was probably Jerry getting home a little early. So, she clicked on the 'send email' option from Chris' profile and sent him a quick, brief six word note before signing off the Internet to prepare for Jerry's return to his castle.

Just a few seconds after Carly disconnected from her Internet service, she heard the garage door start going up. The king was home. She felt her muscles immediately tense up and had to remind herself that it was Friday night and he was undoubtedly drunk. This helped her relax a little bit, but he was also an hour earlier than usual. Change in routine, she had discovered, was usually not good.

Jerry was indeed drunk, spilling what little beer was still left in the bottle he had smuggled out of the bar "for the road" as he stumbled into the kitchen from the garage. His red bowling shirt with "Jerry" stitched over the breast pocket was untucked. Jerry was not fat, but he was a big man--big boned, big muscles, big soft hands, though working with the highway crews had toughened them up a bit. But when he came through the door drunk with his shirt hanging out over his big belly, which had also grown as of late, he simply looked fat.

Normally at this point, Carly would feign a smile and ask, "You boys win tonight?" Normally that was a safe question. Normally he assured her that they had kicked their opponents' butts royally. She suspected that they didn't win quite as often as she was told they did, but certainly wasn't ever going to challenge that fact.

Tonight, however, Carly opted against the routine question. She could already see in his face that the butt kicking had been reversed this evening. She thought making him admit it might not be the best of strategies in maintaining a quiet and peaceful home tonight, if that was even going to be possible. But she didn't have to ask the question tonight to get the answer.

Setting his beer down hard and steadying himself with the kitchen counter top, he slurred, "Fuckin' Dewy's team stole the championship in the third game tonight. Fuckin' John threw a split in the ninth. I got fucked by a slidin' pin that wouldn't fall in the tenth. Fuckin' seven pins short. Fuckin' miniature trophy. Threw it out the fuckin' window at the asshole that fuckin' cut me off. That'll teach the fucker."

As she listened to Jerry's mini-tirade, hoping the kids were sound asleep, all Carly could think was, *oh, fuck.*

"Well, there's always next year," was all she could think to say, knowing damn good and well it wouldn't help.

"Fuck next year," Jerry wittingly replied. "We'll just get fucked again. Got fucked last year. Got fucked this year. I don't know why I still bowl with those fuck-heads."

And if I'm not careful here, Carly thought, *I could get fucked tonight.* She knew she would have to pick her words cautiously, if she had to speak at all, that is. Best when Jerry is toeing the line to try to just stay out of his way. And tonight, he already had an entire foot dangerously over the line.

"You ready for bed?" Jerry slurred.

More a statement than a question. Another break from routine. Not good. Usually Friday nights after returning from his weekly outing drunk, he opened a fresh beer and sat down in front of *The Tonight Show*. After that was *Cheers.* Carly would finish the laundry or dishes or whatever household chore she could find to busy herself with and then go to bed sometime during *The Tonight Show*. After *Cheers* was over, Jerry would come up and join her. She would be conveniently already asleep, or at least pretending to be. And that made for a good Friday night, normally.

Tonight was not shaping up to be a normal Friday night.

"You're not going to watch *The Tonight Show*?" she asked, hoping he was just too drunk to remember his normal routine.

"Fuck *The Tonight Show,*" Jerry said. "Let's go to bed. I've been getting fucked all night, I figure I might as well enjoy it at least once tonight."

How romantic, Carly thought. As feeble as she knew the attempt would be, she suggested anyway, "I had a few more things I wanted to get done first. I'll join you there in a little while. Okay?" *And with any luck*, she thought, *you might pass out before I get there.*

"Come on," Jerry slurred back, "you got all day tomorrow for that shit. Right now, you're needed upstairs by your man. Go on up and put on that cute little orange number I like so much." Jerry moved across the room and wrapped his arms around her waist from behind her as she put away the last of the dried dishes, pressing his groin up against her. "That one gets me hard just thinking about it. I gotta go to the john and I'll be up to take care of you in a minute. Go on," he said, letting go of her waist and giving her a slap on her rear.

It wasn't that she disliked having sex with Jerry, well, normally. But when he was in a mood like this, he tended to be rougher than she cared for, less caring of how she felt as he pounded into her. Whenever he was in a sour mood, she knew it didn't matter who was beneath him. Sex for the wrong reasons, though it may have worked for him, didn't work for her. When having sex for the right reasons, Jerry was attentive to her feelings and needs and desires. It had been a while now since this phenomenon had occurred. She knew it wasn't apt to be reappearing tonight.

Well, let's get it over with, she told herself. *He won't need you to do anything tonight. Just lay there and let him get it out of his system and then go to sleep.* She put the plate in her hand onto the counter and turned to do as told without looking back at Jerry and without protesting the idea a second time.

When Jerry entered the bedroom a few minutes later wearing only his red bowling shirt, Carly was already in bed wearing her lacy orange nightie that he had bought for her on their first anniversary. She was always told to wear it when *he* was feeling sexy. Now more than three years later, it was still the only sexy thing he had ever bought for her. She lay on her back on top of the covers, hoping that her next move would be rolling over as she pulled the covers over her head and silently cried herself to sleep. She did later cry herself to sleep, but it wasn't silently tonight.

The only time Jerry had ever hit Carly before was during an argument about spending time with the kids. This had been six months earlier. Jerry had gone out for a drink after work and didn't get home until after 8 p.m., missing dinner, and the cake and ice cream. That particular night had been Johnny's fourth birthday. Carly had let him know in no uncertain terms that she was angry with him, and that his son was feeling hurt from his thoughtlessness…and that she thought she might be falling *out* of love with him and that some things had to change. That was the last time she had voiced any displeasure about anything Jerry did, at least to his face. After all, she had two kids to think about.

The change from teddy bear to grizzly had been gradual. Thinking back, Carly knew it had actually begun the moment the consummation of their carefree days had become official. She now recognized the fact that marrying for any reason other than pure, simple, passionate love just wasn't worth it…not even for the sake of the kid, which is what her number one reason at the time had been. She knew now that his proposal to "give the kid a name" should have been all the clue she needed to realize this. Under any other circumstances, such a proposal would have sent her into a fit of guffaws while walking away, not even honoring him with an answer. But with one hand pressed against her rapidly swelling belly, she had answered him with an equally generic, "okay." It had not been the proposal she had imagined throughout her years as a young lass dreaming of the big day…but she had a kid to think about.

And now, later, too late, she understood that she had thought wrong.

Before Johnny's birthday, Jerry had never laid a hand on Carly maliciously. They were arguing more often, their voices getting louder more quickly. Despite the fact that the blow had sent her head over heels backwards, tripping over a kitchen chair, there had been more shock from his slap across the face than pain. For Carly, the hurt in knowing that their marriage had at that moment crossed a line they'd probably never be able to fully return from hurt more than his hand had.

He had been remorseful of his action, but when they argued again just a week later about the same damn thing, he had flinched. She could see him struggling between his desire to hit her again and what he had promised her after that first time. "Never again" he had sworn to her. He had won the struggle and managed to restrain himself that time, but though she refused to admit it even to herself, she knew then that it was going to be just a matter of time before the same struggle might be lost.

Tonight he had lost the struggle. Tonight it was over kisses. Why didn't she kiss him before work in the morning anymore? Why didn't she kiss him when they made love anymore? Her response to the latter being, "Oh, is that what you call that?" was enough for him to break his promise…and Carly's nose.

10

Chris woke up April 1st with the sun squeezing through the slats on his bedroom window and warming his face. Spring was in the air. A time when the grass turns a healthy green and the trees sprout new life on their branches. A time when primal instincts shift with the seasons, from survival of winter to love and the serenity of new life. A time when winter bowling leagues are wrapping up their tournaments for the season.

Chris was certainly not looking for a new love in his life this season, but whether due to the seasonal change or basic human instinct or simply time passed, he had begun to feel the loneliness he had recently sentenced himself to. He still didn't feel ready to patch up his injured friendships and resume his pre-accident life. He was still having the dream. He was overly tired all the time. He still didn't feel like dealing with people. But he was beginning to feel very lonely.

This morning as he showered, he found his mind wandering away from his dream without effort for the first time since it had begun six long months earlier. There had been a new elderly man hosting, already well into his fading. He seemed just like so many others now. Not attaching himself to his dream's hosts, accepting his connection to them, for now anyway, as something beyond his control, Chris had been able to draw another possible reason for this incubus.

Over the past few days, Chris had grown more and more attached to the idea that there might be a medical explanation, unknown to most, possibly even undiscovered yet, but due to his concussion in the accident. He knew that people supposedly only used a small percentage of their brains. Maybe the jolt from the fall had kicked a new portion of his brain into action. Maybe once he learned to use it right, he *could* save a person or two. Or better yet, maybe it would react like memory loss does sometimes with head injuries and just stop coming any day now as a memory might suddenly return. The latter was his strongest hope.

But learning to accept his current ailment and attaching himself to the idea that it couldn't possibly last forever, while promising himself if it *did* last much longer, he would see a doctor about it, he had relieved just enough stress to suddenly notice how lonely he had become. Not that he had any solutions in mind, but that was the direction his mind was wandering. He decided if he had someone he could share his thoughts with, he'd begin to feel better. Less alone, at any rate. Someone to tell him he wasn't going crazy. Or that he was. He just felt that maybe a second opinion from someone he trusted would be nice. But who could he trust to believe him about something as unbelievable as this? The detectives who had interviewed him a few months earlier for Officer Worthington obviously hadn't believed a word of it. They had been sent, of course, merely to decide if they deemed Chris any kind of threat to Benjamin, or society in general. Chris assumed they had sent word back to Benjamin's dad confirming the factual part of his story, the accident, and that he appeared harmless. He further assumed they must have missed the news of the tornado because of a poker night or an office party, or maybe they just failed to put two and two together, because he hadn't heard from them after the Worthington family's demise. Even Mr. Worthington admittedly denied believing a word of Chris' outlandishly wild story but had heeded the warning, although to no avail, only because it involved his son.

Chris had his usual skimpy breakfast and was entertaining the thought of maybe using some of the insurance settlement for psychiatric help as he cracked open a can of Mountain Dew and sat down in front of his computer. He figured a shrink would listen, but he still probably wouldn't believe. He tossed the idea aside. Not out. Just aside, for now.

"You've Got Mail!" greeted Chris as he turned on his computer. He clicked on the icon of a mailbox to retrieve his customary Saturday note of news and good wishes from his mom. Her note was of course there with "Write to me!" in the subject line, as well as another one from a *LorettaC* with no subject in the space where one usually exists. He remembered that this note had actually come in the night before and had figured it was probably some sort of advertisement as he didn't recognize the sender's name. At the time it had arrived, he had been busy reading up on the Timberwolves' win from the previous night and figured the ad could wait. Ultimately though, he had forgotten about it and had signed off to start getting ready for work for the night never having opened it. He opened his mom's note first.

After reading and responding to his mother, he opened up the one from *LorettaC*. The only words on the page read:

your fate is in MY hands

It was the last thing he expected to see. The furthest thing from his mind. He stared at the six words without reaction, more confused than anything, before soaking in the meaning of the words themselves. Then he remembered the profile he had set up for his screen name back when he had bought the computer and realized this *LorettaC* person must have stumbled onto it and was commenting on it. Nothing wrong with that, he figured. He had asked the question, after all. But this particular answer certainly wasn't the one he was looking for.

Before responding to this seemingly bold, if not rude, statement and setting the record straight for *LorettaC*, Chris looked up the profile for the screen name using the available method to do so to possibly get a better idea of who he was about to berate for her comment.

Member Name:	**LorettaC**
Location:	**Minnesota**
Birth Date:	**every year**
Marital Status:	**very married**
Hobbies:	**mom, AOL, fantasizing**
Personal Quote:	**HELP!!!**

Chris saw nothing objectionable or perverse or weird. She looked like your average overworked mom according to her profile. This fact made him even more curious for the reasoning behind her slant on his quote.

Seeing that she also used the AOL Internet service, he added her to his buddy list to see if she might happen to be online at that moment. To his surprise, she was. He then double clicked on her screen name from his buddy list and brought up the IM system giving him a chance to question her motives person to person, rather than email to email.

F8meNOT: So what makes you think you control my fate?

Then after a thirty second wait that felt much longer,

LorettaC: oh hi! I was just responding to the question in your profile

F8meNOT: yes, I assumed that much, but my above question remains the same

LorettaC: well I didn't say I controlled YOUR fate, I said I controlled my own…I wrote…My fate is in my hands

F8meNOT: Well I probably would have agreed with you if that was what your note said, but I have it right here hot off the press and it most definitely says that you control mine

LorettaC: I could have sworn I wrote it the other way…oh well, consider it corrected now

LorettaC: however…

LorettaC: if you think about it…

F8meNOT: think about what?

LorettaC: what I apparently wrote wasn't that far off, was it? I mean, if I hadn't sent the message then you wouldn't be talking to me right now. So if fate was that we should meet, then I did indeed just control your fate, in that sense

F8meNOT: that is assuming, of course, that fate even exists and I am of the strong belief that it does not

LorettaC: I tend to believe the same, but then is it really any harder to believe in than God? Or the Devil?

F8meNOT: I don't believe in those two either

LorettaC: well I am certainly a believer in God, or at least in some kind of supreme being that created us in his own image and watches over us to some extent. God is as good a name for Him as any, but I'm not so sure about the rest. Anyway this is kinda heavy shit to be talking about for our first date, don't you think?

F8meNOT: I see by your profile that you are married. What would your husband think if he catches us?
LorettaC: fuck him
F8meNOT: somehow I doubt that would be his desire
LorettaC: HA! Nonono…I mean…you know what I mean!
F8meNOT: marriage on the rocks? Not that it's any of my business
LorettaC: you're right, it's not, but yes, I am beginning to think it is, definitely been on the rocks lately… you ever been married?
F8meNOT: sorry to hear that…no, I haven't
LorettaC: don't…hee…it's not all it's cracked up to be
F8meNOT: well, unless you find the right person…
LorettaC: maybe, but then who's to say they will STAY the right person
F8meNOT: the chance you take, I guess
LorettaC: I suppose you are right, but I did say that I controlled my own fate, or meant to anyway and I do believe that, so why can't I change my life…my fate
F8meNOT: I've been asking myself the same question, believe me
LorettaC: hey…shit! I hear 'Rocky' coming home now, time to sign off…can we chat some more sometime?
F8meNOT: I don't see why not
LorettaC: good deal, I could use a new friend…you want to be my new internet friend? Or am I being too forward?
F8meNOT: I don't see why not
LorettaC: COOL!! gotta fly…laters

With that Chris saw her name on his buddy list blink out before he had a chance to type in his 'good-bye.'

"Well, that was interesting," he said aloud to himself with a smile. A pleasant distraction from his daily boring routine. An Internet friend. He had heard of people meeting over the Internet, but until now, he hadn't actually spoken with anyone on the Internet that he hadn't already met through the more traditional methods of jobs or mutual friends. But the more he thought about *LorettaC*'s final question, the more he liked the idea. An Internet friend.

I don't see why not, he thought to himself as he cybered over to *The Simpson's* web site to see what tomorrow evening's new episode was going to be about. And then added sarcastically, out loud to himself, "maybe it's fate."

11

LorettaC: you been online all day?!
F8meNot: only since we last talked, but I am on a lot
LorettaC: I put you on my buddy list…do you mind?
F8meNOT: not at all…why would I mind?
LorettaC: you know, in case you wanted your privacy
F8meNOT: ahhh, nice of you to consider that but I put you on my list too---figured one couldn't hurt
LorettaC: one?! Is that all you got on your list?
F8meNOT: and my parents out in Seattle…guess that makes two then
LorettaC: I feel honored…you a private kinda guy?
F8meNOT: I do pretty much keep to myself
LorettaC: did ya miss me?
F8meNOT: you were the highlight of my afternoon
LorettaC: flattery will get you everywhere, you know
LorettaC: damn…gotta run again…see ya ;)

LorettaC: tell me you at least took a break tonight!
F8meNOT: well good evening to you too
LorettaC: you ARE online a lot

F8meNOT: passes the time
LorettaC: am I interrupting?
F8meNOT: no, not at all, a pleasant distraction
LorettaC: so I'm a distraction, eh? you sure know how to make a gal feel wanted…shheeesh
F8meNOT: okay, bad word, how's "break from routine?"
LorettaC: does the word "pleasant" still remain?
F8meNOT: still remains…so Rocky is out late tonight? I've noticed you tend to run when he's around. Does he not approve of your computer usage?
LorettaC: he's sleeping…I couldn't
F8meNOT: insomnia?
LorettaC: of a sort, I suppose…sleep has been losing its appeal to me lately
F8meNOT: same here, though I tend to doubt for the same reasons
LorettaC: so what's your reason?
F8meNOT: maybe another time
LorettaC: yeah you're right, that's a tough one to come out of the gate with…here's an easier one… how old are you, Chris?
F8meNOT: how'd you know my name?!
LorettaC: your profile…DUH!
F8meNOT: oh yeah…forgot…29, you?
LorettaC: 24 going on 30…how long have you

LorettaC: Hi Chris! Sorry I bailed on you mid sentence last night…forgive me?
F8meNOT: hi…no problem, had to get ready for work anyway, I work nights…I take it Rocky stirred?

LorettaC: yeah…came down to see why I wasn't in bed "where I belonged"

F8meNOT: and you said…

LorettaC: couldn't sleep

F8meNOT: the truth usually is the best policy

LorettaC: but that was really only half the truth…the rest was that I was hoping to find you online to talk to some more…hee…but I couldn't tell him that

F8meNOT: why not? innocent enough

LorettaC: he wouldn't understand

F8meNOT: that you talk to people?

LorettaC: that I talk to a man

F8meNOT: does he use the Internet, too?

LorettaC: no

F8meNOT: then if he sees you talking to me, just tell him I'm a woman…can't tell from the screen name and I've met a few women named Chris, too, for that matter

LorettaC: yes, I could do that…if need be…but would just as soon rather not have to explain …I'm a terrible liar

F8meNOT: is he the jealous type?

LorettaC: he hasn't ever had the opportunity or need to be, but I have a feeling it is best I don't find out

F8meNOT: he has a temper, eh?

LorettaC: like you said, maybe another time…I don't want to waste my time spouse-bashing right now. I do that with most of my other Internet buddies…getting boring

F8meNOT: okay, so what do you want to do with this Internet buddy?

LorettaC: something different…something better… something new…something WILD!

F8meNOT: lucky me

LorettaC: oh I'm sorry, I'm intruding aren't I?

F8meNOT: no, not at all, what did you have in mind…like I said I could use the break from routine…you have my curiosity now anyway

LorettaC: I don't know…no idea at all really. I just have a…feeling, I guess…sounds silly…what I really want is just a good friend, someone to know me, someone that isn't half way across the planet that I can relate with

LorettaC: someone I can know…you seem like a nice, intelligent sort…am I wrong? you're not some closet weirdo or anything are you?

F8meNOT: well I suppose that depends on who you ask

LorettaC: hee…good answer…hey, you got a pic?

F8meNOT: pic?

LorettaC: picture…online to send me

F8meNOT: ah no not that advanced over here yet

LorettaC: want to see mine?

F8meNOT: okay…how?

LorettaC: I'll send you an attachment with an email, just click on the download in the mail when you get it and there you be…or there I be, as the case may be…hee

F8meNOT: I think I can handle that

LorettaC: give me a sec

LorettaC: okay…sent

F8meNOT: got it

F8meNOT: downloading…

LorettaC: WAIT! I changed my mind! You might not like it! Send it back…hit CANCEL!!!!!

F8meNOT: hehee…too late

LorettaC: don't laugh
F8meNOT: why would I laugh…you are very pretty
LorettaC: you are a good liar
F8meNOT: not at all, you have a nice smile, gorgeous hair, sensitive eyes, cute nose
LorettaC: nose ain't so cute anymore
LorettaC: you sound like a romantic…
F8meNOT: of the closet type…not much to be romantic about for a while
LorettaC: you and me both, kiddo
LorettaC: I could sure use a little romancing in my life
LorettaC: Rocky is about as romantic as a horse's ass
F8meNOT: my life is about as romantic as a John Carpenter horror flick
LorettaC: hey, I got an idea…maybe we could…
F8meNOT: could what
LorettaC: nah, never mind…stupid…you'll think I'm the weirdo
F8meNOT: spill it…I won't laugh…I promise
LorettaC: well, you know I am married…and I have two wonderful kids…but there's no romance in my life…
F8meNOT: I have a policy of not messing around with married women, if that's where you're going with this
LorettaC: Nonono! I'm not ready to throw away my marriage yet, Rocky is doing a fine job of that on his own…but, I don't know… maybe we could kinda, you know, practice together
F8meNOT: practice?
LorettaC: just online, of course…I mean, we don't need

to meet f2f or anything…never mind, I told you it was stupid forget I mentioned it…sorry

F8meNOT: hee…yeah, kinda stupid…and kinda funny… and looking at your picture, not at all hard to imagine

LorettaC: did you just slip a romantic compliment in there?

F8meNOT: who me? I wouldn't know how…but if I did, I sure wouldn't have any trouble running my fingers through that long luscious hair of yours and staring into those sexy eyes as I kissed those soft, wet, hungry lips…

LorettaC: WHEEEEEEEE!!!! xoxoxoxoxoxoxo!!

LorettaC: oh you are good….hee! perfect! god how I miss those corny lines!!

LorettaC: Chris?

F8meNOT: yes?

LorettaC: my name is Carly. I am very pleased to meet you. I would like to get to know you

F8meNOT: the pleasure is all mine, Carly

LorettaC: Chris?

F8meNOT: yes, Carly?

LorettaC: Thank You.

12

When Chris first began his dialogue with Carly two days earlier, he had no idea she was going to be the answer to the question he had been asking himself just moments before opening her initial email. *Someone to talk to, to trust,* he had requested. Though he still hadn't confided in her yet, and still didn't know that he could, he did feel like, somehow, someone had just been delivered to him. Time would tell.

After she had "bailed on him mid-sentence," as she had put it, during their brief third encounter on that first evening their lives had intersected, Chris had skipped the nightly cleaning chores around the house and remained online until hearing his papers being dropped off in his driveway. He had also eaten his dinner from a tray in his lap as he sat in front of his computer just in case *LorettaC* had decided to reappear before he had to begin work.

He had assumed, as was confirmed in their next encounter the following afternoon, that 'Rocky' had been the cause of the sudden and premature halt in the chat. At the time, he didn't give it a second thought. She had certainly been a pleasant distraction from his other mind-consuming affairs of late. If she wanted him to "practice" a little missed romance with her online, well, that was the least he could do in return for the favor she had unknowingly given him. He was grateful to her for that.

Besides, according to the picture she had sent him, she was indeed very cute. He hadn't lied to her, wasn't pretending, when he had told her that practicing a little romance with her over the e-waves would be easy. He had found that, so far, he easily liked her. What might be hard was not wanting more than that. But then, he was in no shape to start anything with anyone these days, policy or no policy, married or not. In reality, offline, he knew he was a mental wreck.

As much as Carly had occupied his waking mind over the last two days, she still proved no match for his sleeping mind. Once again, seemingly as soon as he laid his head down and closed his eyes, Chris found himself trekking up the familiar graveyard path toward the ominous looking sky ahead. The mourners, the Priest, and Randolph awaited his presence at the top of the hill.

Randolph had first appeared the night before meeting Carly, very old and very faded. Chris had already guessed that he wouldn't be back more than another day or two. Randolph was ready to go. Chris felt more and more like a mere observer, like one of the hired mourners. He was the only one that ever spoke to the coffin's inhabitants, and was in turn the only one they ever addressed, as though none of the others were even there. But then they never saw themselves lying in a coffin, either.

Benjamin had best described to Chris what his visitors must see or feel when he said he wanted to "go back to sleep" and that Chris hadn't been invited, he had simply appeared. Chris was a presence in their dreams, with their own backdrops and props, their own story lines and agendas. Benjamin and the others had not seen the mourners or the Priest…or the fact that they were lying in a coffin. The graveyard scene, as well as the eyes he felt following him on his daily journey, belonged solely to Chris.

Or maybe this grisly scene, he thought, *belonged to the Priest.* He chased that idea out of his head immediately, not because he thought it was far-fetched, but because he didn't want to think about what that might mean if it were true.

Randolph had indeed faded to the point of doubtful return by his third appearance and seemed to be quite happy about it, though the fading as Chris saw it was not something the old man was aware of. With a misplaced youthfulness, he claimed that he was dreaming his final dreams, that he was moving on, and saying good-bye. His grin was genuine, stretching ear to ear. He said his pain had already left. Chris was happy for him and told him so.

While listening to Randolph bid his fond farewells to the things and the people that he had loved in his long life, Chris tried to ignore his surroundings. When Randolph took control of the conversation, Chris tried to let his mind wander to his chats with Carly the previous two days. He knew he could not close his eyes in this recurring nightmare. Even if he felt they were closed, it was as if his eyelids were transparent; they refused to shut out the light. The mind's eyes have no lids.

Tonight he stared at Randolph as though he were studying a 'magic-eye,' one of those computer-generated pictures that hides an image beneath a blanket of what appears to be a random splash of colors in disarray, an image unseen by the working eye yet clear to the lazy eye. The image Chris was trying to replace Randolph with was the picture Carly had sent to him of herself. He was recalling the conversations they had typed out to each other. How she had made him smile. How she had…

Chris snapped alert as if out of a daydream, but still within his nightmare. Back awake, yet still asleep. He suddenly thought he had caught some movement out of the corner of his eye and glanced up from Randolph to the Priest. The Priest's head was still bowed as though listening intently to every word of Randolph's prattle. But Chris could have sworn the Priest had just been looking directly at him, studying him as he tried to block out the dream with thoughts of Carly, trying to read his thoughts. For just a moment, he thought he could feel the Priest inside his head.

That thought sent a solid, strong shiver throughout his entire body like a twelve-volt jolt of electricity. The jolt woke him up, this time back to level one, back in his own room, in his own bed, where he was once again sweating profusely on his own pillow. He lay there unmoving for a few minutes, eyes wide, staring at the familiar swirls of plaster on his bedroom ceiling, breathing hard as if he had just made a quick escape. An escape from what, he wasn't sure.

As his pulse began to slow to normal again, Chris climbed out of bed and started his morning ritual. Under the pulsating, hot shower, he tried to scrub the feel of scum off the back of his neck left from the Priest's eyes as they had momentarily seemed to crawl under his skin. Small shivers continued to course through his body like small aftershocks of the major quake that had awakened him. This morning he exhausted the hot water before he was able to exit his small sanctuary and begin another day of seeking distractions from the ever-growing questions that weighed so heavily on his mind.

Just as in the two previous days, Carly had come through with the necessary distraction that afternoon when she sprang to life on his computer once again. The nightmare set aside, Carly center stage. Stupid, silly, insane…no matter. He was more than willing to appease Carly's desire, cater to her need. It was definitely a two-way street.

Over the next three weeks, Chris and Carly fell into the routine of almost daily interaction between one p.m. and four p.m. during the weekdays, and most of the evening on Friday nights. Bowling leagues were done for the season for Jerry (Chris still only knew his name as 'Rocky,' his adopted name for the Internet since Carly and Chris' first night of contact) but now on Friday nights he and 'the boys' got together for poker at Billy's place, or so he had told her. Carly doubted they were dealing out any cards on Friday nights, let alone that they stayed rooted at Billy's, but she looked forward to her free time with Jerry gone so she certainly had no intention of questioning his activities.

Chris and Carly were technically still in the 'getting to know each other' stage of their new Internet relationship, but a true friendship had already begun. Though they still 'practiced' a little romantic flirting and banter back and forth every now and then in fun, as Carly had suggested when they had begun, their connection was genuine, less like the more scripted game Carly played as *LorettaC* with the rest of her Internet pals. More honest. More real. Chris hadn't yet told Carly about his recurring nightmare, nor had Carly yet mentioned her recently broken nose, though both had become sufficiently comfortable with each other to do so when the proper time came up. And both felt that time was nearing as they had covered just about everything else in their respective histories. Chris already knew the full story of how Carly and Rocky had gotten together, something it had taken almost a year for *LadyAvec2* to find out and even then with no real details.

LorettaC: So why didn't you go back to Holiday Inn after you recovered from the accident? You like working nights better than days?

F8meNOT: There's more to it than I have told you

LorettaC: So we still have secrets, eh? That's okay, I have one or two I haven't told you yet too...hee

F8meNOT: it's not that I haven't wanted to tell you, in fact, I want nothing more. But I'm not sure you'd believe me, and if I tell you, it is important to me that you do believe me…completely

LorettaC: Chris, this is Carly, dear. I know we have only known each other a few weeks but I feel like I have known you a lot longer and already consider you a true, close friend…my only real friend, sad as that may be…hee.

LorettaC: I would believe anything you told me if you told me it were true

F8meNOT: well this one would certainly put you to the test on that…it's something that I even have trouble believing myself, but it is very, very true, I assure you

LorettaC: you are actually an alien from another planet?

F8meNOT: I wish it were that simple

LorettaC: Rocky broke my nose the day before we met… 2nd time he ever hit me…told the hospital little Johnny ran in through the bedroom door as I was coming out and slammed it into my face

F8meNOT: oh jeeez, Carly! Are you okay there? safe?

LorettaC: Rocky said I never kiss him anymore like I used to…he's right, I don't…and probably never will again, either…but I am not going to leave him, so don't tell me I should…at least not yet, not until the kids grow older and I can make a living for myself…and he might come around yet and realize what a cad he has turned into… but…

LorettaC: but…um…hee…

F8meNOT: but what?

LorettaC: well…I think about kissing you all the time… hee…ok, I told you both of mine. what's your secret?

F8meNOT: wait a minute! I'm still back at the hospital portion on yours…aren't you afraid of a 3rd time? a pattern has begun to form already with two in the books, you know

LorettaC: I'm fine. I can take care of myself. I don't think there'll be a 3rd time.

F8meNOT: you can't be sure of that

LorettaC: I told him if there was a next time he'd be spending the rest of his life turning his pay checks over to me through the court systems

F8meNOT: I'm not telling you to do so, as you requested, but wondering all the same, why the hell you don't leave him now?

LorettaC: the kids need their dad…they love him…I'm not ready to take that away from them yet. he's had his rough times and is an ass, no argument there, but he has his good points, too. he's good with the kids when he tries to be…he deserves the chance…he's been warned

F8meNOT: as have you been…but you know him better than I do of course. just be careful, okay?

LorettaC: don't worry about me…I'll be ok. Now! I believe you owe me exactly one secret… and a kiss!

F8meNOT: ~~smoooooooooch~~

LorettaC: wheeeeeeeeeeee! I like it! kiss! kiss!

LorettaC: and the secret? I'm not letting you off that easy! besides, now you have my curiosity stoked

F8meNOT: I could never explain it here, like this. It would take all day. I'm not the fastest typist, as I am sure you have noticed

LorettaC: I'll give you my phone number…I would love to hear your voice anyway

F8meNOT: that won't be breaking any rules?

LorettaC: nah…I still don't even know what you look like

F8meNOT: I told you what I look like last week

LorettaC: you still owe me a pic too, now that you mention it

F8meNOT: I should have quit while I was ahead

LorettaC: oh stop that! you sounded gorgeous! don't deny it. I make the rules around here…woman's prerogative, and the rules say you are gorgeous…555-2193…you have one hour to make me believe

F8meNOT: that may not even be enough time for my secret

LorettaC: then you better hurry up and get started…talk to you in a minute…xoxo!!

Carly's screen name instantly bleeped out of sight from his buddy list after her last message appeared on his screen. Chris closed out his own service, took a deep breath, and moved over to the phone next to his bed. He hoped she would believe. He needed her to believe. He knew it wouldn't actually change anything for him. The dream would still come, the questions would still haunt him, the Priest would still scare the bejeebers out of him, and the people would still die. But knowing that someone else knew, someone he trusted, someone who truly believed, someone he liked, seemed to ease the burden a bit. Meeting Carly online, getting to know her, letting her get to know him, had been a wonderful change in the rut he had fallen into over the previous six months. Carly was pretty wonderful herself, actually. *But married,* he reminded himself, not for the first time in these past three weeks.

Many times over the last few weeks and months, Chris had almost broken down and decided to tell his parents the truth about what was happening to him, out of the need to let someone, anyone, know. But he knew they would just get overly worried. They would probably insist on coming to Minneapolis, or worse, insist that he move to Seattle. He would only succeed in turning their lives upside down. And still, he doubted they would believe his experience to be real, to be more than just a dream.

He hoped Carly would believe.

Chris picked up the phone and dialed the number Carly had given him.

At ten minutes past four, Chris hung up the phone, leaned back against the pillow he had propped up on his bed, and let out a heavy sigh. Carly had played her role perfectly. Never once during their seventy-minute call did she question whether what was happening to Chris was real or not. She quietly listened where she was supposed to listen and only asked questions so that she could better understand what he was trying to convey. When the story was done, she hadn't accused him of being insane, she hadn't asked if he was seeing a shrink, and she hadn't pretended to know what he was going through, just as he couldn't understand why she was so adamant about living with a man who had maliciously broken her nose in a rage. What she did do was believe, and that was what Chris needed more than anything, someone to listen, and to believe.

"Wow," Carly said as he finished, catching her all the way

up to the newest host, Miss Gantry, an elderly, never-married housekeeper who had spent the majority of her life caring for her younger brother with Hodgkin's disease. Miss Gantry's brother had finally died a few months earlier at the ripe old age of 42 and after all her efforts to make his life as comfortable as possible, she was now waiting to see if she could find him once again in the afterlife. Chris told Carly her wait was not going to last more than another day or two.

"You know you can't blame yourself for Sherry's or Benjamin's death, Chris," she assured him.

"I know that, at least in Benjamin's case anyway, but I often wonder if I might not have been able to prevent both had I done the right things," Chris replied.

"No. Even Sherry. It wasn't your fault the cord broke. Nor was it your fault the doctors had missed something," she reminded him. "You said Sherry admitted as much in one of your dreams. She was right, you can't take on the burden yourself."

Carly was right. Chris knew that. But up until now it had been easier to accept the presence of the dream by also accepting a good portion of the blame for Sherry's death. It was easier to think of it as a punishment, a price to be paid for his role in the incident, than any of the other possible unexplainable reasons for this phenomenon.

Suddenly a thought occurred to him. This is why he needed a friend who believed, he realized. To bounce ideas off of. To allow himself to think again. He had lived with this problem for seven months by himself now and had never thought of any solutions. Now he had talked to his new friend for one hour and already he had a new idea.

"Carly, I just had a thought. Tell me if this sounds stupid or not," he said. "What if it were my fault that Sherry died. I mean totally my fault. What if this isn't a punishment or a price to pay like I've been thinking, but rather a chance to make up for it. A chance to make something better. You know, like that old TV show *Quantum Leap* where the star bounces from past life to past life altering something to make it better before he can bounce to another life." Chris' mind began to race and his words could barely keep up. "What if the only way I can stop these dreams is if I DO prevent someone from dying. You know, to give back what I took. A life for a life. You know what I mean?"

"But who would be monitoring this action?" she asked. "Who would be the one that decides this is something that must be done? God? I thought you didn't believe in God."

"I don't know what to believe in anymore. I suppose anything is possible. But if I am right about this, or even close, I would have to put my money on the Priest in my dream as the one who is in charge. He scares me," Chris said with a shudder.

"Wow," Carly said again. "Damn. Chris, it's after four. I need to start getting things ready for Rocky…I mean Jerry, that's his real name, by the way. But I don't want to go."

"It's okay. I've kept you too long," Chris admitted. "Thanks for listening, Carly…and believing. You have no idea how much that means to me."

"Hey. What are friends for. You're the best, Chris. Let's talk more about it tomorrow," she said. "Maybe I can sneak online a little tonight and we can toss around that idea of yours a little. It's not stupid. Like you said, anything is possible. But don't sell yourself on it too quickly and raise any false hopes. Let's let it sink in a bit first, okay?"

"Okay. Thanks again, Carly. You're a wise lass, as well as a beauty."

"Hee…God I hate to go…but I got to. Kisses!"

"Kisses," Chris returned, and then heard Carly hang up the phone as he did so himself.

Leaning back against the pillow bunched up against the wall by his bed, he thought about his new 'Quantum Leap' idea. But it only took a moment of thought to toss the idea out as mere wishful thinking. There were too many old people in his dreams. In fact, most of them had been old and ready to *move on*. If his purpose had been to save someone that appeared in his dream, wouldn't they all be of the Benjamin type? Or even the middle-aged insurance salesman who had drunk himself to death? There would be no point in saving someone who had already lived a full life and was looking forward to their next one.

The only part of the idea that had survived his rational thinking, that still made some sense after five minutes of consideration, was the one he wanted to shake off the most. Who was responsible for this nightmare? Who was 'monitoring' this, as Carly had put it? His answer had been the Priest. That thought, that the Priest had more to do with all this than just being a prop for his backdrop, did not sit well in Chris' mind. But there it sat. And it didn't feel like it was going anywhere else any time soon.

13

"I think she's cheating on me," Jerry confided to Billy, leaning in over his beer. It was Friday night, poker night at Billy's place, or so he had told Carly, of course. He was speaking loudly over the music but trying not to let anyone else hear what he was saying at the same time. This is not something Jerry would readily admit to just anyone, but not only had Billy been his best friend since high school, he also had first-hand experience on the subject. Billy had spent four years in prison after beating his ex-wife and her lover to within inches of their lives after catching them in the act one afternoon five years ago.

"Oh, man, Jer," Billy sympathized. "Who with?"

"I don't know. I don't even know if she is or not," Jerry confessed. "I was wondering how you knew when Lori was cheating on you."

At that point, one of the topless dancers, wearing only a purple, glow-in-the-dark G-string, strolled over to the table and sat on Jerry's lap facing him, squirming erotically and kissing his neck.

"Not now, bitch!" Jerry yelled at her over the screaming voice of Billy Idol's *White Wedding* on a sound system playing too loudly for the small strip joint. "Can't you see I'm tryin' to talk here?"

"Sorr-r-r-EE!" the stripper sarcastically said with a scowl as she pushed herself away from him. Three seconds later she had her seductive smile back in place and was working the next table, stretching out her G-string to receive a few singles as she rubbed her over-sized breasts in the next patron's face.

"Jesus, man. You really are worked up about this, aren't you," Billy laughed.

"It ain't funny, man," Jerry returned. "And yeah, this is really pissin' me off."

It wasn't like Jerry had never cheated on Carly…but that was different. He had twice. Well, once, sort of. One time didn't count, and the other time was a meaningless two-hour stand. That's where the difference laid, in Jerry's mind. What he had done had been harmless. The time that didn't count was a year ago when he had paid for it. Bought himself a service, just like buying a pizza…a very expensive pizza. He had four hundred dollars cash that night, income tax returns, burning a hole in his pocket. He had been flashing it around, buying rounds for his buddies here at the Hot Times Gentlemen's Club, though few, if any, true gentlemen would ever frequent a place like this. It was another Friday night of many after a good bowling night when one of the dancers working the floor caught sight of his wad, the green wad, and told him she could help him put some of it to good use. The two had run across the street to the little no-tell motel, checked in, and returned an hour and three hundred dollars later. Jerry with a big grin, ear to ear, plastered on his face, buying another round for his buddies as he gave them a detailed account of how he had spent it.

The time that sort of counted, but still wasn't an all-out cheat in Jerry's mind, had come four months later. He and his bowling buddies, in this same establishment, on another Friday night escapade, had invited themselves to sit down at a table of four women and started buying them drinks. As the night wore on and the drinks took hold, Jerry managed to talk one of the women into crossing the street with him. He couldn't remember her name, wasn't even sure she had given it, but what's in a name, right? This time it only cost him twenty-five bucks for the room and he got in a couple hours of romping fun. But it was nothing. Just a man doing what a man does. The woman meant nothing to him. He wasn't going to see her again. He certainly wasn't going to let Carly know about it, or leave her for the tattooed slut. He was just getting in a meaningless quicky. End of story.

But if Carly was cheating on him, well, he knew it would mean something to her. Not that he thought it was okay for her to have meaningless sex, that would be a direct insult to his manhood. That would say that he wasn't good enough for her. And he knew beyond a shadow of a doubt that he was certainly good enough for her, or for any woman, for that matter. But if she were to cheat on him, if would involve feelings beyond the simple sexual stimulation. It would mean more. And she might even leave him for this yahoo she was balling. That was something Jerry just couldn't allow to happen. The more he thought about the possibility, the madder he got. It was beginning to eat him up inside.

"So how'd you know?" he asked again.

Billy was a sandy-haired, square jawed, scrawny stick of a man with biceps that were so big they seemed out of proportion with the rest of his skeletal frame. It was obvious he worked out with weights, but little else. He also sported a barbed wire tattoo around his left bicep. He had been working the road construction crews since straight out of high school, except for his four-year vacation paid for by the state of Minnesota, anyway, but had the leathery, dark brown skin of one who works under the sun without a shirt for a living. He was also missing a couple of teeth in front from a fight or two and, at age 29, was just beginning to sprout what would probably turn into a good-sized beer gut by the time he got through his thirties. He was the one who had convinced Jerry to work road construction with him, for the great benefits packages, once Jerry had happened into his unplanned family.

"She quit fightin' with me," Billy explained. "We were fightin' and arguin' all the time, and then one day it just quit. She wasn't bein' nice all of a sudden or nothin', but she didn't seem to care what I did anymore. Then after a couple weeks, I noticed she actually seemed happy and that's when I knew. Turned out she met this asshole on the Internet that worked nights and she'd been ballin' him during the day while I was at work. I ain't dumb. I knew she musta been gettin' somethin' on the side. I called in sick for work, stayed around the corner and watched the house and sure enough, not an hour later he walked right in the house without even ringin' the bell first. So I knew it wasn't somethin' new, that it wasn't the first time. And well, you know the rest of the story from there."

"Yeah, you did him up pretty good there. He was in the hospital for a month, wasn't he?" Jerry snickered, almost forgetting his own problem for a moment.

"Lori, too. She didn't get out for a couple weeks. But then she went and married the faggot after she divorced me while I was in the joint," Billy said. "But that ain't gonna happen again. Nobody'd wanna fuck with Jeana. She's too damn fat and ugly. But I tell ya, Jer, she do what ever the fuck I tell her to do 'cause she knows damn good and well she's lucky to have a man to fuck at all," Billy said, laughing and almost knocking over his beer on the table while trying to pick it up. He took a quick swig, wiped his mouth with his sleeve, and then added with a devilish grin, "An' there ain't nothin' she don't do, too, man. I tell you. I just come here and get those faces up there in my head and go home with them fresh on my mind and you can't even tell the difference."

"You're fuckin' pathetic," Jerry said with a laugh.

"So Carly been actin' all happy without you lately?" Billy asked.

"No, not really. But she called me 'Rocky' once last week. Not that I can see her screwin' anyone named Rocky," Jerry said. "She got all flustered and stuttered, then said she was thinkin' about the movie Rocky because of the way I had punched her the week before."

"You hit her?"

"Broke her nose."

"Damn, man. You better be careful there. I tell ya, the joint ain't no fun," Billy confessed. "I couldn't wait to get out. Can't get laid in there, man. At least you better hope you don't get laid while in there."

"Yeah, yeah. You were in county. It wasn't that bad," Jerry said.

"No. But bad enough. I stayed outta trouble, but it still cost me plenty to stay that way."

"Well I ain't gonna go bustin' Carly up and getting' thrown in jail, man. I got a couple kids to think about," Jerry said. "But I *am* gonna find out if she's fuckin' around on me."

"And what are you going to do if she is?" Billy asked.

"Scare 'em into stoppin' somehow, I guess. Hell, I don't know. She just better not be doin' nothin' she gonna regret. And maybe she ain't, but I just got this bad feelin'. Fuck. I can't deal with this shit, man," and then Jerry did knock his half full glass of beer over as he tried to grab it for another a swig. Beer flowed over the table into Billy's lap, making him jump out of his chair.

"Shit, man!" Billy yelled at Jerry.

"Fuck. Sorry, man. What am I gonna do, Billy?" Then seeing how Billy was actually pissed, "Sit down, man, let that wench with those big fake titties lick you dry. She'll love it."

"Fuck you," Billy said, but he was laughing again and sat back down. Then putting on a serious face again, "Okay, man, we'll figure this out. Why do you think she's cheating on you? And when?" he asked.

Jerry called over to a waitress and ordered two more beers. When she walked away, he looked at Billy like a light had just gone on inside his fuzzy brain. "She's been spending a lot of time on the Internet, I think. You know, 'chatting with friends' she says. You said Lori met that guy on the Internet?"

"Yep. Everybody's meetin' everybody that way these days. I don't even have a fuckin' computer anymore," Billy slurred as he polished off his beer making room for the one Jerry had just ordered for him.

"And she knows I never get home 'til late on Fridays," Jerry continued. "Fuck! She could be balling some asshole right now!"

"Come on, man. Just cause Lori met her faggot on the computer don't mean Carly did too," Billy said trying to calm Jerry down. "Hey, I got an idea. It'll at least help give ya a clue, man."

"We should go there now. Maybe catch her in the act," Jerry said, not really hearing what Billy was saying.

"Yeah, right. Then you can kick the living shit outta both of them and take my old cell over in county for a while. No, man. Take it from me. That ain't the way to go. It's getting late anyway. Even if she were tonight, he'd probably be gone by now. I gotta better idea," Billy said.

The waitress brought over their fresh beers. Jerry thanked her as he stuffed ten bucks down her cleavage while grabbing as much breast as he could in the brief contact and patted her on the rear. "Tell me," he said as the waitress left them alone again.

"Okay, listen up." Billy slid his chair a little closer so he wouldn't have to talk so loud. "She thinks you're playin' poker at my place every Friday now, right? Okay. Next week, we'll actually play poker. But we'll use your place! I'll call Brad and Gary and Buzz, they ain't got nothin' better to do. I'll make sure they know it's supposed to be somethin' we been doin' every week since bowlin's done. Don't tell Carly. We just all show up right around six. I'll say Jeana was sick and didn't want all the racket this week so we needed to play at your place. If she's got some asshole lined up to pop over, or if she was gonna go somewhere without tellin' you, well, you'll be able to watch her squirm and try to change plans. Or maybe a babysitter will suddenly show up. Wouldn't that make her sweat. Then you'll know somethin's goin' on if she gets all nervous about it. At least you'll know if you got a problem to work out or not. You know what I mean?"

"Oh yeah," Jerry smiled. "And I'd have witnesses, too! Let's do it. She ain't gonna be happy about it. But it'll serve her right if she got anything to hide."

Jerry felt a little better now with a plan. He waved a fiver in front of the near naked nineteen-year-old girl walking by their table. When she turned his way, he pulled the five back, holding it up above his head. The girl stepped closer and took the five from his hand in her mouth while he took a supple nipple in his. He still didn't know if Carly was messing around on him or not, but having a plan made him feel more like his old self again. He was looking forward to the poker game next Friday night.

14

For the last year and a half or so, Friday nights had been Carly's favorite time of the week because it gave her some good quality time to spend with herself while Jerry was off tossing a sixteen-pound ball at a bunch of fat wooden sticks. But it hadn't always been her favorite time of the week. There had been a time, not too long ago she remembered, when the weekends had been her favorite time of the week, and for quite the opposite reason. Jerry was home, off work, and the quality time was spent with her little family, instead of alone. They explored the parks around the Twin Cities and sat arm in arm in the grass while watching Johnny get all dirty in sand boxes or sliding down slides or playing in playgrounds at neighboring elementary schools. She had a child seat put on the back of her bike and the three of them would go for a ride on some of the bike trails that weaved throughout the southern suburbs. They even occasionally hired a baby sitter and actually went out to a movie and dinner, like a real date.

Now she just waited for the videos to be released. Now she was waiting for Johnny to learn to ride his little bike with the training wheels so she could take Sasha out for rides in Johnny's old seat, hopefully later this summer. Jerry hadn't gotten on his bike for two years and it was getting rusty in the back of the garage, the tires flat from lack of use. Yes, once upon a time, in a happier, simpler time, she had looked forward to her weekends. She wondered where that time had gone.

These were her thoughts this Saturday morning as she awoke next to her snoring husband who was still 'sleeping off' the previous night's 'poker game.' As she looked at him lying next to her, calm, serene, facial muscles relaxed in a comfortable slumber, it wasn't hard to imagine the man she had once loved. She knew he was still in there somewhere.

As Carly had relayed to Chris early on in their new friendship, she did believe in God. She wasn't a church goer, hadn't in fact been to a church since she left her parents' home to find a life for herself. She didn't claim to be of any particular denomination, and didn't even own a Bible. But she still believed. She believed in the Golden Rule, to do unto others as you would have them do unto you. She believed in the Ten Commandments. She believed that all people, at least most all people, were basically good deep down inside, but that some just get a bit sidetracked or misguided as they trudge through daily life trying to make ends meet.

And she also meant what she told Chris about not wanting to throw away her marriage yet. She still felt that the Jerry that had charmed her into bed, the Jerry that had wanted to "do the right thing," though maybe not the most romantic of men, was still in there, still retrievable, still worth saving.

She envied her children and their natural, unconditional love for their parents, wishing her marriage held the same trait. She felt the same way for them. No matter what, she knew she would always be there for them in any way they needed her for as long as she lived. She was sure Jerry felt that way too. He wasn't as open with his emotions as she was. And maybe he didn't spend the time with them she wished he would or thought he should, but she was still sure that they meant the world to him. She would occasionally catch him watching them play and see a certain smile in his eyes that assured her that the Jerry she thought she had married was still indeed in there somewhere. He just didn't seem to be surfacing very often any more. Why? She hadn't a clue.

Another thing that Carly and Chris had spent many hours discussing over the last few weeks, the subject that had brought them together, was fate. Did it exist? Could it exist? Both had agreed over and over that it could not, although they had gotten quite a laugh out of the fact that even if it did not exist, it was still fate that had brought them together, not the reality of it, but the mere concept of it. If she hadn't typed the word 'fate' into her search, and if he had not had the word "fate" in his profile, they never would have connected. Therefore, fate had indeed brought them together, via the very existence of the word. It had certainly been their own individual choices to use the word.

So if it was not in Carly's fate to have a failed marriage, and if it was not in Jerry's fate to become a wife beater, then it was a matter of choices, as she and Chris both believed. And if she had her choice, she would repair the fabric of her marriage, tear down the walls that had been erected over the last couple of years, dig deep and find the Jerry she knew was still living somewhere inside.

She fully understood that she would need Jerry's help on this. You just don't change another person's attitudes and habits on a whim because you want to or think it best. It would take efforts on both their parts. Give and take. Understanding. Recognition and a desire to make things better. But she also knew that if she didn't decide to take the first steps, to take her fate into her own hands, then there was no hope at all to fix what she felt was broken.

This morning, looking at her husband sleeping beside her, she decided to do just that. Take her own fate into her own hands, and consequently, that of her children and of Jerry at the same time. She decided to make a genuine effort to right the ship, to prevent it from sinking, as it seemed to be doing as of late. She would talk to Jerry. Communicate her feelings and concerns to him.

Not that she hadn't tried before, which had been the cause of many an argument. She would tell him what she thought the problems were, he would get all defensive and next thing you know, voices were raising, words not meant were spat out, and walls were erected.

Choices. It was all about choices. She needed to choose her strategy better. Maybe not blame him and talk about problems so much as merely changing a few of her habits and trying to include Jerry in some new ones. Act. Yes. Actions, she thought to herself as she lay awake in bed this Saturday morning, she had always heard and believed, speak louder than words. This would be her new strategy. She knew what she wanted out of life, in her life, and it was time to start acting like it, rather than sitting back and letting 'fate' dictate life for her. And what better time to start than now?

Slowly she snuggled up next to her sleeping husband who stirred, ceased snoring, but didn't wake. It was just after nine a.m. He hadn't gotten home until shortly after midnight and she knew he had been drinking all night. He still smelled like stale beer and cigarettes, even though he didn't smoke. She knew he had probably been at a bar, as opposed to being at Billy's playing poker as he had told her. But to err is human, to forgive is divine, or so she had been brought up to believe. And she was more than willing to forgive, especially if it meant succeeding in making things better between them, for her children as well as for themselves. She didn't think about what might happen if this new strategy didn't work. She didn't think about what she might have to do if Jerry just didn't want things to be better, or worse, if he simply didn't love her any more. Or maybe she just didn't want to think about those things. She had told him once that she thought she might be "falling out of love" with him, but that was one of those spiteful spewings of anger in the heat of a bad moment. She still loved him, she thought, she just didn't like the way their relationship had grown, or not grown, as the case may be. And giving him the cold to colder shoulder as she had over the last few months, and especially the last few weeks since the broken nose, was not the way to make things better. She didn't want him to think she had forgotten and that he could get away with stuff like that in the future or whenever he got mad at her, but maybe if they were closer, more intimate, better friends again like they were once upon a time, he wouldn't feel the need to express his anger as he had lately.

She did the math. Nine hours of sleep for Jerry after stumbling home. Hopefully he drank a couple of glasses of water and took some Advil before passing out in bed. She didn't want him to be hung over. Nine hours should be enough either way, she hoped.

Carefully, softly, she rolled over onto his chest, the weight of her body on his, one hand caressing his hair as with a child with a headache, the other resting on his shoulder. Her face hung inches above his and her eyes were the first things he saw as he awoke moments later.

"Good morning," she said softly as his eyes focused with a hint of surprise in them.

"It'd be better if my head wasn't pounding. What time is it?" he asked.

She almost replied with, *well it wouldn't hurt so much if you didn't drink so much,* but stopped herself just in time. That was the way the conversation might have gone last week. This was a new week. A new beginning, she hoped. A new strategy. A new fate.

"Oh, poor baby," she said sympathetically, managing to keep the sarcasm out of it. "Anything I can do to help?"

He looked at her a bit confused for a second, then asked, "So why do you care all of a sudden? I would have thought you would have said something like it's what I deserved."

"Well do you deserve it?" Carly asked, trying not to sound motherly and not removing her hold on his eyes.

"Well," Jerry replied cautiously, searching her face for the sarcasm he expected to hear in her tone that she was successfully keeping out, "I suppose I do," he conceded. "I probably had a few more than I needed last night."

"Did you take any Advil before bed?" she asked.

"No."

"Let me get you some, with some water. You'll feel better in a few minutes."

"So what gives, Carly?"

"What?"

"You know what I mean," he said, now taking the offense. "This ain't the first time I've waked up with a hangover, but it's the first time I can remember you offering to make it better."

"We'll talk about it later when you feel better. Nothing for you to worry about," she assured him, noticing the concern on his face at the mention of 'talking about it.' "I'll be right back." She gave him a smile and pushed herself off the bed heading to the bathroom for the Advil and some water.

Jerry laid back and smiled at first. Then he suddenly remembered some of the 'clues' Billy had told him about the night before. Was this one of the signs, he wondered? Maybe, but she wasn't just ignoring him uncaringly as Billy had suggested, she was being downright nice. He figured there had to be a catch.

Carly returned with a glass of cool water and two Advil.

"Here," she said, handing him the tablets and sliding back into bed again next to him.

Jerry hesitated. He simply could not understand why she was suddenly catering to him. The thought even crossed his mind that maybe she was trying to poison him. Maybe this wasn't Advil at all, but some kind of poison she had found with her time on the Internet. He looked at the little red tablets and saw "Advil" clearly printed on each tab.

"Go ahead," she urged and held the water closer to his face so he could swallow down the pills. "And drink the whole glass, too. It'll help with the dehydration from last night's beers."

Ah, he thought, *it's the* water *she has slipped something into.* Not that he believed it. He didn't think Carly could maliciously harm any living creature, let alone a fellow human being. But the thought couldn't help but surface anyway as he swallowed the pills and drained the glass of water.

"There," she said, taking the glass from his hand and setting it on the night stand next to the bed. "That should help. Maybe this will help a bit too," she added as she leaned in and gave him a soft kiss on his neck. Then on his cheek, his forehead, and gently on one of his eyes. Slowly, seductively, her lips found his and she began to kiss him like she hadn't in months.

Jerry responded, cautiously at first. He still felt sure the punch line was coming any minute. But wow. Her lips felt so good. He forgot his pounding head and succumbed. He grabbed the straps of her nightgown and started to pull them down, aggressively.

"No," she said softly. "Slowly. Gently. Take your time. Love me."

Jerry obeyed.

An hour later, the two lovers laid side by side, breathing heavily, feeling like they hadn't felt together in a very long time.

"Wow," Jerry sighed. "That brought back memories."

Carly couldn't have planned a better segue. Taking immediate advantage of his comment, but trying to remain casual in tone, she propped up on one elbow and facing him said, "Exactly what I wanted to talk about."

"What?" Jerry asked. "Sex? I thought you were losing interest in it. At least with me."

"No, Jerry," she said. "Not sex. Love. And it extends farther than just the bed." Now she was building up steam and let her thoughts out. "We used to take walks, play with the kids together, go for bike rides. We used to date, Jerry, even after we were married. When was the last time we had a date?" She felt her voice quiver a little and raise a notch in volume. She consciously reeled it back in to a soft level, took a breath, and continued. "What happened to us, Jerry? No, don't answer that. Just help me fix it. I want it like it used to be. I want to be a family again."

"So what brought all this on?" he asked, still sounding suspicious.

"Does it matter?" she returned without answering. "Do you think we can try to find what we lost?"

So, something did *bring it on,* Jerry thought. *She doesn't want to tell me.* Thoughts started to race through his head. What had happened to cause Carly to make this sudden attempt to repair their injured marriage? And then it hit him. She had had an affair. That had to be it. She had an affair, it went sour or wasn't what she had expected, and now she was running back to him trying to escape her guilt. She had cheated on him with someone she'd met on that damn computer and was now trying to cover it up, to make it up to him. This was the only explanation he could think of. Now the question was, could *he* forgive *her*? And, *who* had it been? And *how long* had it been going on? The second one he didn't know if he wanted to know the answer to. The first one might depend on the answer to the third.

Jerry decided he didn't want to ruin a good morning by asking these questions, at least not yet. He figured with Carly in her current mood, a nice breakfast would be coming next and no telling for how long she'd remain in it. But he was going to find out the answers. The questions lingered in his mind, leaving a sour taste on what should have been a sweet morning. Yes, he thought, one way or another, he'd find out.

Part Three

"The past is only proof that we know not what the future will bring."
---Classified Trash

15

Chris stood beside the gaping hole above the casket with the Priest and his small band of black robed mourners across from him, waiting for the lid to open and reveal his dream's newest host. The previous resident of what Chris still thought of as Sherry's coffin, Gloria Bitterman she had called herself, was not expected to be returning. She had been looking forward to meeting God and rejoining her family. She had been relatively young compared to most who had known their time was coming, 34 lonely years old, she had said. She had also been healthy, at least as far as Chris could tell. Her parents had died a year earlier in a car accident, her father having a stroke while driving and losing control of the car, taking her mother with him as the car careened into the base of a bridge at fifty miles per hour. Her younger brother had died a month before that while sitting on the front porch watching the sun go down, as he liked so much to do. He had met a stray bullet from a gang dispute a block from their home on the south side of D.C. That had been the second strike of lightning in the same place, so to speak. He had already spent the last twelve years of his life, since the age of 14, in a wheel chair, mostly under the constant care of Gloria, paralyzed from the neck down, again from a gunshot, this one from a robbery gone bad at the convenience store a block from the Bitterman's home.

Now for almost a year with the small house to herself, Gloria had told Chris that she was planning on going to sleep soon, never to wake up again, and rejoin her family in Heaven. She was cleaning up the house first. She didn't want to leave it messy for whoever was going to discover her later. Then she planned on taking a bottle of sleeping pills, along with a bottle of her father's favorite whiskey, and go to sleep. Chris knew she'd go through with it. She had only been a host for three days but was already fading fast. He might have tried to talk her out of it during his dream, if he thought it might have helped to save her. But at this point he had pretty much decided he didn't have the ability to do so even if he had wanted to. Listening to her tell her story and explain her reasons for wanting to take her own life was all he could do. Her life had been a living Hell, one tragedy after another, according to her. Maybe in death she would find her peace. Who was he to try to deny her that, he thought, her escape to Heaven?

As the lid began to open, Chris wondered if the Priest standing stoically at the opposite side of the hole didn't already know who was about to introduce themself to Chris. If he had to guess, he thought the answer was yes, but he didn't want to think about what that might mean and he forced his thoughts back to the presumed newcomer.

Ever since his failed attempt to intervene with Benjamin's fate, Chris had given up on the idea that he could have a role in the lives, or the deaths, as the case may be, of his visitors other than as observer, listener, and comforter for those who were moving on. *He hadn't allowed himself to get emotionally attached to any of them as he had to Benjamin.*

But that was about to change.

The lid slowly opened, revealing the sweetest, bluest eyes he had ever seen. Her long, straight black hair lay over her shoulders, her bangs resting neatly just above her brow. Her dimpled smile as she looked up at Chris was playful, bordering on seductive. She was wearing an extra-large, bright orange T-shirt with the letters "U of I" on it, that came down to just above her knees revealing sexy but strong-looking calves. She looked to be in her mid-twenties, close to his own age, Chris thought, and full of exuberant life. Her toes were wiggling and she was giggling as she spied Chris looking down at her.

Chris' heart sank, hard and fast. He could see no sign of the telltale fading. He knew he was going to have time to get to know his new visitor. He knew his emotions were going to be hard to keep in check. Her voice, as she spoke, sounded friendly and pleasant, like a favorite long-forgotten song.

"Oh!" she said, eyes gleaming like none before in her place on the hill. "One of these dreams."

Chris couldn't help but smile, a little embarrassed from the insinuation in the tone of her voice. He stood speechless, admiring the curve of her cheek bones, her long, slender neck. He had almost forgotten what her presence here implied of her future as she spoke again in response to his silence.

"Well?" she asked, her smile unwavering. "Is this one of those dreams, or are you going to just stand there making me dream about it?"

"I, um, I'm not sure I know what you mean," Chris finally forced himself to say. Actually, he knew exactly what she meant by "one of those dreams," and as much as he would have loved nothing more than for it to be one of those dreams, he knew that somehow, he needed to let her know that this was most certainly not the dream she thought it was. In fact, it was more than a dream. More real than she obviously realized.

"Sure you do," she said, a playful pout forming on her full lips. "I dreamed you up, so you know what I know. Isn't that how it works?"

"I'm not sure how it works," Chris admitted honestly. "But I don't think this is what you think it is."

"Damn," her smile in her eyes still overpowering the pout on her mouth. "And you looked so cute, too. Are you sure? Lord knows I haven't been able to find you when awake. And now you are going to be equally elusive in my dream, too? Just my luck," she said as she *stuck out her tongue at Chris. "So," she continued, "if it's not what I think it is, then what is it? Why are you here in my dream, in my bedroom, if not to make passionate love to me? Tell me. I mean, is this my dream or not? Don't you have to do what I want?"*

This wasn't going to be easy. Under any other circumstances he would probably have wanted nothing more than to make sweet, passionate love to this beautiful young woman. On the one hand, it wasn't even real. He was in his bed at home, she in hers. If he were to succumb to her wishes, it would just be their minds, right? No physical contact would actually be made. And in this day and age of 'safe sex' necessities, Chris thought, what could be safer!

But even if he wanted to, which he did, he wouldn't have been able to. There was still the other hand, him knowing what he knew, knowing that he would remember and she wouldn't, knowing that this is probably more real and less dream than she is aware. He would have felt like he was taking advantage of her, possibly doing something she wouldn't do if she knew the facts as he knew them. And of course, there was also a matter of the audience, the audience she could not see but Chris was ever aware of.

"Yes," Chris replied, trying to choose his words wisely. "This is your dream. But it is also mine. Our dreams have somehow collided, gotten mixed together. I don't know how else to explain it. But I am real," he continued, "not just a product of your imagination."

Chris saw her face redden in embarrassment as this fact sunk in. But it quickly passed as disbelief replaced it.

"How can we both be having the same dream?" she asked.

*"I have no idea how the mechanics of this phenomenon work, but I can guaran*tee *you that things aren't as they seem to you," he said.*

"So, what makes you so sure they aren't what they seem to you*," she challenged.*

"Because you are not the first one whose dreams I have been a part of," Chris tried to explain. "I will remember all that happens in this

dream, yet from my experience so far, I don't think you will remember any of it."

"So you just travel around invading people's dreams? Who are you? Some kind of psychic Peeping Tom?" She tucked her legs under the blanket and pulled it up to her neck, though all Chris could see was her knees bend and her hands raise up to her neck. He couldn't see the blanket she held on her side of the dream. Chris could tell she was beginning to feel uncomfortable. The smile in her blue eyes vanished, the playful pout in her lips changed to a serious frown. She appeared to be trying to figure out if this was a dream, or rather, a nightmare.

"No, no," Chris assured her. "Nothing like that. You don't need to be afraid of me. But your being here is not a good sign, at least as far as I can figure from the others that have been in my dreams."

Chris made up his mind, without giving any time to thinking about it, that he was going to try to help her. He knew he was setting himself up for another disappointment, but the price she would have to pay if he could have helped and didn't was tenfold worse. What choice did he have? She appeared to be another Benjamin, healthy, young, full of life, a life that was about to be taken from her. If there was the slightest chance that he could help save that life, he had to try.

"You're scaring me," she said looking up at Chris, her lower lip slightly trembling as she spoke.

"I don't mean to scare you. Damn. This isn't easy to explain, but it isn't me you have to be afraid of," Chris said, trying to ease her obvious growing fears.

"Who do I need to be afraid of? And why?" she asked.

"I don't know," Chris said, but he glanced up at the Priest as he answered her, silently naming him as the one whom they should both *be afraid of, if he had to name anyone.*

Disbelief began to overpower fear on her face once again. Such a pretty face, Chris thought. A face he could get used to looking at, but wished he had never seen. At least not here, not in his dream.

She was an adult, unlike Benjamin. He would have to try to be straight with her at the risk of scaring her. He knew no other way to let her know the danger he felt sure she was in, yet had no real way of proving. It had been a tornado, of all things, that had taken Benjamin. A natural disaster that could not possibly have been foreseen. Yet somebody had to have known. Benjamin wouldn't have been in his dream if somebody hadn't known. So how could he help this new woman? How could he forewarn her of a tragedy that can't be predicted? He could tell her to leave town. But what if she died in a car crash while leaving? Then he would have caused her death instead of preventing it. He could tell her to hide out in a bomb shelter until she didn't appear in his dream anymore, as if she would actually do that. All he could do, he decided, was level with her, and then let her make her own decisions.

And would she even believe him? And would it matter if she did? Because supposedly she wouldn't remember anything he tells her in the dream anyway. How could he possibly help? He could get her phone number, he thought, like he did with Benjamin, if she'd give it to him. Then he could try to convince her when she's awake. Convince her here in the dream that she needs his help when awake. This, Chris decided, was all he could do. But even that, he felt, was probably not going to be enough. It hadn't been enough for Benjamin. But he had to try.

"Well?" she said, relaxing her grip on the blanket a bit, letting it fall back below her neck line. "What good are you then? Why are you here?"

"I don't know," Chris said again, shaking his head in frustration. "But I want to tell you what I do *know and maybe together we can decide what to do. I need to ask you some questions first though. And I need you to trust me."*

"And what if I don't want to answer them?" she fired back, starting to show the candidness in her face and spunkiness in her voice

that Chris witnessed when she had first appeared. "How can I trust you? I don't even know you. And none of this is real anyway," she said in defiance. "You are just a dream. Or maybe a nightmare, but you aren't real."

Chris didn't want to argue with her. He had already told her that he was indeed real, that this was more than simply a dream.

"Are you healthy?" Chris asked, ignoring her question.

"Yes, why do you ask?"

"You don't have any diseases or cancers or something not noticeable that you have been treating or are worried about?" he asked.

"No. I run every morning. I am 27 years old. I don't smoke. I am in perfect health," she reported.

"What's your name?" Chris asked.

"What's yours?" she replied stubbornly.

"Christopher Battles. And I wish I could say that I am pleased to meet you, but I'm afraid I'm not. The fact that I have met you here in this manner means that you are in danger." Chris blurted out.

"Danger? What kind of danger?" she asked.

"I'm getting to that, but it isn't going to be easy to explain. And you may not believe me anyway, but I assure you that everything I have to tell you, to the best of my knowledge and as best as I can figure out, is very, very true. But it might be easier if I at least know your name," Chris said.

"Kimberly," she answered. "That's all you need to know for now."

"Fair enough, Kimberly. I wish I could have met you under different circumstances," Chris admitted.

"What kind of danger do you think *I am in?" Kimberly asked.*

Even though she was an adult, Chris still couldn't just blurt out that he thought she was going to die soon. He didn't know where to begin in order to best make her believe.

"You said you are in your bedroom, right? That's where you see yourself in this dream? Where am I in your dream?" he asked.

"Yes. This is my bedroom," she said looking around. "You are standing at the foot of my bed. I thought I dreamed you up to make love to me, but then I guess if that were true, you wouldn't have that shaggy stuff on your chin. I prefer my men to be clean shaved. And your hair would be more trimmed. In fact," she added, "I don't know why I even thought you were cute at first. You don't actually look like my type at all."

The critical words did not go unnoticed to Chris, but he wasn't going to worry about it. Her life was what was important here, not whether or not she liked him or thought he was cute, although at some other level, he still wished she did. But it wasn't like he was trying to impress her. He was trying to save her.

"I don't see your bedroom. That is not a part of my dream," Chris said, trying to ignore her commentary on his appearance. "My dream appears the same as it has for all the others that I have dreamt of over the last half a year or so. It started after I had an accident," he explained, figuring he had to start somewhere. "My girlfriend died in the accident. She was the first one I saw in my dream."

"I assure you that I am not dead," Kimberly interrupted.

"That's not what I mean," Chris continued. "I saw her here in my dream, where you are, before she died. She was asking me to help her, and I couldn't. She died three days later. That's what I am trying to tell you, but I can't think of an easy way to do it. Everyone that has been here in my dream has died soon afterward. Most were old and ready to die, even welcoming death. But some, like you, were young and healthy." Chris looked down at his hands before him, not wanting to look into Kimberly's eyes as he said what he had to say next. "By appearing in my dream," he explained, "I think you are supposed to die soon. But I want to try to help you live if I can. I don't know how, or even if I can, but I have to try. Do you understand?"

"No! I do NOT understand!" Kimberly yelled. "This is ridiculous! No, it's just a nightmare! Go scare someone else! I don't need this shit!"

Chris woke up.

Damn. He remembered everything, as he always did. He hadn't convinced her. She had chased him out of her dream, or nightmare, as she had deemed it. His one consoling thought was that she had had no sign of the fading, which meant her death was not near, at least not in the next few days. He had some time. How much time, he could only guess. At least a couple weeks, maybe more. But he knew the fading could start at any time.

It was Sunday, late morning. He'd only gotten about four hours to lay down before snapping awake. He was tired and sore, even more so than usual as the Sunday paper is always a bear to deliver. He thought about trying to get some more sleep before getting up but knew he wouldn't be able to find a wink. Thoughts were racing through his mind a mile a minute. He wanted to talk to Carly. He needed some feedback, some input. He wanted a second opinion on what he wanted to do and how to go about doing it from the only person he could trust. But he knew Carly usually wasn't online on Sundays and he didn't want to call her in case 'Rocky' answered the phone. He had already spent the morning causing grief in one woman's dream; he didn't want to accidentally cause even more grief in another woman's reality. Her opinions would have to wait until Monday afternoon. He would still have to see Kimberly one more time before then.

Chris headed for the shower and began thinking of his next strategy to try to convince Kimberly of her danger. Looking in the mirror, he recalled her comments on his appearance. She was right. He was looking pretty ratty these days. His appearance had been one of his least concerns over the past seven months. Only now for the first time, he realized it showed.

Opening up the medicine cabinet, shoving aside the *Tylenol PM* and the *No Doz*, neither of which ever really seemed to do what they were supposed to do, he pulled out an old disposable Bic razor and shaved off his scraggly beard. He also decided, because he really didn't have anything better to do with his day, that maybe it was time to get a haircut.

16

Chris didn't think Carly would know what should or could be done about Kimberly any better than he did, but he missed not having her to bounce ideas off of. All day long, as he showered, ate, drove downtown for a haircut and some much needed new jeans, surfed the internet reading obituaries and local news, all he could think about was Kimberly and her tentative future. He even watched the National Weather Channel for an hour looking for anything that looked ominous or potentially life threatening in the forecasts. Nothing looked particularly nasty, but the forecasts didn't span beyond a week and he was fairly confident Kimberly had longer than that.

Although he could think of nothing but Kimberly and her dilemma, none of his thoughts came to any conclusions. He still had no idea how to proceed, how to convince her that she was in danger. And even if he did convince the dreamland Kimberly enough to hand over her phone number to him, he would still have to re-convince the conscious Kimberly. And even then, what would he accomplish? Scaring her? Making her life miserable, or what's left of her life? And if he couldn't stop her impending death, as he still felt was most likely the case, why should he make what little time she had left a living nightmare?

As midnight approached, he heard the truck back into his driveway outside and start unloading his newspapers for the night's deliveries. Chris closed out the Internet service he had been sitting idly in front of, watching and hoping that Carly might sign on before he had to go to work, and went to make some dinner before beginning his routes.

Throughout the day he had been thinking about Benjamin and the tornado and what that meant for Kimberly. It meant anything was possible. It meant that what he wanted to do was probably impossible. Everywhere he looked he saw potential death. He realized that every day, every person faces death a hundred times over in their daily routines. Every street one crosses risks someone stepping on an accelerator instead of a brake. One risks slipping in the shower and banging his head on the hard ceramic tub. We trust electricity to be properly wired and insulated every time we flip on a switch or plug in an appliance. There are robberies and muggings and carjackings going on every day throughout the country, common everyday people doing routine everyday things suddenly becoming victims of random crimes. There are drunk drivers, strung out drug users, serial killers. Add to that Mother Nature with her tornados, floods, earthquakes, hurricanes, lightning…the list is endless.

As he pulled out his Tator Tots from the oven to flip them over, he imagined the gas line in the oven exploding in his face. As he sunk his teeth into the hamburger he had bought at the grocery store, he thought of salmonella. As he swallowed, he imagined choking to death on food not thoroughly chewed. Reading the obituaries on a daily basis for the last few months, he had become quite aware of the countless ways one can meet with an untimely demise. By the time he had his papers loaded into his van and started out into the night to deliver them, he had almost convinced himself to abandon any hope of saving Kimberly.

Almost.

He knew, despite the overwhelming odds against it, he still had to try.

As Chris drove through the night shoving the newspapers into the tubes, he kept returning to the same conclusion. He had to convince Kimberly to give him her phone number. He had to talk to her. He had no idea what he would say, but he had to make contact.

The night was slowly beginning to give way to the light. It was 6:15 a.m. and Chris was in his final neighborhood before turning towards home to go to bed and meet Kimberly again. He had decided not to push things too much this morning in his dream. He might make a stab at getting her phone number, but he knew that first he would have to win her trust. He still had time. She hadn't been fading yet. No sense in scaring her too early, giving her time to lower her guard after a few days of being alert and nothing happening. He also still wanted to talk to Carly and knew he wouldn't be able to do that until after his next journey up the hill.

Chris left St. Charles Place and turned down Baltic Avenue, the second to last street of his route. Boardwalk Avenue was the last street for the night. All the streets winding through this neighborhood were named after the Monopoly game board. It was a quiet, pleasant area, in Eagan, the same city he lived in himself, a suburb just south of St. Paul. In this particular part of town, most of the houses were split-level, with two- and three-car garages. All summer long, young kids played soccer and baseball in the middle of the streets. Parents sat on porch steps drinking tea and lemonade, talking to neighbors, keeping an eye on their kids in the streets and neighboring yards. Every morning, even more so now that winter had passed and spring was in full bloom, as Chris finished his night's work in this area, joggers began their workouts. He generally hit this area at about the same time every morning and some of the more dedicated joggers in their morning ritual would recognize Chris as he drove up to the mailboxes to insert the newspapers and wave. Chris always managed a smile and wave back in return.

Ten stops left. On Boardwalk Avenue, one customer had a wheelchair ramp leading up the front steps of the house. They had made the request that their newspaper be delivered to the front door of the house, bagged and hung on the doorknob of the door at the top of the ramp so that the wheelchair-bound resident wouldn't have to roll all the way out to the mailbox next to the street each morning to retrieve the paper.

Chris pulled his van up to the curb and parked, grabbed a paper from the passenger seat, slipped it into a plastic bag and exited the van. The sun was just beginning to peek over the horizon. Birds were busily chirping. The day promised to be a beautiful spring day, though Chris rarely spent anytime outside beyond his job anymore. The grass was turning its suburban green, dew moistening the toes of his shoes as he walked through the yard towards the ramp leading to the front door. The crisp, clean morning air filled his lungs. A night's work moments from being done. His favorite time of day.

He wasn't looking forward to going to sleep but couldn't suppress the smile that a morning like this effortlessly inspires. A beautiful day can instill hope to hopeless situations. He thought about finally being able to talk to Carly again after a long weekend. He missed her on the weekends. He looked forward to being able to hear what she thought of his newest mission, to try to save Kimberly despite the conclusions that he and Carly had come to in their many discussions about the subject.

Suddenly thinking of Carly again gave Chris an idea. Maybe she could help in his new mission. Maybe *she* could make the initial call to the conscious Kimberly. Maybe Kimberly would be more willing to believe, or at least listen, if she was aware that someone else already believed him. He knew he had to be the one to ultimately spell out what the danger was, to be the messenger of the ominous news. He had no intention of passing on that burdensome task to Carly. But maybe Carly could break the ice, prepare Kimberly for the fact that he had some urgent, important, life and death information for her. That she, Carly, believed what he had to tell her about and that she believed Kimberly should keep an open mind to what he had to say, no matter how absurd or unbelievable it sounds at first.

The news was going to scare Kimberly, Chris had conceded. There was no way to help her without scaring her. And she should be scared. He just hoped she was strong enough to keep a level head after hearing, and believing, the news he had to offer. He hoped she wouldn't hold the news against him and understand that he was just trying to help, not turn her life upside down, which he was probably going to unavoidably do anyway.

Of course, first he had to get her phone number out of the dreamland Kimberly. Then, if this was to be his new plan, he had to talk to Carly and see if she was willing to help. Carly had her own life, her own problems. Talking things through to help another out with their problems and dilemmas was one thing. Getting involved, diving in where the waters are over your head, where little is understood, taking a stand on something that you know is not going to be readily believed by anyone else, this was something else altogether.

But he and Carly had become very close. Though they had still never actually met face to face, they had talked on the phone several times and over the Internet more times than he could count. They had shared secrets with each other that they had shared with no one else. They knew each other better than their own families knew them. He thought she would help. He thought she would be pleased to help. He knew she would want to help in any way she could, as Chris would certainly do for her if she ever asked. They were good friends, the best of friends, despite never having been together in the same room and only actually knowing each other for a handful of weeks. A different time and a different place, they openly admitted and agreed that they might have been more than good friends, but that hadn't been their 'fate,' they had jointly concluded. And they were content to have what they had, a solid friendship, someone to trust and confide in. Someone to believe in each other.

Chris looped the hole in the top of the bagged newspaper over the door handle at the top of the ramp and turned back down the ramp towards his van. The beautiful morning, the crisp fresh air, his new plan, looking forward to talking to his only true friend, Chris felt hope.

As he stepped out into the street, rounding the front of his van, he caught sight of a jogger nearing on the far side of the street still a few houses away. He rarely initiated the first wave to the local joggers, but he was feeling pretty good this morning. He began to raise his arm to wave to the oncoming jogger as he jumped into the van, but froze with his arm half way up still standing in the street beside the driver's door.

He noticed the long dark hair swinging back and forth with the jogger's long strides. She was tall, young, very shapely and pretty…and very familiar looking. She was now approaching the house across the street, Chris still standing with his arm half raised, mouth half open, staring at her in disbelief. She saw him standing there motionless, watching her, and for an instant their eyes locked. She slowed her pace a moment, smiled a little uneasily, waved, and then picked her pace back up and moved on by.

Still frozen in place, unable to move, unable to lower his arm, unable to think, Chris stood and watched as Kimberly rounded onto Baltic Avenue and then out of sight in the direction that he had come from.

17

Kimberly Stringer rolled out bed at five a.m. as she did every morning. Shedding her extra-large orange University of Illinois sweatshirt that she used as a nightgown, she slipped into another sweatshirt from her old alma mater that was more her size as well as some bright orange sweat pants, thick white sweat socks and her Nikes. She thought the outfit made her look like an over-sized carrot stick, but the orange showed up in headlights well when out jogging before the sun came up. Better to be a visible carrot than to be run over by a tired early morning commuter.

After a quick *SlimFast* shake for breakfast, she stepped out onto her four-season porch in the rear of her new home for some pre-jogging warm-ups. A healthy body makes for a healthy mind, she had always believed. She ran four miles to begin each day, seven days a week, rain or shine, snow or bitter cold, a ritual she had begun her senior year at the U of I and had managed to continue ever since. Though the run itself was usually completed in just over thirty minutes, she always took another full thirty minutes to loosen up before she began.

One of the main reasons she had chosen this particular house when she had been in the market for a new home three months ago had been the screened porch in the back, perfect for her morning warm-up routine. The back yard was shielded from the neighbors by a natural barrier of large pine trees and bushes so she didn't have to worry about being watched under the light during her pre-dawn stretching exercises. Although her neighbors all seemed quite friendly and harmless, mostly young families in this young growing suburban city of Eagan, and she was far enough away from the city itself that peeping toms and crime in general were not normally a concern in the area, she still didn't like the idea of warming up in view of others. Before her move out of the city to the 'burbs, she had done her loosening up in her apartment, but the open, fresh air made her morning ritual much more enjoyable.

Finishing her warm-ups, Kimberly went out the back door of her porch and rounded the side of her house to begin her morning run in her new neighborhood. The area was perfect for jogging. Winding streets, slight hills, trees and parks and a lake were on the route she had mapped out for distance in her car when she had completed her move. The old city route had been straight, flat, square blocks with apartment buildings and aging homes in need of paint and repair crammed as close to each other as space would allow, with few trees and never the scurrying rabbits and occasional deer she now saw on her morning run in the quiet suburb.

She loved running at this time of the day. The sun was just coming up, the air crisp and new. And it was peaceful, quiet. Aside from the occasional barking dog, the only sounds coming from her Nikes slapping the pavement with her long easy strides, the beat of her heart and the trained rhythm of her breathing. This was her time to plan her day, to reflect on days past, to think, or sometimes to not think at all. It was a soul-cleansing experience for her each morning.

This morning was especially nice. Spring was in the air. The changing of seasons always exhilarated her. She welcomed each, but favored spring with its promise of new life and fresh green smells. It always managed to put an extra bounce in her step as she ran. This morning was a perfect running climate of forty-eight degrees outside with a few scattered white fluffy clouds coming into view with the morning light, promising to be a beautiful day. She thought she might try to move her small spare desk out to her porch and work from her laptop outside after the sun started spreading its warmth over the day.

Kimberly was a writer. She worked at home. She wrote children's books. She loved her job. She had majored at the University of Illinois in Child Psychology, had always loved working with children and had even thought about going on to medical school and becoming a pediatrician after graduating, but had been deterred by the thought of having to learn all the technical medical terms and jargon that would involve. Psych had enough Latin terms and fifteen-plus letter words as it was. Medical school was like learning a whole new language, not to mention at least eight more years of school.

As it had turned out, fate had a completely different idea about what her contribution to the little people of our world would be. At the end of her junior year at the U, for her final paper in her Child Psychology class, she had decided to do something different. She was tired of writing reports regurgitating all that the professors were trying to teach about the make-up of the pre-adolescent mind. Her final was to be about the effects on young children of their transition from home to school. Always one of the more traumatic periods of time for any child, leaving the familiar and comfortable wing of the parent and the familiar surroundings of home, and venturing out into an unfamiliar, new and complicated world full of new experiences and demands. An important time in their lives, a time which will have a very heavy impact on the rest of their lives. Their personalities, social abilities and acceptance, their fears and much more depend on how well the transition is made and the experiences they go through in the process.

Kimberly, in her attempt to bypass the tedious task of yet another technical report filled with the expected jargon of the field, wrote a series of three short books geared to the first and second grade reader. "My Friend in Me," "A Different Difference," and "A Home Away From Home" were their titles, each being a learning tool for the young reader as well as an instructional tool for parents and teachers to use to help their young ones in their transition. Though she wasn't much of an artist, she did her best to draw in the pictures relating to the words on each page. She hoped she wouldn't be graded on her art work, but rather on how well the professor thought the stories she had written would actually help the early student in their transition. And she actually had fun putting together the stories, something that had never happened before while writing a term paper.

As it turned out, though her art work had left a lot to be desired, her professor had loved her creative approach. She had two young daughters herself, 5 and 6 years old, who were currently just beginning their own school careers, and she had given them Kimberly's books to read, asked them what they had thought, and part of Kimberly's excellent grade, though she had not told her this fact, had been due to how thoroughly her daughters had enjoyed the books.

Next Kimberly's professor showed the books to a friend of hers, a publisher. The publisher hired an artist who drew for another writer specializing in children's books, to rework the pictures. By the time Kimberly had gotten her exam back from her professor, it had been type-set, put into a colorful hard cover binding, had an 'A' from her professor and a note attached to the cover from the publisher asking if she thought she could write more. A lot more.

By the time Kimberly graduated a year later, she was working on her ninth book. The publisher had hooked her up with an agent, and elementary school libraries and book stores around the country were ordering her books by the truckload. The royalties for each book sold were small, a scant ninety-three cents, but the quantity that were being sold were quickly ensuring Kimberly a financially secure future. When it came time to decide on graduate school and which direction her career was going to go, she realized she had already begun her career--as a writer.

Now six years later, at the age of 27, Kimberly Stringer had become a household name in homes with young school-age children with fifty-six instructional, fun stories published. Also, at the suggestion of her publisher, to help maintain her writing career, she was currently trying to broaden the age group of her audience. She was almost done with her first short adventure novel, "Missy's Summer Vacation," written for the pre-teen.

Kimberly jogged off her street, Pennsylvania Avenue, and turned left down Marvin Gardens smiling and thinking to herself that life was pretty good. She loved her new running route through her new neighborhood. She was thinking about maybe finding a new dog, a golden retriever or a shepherd or something to keep her company. She hadn't felt lonely in her small apartment near downtown amid the hustle and bustle of Minneapolis, but out here in her new suburban home in Eagan, surrounded by two-car garages, tricycles and bicycles laying in the yards, the sound of balls bouncing in the streets, dinner chimes on front porches ringing in the evening, she had begun to feel more alone in her new little house. She often reminded herself that she had nothing to complain about, that life had been kind to her, but *if* she did have one complaint...

Kimberly had worked on her career. When she got her first royalty check, along with an advance for her next three books, she hardly felt like she had earned the money and had dug in hard to make sure she met what she felt was expected of her. She rarely dated. She did her best writing late afternoon into the evening, sometimes late into the night when 'on a roll' and not wanting to break the flow, prime time for dating, so she rarely allowed herself the opportunity. Then of course, working alone and at home didn't give her the chance to meet too many new people either.

Yes, she thought, a good dog might be just what she needed.

Many of her new neighbors had come by and introduced themselves and their families. No one had come out and said so, but she could see in their eyes the same question, *Why aren't you married?* Or, *Are you a lesbian?* She knew that was what Tammy Anderson next door had wanted to ask, but had refrained from doing so. She had looked almost confused when Kimberly told the young mother of three that she wasn't married, and then her facial expression had suddenly changed. Tammy had just come up with a reason in her mind why Kimberly, a successful, young, intelligent, very pretty woman must be single. "Ohh," Tammy had said somewhat absently, probably not even realizing she had said it out loud, as if in response to an explanation Kimberly had voiced. Then Tammy stuttered over her next couple of words, eyes looking everywhere but at Kimberly, where they had been focused throughout their conversation up until that moment, and quickly changed the subject. Kimberly almost laughed knowing what was running through Tammy's mind, but she didn't bother trying to correct her.

Kimberly figured she'd meet Mr. Right someday, when the time was right. She wasn't sure how she'd know when the time came, but things were moving along nicely in her life. She had no complaints. She was in no hurry.

Turning down Boardwalk Avenue, finishing up her first mile of four, she saw the paperboy walking towards his van parked in front of the Billows' place. Well, not really a paper*boy,* she thought. Even out here in the suburbs, the paperboy had grown extinct. Now it was the paper*man*, like the mail*man* and the milk*man*, or *person* in the politically correct world. Now they drove cars instead of bicycles and they paid taxes. She had seen him a few times before, driving slowly down the wrong side of the street stuffing papers into the tubes. She would give a neighborly wave as she jogged by from the opposite side of the street but usually, he seemed to be concentrating on his job, occasionally nodding and returning her wave with one of his own.

This was the first time she had seen him out of his van, however. She noticed he was about her age, tall, clean shaven, kinda cute actually, she thought. Then she noticed he had stopped walking at the front of his van and was literally staring at her as she got nearer.

Kimberly knew she was a pretty good-looking woman and was used to men she'd never seen before staring, their cat calls and whistles and tongues hanging out. She was good at ignoring them. But this wasn't one of those stares. He had a weird, almost haunted look on his face, one of disbelief mixed with recognition. Did she know him from somewhere else, she wondered? The university maybe? She didn't think so. She had run into a couple of old classmates over the last few years, Illinois and Minnesota aren't that far apart, but she didn't think she recognized him at all. Although it certainly appeared that he recognized her…and that he couldn't believe it.

As she got close, just across the street from him, as she tentatively waved a neighborly hello in passing, she almost decided to stop and ask if she knew him from somewhere. That was when their eyes met and locked for an instant, and for that split second, she thought she did recognize him. But on another level, she knew she'd never met him before. This was too weird.

She picked up her pace a bit and jogged past quickly, not looking back, although the urge to do so was very strong.

"What was that all about?" she huffed to herself out loud, turning onto Baltic Avenue and out of his view.

Increasing her pace more than usual, she tried to concentrate on her running and put the brief encounter out of her mind, but found that to be impossible. She could still see his eyes, the way he was looking at her, the way he had frozen in place as she neared and passed. She couldn't shake the feeling that he had known her, but for the life of her, she couldn't think from where. She was sure she recognized him only as the paperboy she had seen a few times before on her morning run in her new surroundings but wasn't sure he had even really noticed her on those occasions. Certainly not to the extent that he just had this morning.

Unable to quiet the uneasiness stirring in her belly, Kimberly cut her run short and turned towards home rather than going around the far side of the lake. She ran back the same way she had come, half hoping that he would still be there so she could confront him. What she would say, she hadn't yet figured out, but she knew she wouldn't be able to let it rest in her mind until she knew from where he thought he had recognized her. And why he had looked so afraid.

Afraid. That was how he had looked. The more she thought about it, the more she was sure of it. He looked like he had just seen a ghost. That was why his stare seemed so strange.

As she turned back onto Boardwalk Avenue, running more than jogging now, the street was empty. He and his van were gone. She slowed her pace back to a jog, then stopped in the middle of the street where she had seen him in front of the Billows' place, bending over, hands on her knees, breathing heavily. She knew what she had to do. She knew she wouldn't be able to let it rest.

She knew she was going to have a tough time today concentrating on the novel she was trying to finish. She checked her watch and made a mental note of the exact time. She knew that tomorrow she would be back on Boardwalk Avenue at the same time.

18

"You back to haunt me some more?" Kimberly asked as her eyes fell on Chris standing over her. "I see you shaved. I must be getting better at this creative dreaming stuff."

"You don't remember seeing me today, do you?" Chris said more than asked. "While you were jogging. On Boardwalk." Benjamin hadn't remembered, Sherry hadn't remembered, he knew Kimberly wouldn't have either, but there had been that moment when their eyes locked that he'd thought she almost did.

"No. Should I?" she replied nonchalantly. Apparently, she wasn't afraid of him anymore. Apparently, she had convinced herself that this was in fact just a dream. Why else would he appear changed from one night to the next and even more according to her tastes, minus the facial scruff and hair trimmed up off the shoulders? He certainly didn't look as menacing as he had the previous time when he popped in with the ominous news of her upcoming premature death.

"You waved," Chris told her. "I thought for a moment you might have recognized me. I was delivering papers when you jogged by. You slowed for a second, but then went on without stopping."

"It's not good form to stop when you're jogging," she said indifferently. "You gotta keep your rhythm going. So when am I supposed to die?"

Maybe you should be asking him *Chris thought, glancing up at the solemn figure chaperoning this conversation. But he knew she couldn't see him. He wished* he *couldn't see him. The only good thing, Chris thought, was that the tall figure in black seemed content with being an observer. He hadn't interfered in his questioning Benjamin, which Chris had thought he might, as if he had been breaking rules of some kind. Maybe he was just an eerie backdrop Chris' mind had created for this macabre scene after all. Though deep down, Chris couldn't quite bring himself to actually truly believe that.*

"I don't know the why's, when's or how's of any of this," Chris confessed. "I just know from the others that your life is in danger. I wish I could tell you more."

Chris looked down at his hands, fidgeting his fingers together nervously in front of his waist. It hurt his heart to look into her eyes. Such blue eyes. Her long, silky black hair tied back in a pony tail tonight, curving around her slender neck and over her right shoulder. She was wearing a blue one-piece swim suit this time that matched her eyes and hugged her firm, neat body. Her toes at the end of her long legs, he noticed again, were always in motion as she talked and listened. He figured maybe this time her backdrop for her dream was at a pool or a beach. Once again, he wished he were meeting her under different circumstances, in the real world, maybe at that pool or beach. Anywhere but here.

"What others?" Kimberly asked. Then, "Oh yeah. You said yesterday that you make a habit of invading people's dreams. But then you also said this wasn't a dream, didn't you? What is it then?"

She certainly remembered their last dream encounter very well, Chris realized. Chris decided, as long as the Priest wasn't going to object, and it appeared he wouldn't, he might as well tell Kimberly the whole story and try to get her to believe. He couldn't help her if she didn't believe she needed help.

But he wasn't sure he could help her even if she did believe. In fact, telling the whole story would make it sound like there was nothing that could change the outcome, given belief in the past outcomes. And that would only make matters worse for her. Carly and he had discussed this very thing in great depth, and had come to the conclusion that Chris simply could not change things. But that was, at the same time, contradictory with their other major conclusion, that fate did not exist. Suddenly Chris didn't know what to believe anymore. He felt like his mind had been running in circles on high rev, getting nowhere fast.

His head ached from the questions he couldn't answer. His heart ached for Kimberly. How could she possibly deserve this fate? He had to help her. He had to try.

"I am going to tell you everything I know," Chris finally conceded to himself as he spoke. "It's not easy to believe," he warned her, "but if we have any hope of defeating this…this…whatever it is, you have to believe me. And we have to get together when awake. You have to trust me. I am only trying to help."

"I am anxious to hear your story," Kimberly told him. "But I'm reserving the right to believe and trust for afterwards. No promises."

"Fair enough," Chris smiled, though it quickly faded. He couldn't help but like her. It had hurt deeply when he had heard of the tornado sweeping through Kansas, when he realized he had failed Benjamin despite the success he had had in making contact with him. He knew he was setting himself up for a much deeper hurt if he failed Kimberly too. And she was here, local, closer, within his reach. He knew that if she even somewhat believed the story he was about to tell her, he would get her phone number, he would meet her, he would have time to get to know her, and in the end, he would probably lose her in some way that neither of them could have possibly seen coming. But what choice did he have? He had to try.

Chris began with the fateful bungee jump with Sherry and his first dream communications with her, and continued with an abbreviated version of the months that followed. He left out the details of the backdrop to his dream. He didn't feel the need to reveal to Kimberly the grisly fact that she appeared to him in a supposedly predestined casket. Nor did he feel comfortable talking about the Priest and his band of mourners while they stood next to him and silently listened.

Kimberly listened to Chris' story patiently, not asking a single question. Occasionally he would glance up at the Priest as though looking for insurance of getting a detail right, as if the Priest might jump in with a correction, but the Priest didn't appear to care how Chris told his story. His gaze, as far as Chris could tell, and the gaze of his company, never seemed to rise from the coffin before them once it had opened.

As he finished describing his encounters with Benjamin, the phone contact with his father, the visit from the police, the tornado that finally put an end to Benjamin's visits to his dream, Chris noticed concern in Kimberly's eyes. He knew she didn't want to believe this wild story that she had unwillingly become a part of, but that she was beginning at that point to consider the possibility that it was true. But she still remained silent until he finished up with his sighting of her jogging that morning.

"So now what am I supposed to do?" she asked Chris when he fell silent. "I don't think any tornados are going to come along here in Minneapolis, but if I get what you are saying, anything *could happen." Her lower lip quivered a bit as she spoke. A tear had formed in her right eye and was slowly sliding down her smooth cheek. Chris knew she believed. He hated himself for causing that tear.*

"I have no idea what we can do, Kimberly. But we need to be able to discuss this in person. I mean when awake," Chris corrected himself. "I told you about the fading. You don't seem to be fading right now, so I think we have some time to maybe figure something out. Maybe you could give me your phone number and I can call you."

He knew she would give him her phone number. She hadn't wanted to believe, but she did. But she wouldn't remember giving it to him.

She began rattling off her phone number but Chris wasn't hearing it. He was already thinking about the call. What could he say to the conscious Kimberly to make her take a phone call from a total stranger and then agree to meet him? He couldn't tell her that they had met in a dream and she had wanted to meet with him to discuss saving her life.

Then he thought of Carly, his idea before about trying to get her to help, to get her to make the initial call, maybe even join them at their first meeting. She might feel less threatened, less like he was simply trying a new, though certainly original, come-on line to get to meet her if Carly were to break the ice.

Chris knew she would remember none of this, but he explained his idea to her anyway.

"I have a friend," he told her, "her name is Carly. She knows what is going on, too. You won't remember any of this and I will have to explain it to you all over again. Right now, here, you had to listen to me. You couldn't just hang up on me because what I have to say is not pleasant. But given the choice, when I call you, it is likely that you might not want to listen. I want to have Carly call you first. I need to talk to her first, too, and then I will have her call you tomorrow and try to set up a meeting for all of us, if Carly can do it. What do you think?"

"Okay."

"Good. What's your phone number."

Kimberly repeated her phone number to Chris who repeated it out loud to himself, committing it to memory for when he woke up.

"Okay then," Kimberly said hesitantly, "I guess I'll wait to hear from Carly."

Chris didn't want to let her go. He wanted to talk more with her, but he knew she was going to be cutting whatever connection they had now. Benjamin had "gone back to sleep" once at will. Sherry had chased him out of her dream once, as Kimberly had actually done the day before, Chris realized, now that he thought about it. He didn't seem to be able to end his dream at will; he had tried before. But his guests appeared to be able to do so. However, they couldn't remember the dreams, and he could.

More questions raised. No new answers. His head ached as he suddenly awoke without saying good-bye to Kimberly.

19

Carly kissed her husband as he headed out the door for work. Not just a peck on the lips and a "have a good day" kiss, but a long, sensual "something to remember me by" kiss. It had been a wonderful weekend. She didn't know if it would last, but she thought maybe now they had a chance, quite the opposite of what she had thought only a week ago. Jerry still appeared a little confused and shell-shocked from the sudden affection Carly had bombarded him with all weekend as he turned towards the car, but he certainly hadn't complained. He even managed a smile and a wave to Carly still leaning against the door frame watching him go as he backed the car out of the garage. The grizzly bear had at least temporarily gone into hibernation and the cuddly teddy bear Carly had married appeared to have resurfaced.

So far so good, Carly thought with a sigh as she watched him leave. There was still a lot of work that needed to be done to get their relationship back to where she felt it belonged, but she had taken control of her fate.

She smiled at this thought and thought of Chris. It had been her talks with him that had steered her in the direction she was now headed. She couldn't wait to talk to him, to tell him of her taking control of her fate, to thank him. Now if only she could figure out a way to help Chris regain control of *his* life, too. But his was a different story altogether.

It was 7:30 a.m. She knew Chris didn't usually sign on until close to noon. She'd have to find a couple of hours of chores around the house to keep her busy until the kids woke up demanding her attention. Laundry was always available and vacuuming was necessary after their weekend romp in the park down the street. Even though she had the kids remove their shoes upon returning home Sunday afternoon, they still managed to leave sand from the playground throughout the house. Of course, some of it probably came from Jerry who hadn't removed his shoes even though he had spent some of his time in the sand pushing the swings. But she wasn't complaining. It had been a lovely day. The messy house was just a reminder of what a wonderful weekend it had been. It meant she had been doing something other than trying to keep busy with chores…and trying to stay out of Jerry's way.

At 11 a.m., she fixed some lunch for the kids and then got them settled down with coloring books and crayons in front of a Disney movie, *The Little Mermaid*. They'd seen if at least fifty times but never seemed to tire of it. They knew all the lines by heart and sang along with all the songs.

After cleaning up the lunch dishes and looking back into the family room to make sure the kids were keeping their crayon work in the books, she sat down in the den where she could still hear her young crooners singing and signed on to her Internet service. Chris wasn't online yet. It was 11:45 a.m. She knew he would be along very soon.

She wasn't disappointed. Not five minutes had passed before she saw *F8meNOT* magically appear on her buddy list with the sound of a door creaking open. When one of her buddies from her list went off line, her computer would accompany it with the sound of a door slamming shut.

LorettaC: POUNCE!!!!
F8meNOT: hey Carly…how's it going
LorettaC: good…very good actually…how was your weekend?
F8meNOT: you first…I'm still trying to figure out where to start
LorettaC: really? Now you got my curiosity up
F8meNOT: so you had a good weekend?
LorettaC: gonna make me wait anyway, eh…ok I'll start…
LorettaC: you know how we said we control our own fate and shouldn't complain about our lives if we don't take the initiative to change them? Well I took some initiative
F8meNOT: that simple? I wish
LorettaC: that simple…at least so far. I just did everything the way I wished it would be done and things kinda fell into place…namely Jerry
LorettaC: but the result was a very nice family weekend… and all I had to do was have fun
F8meNOT: so you think if I start having fun in my graveyard it will get easier to deal with? maybe I could ask the Priest if he wants to go out for a beer after the guest dies
LorettaC: rough weekend, eh?
F8meNOT: yeah…sorry…I am very glad you had a great weekend, Carly, really I am
LorettaC: I couldn't wait to tell you about it…but my very next thought was a wish to help you find some peace, too
F8meNOT: you are so sweet, Carly…but you know, I was going to ask you for some help today…if you are willing, that is

LorettaC: of course I am willing! I would do anything to help you out. you know that…don't you?
F8meNOT: Things got pretty weird this weekend
LorettaC: as if they weren't already pretty weird?
F8meNOT: weirder…Carly I can't think…we need to talk…I need your input, some ideas, and some help…something happened this weekend
LorettaC: what is it?! you want to call me?
F8meNOT: actually, if you can swing it, I would like to meet with you, if that isn't breaking any rules. this is some deep shit
LorettaC: no, I mean yes, I'll meet with you, of course. no, it's not breaking any rules…we don't need rules any more, Chris…you are a friend, a very good friend. did you want to meet today?
F8meNOT: as soon as possible…my head is swimming
LorettaC: well I need to find a baby sitter, but I have a neighbor who is usually willing… let me check with her and I'll be back in a few minutes
F8meNOT: I'll pay for the sitter
LorettaC: don't worry about it…she won't charge she has three little ones, we help each other out when ever we can, you know sit for each other, our kids get along great together, they make it easy…I'll go see if she's home.
F8meNOT: okay, great thanks Carly I'll be here
LorettaC: brb
LorettaC: back…she said give her a half hour and bring 'em over…where do you want to meet
F8meNOT: anyplace convenient for you…I really appreciate you doing this

LorettaC: not a problem, really, dying to see what you really look like anyway…hee!

LorettaC: there's a cute little coffee house/deli just a few blocks from where I live…called 'X', corner of Lyndale and 42nd N. in north Minneapolis. you know of it?

F8meNOT: no, but I can find it

LorettaC: big brick building, back side off 42nd Ave has couches and coffee tables and comfy chairs instead of booths…like being in someone's living room…all the local starving artists hang out there…cool place

F8meNOT: sounds nice…I'll buy you lunch

LorettaC: I just ate…but they have the best hot chocolate in the state…you can buy me one of those

F8meNOT: deal…give me about an hour, I'm down in Eagan

LorettaC: I'll see you then…xoxo

F8meNOT: thanks Carly…kisses

Carly heard the door slam shut as Chris' screen name disappeared from her screen. She couldn't help but smile and felt guilty for it since Chris had obviously been quite distraught about something. "Serious shit," as he had put it, and it must have been because he rarely swore. She hoped she could help. She liked Chris a lot, probably more than she was even willing to admit to herself, and it pained her to know he was in pain. She couldn't imagine what might have happened this weekend to cause this need to see her. But then she knew she'd know in an hour so she didn't need to try to imagine what it could be.

She called to the kids and told them they were going to get to spend some time with the Claybourns next door this afternoon.

Johnny cheered and Sasha got excited because her big brother appeared excited. She got Johnny to go potty and changed Sasha's diaper and put together the diaper bag for Nancy Claybourn in case she needed more. Then they all walked next door where they were greeted by three more excited children under the age of five.

"Thank you so much, Nancy. I owe you big time for this one on short notice," Carly said as Nancy opened the door and Johnny and Sasha ran inside.

"Don't worry about it, Carly. My pleasure. Your kids are never a problem," Nancy smiled genuinely. "Take your time and have a good afternoon, Carly."

Carly wondered from Nancy's smile what she thought Carly was doing with her afternoon. She had told her when she asked if she could watch the kids that she needed to go see a friend who was troubled and in need of talk. Hardly the setting for "a good time." Nancy knew things had not been the greatest between Carly and Jerry over the last couple of years. Carly had sensed that Nancy hadn't believed the door story when her nose had been healing, but Nancy hadn't challenged it. Judging from her somewhat sly smile, Carly didn't think that she was buying her current story either.

But that didn't matter. And besides, she was planning on having a good time. She was very excited to finally be meeting her newest and best cyber-friend f2f. She wished it could have been under a less stressful situation, at least in Chris' case, but she was looking forward to it all the same. He had helped her, now he was asking for help.

A great weekend with her hubby, and now getting together in person with a best friend in need of her help. Yes, Carly thought, life was definitely on an upswing.

Chris pulled into the gravel parking lot behind 'X' and walked around to the entrance door. He would never have noticed this place if he hadn't been told it was here. A plain glass door on the back side of an old three-story, red brick building that looked like a rundown warehouse. 'X' occupied a large space on the ground floor in the back of the building. A little hand-painted sign that read 'X Deli and Coffee' was above the door.

Inside was just as Carly had described it, couches and La-Z-Boy chairs with coffee tables and end tables instead of booths and counters. Floor lamps of a wide variety, no two alike, were sporadically spaced around the seating areas and atop end tables. A deli counter and a cash register along the right-hand side wall were the only things resembling a business. The rest of the walls were decorated with an assortment of art by local artists, many of whom probably hung out here with their work. Each piece hanging on the walls had a small business card stapled to the plaster underneath it naming the work, the artist, and the price it could be purchased for.

There were half a dozen patrons in the quaint shop, none of whom appeared to have made it past their twenties yet. Two were lounging sprawled out on a couch reading books, coffees on the end tables next to them. Another had papers spread out on a coffee table, deep in concentration, sandwich crumbs sprinkled over his papers. A very young-looking couple on the couch furthest from the door were making out, untouched pastries and coffee growing cold on the table in front of them.

Chris spotted Carly seated in an old-looking overstuffed chair with a rip in the arm rest. She hadn't recognized him as he walked in the door. She was still looking past him at the door expectantly until she noticed he was heading her way. A smile stretched across her face as he approached her and she stood up to greet him.

"Chris?" she asked as he rounded a couch towards her chair.

Chris thought her picture online, though she appeared pretty in it, hadn't done her justice. She was very pretty, very down to earth in her blue jeans, white blouse and tan sleeveless vest. She wore no make-up on her round face. She certainly didn't need it. Her reddish hair had been cut since her picture, sweeping the tops of her shoulders, parted on the side now instead of the middle as it was in her online pic. Her nose and cheeks were lightly spattered with faint freckles not picked up by the camera's eye. She was pretty, even beautiful, he thought, and very girl-next-door*ish* cute too, all at the same time. He still had no problem recognizing her despite the changes. He had spent many hours looking at her pic while chatting with her on the computer and her soulful brown eyes he would have recognized anywhere. He also noticed her nose had changed a bit since the pic, probably thanks to Rocky, he figured.

"Carly. Hi," Chris said, holding out his hand for her to shake. "Thanks for coming."

Carly looked at his hand but rather than shaking it, she took a step closer to him and slung her arms around him and gave him a squeeze. She was a full eight inches shorter than he was, standing at 5'6" compared to his 6'2" frame, and her head rested comfortably and naturally at the top of his chest just below his chin. He hugged her back, soaking in her warmth and a feeling he missed more than he had realized.

"No problem. I'm glad you asked me for help, though I don't know that I will be of any," she said, looking up at him, releasing the hug and sitting back down in the chair.

"Can I get you one of those hot chocolates you raved about?" Chris asked.

"That would be wonderful," she said. Her smile was radiant. Her eyes shined.

Chris walked over to the counter where a young white kid in dreadlocks and a tie-dyed tee-shirt with several holes in it, as well as a few holes in his face where he had multiple piercings, asked for his order. He ordered two large hot chocolates and returned to Carly. Handing Carly her drink, he took a seat on the couch next to her chair, a putrid green threadbare but remarkably comfortable three-seater, propped his feet up on the coffee table in front of him and sipped his hot chocolate. It was every bit as good as she had said it would be.

"You sounded awfully stressed when you IM'ed me today," Carly said after a sip of her hot chocolate. "What happened this weekend?"

"I met someone that is appearing in my dream," Chris told her.

"Live and in person?" she asked, her big brown eyes getting even bigger.

"Yeah. Just this morning."

Chris then told Carly about his first dream when Kimberly had appeared, how she had responded to his first attempt at explaining his presence in her dream, or her in his, he still wasn't sure which was more accurate. Then he related the sighting while delivering his papers and the following meeting at the gravesite earlier that morning.

"I know we kinda concluded that I was nothing more than a spectator, that I probably couldn't save anyone, but what if I can? She's here in town. I've seen her. What if she doesn't have to die? She's scared, Carly. I saw it this morning in her eyes. She believes me, and she's scared. I have to try to do something."

"But what can you possibly do?" Carly asked, knowing he couldn't answer. "Literally anything could happen."

"I know," Chris said, staring into his cup absently. "But I have to try."

"I have a question," Carly said cocking her head and waiting for Chris to look back up at her. When she had his attention again, she continued, "This doesn't seem to make sense. You saw her running this morning, then you went to bed and met her in your dream again. It must have been mid-morning by then. She goes to sleep after jogging? Wouldn't that be unusual?"

"Yeah, I thought of that too this morning in the shower after I woke up," Chris said. "I had thought of it before too, but I just figured that I was seeing late sleepers. I mean, most were fairly old, probably retired. The others that obviously had jobs and such, I just figured were in an earlier time zone than me. Made sense at the time."

"So now what do you think?"

Chris took another sip of his hot chocolate, laid the cup on the table and sat up resting his elbows on his knees. "Maybe it's like I told Kimberly the first night," he said. "It's more than just a dream. Maybe it isn't a dream at all. A dream is just our subconscious working while our consciousness sleeps and rests. Maybe I am reaching a level farther, deeper than that. Kind of a sub-subconscious.

"Kimberly was most likely doing whatever she usually does Monday mornings this morning while our sub-subconscious minds were connected." He shook his head as if he was having trouble believing this himself. "Maybe because of my accident I opened up a direct line to that deeper level which allows me to remember it, makes me aware of it at a conscious level. Maybe peoples' minds are connecting all the time like this but we just don't know it. Maybe our minds shut it out from us because if we were constantly in touch with the minds of others at this level, it would drive us all insane."

"Or maybe it is your souls communicating," Carly suggested.

"Maybe," Chris conceded. "I suppose at this point I would believe just about anything. But at any rate, I think my dream, or whatever it is, communicates to an inner part of the mind that we aren't usually in touch with. It would explain how the dream Sherry knew she had internal bleeding but the conscious Sherry didn't know. The sub-subconscious, or soul, if you want, would be more in touch with the body's voices than our conscious mind could be with all the distractions of daily life. It's like, we don't think about breathing, but we do it. We don't make our heart beat by thinking about it, but it beats anyway. I think it is at that level somewhere that I have tapped into. But only when my consciousness shuts down. Only when I sleep."

"You know," Carly said, "that almost makes sense."

She smiled, drawing Chris' eyes back to hers again and leaned forward placing a hand over one of his own hanging off his knee. Her touch felt good. Too good. "You said you wanted my help. Did you have something in mind already?" she said.

Chris explained his idea about her making the initial contact with Kimberly and about her possibly joining the two of them when they first met. "I think she might feel less threatened if you are there," he finished.

"Of course, I can do that," she said. "But do you really think you can save her?"

"No," Chris said slumping back into the couch again. "But I can't not try."

Chris was feeling quite stressed from this new glitch in his dream, the live meeting of his newest guest, not to mention her youth, her beauty and his natural attraction to her. He felt if he failed to save her, he would be letting her down, like he had let down Sherry and Benjamin. He didn't want to let her down. He wanted so much to beat this thing, this dream, (*the Priest*?). He pushed the last part of that thought out of his head.

Talking things out loud with Carly over the last three hours, and three cups of creamy hot chocolate, helped ease his tension tenfold. They discussed many theories and doubts and possibilities. Hearing his thoughts out loud, some sounding absurd, others gaining credence, and hearing Carly's responses and added ideas made him feel so much less alone. Even more so than the many phone conversations. Having Carly in front of him here, seeing her belief and the concern in her face as they talked, seemed to lift a weight off his back. Not a lot, but some.

"Have you given any more thought to confronting the Priest in your dream?" Carly asked cautiously. She knew Chris didn't like talking about the Priest. She figured he was just part of his backdrop, something Chris' mind thought belonged at a gravesite, and had told Chris so, but she also knew he scared him too.

"All the time," Chris responded to the cup warming his hands. Then looking up at Carly, he almost whispered, "But what if he answered me? I would rather believe he is just my own creation, like you suggested."

"But that's not really what you believe, is it?" Carly pushed a little.

"I don't know," Chris sighed. "At least not while I'm there. He seems very real, as real as the people in the coffin. He *feels* real. But like you said the other day, how can he be? But then, if the people in the coffin are real, couldn't he be real too?"

Carly saw the shiver run through Chris as that last thought was voiced. He quickly put his cup on the table in front of him as if to avoid spilling it even though it was almost empty. She decided not to push it any farther.

Carly glanced up and noticed the clock on the wall behind the deli counter. "Oh shit, it's 4:30 already. Damn. I need to get home and get the kids and start some dinner before Jerry gets home."

"How'd you get here?" Chris asked. "Do you need a ride home?"

"I walked. It's only about four blocks, but a ride would be nice. I didn't realize it had gotten so late."

They stood up and headed for the door.

"When do you want me to make the call?" Carly asked as they stepped outside.

"Not right away," Chris stopped to think. "Too soon and she might put up her guard thinking we're full of it. She's not fading yet so I'm pretty sure we have a little time. I'll let you know, send you an email if I don't see you online. You know what you're going to say, right?"

"Pretty much like we talked about," she said, linking her arm in his and walking him towards the parking lot. "But I will probably type it out so I don't screw it up. I don't think she'll freak. Which one is yours?"

"The van over there," he pointed. "Thanks a million, Carly. You really are a true friend, you know?"

"As are you, Chris. But you did lie to me," she said.

"When?!" He stopped in his tracks, looked almost hurt.

"You didn't tell me you were so sexy looking," Carly winked up at him and tugged him in motion again towards the van.

"You're such a tease," he smiled. "But believe me, if you weren't already spoken for…" He left his words hanging there.

"I know, I know. Just my luck. Sexy but with scruples." She stopped in front of the van, stood up on her tippy toes and kissed his cheek. "I forgive you."

Chris walked to the passenger side with Carly, unlocked and opened her door. "Thanks. You're too kind," he said with a laugh, standing aside for her to climb in.

For just a moment, as she brushed past him into the passenger seat, as he caught a whiff of her hair, her fresh scent, he let his mind wander, to a time and place where she wasn't spoken for. The look in his eyes did not go unnoticed, or unappreciated, by Carly as he shut the door.

She was smiling as Chris climbed in the opposite side and asked, "Where to?"

"That-a-way," she pointed. "But I think I am going to have you drop me off a block away. You know, just in case."

"Just in case?" Chris raised an eyebrow.

"Not that she would ever say anything, but I think the lady next door, the one watching the kids, was kind of suspicious of my mission here."

"What did you tell her?"

"Just that a friend needed to chat. But she had a sly grin on her face when I left. I didn't give my 'friend' a gender," Carly said with a snicker. "And I don't have the time or the desire to explain anything to her right now, not that I could even…hee."

"Yeah. Tell her the truth about this one and she'd *know* you were lying. A block away it is. You say when." Chris started the engine and drove out of the gravel lot.

"Three blocks down, you can drop me there. "Carly pointed again. "Mine's the stucco place four houses down on the left, around the corner there. You can drive by and peek after you let me out."

Just before reaching the corner, Chris pulled up next to the curb. "Here you go," he said, turning to face her in the passenger seat. "You really are wonderful to help me like this. It's so weird. Yet you believe. You have no idea how important that is to me. I really needed a friend like you, you know. I can't thank you enough."

"Don't worry about it. I am happy to help," she said, opening her door. She reached across the van and touched his hand again before getting out. "We'll do what we can, okay? That's all we can do, you know."

"Yeah. I know." He squeezed her hand on his with his other and then reeled both back in, reluctantly, so she could leave. "You take care, okay? I'll be in touch online." He blew a kiss through the van to her. She caught it with her hand, touched her lips, smiled, and hopped out of the van.

Chris watched as she hurried around the corner and out of sight. Her smile still replaying in his mind, still melting in his heart. *A different time and a different place,* he thought, *wow.* It was several minutes before he felt ready to put the van back in gear and then he drove straight ahead, heading home.

20

Tuesday morning, 6:10 a.m. Chris turned into the Monopoly neighborhood, the last neighborhood of his night, the one in which he had seen Kimberly jogging yesterday. The night was just giving way to a late dawn, revealing the dark clouds in an overcast sky above, a light rain coming down in a steady soft rhythm, but the threat of a serious thunderstorm looked promising.

Chris felt on edge. He was tensed and watching for Kimberly, paying more attention to the deserted street in front of him than to the addresses for the tubes he was absently stuffing newspapers into. He had all the stops memorized and didn't need to use his route list for anything other than checking it briefly before beginning each night for new stops and starts, so despite his lack of attention to what he was doing, he was still managing to get all the papers in their proper tubes.

He wanted to see Kimberly jog by, to see that she was fine, even though he knew it was too soon for anything to have happened to her. He hoped that the potential stormy weather hadn't deterred her from her morning run. He also didn't know how regular she was--every morning, every other morning, two or three times a week. He decided to try to find out from her deeper consciousness when he met her after work in his dream. That way, at least until Carly had made the call to her and they had all met, he would be able to confirm that she was okay each morning, or at least each morning that she regularly went for a run.

After their planned meeting with Kimberly, providing they were able to convince her of its necessity, not to mention the task of making her believe the threat to her life was very real, things would probably change. Chris had already thought one of the things he would suggest to Kimberly at this meeting would be to stop jogging for a while. This would eliminate the threat of a car losing control and running her over, or a vicious dog getting loose and attacking her, or maybe just twisting an ankle and falling, cracking her skull on the hard concrete curb. There were probably a lot of ways one could die while out for a morning jog. Jogging would definitely have to stop once her fading had begun, Chris figured. Of course, his strongest suggestion to her once the fading started was going to be to lock herself up inside her home and not come out until she was no longer hosting his dream, assuming she was still alive at that point. But then even that wouldn't have been enough to save Benjamin, he reminded himself.

Chris was running a little later than usual due to the rain and the extra time he had to spend bagging all the newspapers he delivered to keep them dry in their tubes. It was 6:40 when he finally rounded the curve off Baltic Avenue onto Boardwalk Avenue, his last street to be delivered. He guessed that he and Kimberly simply hadn't crossed paths due to his being later, or perhaps the rain had indeed kept her inside this morning. No telling if she was consistent with the time she ran either, as he usually was with his deliveries. Something else to try to remember to ask her later in his dream.

The rain picked up, soft and steady becoming an all-out downpour. Chris had to increase the windshield wipers to full speed just to catch glimpses of the street in front of him as the rain pounded and splashed against the glass. He was three doors down from the place where he would have to sprint up the ramp to hang the paper on the door when he caught a blurry glimpse of the orange figure sitting on the curb across the street from the stop.

He knew instantly it was Kimberly. And though it didn't make any sense to him as to why, he also knew she was waiting for him. In the rain. And he was late. How long had she been sitting out here in the rain waiting for him? He was a good half hour behind his usual schedule. Maybe this was it, he suddenly thought. Maybe she was going to catch pneumonia from sitting out in the chilly rain waiting for him, because he was late. Maybe instead of saving her like he so wanted to do, he had just killed her. But why was she here?

He was about to find out. As he pulled up in front of the house and parked, she stood and approached his van. This wasn't supposed to be how it worked. He wasn't ready to tell her anything. She wasn't ready to hear it. He leaned across the van anyway and pushed the passenger door open as she crossed the street so she could get out of the rain.

"Thank you," Kimberly said as she jumped in pulling the door shut. "It just now started to pour. I'm glad you came along when you did."

Her orange sweat suit was soaked through. Her hair was drenched and water dripped from her slender nose and smooth, pointy chin. In his dream, she was in a coffin, in a hole in the ground, while he stands at the grave's edge looking down at her. Yesterday she had been across the street jogging by. This was the closest Chris had been to her, sitting right next to him in his van, just two feet away, close enough to touch. It struck him anew how utterly gorgeous she was. A pain inside somewhere suddenly doubled at the thought that she might not be alive in two weeks.

"Here," he said, handing her a towel. He always brought a

couple with him on rainy nights to wipe dry the inside of the door since he delivered with his window down even when it rained. He stuffed a newspaper in a plastic bag and said, "Dry yourself off some. I'll be right back."

It wasn't exactly cold outside, but the rain still had a chill in it. Chris turned on the heater before opening the door and racing up the ramp to the porch with the morning paper. *What the hell is she doing in my van?* he thought as he ran up the ramp getting soaked himself even in his short sprint. This was too weird.

"Thanks again," she said, handing the towel back to Chris as he climbed back into the van and shut the door.

Chris took the towel and patted his own face dry. As he put down the towel, he noticed she was staring at him, studying his face.

"I don't always jump into the van of a stranger whenever it gets a little wet out, I hope you know. In fact, this would be a first," she said with a shy smile. She could easily see the confusion and surprise on his face, though he looked friendly enough. She knew she hadn't jumped into the van of a psycho killer or rapist, but she still felt like she had taken a risk being so outwardly bold and direct in her approach. She hadn't planned on jumping into his van when he came to deliver the paper to the Billows' this morning, but the sudden rain had limited her options. He had opened the door, and here she was.

"I saw you yesterday here," she continued. "I was waiting for you. You looked almost familiar, like I should know you, but I don't think I do. Should I? You looked like you knew me, or were at least surprised to see me. Actually, to be honest, you looked more like *shocked* to see me. Kinda the way you look right now. Why?"

He was shocked. He was shocked that he had stumbled onto

someone from his dream, live and in person. He was shocked that she was sitting next to him. He was shocked at her beauty. And she must have known he was in shock as well because he just sat there staring at her, unable to speak, unable to respond to her questions, not that he had any idea how to answer her.

"Are you okay?" Kimberly asked.

"Oh…um…yes. Sorry," Chris finally responded, forcing the words out of his mouth. "I just don't know how to answer you," he admitted.

"Well, do you know me or not?" she asked again.

"Yes…I mean, sort of…I mean, no, not really," Chris stuttered. Then finally collecting himself, "I have seen you before."

"Where?"

Damn, Chris thought, *no way around it.* "You wouldn't believe me if I told you," he tried.

"Hmmm," she said, trying to decide if her first assessment of him had been accurate or not. Maybe he had been stalking her, she thought. That'd be why he knew her but didn't. That'd be why he would have seen her before but was unwilling to divulge from where. That might also explain why he was so tongue-tied, to all of a sudden be confronted by his subject. But he really didn't strike her as the stalker type, not that she knew what the stalker type looked like, but she was pretty sure he wasn't it. "Try me," she said.

Well, here we go, Chris thought. He was never good at lying. Sure, he had been lying to his parents about his job and his well-being for better than half a year, but that was through notes and emails and a rare phone call from sixteen hundred miles away. If he had had to lie to them face to face, well, he would have been unable to. He would have simply told them the truth. And that's what he did now. "I met you in a dream two days ago. And then again yesterday," he told her.

"Oh, right," Kimberly laughed. "Is that the best you can do?"

"I told you that you wouldn't believe me," he shrugged.

"No really," she said. "Where have you seen me before?"

"It's true. You told me your name is Kimberly. You didn't give me a last name."

Oh God! Kimberly thought. *Maybe he* has *been stalking me!* "How do you know my name?" she demanded.

Chris smiled. "I told you that you wouldn't believe me," he repeated.

Kimberly stared ahead out the windshield. The rain continued to pour. She glanced at the door handle, just to make sure she knew exactly where it was if she decided she needed a hasty escape. Chris followed her eyes and guessed what she was probably thinking. He didn't want to tell her everything, not yet. He needed her trust first. But he didn't want her leaving now, thinking he was some kind of kook. It was obvious she was nowhere close to believing him yet.

"Okay," he said slowly, thinking. "I told you my name in the dream, too. Think really hard about it. Can you guess my name?"

"I'm not the one that had the dream," she snapped back. "It's your dream. How would I know your name?"

Chris could see she was already getting agitated with this. She thought he was lying to her. He thought she might leave at any second if he didn't score a point quickly.

"Maybe dream is the wrong word," he said. "But it is something we have shared. That's why I know your name. It is Kimberly, isn't it?"

"Yes," she answered, but the concern in her face remained.

"I have a friend," Chris continued, "who knows about this 'dream', for lack of a better word. She suggested that maybe it was our souls communicating."

"Ahhh," she said, smiling wryly. "So now you're saying we're soul mates or something. Is that it?"

"No," Chris said, a bit reluctantly. He certainly wouldn't have minded if that were true. "To be honest, I don't understand it all myself, but for the sake of argument, let's say this is all true. Humor me. Look at me," he said, pointing directly into his own eyes. "Concentrate. Try to guess my name."

She directed her bluer than blue eyes directly into his. He thought, given the chance, he could get very used to looking into those eyes. But then, he figured, trying to let himself down easy, he probably wasn't her type. He was just a paperboy after all. Then he saw the tense line in her forehead smooth out, as if she saw something in his eyes that allowed her to relax a bit. Recognition, maybe?

A long thirty seconds later, Kimberly broke her stare into his eyes. "I don't know," she said, sounding frustrated. "Nothing comes to mind, but if I had to guess, I'd say you look like a Christopher or something."

Yes! He exclaimed excitedly in his mind, but outwardly, he tried to remain cool. "Well," he said with a smile, "my friends just call me Chris."

"No way! You mean I was right?"

"On the money."

"That's too weird," Kimberly said, leaning back in her seat and staring out into the rain. Now she not only didn't believe him, she was having trouble believing herself. "Then show me your driver's license," she said looking back at Chris.

Chris pulled his wallet out of his back pocket and flipped it open, handing it to her.

"Christopher P. Battles," she read. "What's the 'P' stand for?"

"Paul."

"But how did I know your name?" Kimberly asked, handing his wallet back to him.

"Like I said," Chris said, stuffing his wallet back into his jeans, "I told you in our dream…or whatever it is."

"I don't know what to say," Kimberly said, shaking her head. "Why don't I remember the dream like you do?"

"That's a good question," Chris said. "And I don't really have a good answer."

The rain started to lighten up a bit. Chris slowed the wipers.

"I have just a few more deliveries to make here," he started.

"Oh! I'm sorry. I should let you get back to work," Kimberly said, reaching for the door handle.

"No. It's okay. This is my last street. I have only five more here," he said, pointing down the street. "I was going to ask if you wanted to go get some coffee or something. We could sit down and talk about this."

"I'm all wet," she said, looking down at herself. "How about if we make it lunch. Are you available later today? We could meet somewhere."

"That would work. I need to go home and clean up anyway." He raised his hands showing her his inky dark palms. "Rain and newsprint don't exactly mix well. And it'll give me a chance to rest a bit."

"Okay. Does one o'clock give you enough time?"

"Yes," Chris replied. "That'll be more than enough time. I am usually up before then. Where would you like to have lunch? My treat."

"You don't have to do that," she smiled.

He liked her smile. "I insist. For not walking out on me here thinking I was a kook."

"Well, I'm not totally convinced you're not yet," she said with a chuckle. "But I think this name guessing thing earns you at least the benefit of the doubt, for now. You know Applebee's over on Town Center Drive?"

"Yes," Chris said, trying to contain his own smile within the boundaries of his face. "I know where it is. One o'clock. I'll meet you there. Do you need a ride home?"

"No, thanks though. I need to finish my run. The rain seems to be letting up, too. Just in time."

"Well don't catch a cold," Chris said as she opened the door and stepped back into the rain. "Take a hot shower when you get done."

"Thanks, Mom," she giggled. "I'll see you at one."

"B'bye."

Chris waved and watched as she trotted off into the rain. *Well, that didn't go too badly,* he thought. He didn't start with his last five deliveries until she had jogged out of sight. He was still smiling broadly when he put the van into gear and inched towards the next mailbox.

Suddenly his smile faded. He had just remembered what had brought them together to begin with. He remembered that she might very well have only a couple of weeks left to live…unless he could manage to do something he didn't think he could do. And he didn't even know what that something was. Suddenly he felt sick to his stomach.

21

It was already approaching 9 a.m. by the time Chris had gotten home, showered and eaten a bowl of cereal to quiet his stomach. He was meeting Kimberly at Applebee's in four hours. He was tired as hell, having been up the last twenty-one hours, but then what else was new? He had no intention of trying to go to sleep for only three hours. He'd be better off just catching sail with his second wind and going with it.

Thoughts were traveling through his head faster than he could keep up with them. One of them was that Carly wouldn't have to make the call to Kimberly as they had planned. He no longer needed the introduction. He still wanted to have Carly with them when he informed Kimberly of the actual danger she was in. And once the two of them had convinced her that the threat was indeed real, well, if two heads are better than one, three must be even better yet when they start trying to come up with ideas on how to beat this predicament.

Thunder boomed outside as the skies opened up once again, rain coming down in sheets as opposed to drops. Dawn had seemed to move right into dusk in a matter of two hours. It was darker outside now at 9:30 a.m. than it had been at 7:00 when Kimberly and Chris had sat in his van in front of the Billows' place. Chris pulled open the shades as he sat down at his computer. The sun's glare on the screen was not going to be a factor today.

He was hoping Carly would be online so he could update her on the latest events and find out when she might be available, maybe at the end of the week, Monday at the latest, to meet with him and Kimberly. Then he figured he could try to set that meeting up at lunch today. Timing, he thought, was going to be important.

As his Internet service connected, he didn't see Carly's name on his buddy list so he went to a weather website looking to see how long this rain was supposed to last. He wasn't worried about tornados in Minneapolis; though it had happened once several decades ago, they tended to stay away from the larger cities. Eagan however, and the surrounding area, about this time of year, had flooded just three years ago as the snows from the north had melted and the Mississippi had overflowed its banks, though there had been no casualties.

The rains weren't supposed to last more than another day at most and the Mississippi River, Chris discovered, was still about fifteen feet below flood levels. Shouldn't be a problem there.

Chris was just pulling up the Minneapolis Star Tribune site to check local news when he heard a door creak open and saw Carly's name pop up on his buddy list.

F8meNOT: Hey there sexy
LorettaC: hey! what are you doing up so early?
F8meNOT: got a date
LorettaC: no way!…I'm jealous! who with?!
F8meNOT: one guess
LorettaC: NO WAY!! with HER?
F8meNOT: yes…Kimberly…met her again on my route this morning…she was actually waiting for me
LorettaC: jeez louise Chris…you are a fast operator
LorettaC: so is she prettier than me?

F8meNOT: you're still the sexiest lass I know
LorettaC: you are tooooooooo sweet xoxo
And a good liar…thanks
F8meNOT: we're meeting at Applebee's at 1
LorettaC: did you want me to try to be there? or would I just be cramping your style, Romeo?
F8meNOT: very funny…not yet, though. I don't want to scare her too early. But I did want to find out when might be good for you. I was thinking I might try to schedule one for the three of us when I see her
LorettaC: so I guess I don't need to call her then, eh
F8meNOT: right…I was thinking if I don't see any fading before this weekend, Monday would be a good time for us to meet… we could even do it at 'X' again…I liked that place
LorettaC: that should work for me
F8meNot: great…if we need to get together sooner, I'll make sure to let you know, but right now Monday should be cool
LorettaC: uh-oh…one of the kids just made a bang in the kitchen…brb

Carly jumped up from her computer and raced towards the crash in the kitchen. Johnny was on the floor crying, a wooden kitchen chair lying on its side and on top of Johnny, the cookie jar on its side on the counter, the ceramic lid beside it in two pieces.

Busted, Carly thought, but it looked like Johnny had already paid the price. She picked him up off the floor looking for bumps or cuts while caressing his hair trying to calm his tears.

"Oh honey. What happened?"

Between tears and heavy breathing, little Johnny said, “I was trying to put away the cookies and I fell.”

Carly couldn’t help but smile. He looked like his young pride had been what was hurt the most. “You were trying to put them away?” she asked.

“Uh-huh,” Johnny said, sobs simmering to a runny sniffle.

Carly grabbed a paper towel from the rack hanging over the sink and wiped his tiny nose. “So how did the cookies get out before you wanted to put them away?” she asked, still smiling.

“I don’t know,” he sniffed. “They were just out.”

“You didn’t take them out?”

“No.”

“Do you remember what Mommy told you about lying, dear?”

“That it only makes things worse,” he answered, now sniffing purely for sympathy. He wasn’t hurt.

“And are you trying to make things worse now?” Carly asked.

“I just wanted one,” he finally confessed.

“Well, you could have had one after lunch,” Carly said, making sure he was looking at her. “But since you decided to tell me the truth, you only made things a little worse instead of a lot worse. Now I guess you’ll have to wait until after dinner before you can have a cookie. If you didn’t tell me the truth, you wouldn’t get one at all. Do you understand?”

“I’m sorry,” Johnny sniffed. “But does Sasha get one after lunch?”

“Well sure she does. She didn’t tell a little lie.”

“But that’s not fair!” Johnny said, starting to cry again.

“Is lying fair?” Carly calmly asked, still stroking his hair.

“No.”

“Then after dinner. And if you argue with me about it, then there’ll be none for you then, either.” She set him down on his feet. “Now help me pick up this chair. Are you okay?”

"Yes, Mommy," he said dejectedly, lifting one side of the chair while Carly picked up the other, setting it upright again.

"Thank you for your help, Johnny. Now go back in the living room and color with your sister. And make sure you two keep the colors in the books. I'll fix some lunch for you pretty soon. Okay?"

"Okay." Johnny hung his head and turned towards the door.

"Oh, one more thing, young man," Carly said, waiting for him to turn back around and look at her. She put on a big smile for him, then said, "Thanks for telling me the truth. I love you, Johnny."

Johnny smiled. "I love you, too, Mommy." Then he turned and ran out the door looking happy again, the lost cookie already all but forgotten.

Carly looked at the broken lid on the counter top and sighed. The price for having kids, she thought. But still well worth it.

She was throwing the two-piece lid into the trash as she heard Johnny exclaim from the living room, "Hi Daddy!"

*Jerry's home? What's he doing…*and then she remembered she had left Chris online waiting for her to return. She ran out the kitchen door into the den. The IM was still sitting on the screen. She looked to her left and saw Jerry kneeling down to the floor with his children in the family room. Walking by the computer, she quickly clicked on the 'x' in the corner of the IM canceling it off the screen and walked into the living room where her family was.

"I didn't hear you come in," she said to her husband.

"Yeah. We sat around in the trucks for a while waiting to see if the rain was going to let up," Jerry explained. "But once the thunder and lightning started, boss said wrap it up and call it a day."

"Oh, well, good," she said, trying not to sound surprised.

"Not really," Jerry said, as he absently picked up a crayon to color with his son, not looking at Carly. "No work, no pay. Might have to work Saturday to make it up."

"Well, we have today then instead. I was just getting ready to make some lunch. You hungry?"

"It's only 10:15," he said, looking up at her for the first time since she walked into the room. "Maybe later," he added, turning his attention back to the Spiderman coloring book.

"Okay," was all Carly could think to say. She was trying to recall what the last couple lines on the IM had been. That was all he would have been able to see in the little dialogue box if he had looked. She didn't think there had been anything there that would have looked bad, but she couldn't remember for sure. And she had already destroyed the evidence. And she couldn't tell from his demeanor.

Damn the rain anyway, she thought. She hadn't heard his car pull in over the pounding pulse of the rain beating against the house. She turned back to the computer and disconnected her Internet service. She hoped Chris would understand. It wasn't the first time, of course, that she had broken their line of communication unannounced. And now she'd have to wait until tomorrow to hear how his lunch with Kimberly went. *Damn the rain.*

Carly put on a smile and walked back into the living room. She pulled up a piece of the floor next to Jerry and watched her family color.

22

Chris pulled into the Applebee's parking lot ten minutes early. Kimberly was already standing in the entryway under a canopy keeping out of the rain, watching for him. The day had grown warm and humid despite the lack of sunshine. She had changed into a pink sleeveless pull-over blouse with small ruffles around the collar and a strap tied to a bow in the back, and blue denim jeans. Her hair, now dry, looked soft and shiny covering her shoulders. Chris couldn't help but smile as he realized this pretty vision was waiting for him to arrive. He felt a slight fluttering in his belly. It had been a long time since he had had a case of nervousness when meeting a woman. She certainly had an effect on him, that he could not deny.

Which made him think about the effect he was going to have on her. He hated the idea that he was going to have to be the bearer of such unwanted, not to mention unbelievable, speculation; that he was probably going to turn her world upside down. Maybe not today, but before too long, he would have to tell her. He doubted she'd look quite so radiant seeing him approach after he passed along all that he felt and knew.

"Hi, Christopher," she said as he approached.

"Hi, Kimberly," he said trying to sound less depressed than he suddenly felt. "Just Chris is fine," he suggested again as he opened the door for her.

"Ah, but you said your friends call you Chris," she responded, smile unwavering. "I still don't even know you. Are you telling me I am your friend?"

A hostess greeted them inside the door before he had a chance to answer her. "Two?"

"Yes. Thank you," Chris said to the hostess.

"Right this way, then."

The hostess turned, Kimberly and Chris followed. She started to seat them at a table with tall chairs in the center of the dining room when Kimberly asked the hostess, "Can we take a booth by the window? I love the sound of the rain beating against the glass."

"Certainly," replied the hostess, smiling as she led them to a table next to a window and handed them each a menu.

No sooner had they sat down when a waitress replaced the hostess and asked if they wanted to order a drink.

Chris nodded to Kimberly. "I'll just take a Coke," she told the waitress.

"Make that two," Chris added.

The waitress said she'd be back in a few minutes to take their orders and turned to get their drinks.

"Well?" Kimberly asked, elbows on the table, head resting in her hands. Her eyes sparkled. So full of life.

"Well, what?" Chris asked back.

"Is this the beginning of a friendship?"

What a question. If only he knew the answer, but he didn't know if she was going to even live long enough for them to become friends. If he had anything at all to do with it, he silently vowed, she would. Before he had met Carly, he wasn't sure he was even capable of having friends anymore. He had lost touch with all his old friends, and to be honest, he didn't think they would have wanted to be burdened with his new problems. But then

Carly was special. Carly would always hold a special place in his heart, married or not. Looking at Kimberly, he wondered if she might be special, too.

"Time will tell, I suppose," he answered, trying to sound nonchalant, but not quite pulling it off. He was glad he hadn't been holding a tea cup and saucer. He knew they would have clinked, giving his nervousness away. "So," he said opening up his menu, "what would you like for lunch? My treat, as I said."

"You married?" she asked casually, head still cradled in her hands.

Chris looked over the top of the menu at her smiling face. *Damn, if only circumstances were different,* he thought. "No. You?"

"Nope." She finally picked up her menu. "I think I'm going to have the baby back ribs. It's what they do best here."

The waitress stepped up with their Cokes. "Are you ready to order?" she asked.

"I think so," Chris said. "I guess we'll have two orders of baby back ribs."

"Fries or baked potato?" the waitress asked looking at Chris.

Without hesitation he said, "Fries with both, please."

"Will that be all, then?"

"That should do it, along with plenty of napkins," Chris said, taking Kimberly's menu and handing both to the waitress.

After the waitress turned away, Kimberly said, "Oooh. Such the gentleman. You even got the fries part right!"

"Lucky guess," Chris said chuckling.

"So," Kimberly said, very businesslike, clasping her hands together on the table in front of her. "Did you want to talk weather first and various other forms of chit-chat to feel each other out, or are you ready to dive right into the meat of the matter?"

Chris smiled. He couldn't help but like her.

"I not sure where I would begin," he said. "Or how," he added honestly.

"Okay, how about starting with this dream you say we met each other in," she said. "I could think of a lot of ways you might have known my name, but my guessing yours kinda blew me away. That's the only reason why I am here, you know. I'm curious."

"Curiosity killed the cat," he said, trying to be humorous… then immediately wished to hell he hadn't. *Bad choice of words*, he thought. *Very bad.*

"You're stalling," she said, but she still seemed to be enjoying herself.

Chris knew this was going to be hard. It seemed to be getting harder by the minute and he wasn't even planning on getting to "the meat of the matter" today. He wasn't ready. Nor did he think Kimberly was ready. That talk he wanted to put off until he had Carly's support present.

"The dream," he said sighing, stalling, "and I'm not even all that sure a *dream* is what it actually is, began for me last August after I was involved in an accident. I was at the State Fair, did the bungee cord jump, and it broke. My girlfriend at the time was with me. We had jumped together. She died in the accident. I was out cold for a while with a concussion, but otherwise came away unscathed. That was when this *dream*, for lack of a better word, began."

"Oh, wow," Kimberly said sympathetically. "I'm so sorry."

"Anyway," Chris said, trying to get away from the 'death' part of his story, there'd be plenty of that to come later, he thought. "I seemed to have opened up a channel to a deeper subconscious in us that we are normally unaware of. I have a friend who thinks maybe I have made a more conscious contact with my soul, or something like that."

"And this is why you remember our meeting and I don't?" she asked.

"I think so," Chris said. "Because of the accident, for some reason. But I need to ask you a few things to maybe better understand."

"Okay," Kimberly said, taking a draw of her Coke through a straw.

"You see, I deliver papers all night," Chris explained. "My dream comes to me every day when I sleep. I meet people in these dreams. But I sleep usually between seven a.m. and noon, when most people are awake." Chris wet his lips with his Coke before continuing, watching Kimberly's eyes to make sure she was following him. She appeared to be fascinated, giving him her full attention.

"I've met you twice in the dream, as I told you this morning," he recapped for her. "The last time was after seeing you jog by yesterday. So, my main question for you is, did you get some sleep later in the morning? Or were you awake all day?"

"I was awake," Kimberly told him. "What does that mean?"

"Well," Chris said, "it means we are not sharing a dream. But our minds are definitely connecting at some level."

"This is really weird," Kimberly said. "What am I thinking right now?"

Chris smiled. "It doesn't work like that. I think when my consciousness shuts down, when I am asleep, that's when this other level surfaces. It is possible that maybe people are constantly connecting like this without being aware of it. You've heard that thing about how we only use a tenth of our brain, or something like that. Maybe this is actually a part we usually don't use or aren't aware of, but because of my head injury from my accident, I have some partial awareness of it."

"So why me?" Kimberly asked.

The waitress appeared at that moment with their food. They each leaned back away from the table to make room for the plates of ribs. Chris was thankful for the extra minute to formulate in his mind his answer to her last question.

When the waitress walked away, Chris noticed Kimberly still looking at him instead of her food, still waiting for his answer.

"I don't know why you," he said honestly enough. "I don't know why I have connected with any of the people I have met in this dream."

True, they were all dying, a fact he wasn't ready to reveal yet, but many people died every day and why he had met the ones he had met, he honestly had no idea.

"But," he continued, "you are the first one that I have then met in person."

"So now what?" Kimberly asked as she started in on her ribs.

"Well," Chris said, "there's more to it than I have told you."

"It gets weirder?"

"Yeah." *Much weirder*, Chris thought.

"Well? Are you going to tell me?" she asked.

"No. Not right now," Chris said between bites.

He figured he could tell her everything right now and she would never believe him. He still clung to the idea that Carly should be present. And even if she did believe, here and now, he didn't know how she would react to the news that he thought she might only have a couple weeks before some unforeseen accident was going to take her life. He also still thought it best if she not found this out too soon. He didn't want her dropping her guard in a week when nothing unusual had happened yet.

Suddenly she put down her ribs and, wiping her mouth with a napkin, revealed a coy smile and said, "What exactly are we doing in this dream of yours?"

"Oh, no, no," Chris said, blushing, following her thought. "It's nothing. We just talk."

"What do we talk about?"

"I told you all about my accident and about a lot of the other people I have seen in my dream," he said.

"I wish I could remember it the way you do," she said.

"Look," Chris said pushing his plate away. "The friend I told you about, the one who thought our souls were connecting, her name is Carly."

"Is Carly like, um, your girlfriend?"

"No, no. I wish," he let slip. Then added quickly, "She's just a good friend. She's married, has two kids. But she's the only other person I have ever confided in about this dream. The weirder stuff." Chris paused, washed down his lunch with his Coke, and swallowed, stalling. "She has some ideas, too. I kinda wanted to have the three of us together when we get into that."

"Wow. Now you really have me curious," Kimberly said, smiling.

"Do you jog every day?" Chris asked.

"Every day," Kimberly said. "Usually from six to six-thirty."

"And when do you work?"

"I work at home," she told him. "I'm a writer."

"Really? Anything I would know?" Chris asked.

"Not unless you just recently graduated from kindergarten," she said with a chuckle. "But anyway, my schedule is pretty much my own. If you want to set something up with Carly, I'm usually available. I'm dying to hear the rest of this story."

Ouch. Another bad choice of words, Chris thought. But he said, "I was thinking maybe next Monday we might meet at this coffee shop in north Minneapolis. It's close to where she lives. I can pick you up and drive if you like."

"You're gonna make me wait a whole week?!"

"Timing is important, I think," he confessed to her. "You'll understand better then."

"Okay, okay," she conceded. "But it's going to be a long week, I can tell you that much."

Chris figured it was going to be a long week for him, too. He would still have to see her every time he went to sleep.

"What?" Kimberly asked, sensing something else on his mind.

"Nothing," he said. "I'm sure I will be seeing you again before next week."

"Yeah, but you'll remember it. Apparently, I won't," she said dejectedly.

"No. I mean I'll look for you in the mornings, when you're jogging. We can talk some more, I mean, if you want." Chris could feel his cheeks redden.

"But not about the weird stuff."

"Yeah. I really want to wait on that. I promise you'll understand," he said.

They each declined the waitress' offer for desserts as she cleared away their plates.

"Well then," Kimberly said, "if you're not going to tell me any more for now, I should probably go try to get some work done. Though it's not going to be easy with this mystery hanging over me, thank you very much."

"Sorry about that," he said. "I wish I could tell you more now, and I can promise you I will tell you everything when I do, but really, we'd better wait."

"And you look like you could use some sleep," she told him. She pushed back from the table and stood. "So, I guess I'll see you in a little while?"

Chris stood and smiled. "Yeah. I'll tell you that you said hi."

"Very funny," she said sarcastically, but with a smile.

They walked to the register and Chris paid for the lunch as promised. Kimberly gave one more polite "you don't have to," and then offered to at least leave the tip. He agreed to that and they made their way together back to the front door, looking out at the pouring rain.

"Thanks for meeting me, Kimberly. I'll let you know if Monday works for Carly," he said.

"But what if we don't run into each other on the run? I won't remember if you let me know in your dream," she pointed out.

"I have your phone number," he confessed. "You gave it to me yesterday when we met on the other level."

"Oh really!" she said, eyes wide. "I'm gonna have to have a talk to that girl about handing my number out to strangers," she snickered.

Chris laughed. "Drive carefully in this rain, Kimberly," he cautioned.

"You, too. And you can call me Kim," she said as she ran out into the rain towards her car.

23

Chris got home from his lunch with Kimberly at 2:30. He was dead tired, dragging his feet as he walked, struggling to keep his eyes open, not that that was anything too far from the usual, but it was eight hours past his normal time to attempt rest, and he was feeling it. He wasn't looking forward to sleep. He knew Kimberly would be there, the Kimberly that was worried. The Kimberly that knew. The Kimberly that was scared.

Chris stood at the foot of his bed, looking at it for a moment, stalling, listening to the rain ping against his bedroom window, reflecting on what he had told Kimberly at lunch, and what he was yet to tell her. He thought about calling her to make sure she had gotten home okay. He wanted to ask her out to dinner. He wanted to arrange to get together again tomorrow. He wanted to watch over her, to protect her. He knew he had to restrain himself so he didn't appear obsessed or desperate or just a pest. But he was obsessed. And the more he knew about Kimberly, the more desperate he was feeling with the idea that he had to prevent her upcoming tragedy.

He decided to try to contact Carly before trying to get some sleep. He needed to take his mind off Kimberly and the task that lay before him. He was also curious as to what had happened to Carly earlier when they had been IM'ing. She had signed off abruptly without saying good-bye. And he wanted to make sure

Monday would work for her to meet with him and Kimberly at 'X'.

Chris sat down at his small computer desk and signed online. Carly was not there. As much as he wanted to, he was too tired to hang out and see if she signed on before Jerry was due home shortly after five. He would have to wait until tomorrow after his routes to talk to her. He closed out his Internet service and dragged himself back into the bedroom.

Too tired to bother changing out of his clothes and into the old tee-shirt he liked to sleep in, too tired to pull back the blanket and covers on his bed, he laid down on his bed and was asleep before his eyes had even fully shut.

Chris stood before the hole in the ground and waited for the coffin to open revealing Kimberly. He wondered if this version of Kimberly would remember the lunch date they had had earlier that day. He didn't think she would. Sherry had known who he was without introduction when they had first met atop the ominous hill. Chris figured the impact he had had on Sherry's life was the reason, the sub-subconscious needing an explanation for her body's condition, Chris' existence being a major part of that explanation. Yet the dreamland Sherry had not remembered his visits to the hospital when he had tried to see if she was okay. The two levels of consciousness, although in essence the same person, apparently worked independently of each other, information being shared only on a need-to-know basis.

The coffin opened and Kimberly's blue eyes fixed their gaze on Chris. Chris was once again struck by the beauty and passion he saw in those eyes. Were they less shiny than they had been when he last saw them here in the dream? Or was it hard to tell since he had seen the live version up close so recently? He wasn't sure.

Today she wore a summer sundress, dark green and flower print, no shoes. Her raven black hair was loose and windblown. Chris' heart ached with the thought of any harm coming to this vision lying in front of him.

"I'd say I'm happy to see you again," Kimberly said, "but that'd be a lie. Am I fading yet?"

"I don't think so," he told her. Then, although he already knew the answer, he asked anyway, "Do you remember us having lunch today?"

"We had lunch? Together?" she asked.

"Yes, Applebee's. We both had the ribs," he said.

"Why do I not remember this and you do?" she asked.

"It has something to do with my accident," he said. "I can think of no other reason."

"Will we be seeing each other again?" she asked.

"Yes," Chris told her. "I am going to try to help you through this. We're gonna beat this thing," he said, unconsciously tossing a glance at the Priest across the hole as he said the last part.

"I hope so," she said sadly, but Chris wasn't sure she believed him. She may have already, sub-subconsciously conceded to what Chris had told her the most probable outcome would be, her death.

"So where are we today?" he asked her, trying to change the subject. There wasn't much good he could do for her here anymore. The task of saving her was in the real world. Here he could only console her and try to keep her from getting depressed.

"We're in a park, by a lake, walking a path around it. It's too bad you don't see it. It is very beautiful. It's a gorgeous day out." Her eyes narrowed, and she asked, "You've never told me what you see. Where are we in your dream?"

Chris looked up at the Priest and his smaller hooded followers at his sides. He hadn't wanted to tell her what he saw, but he couldn't lie to her either.

"We're in a graveyard," he said solemnly, "This is where all my dreams have been since they started after the accident."

"Can you see my tombstone? Is that it?" she asked, trying not to sound scared. "Is that how you know I am supposed to die?"

"No," Chris said quickly. "Actually, you are lying in a coffin. There is a Priest here and a group of mourners, all wearing black robes with hoods. But you are not going to die, Kimberly. I won't let you die. I promise you."

Suddenly Chris heard a soft, deep, throaty chuckle. He shot a look up at the Priest whose gaze appeared to remain on Kimberly. The sound had seemed to come more from within his own head than from across the hole, but Chris couldn't help but think it had been the Priest laughing at Chris' promise to keep Kimberly alive.

Putting aside his fears, feeding off his determination to keep his promise to Kimberly, Chris finally gathered his courage and resolved to face the Priest. His voice trembled a bit as he asked the question that had been dogging him for half a year now, "Who the hell are you, anyway?!"

The Priest did not look up right away. He looked as if he hadn't even heard Chris' question, or hadn't known it was directed his way. But then something new happened. Chris noticed the coffin lid was slowly closing. It had opened every day upon his arrival on the scene, but he had always awakened before it had closed. He watched Kimberly disappear under the lid and wondered if he hadn't just made a mistake.

Once the lid had fully shut, Chris looked back at the Priest. The Priest raised his shadowed head towards Chris. Chris had time to wish he hadn't snapped at the Priest before he heard the same gravelly voice as the chuckle, still seeming to come from inside his own head, but now thundering loudly enough to rattle his bones.

"I am the one whom you deny!"

Chris bolted awake with a start, sitting straight up in his bed, his entire body trembling, sweat seeping from his every pore despite the goose bumps covering his flesh. He stood on wobbly legs, the Priest's voice still echoing in his head, the words still lost in their meaning, and headed towards his sanctuary in the shower. He wasn't sure if for better or for worse, but he realized that for the first time since his dream had begun, something other than the face in the coffin had just changed.

24

The rain, though no longer coming down in buckets, continued to steadily fall throughout the night. Chris didn't mind. It made him think a little harder about what he was doing, putting the papers in the proper tubes and keeping them dry, as opposed to dwelling on the shock he had had earlier in the evening.

He had been jolted awake at 10 p.m., showered, gone looking for Carly online, hadn't found her, ate dinner, and paced the floors of his small home until he heard his papers dropped in his driveway for delivery. He was trying not to think about what the change from routine in his dream could mean.

On the one hand, any change could be good because it meant things *could* change, and maybe he *did* have a chance at changing Kimberly's presumed fate. On the other hand, he knew from experience that change wasn't always for the better.

On the one hand, if the Priest and his band of half-sized followers *were* just a backdrop to the scene for his dream, his own creation, then the words were also of his own imagination, and their meaning had to be figured out from within himself. On the other hand, well, that was the hand he really didn't want to think about.

As the black night began to change to a dreary gray morning, slightly off schedule again due to the rain, Chris turned down his final street still searching unsuccessfully for Kimberly. It was

Wednesday morning now and Monday was beginning to seem too far away. He was wondering if maybe he shouldn't be laying it all out for Kimberly before then. He felt it was already time to start keeping a closer eye on her even though her fading had not noticeably begun yet. He wished he had gotten her address when he had spoken to her. Then he could at least drive by a few times a day to look in on her. Of course, that would make her suspicious and he would need to tell her why, which he simply wasn't ready to do yet. Maybe he'd call her later.

Or maybe he should try talking to the Priest some more first. Not a comfortable thought.

But what he really wanted to do was talk to Carly. He needed her input, an unbiased opinion, or at least a second opinion, on this newest development. He needed to talk to his only real friend, the only person he knew that somewhat understood what he was going through.

Chris returned from his routes and showered off the inky film the rain had helped coat him with through the night. Although tiredness was now an ever-present condition for all his recent memory, he wasn't tired enough to go to sleep after sleeping all evening just before he had started his deliveries. And he also had no desire to return to the dream site, at least not until he had a chance to talk with Carly and hear what she thought of the new twist.

By 8:00 a.m. Chris was online reading the local news and weather reports, trying to pass the time, watching for Carly. At 8:15 a.m. he saw her screen name pop into view.

F8meNOT: Good morning
LorettaC: it used to be "good morning sexy"
F8meNOT: you're still the sexiest married woman I know, love

LorettaC: okay, I guess that'll have to do. ;-) so how was your night? talk to Kimberly again this morning?
F8meNOT: no…worse
LorettaC: ???
F8meNOT: the Priest
LorettaC: NO WAY!!! What'd he say?!
LorettaC: no wait!! don't answer that yet. you wanna meet me at X again? can you?
F8meNOT: yeah…I can…would like to…need to
LorettaC: hang on…brb

Carly jumped up from the computer, found her cell phone in her purse, and called Nancy next door.

"Hello?"

"Nancy. Carly. It's not too early is it?" she asked.

"Oh, heavens no," Nancy replied. "These kids got more energy than General Electric. I don't even know why we set the alarm clock any more. I've forgotten what it sounds like. What's on your mind?"

"I hate to bother you so early, Nancy, but I need a really, really big favor," Carly said.

"Bring 'em on over, honey," Nancy said without even being asked. "You know I love Johnny and Sasha. Have they had breakfast yet?"

"They're not even awake yet," Carly admitted sheepishly. "Let me get them up and dressed and fed first. I really, really appreciate this, Nancy. I owe you big time."

"I tell you what," Nancy said. "You sound in a hurry. Just get them up and dressed and bring them over. I was just getting started on breakfast here, Randy's already gone to work. You can get to where you need to go."

"I don't know how to thank you," Carly said, feeling guilty for imposing again on such short notice.

"I do," Nancy replied with a smile Carly could almost hear over the phone. "When you pick them up, I'll make us some coffee and you can tell me what's going on! Twice in three days! I mean, I don't mind, really. And I don't mean to be nosy, but you looked aglow Monday when you came to get them. I know something's going on. Do I know him?" she asked with a giggle.

"It's not what you think," Carly said. Then added, "And no, you don't know him. But it's a deal. You won't believe me, but I don't think he'll mind if I tell you. But for now anyway, promise to keep it to yourself?"

"Cross my heart," Nancy said, sounding quite satisfied. "See you in a few."

"Thanks again, Nancy. Gimme about half an hour."

"Oh! Dress them in rags," Nancy said before hanging up. "I promised Mikey he could finger paint today since it's still raining. Okay with you?"

"I owe you big," she said again and hung up.

LorettaC: back…an hour good? you bought the hot chocolates last time, I'll spring for breakfast this time

F8meNOT: deal…thanks Carly…see you in an hour

They sat in the same place they had sat on Monday. It was 9:30 a.m. and there was only one other customer in the shop, busily writing in a journal. Chris wondered how the place stayed afloat.

"Eat first," Carly said. "We'll be able to think better if we aren't thinking about being hungry."

They ate bending over the coffee table, silently glancing at each other between bites, offering bashful smiles as they chewed. They looked like a couple on a first date, too nervous to say anything for fear of not saying it right. Chris ate ham and eggs and home fries. He was surprised at just how hungry he was as he all but licked his plate clean in record time. Carly allowed herself to indulge her sweet tooth, something she usually only allowed herself to do on holidays and the rare special occasions, with an order of chocolate chip pancakes smothered in maple syrup. Chris took their empty plates back to the counter when they had finished and ordered two of the infamous large hot chocolates to wash it all down with while they talked.

"Okay," Carly said as she sat back in the La-Z-Boy with her cup. "What did He say to you, the Priest?"

"I asked him who he was, or actually, who 'the hell' he was, to be precise," Chris explained. "And then he said, 'I am the one whom you deny.' And then I woke up. Kinda shaking, truth be told."

"Holy shit! Pardon my French," Carly said, putting her hand in front of her mouth. "So, what are you thinking?"

"I've been trying not to think," he confessed. "I wanted to know what you thought."

"Weird. That's what I think," she said. Then, "I'm sorry. I know that's not what you mean."

She looked thoughtful a moment. Chris waited.

"I think," she finally said, "that you need to talk to him more. Why did you wake up?"

"I think I was just shocked awake," he said. "I don't seem to control anything. The coffin closed before he answered me, too. That was the first time I had seen it close. It really was eerie."

He told her how the voice seemed to be inside his head, of the possibility that it was all from his own imagination.

"Wait a minute, Chris," she interrupted. "I remember when you were first describing everything to me, before you climb the hill. Didn't you say that the Priest is reading from a book or something?"

"Yeah," Chris said, thinking. "Every night He is reading as I approach, but I hear him from where he is, not from in my head like it was when he answered last night."

"What is he saying?"

"I can't tell. I'm too far away. But it doesn't sound like English," he recalls.

"And do you speak any other languages?" she asked.

"No," Chris said putting his cup on the table, looking up at Carly. "No, I don't. Which means what?"

He thought he had a pretty good idea what that meant, but he didn't want to admit it, out loud or to himself.

"I think it is time to open your mind up, Chris," Carly said looking at him seriously. "You have already proven and accepted that what you are having is more real than a dream. These people you see actually live, and they actually die. It might be time to accept that this Priest guy might be more real than you thought, too. But I think, if you can, you need to talk to him more."

Chris was listening, but looking at his feet, shaking his head as if in disbelief. How can any of this be happening? How can any of it be real? His whole life has been a long nightmare ever since the accident. Maybe he will awaken any minute from what seems like the longest dream of his life. Maybe he's still in a coma from the accident and this is all happening inside his head, the Priest, the dream, Benjamin, Carly, Kimberly.

But he knew better. He wasn't going insane, though he wondered if that might not be a better way to go. Carly was confirming exactly what he was trying not to let himself think about. He knew she was right. He had already thought the same thing, but had tried telling himself there must be another explanation. But Carly wasn't giving it to him. She was giving him that second opinion, but it was the same one as the first that he had given himself, the same as the one he wanted to discredit. The people he met in his dream were real. No question. And now, he had to accept, no question, the Priest, or whatever he is, is also very, very real.

"Shit," Chris said without looking up. "I know you're right." Then looking up, trying to smile, weakly, "You sure you don't want to come with me?"

"I know it's easy to say, but I wish I could," she said. Then, "Maybe I can."

"Yeah, right," Chris said sarcastically. "Like you can join me in my dream. I appreciate the offer, Carly. I know you mean it, but I don't think that is possible."

"I can't be in your dream with you," she explained, "but maybe I can be there for you. I don't know. I'd have to think of something to tell Jerry, but I could come over and, you know, be there in case it gets weird."

"You're a true friend to offer. Really. But I don't want to get you in trouble with a jealous husband," Chris said, genuinely touched by her suggestion. Actually, he wanted more than anything else in the world to take her up on her offer. *She's married,* he silently reminded himself for the umpteenth time. "I'll be okay. I just need to psych myself up for it. I'm not looking forward to it, but if it might help save Kimberly..."

"You like her, don't you," Carly softly said more than asked.

Chris thought he sensed a touch of jealousy in her voice, but couldn't be sure, not that it mattered. *She's married.* "She's nice," he said. "You'd like her, too."

"Don't set yourself up to get hurt, Chris. You said yourself that odds are against being able to help her. What if there's nothing you can do? Don't let it destroy you, too."

"Maybe that's what he wants," Chris said calmly. "Maybe that's what the Priest is after. Maybe that's all he's ever been after. Me."

A shiver ran through his body as the thought sunk home… and almost made sense.

25

"You still up for the game Friday night?"

Billy and Jerry were sitting in their orange maintenance truck on the side of Interstate 94 waiting to see if the rain was going to let up for the afternoon or not. The weather forecast had called for light rain, no thunder and lightning, but so far, the light rain had still been too heavy to work in.

"Yeah," Jerry said. "But I don't think we're going to surprise her."

"What did you do?" Billy asked. "You fuckin' chicken out an' ask her for permission?"

"I don't need no fuckin' permission," Jerry said. "But I saw her talkin' to someone on the Internet yesterday when I got home early. Looked like she was meeting someone on Monday. I didn't see much, just a couple lines when she was in the kitchen. I didn't want her to see that I saw."

"Really!" Billy raised his eyebrows. "So who was the dude? Could you tell?"

"I couldn't tell, but I don't think it was a dude," Jerry told him. "They don't use their real names on that damn computer, but it looked like some flowery bullshit name like 'forget-me-not' or something, 'cept spelled weird." Jerry shifted in his seat, stared out the windshield at the rain. "I might have been wrong about her," he said. "She's been real good to me ever since last weekend.

I mean, all of a sudden like, it's as if we never fought. She's bein' real nice."

"Uh-oh," Billy said shaking his head. "That ain't good. Man, that's a dead giveaway that somethin' is goin' on. She's feelin' guilty, man. Don't you see it?"

"I don't think so. I think she just wants things to be like they were when we got married," Billy said in Carly's defense. "I don't think she could cheat and still look me in the eye. She just ain't built that way."

"Why the hell do you think she's meetin' with someone Monday, you idiot? If it's a woman, she needs someone to talk about it with. If it's a man, 'cause you said yourself, you don't know, then I don't need to tell you why they're meetin'," Billy chided. "Just answer me this, man. Did she tell you about this meetin'?"

Jerry shook his head.

"And how many other meetin's you think she's had while you're at work all day that she never told you about?" Billy continued. "I mean, I ain't sayin' she done it for sure. Maybe you're right. Maybe. Only she knows that right now. But if you suspected before, you were probably right. And if you are thinkin' now you were wrong to suspect because '*all of a sudden like*' she's bein' nice, then it sounds to me like she's gettin' done what she wanted to get done. Foolin' your dumb ass. You followin' me?"

"Fuck you, man," Jerry said, fighting back the urge to hit something. "Yes, I follow you. But you don't know her like I do." But silently, he wondered if he himself knew her like he thought he did. Maybe she was more capable of lying to him than he gave her credit for. Why *was* she meeting someone on Monday? And why *hadn't* she mentioned it to him? And most importantly, why was she all of a sudden being so loving after such a long dry spell?

Jerry picked up the walkie-talkie sitting on the seat between them and pressed the talk button. "Hey, Jack. You gonna make us sit out here all day or you gonna call it!"

Billy snickered hearing the anger in Jerry's voice. "What's the matter there, pal?" he said. "Got someplace you need to go?"

"Shut the fuck up," Jerry snapped. "I heard enough of you. Just you bring a lot of money Friday night 'cause I'm gonna take you for every penny you got."

The walkie-talkie crackled back finally, "Reel it in, guys. No more work today. Check in at the office for weekend make-up schedules."

"'bout fuckin' time," Jerry said as he threw the truck in gear and peeled out too fast, fish-tailing slightly and showering the truck behind him with loose gravel.

Chris and Carly sat silently sipping their hot chocolates, reflecting on their new conclusions. The idea that the Priest character in Chris' dream was real seemed to change everything. But as much as each of them were trying to think of a way to discredit this concept before speaking again, neither was able to do so.

Finally, Carly broke the silence. "Do you think he's dangerous?"

"No," Chris replied quietly, still deep in thought. "He isn't the one killing these people I see. I think he's more like a mediator or something." He looked up at Carly. "But I think he knows exactly what's going on."

"But who is he?"

"The one whom I deny," Chris replied.

"God?" Carly suggested.

Chris laughed a beat or two. "No," he said with a smile. "Not God. God wouldn't be torturing people like this. I do deny God's existence, or at least I always have. I'm not sure I can deny Him now as strongly as I used to, but even so, this isn't God. I'm sure of that."

"Do you think he will tell you who he is if you ask?" Carly asked.

"I already asked him once and he answered me with a damn riddle," Chris said. "I just know that somehow this guy, this thing, can get into my head." Chris was thinking out loud now. "The others don't see him, don't hear him, so it *is* my head he is in. The others are going to die with or without my knowledge. It *is* me he is trying to torture. He knew a tornado was going to kill Benjamin, so as much as I want to deny the possibility, he must be able to see the future."

"Maybe not," Carly interrupted. "What if he just knows they are going to die but not how it is going to happen? Does he still have to be able to see the future to know that?"

"That's still seeing the future," Chris pointed out, "knowing that they are going to die. I guess if he knows that, it really doesn't matter whether or not he knows how."

"Maybe it's not telling the future though," Carly said. "You know how a dog will sometimes go sit in front of a door ten minutes before his master comes home? Maybe it's like that. A kind of ESP thing. He senses death in certain people. He may not know how they are going to die because he *can't* see the future. But he just knows that their time is coming."

"The Grim Reaper," Chris said leaning forward on his knees, speaking to the floor. "Another one I deny exists."

"Geez," Carly quietly exclaimed. "You think?"

"Shit, I don't know," Chris said, throwing his hands in the air and leaning back on the couch. "It's obviously someone that I don't believe in so I guess now I gotta believe in everything. This really sucks."

"Okay, let's start over," Carly said, seeing his frustration starting to cloud his mind. She knew they had to remain level-headed as well as open-minded if they were going to figure anything out at all. "What do we know?" she asked. And answering herself, she continued, "We know the people you see are real. We know that so far, they have all died. We know that the Priest is real and that he knows the people are going to die."

"Wait a minute there," Chris interrupted this time. "We don't know that he *knows* they are going to die. All we know is that *so far,* they all have died. For all we know, he only *thinks* they are going to die. If he can't see the future, and I really don't believe that is possible because you can't see what hasn't happened yet, then maybe it's just that *odds are* they are going to die. *That* might mean that they might not *have* to die." Chris looked up and felt his first real pang of hope in a long time.

"Benjamin," Chris continued to explain, "didn't necessarily have to die in the tornado. If I could have talked his father into taking Benjamin away, right then and there after we spoke on the phone, then he could have lived. He didn't *have* to die, but maybe the odds just weren't in his favor."

"Are you thinking you should tell Kimberly to go away for a week or two?" Carly asked.

"No," Chris said. "I already thought of that. What if she did and then got hit by a truck on the highway while fleeing in a panic for her life? Then I would have killed her by telling her to go. There's no way of knowing how they might die. But if I can be there when it is supposed to happen, maybe I can prevent something from happening."

"If you had been with Benjamin," Carly pointed out, "then you would only have died with him instead of saving him."

"I know, I know," Chris admitted. "But there's not going to be a tornado here. I think we need to tell Kimberly now. I think we need to move up the time that we all get together. I think I need you to help me convince her that she needs to be watched. She needs to be ready, and I need to be ready. I want her to be with me starting very soon, maybe even before she starts to fade in my dream, now that I think about it, until this is over. It may be the only chance she's got."

"How about Friday night," Carly offered. "Jerry always goes out with his buddies. You can bring her over to my place. You already told her about me, right?"

"Yeah. I told her. She knows I want us all to meet. She doesn't know why yet." Chris was silent a moment. Then added, "And it might be better to be in a private place than a public place when we break all this to her. No telling how she will react."

"I agree," Carly nodded. "Let me know if she will do it. I'll need to confirm that Jerry's doing his normal Friday night thing, whatever that is. We'll plan on my place around eight after I get the kids to bed. Jerry's usually not home until midnight or so. We'd have until eleven for sure. And if he comes home early, so what, we'll just explain what we're doing. Of course," she laughed a little to herself thinking of explaining all this to Jerry, "he'd probably try to have us all committed after we told him. Me at any rate, after you left."

"I like the idea of meeting at your place," Chris confirmed. "If you are sure it's okay."

"I'll find out and let you know," Carly said. "You just try to get Kimberly to come."

"I don't want to go to sleep again," Chris said. "I don't know if I can face this Priest again now believing he is real. But I have to go. I have to watch for Kimberly's fading. I wish I knew who the hell he was."

"And why you?" Carly asked. "Why did he pick you to torture?"

Chris didn't know the whole answer to that, but he did know part of it. "Because of my accident," he told her. "It started after my accident. I'm being punished or something for causing Sherry's death."

"You didn't cause her death, Chris. The bungee cord company did," she reminded him. "And they paid quite a hefty amount for it, too. I don't buy the punishment angle."

"Well," Chris sighed, "I'm fresh out of reasons. But I know it has something to do with the accident. How could it not?"

Carly looked at the time. Almost one o'clock and she still had a lot to do before Jerry was due home. She looked at Chris' tired, sad eyes and felt so helpless. She wanted so desperately to make things better for her friend. It seemed the more they learned, the more they didn't know. She hoped, for Chris' sake even more than Kimberly's sake, that they could manage to delay Kimberly's destiny with death, at least this time around. She didn't want to think about the effect Kimberly's death would have on Chris' sanity if they failed.

"I should probably get going," Carly finally said reluctantly. "Are you going to be okay?"

"Yeah. I'll be fine," Chris assured her. "It's Kimberly I'm worried about. The idea that the Priest actually exists is very disturbing and kinda tears apart my entire belief system, but I don't think he is any threat to me directly. Just scary." He smiled weakly, "You want a ride down the street again?"

"Yeah," she said. "I better get going. But I don't really feel like I've been much help."

"You've been a godsend, Carly," he chuckled at his choice of words and saw her smile at the irony, too. *A different time and a different place,* he thought again looking into her beautiful brown eyes. *Damn my luck. One married, the other about to die.* "I'd be even more lost than I already am through this without your friendship. I'd be going certifiably insane without you to talk to. I really can't thank you enough, Carly," he said as they stood.

She took his hand, pulled him close, gave him his second quick kiss on the cheek. "We might not be able to save her, Chris," she said. "But if anyone can, it'd be you. I truly believe that." She gave him a smile and, keeping his hand in hers, headed towards the door.

26

Chris dropped Carly off a house before the edge of her street corner, just as he had done two days earlier.

"Thanks for the ride," Carly said, reaching out and touching his hand with hers before getting out of the car.

"Thanks for breakfast," he returned, giving her hand a squeeze before she pulled it away. "I'll try to find Kimberly tomorrow morning when I do my routes and then look for you online after I wake up, probably around noon or so. Hopefully Friday night will work."

"Sounds good," she said as she climbed out of the van. "Good luck."

Carly closed the van's door and jogged around the corner towards home, stopping a house before hers, at Nancy's, to pick up the kids. Nancy opened the front door before she had reached the top step of the front porch. She could see that Nancy looked worried. Carly hadn't realized she'd been smiling as she jogged home until she felt it fade at the sight of Nancy's concerned look.

"Are the kids okay?" Carly asked as she made the top step.

"Yes, they're fine. Come in real quick," Nancy said, glancing towards Carly's house next door.

"What's wrong?" Carly asked as she came through the door.

Nancy took two steps back allowing room for Carly to enter but stood right there. "Jerry came over and got the kids about fifteen minutes ago. He wasn't too happy. I thought I should warn you of that."

"Oh, shit," Carly said out loud, but more to herself. Then to Nancy, "What did he say?"

"Well, he didn't seem mad at first," Nancy told her. "He said he got home early because of the rain and came over here to see if you and the kids were here. Then Johnny comes running up to him and he says, 'I thought you guys would be over here playing.' Then he notices that only the kids are here and asks where you are."

"Uh-oh. What did you tell him?" Carly asked, clearly unnerved.

"I didn't know what I should say," she confessed, "so I just said you had to meet a friend. He asked who and I said you didn't say. Then he asked if you did this often, you know, dropped the kids off with me and went off to meet someone. I told him no, because you don't, but all I could think of was that if he asks Johnny the same thing, Johnny will say he was here two days ago."

"Did he say anything else," Carly asked.

"No. He just told the kids to go home, gave me a nasty look like he didn't believe me and then followed after them."

"Okay," Carly said, taking a deep breath. This shouldn't be a problem, she thought. She's done nothing wrong. But she still didn't want to have to tell Jerry she had met a man down at 'X' two out of the last three days. That probably wouldn't be a wise thing to admit in his current state. And even if she tried to explain the whole story, the entire truth of it all, there's no way he'd believe her, let alone understand. She was going to have to lie. She didn't want to lie, she knew she was a lousy liar, but it seemed the lesser of the two evils at the moment, providing she could pull it off. "Damn," she muttered, glancing out the door behind her.

"You gonna be okay, honey?" Nancy asked.

"Yeah, sure," she said, trying not to sound as worried as she felt. "Why shouldn't I be?"

"Well," Nancy said, genuine concern in her face, "I know you haven't had a chance to tell me what's going on yet, but you did say it was a *him* this morning…"

"And I also said it wasn't what you thought," Carly reminded her.

"I know. I remember, honey. And I believe you. Really," Nancy said, placing a hand on Carly's arm. "I just don't want to hear of your face running into any more doors. You know what I mean?"

At first Carly was offended that Nancy hadn't believed her about the broken nose and the door. She had told it that way so many times, she had almost convinced herself that that was really how it had happened. But in the next instant, she realized what a good neighbor she had in Nancy. Nancy had seen through her lie, of course. She was a bad liar. She hoped she wouldn't be as bad in a few minutes.

"I'm here if you need me, Carly," Nancy said. "Don't hesitate to come knocking on my door, you hear?"

"Thanks, Nancy," Carly said, trying on a smile, practicing a smile for her long trek next door. "I really appreciate your concern, but I'll be fine. Really. It's okay."

"Let me know later, okay?" Nancy said, clearly not willing to take no for an answer.

"I will," Carly smiled, a little easier knowing she had an ally. "Why don't you bring the kids over tomorrow. You and I can talk while the kids mess up my place for a change."

"Deal," Nancy said, letting go of her arm. "Now you better get home and cool the fire. Be careful, dear. Okay? And I'm right next door, remember."

"I'll be fine," Carly said again. "And thanks for watching the kids. I'll see you tomorrow."

Carly turned and went out the door. Nancy waved through the screen door from inside and watched her walk slowly back to her home.

Carly took a few deep breaths, started to try to think of what she was going to say, but couldn't think of anything she thought was good enough in the sixty seconds it took her to reach her own front door. She decided she'd just have to wing it, take it one step at a time, keep her cool…

Jerry opened the door for her as she was reaching for the handle.

"Where the hell have you been?" he asked, accusation heavily tainting his tone.

"Didn't Nancy tell you?" Carly said, trying to sound nonchalant. "I met a friend down at 'X' for hot chocolates. She's having some personal problems and wanted to talk." She sidestepped past Jerry in the doorway, avoiding his angry accusing eyes.

"What's her name?" Jerry asked, closing the door a little too loudly, but not quite slamming it.

This was the hard part about lying and her mind went blank for a moment. So far, all she had done was replace a 'he' with a 'she.' Not too difficult. But to come up with a name on the spur of the moment, a fictitious name, that was another story.

"Julie," She said, plucking *LadyAvec2*'s name out of the air, her back thankfully to Jerry as she headed towards the kitchen with Jerry following.

"What's her problem?" Jerry continued to pry, but a little bit of the anger had already faded from his voice.

"Well, it's personal to her," Carly said, finally risking to turn around and face her husband. "But since you don't know her, I guess I can tell you. She found out her husband is cheating on her." *Damn*, she thought, *why did I have to bring up cheating.* But then, *So what. It's not like* I *am cheating.*

"How did you meet her?" Jerry pressed.

"What is this?" Carly said, trying, but meekly, to sound a little angered herself by all his questions. "I don't drill you about your day every day. I met her on the Internet about a year ago. We talk a lot online. This time it was serious and she wanted to talk in person."

"You couldn't help her on Monday?" he shot back.

"No, I couldn't. And I probably didn't help her much today, either," she said, gaining a little confidence in her story. "All I can really do is lend a sympathetic ear. But it kind of rocks your world when you discover your spouse is cheating on you, you know? She's hurting. I'm trying to be a friend. Okay with you?"

Jerry was studying her face. She could tell he was trying to decide if she was lying or not. She could also tell he wasn't sure of the answer.

"Have the kids had lunch yet?" Carly asked, trying to change the subject and break his probing stare.

"Um, I don't know," he said. "They're playing upstairs in their rooms."

"Rain make you quit early again?" Carly asked. "Thought you guys only gave up when lightning was around." Then she added, "But I'm glad you're not working out in the rain. You could get sick doing that."

"Yeah," Jerry said, giving up, for now. "Usually, but we're laying the tar. Can't do that in this much rain. I'm gonna have to work Saturday and Sunday though to make up for the hours lost."

"You eat lunch yet?" Carly asked him.

"Not really. Ate lunch at ten this morning while waiting to find out if we were going to get anything done today or not."

"You want a grilled cheese sandwich? And you should get out of those wet clothes." They weren't real wet, in fact they were barely damp, but she wanted to get him busy at something. That was the first thing that came to mind. "And ask the kids if they have eaten yet."

"Um, yeah. Grilled cheese sounds good," Jerry said. Then yelling at the stairs, "Hey Johnny! You eat lunch yet?"

"Well, I could have done that much," Carly said, adding in a laugh, hoping it didn't sound as full of relief to him as it did to her.

Johnny came barreling down the stairs. "Yah! Lunch!"

"Let me make it first," she told him as he bounded down the stairs two steps at a time. "Why don't you go help your Dad get into some dry clothes first while I make us some grilled cheese and Frito's. K?"

"Okay," Johnny said enthusiastically. "Come on, Daddy," he said, grabbing his Dad's hand and starting to tug him back up the stairs.

Her two men trudged up to the second floor and Carly turned back towards the kitchen, sat in one of the wooden chairs at the dining table, let her arms fall limply to her sides, and let out a long breath of relief. *Round one, advantage Carly*, she thought. She hoped that was the only round. She didn't know if she could do it again.

After a moment of calming her mind, she stood up and began making lunch for her family. She had nothing to feel guilty about, she told herself. She'd done nothing wrong and her lying just then had only been for the good of keeping the peace. She'd worked hard this past week on trying to mend their marriage, to get it back on the right track. She didn't want it all to be for naught just because Jerry wasn't ready to understand her innocent friendship with a member of the male species. And things had been good so far since her extra efforts to remold her own destiny and fate. Very good. She thought maybe after lunch, if Jerry was good, maybe they could get the kids into a movie downstairs and the two of them might try a little private rain dance in their room upstairs.

27

After Chris dropped off Carly, he went driving around the Monopoly street neighborhood in Eagan where he had seen Kimberly jogging. He didn't think he would be lucky enough to spot her out in her yard with the rain still coming down or even through an undraped window, but he hoped he might see her car sitting out in a driveway or on the street in front of her house. He had watched her run to one of those new era Volkswagen beetles, a metallic sky blue one, after their lunch on Monday. He had no plans on dropping in on her, he just wanted to know where she lived. Of course, if he couldn't find her house this way, he figured he could ask her for her address in his next dream.

His next dream. That was the other reason he was out driving around instead of going home. He was very tired, but had already decided he wasn't ready to return to the gravesite yet. He wasn't ready to face the Priest, believing now that he was his own person, or whatever he was, and not just a part of Chris' imagination. Chris planned on staying awake the rest of the day, doing his routes, possibly finding Kimberly out jogging in the morning, arrange the Friday night meeting with Carly, and then, finally, get some sleep.

After an hour of aimlessly driving around the area, Chris gave up on spotting her car. With all the rain the last two days, few cars were out of their garages and all the garage doors were closed keeping the dampness out. By three o'clock, Chris was pulling his van into his own garage and shutting the door behind him.

Inside, Chris took two *NoDoz* and sat down at his computer to pass a few hours surfing his usual sites. The *NoDoz* didn't make him any less tired, it just gave his body a small tingling sensation that seemed to keep it from shutting down. Between that and the six-pack of Mountain Dew he drank, he managed to stay awake until he heard the truck with his papers back up into his driveway.

He went outside and helped the driver unload the papers directly into his van in the garage so that the driver didn't have to deal with putting them under a tarp to protect them from the rain that had continued to fall throughout the day and into the night. The physical exertion of this task also helped re-energize his system for the job in front of him. He took two more *NoDoz*, just in case. He didn't want to be finally falling asleep near the end of his routes and, say, run over some poor innocent jogger dressed in an orange sweat suit running with her back to him while he coasted down the wrong side of the street nodding off.

The night seemed to take forever. The lightning was back, accompanied by a booming thunder to accentuate the flashes that lit up the night every few seconds. The rain was coming down full force again through most of the night. By morning, he was soaked through and through. His feet squished in his tennis shoes on the floor of the van. The two towels he had brought were full of water, weighing about ten pounds each. His hair was matted to his skin which was smeared with black ink from his hands as he'd wiped the rain from his face. Kimberly had predictably not been seen.

At 7:15 a.m., his eyelids feeling heavier than the soaked towels had, Chris finally stretched out on his bed and allowed his eyes to close.

Chris stood at the foot of the small hill, the tombstones and their watching eyes behind him; the Priest, his book already closed and clutched to his chest, and his party in black, stood before him awaiting his arrival. Even as he told himself to hold his position, to go no farther, his feet began to climb the hill, the wind pushing softly but firmly at his back. As familiar as this entire scene was to him after months and months of daily visits, everything seemed different now that he believed all those present were as real as he and the coffin's guests were.

Chris tried to peer into the shadow of the Priest's hood, trying to get a glimpse of his face, wanting to learn anything that might help him discover the identity of the tall robed man…if indeed he was even a man. Chris was not jumping to any unproven conclusions at this point. But the face remained unnamed, just out of sight.

Chris obediently stepped up to his side of the grave, daring to continue looking directly at the Priest on the other side. The Priest paid him no mind, concentrating on the closed coffin as he always did. Chris wanted to speak to him, was trying to manufacture the courage to do so, when the coffin began to open with the faint creaking sound of old wood, drawing his attention away from the Priest.

Kimberly was still there, but Chris was unable to hide the anxiety on his face after the lid had fully opened. The whites of her eyes seemed to bleed into her irises which were no longer the bright blue that he had first seen but now looked more like a cloudy day. Her pupils were more gray than black. She was wearing a silky sheer blue nightgown that looked somehow thicker than her skin. Her lips, full and red before, were now thin and pale. Her fading had not only begun, it had become advanced since the time he had last seen her here.

Which had been when? he wondered. Only two days ago. Not

even that, he thought. A day and a half. A panic slipped under his skin and struck him bone deep. And it showed on his face.

"What's the matter?" Kimberly asked as soon as her eyes fell on Chris, who had turned about as pale as Kimberly. Then she remembered. "I'm fading, aren't I?" she said with a sadness in her voice that made Chris' heart skip a beat.

"Yes," he said feeling completely helpless.

"Am I going to die?" she asked, trying to sound brave.

"Not if I can help it," Chris said, looking up at the Priest as he spoke. And then speaking directly to the Priest, "I am not going to let her die. I don't know who you are or why you are doing this," he said, without giving thought to the words he was saying, letting his anger take control, "but I am not going to let you take her!"

Slowly, the Priest raised his head and directed his attention to Chris, but said nothing. Chris tried to hold on to his anger, but felt fear creeping in as he waited out the silence for a response.

The coffin again whispered a quiet creak as the lid began to close and Chris braced himself for the Priest's words. He caught a glimpse of Kimberly before the lid snapped shut, agony and worry dominating her soft, pale face, and briefly wondered if it would be the last time he ever saw her. Forever passed in a minute before Chris' wait was over.

"I do not take," the gravelly voice finally said, seemingly again from inside Chris' head. "I only receive."

"You cannot have her!" Chris cried back, putting his fear aside. "You don't need her!"

"It is not for you to decide her fate," the voice replied calmly. "Her time has come."

"No," Chris challenged. "Her time has not come. We control our own fate. Not you. Her destiny, just like mine, is in our hands, not yours." And then remembering what the Priest had said last time he had been provoked into speaking, Chris added, "I will *deny you. You cannot exist. You are not real!"*

"You may deny me, for you are a fool!" the voice boomed in anger inside Chris' head, making his eye sockets ache at the sound. "But you will not defy me again! I will *have her!"*

The next moment, Chris was sitting up in bed, tears flowing down his face, his chest heaving, gasping for breath.

"You can't be real!" he screamed before he realized he was alone in his room. The Priest, his followers, the coffin, all gone. The thunder and the pounding rain outside his bedroom window, along with his pounding heart, were the only sounds that remained.

28

At 7:15 a.m. Thursday morning, just as C
eyes, Jerry was hanging up his bedside phone.

"That was Jack," he told Carly who wa
to him still warm under the sheets. "He said
coming in today. S'posed to be storming all d
hurtin' come payday with all this time off."

"Can't you claim some vacation time o
asked.

"Yep. Gonna have to, looks like," he said.
na get paid, anyway."

She snuggled a little closer, lining his bod
she whispered seductively into his ear, arm
around his chest, "looks like we got ourselve
kill here before the kids get up. Any ideas o
start your vacation day?"

"Oh, I can probably think of one or tw
with a devilish smile as he slid back under the

Shortly after 9:00 a.m., Carly climbed
feeling refreshed and new after an invigorat
isfying morning workout. Jerry was lying n
diagonally across their bed, sleeping again.
at him and smiled to herself before going t

get the rest of the day under way. He wasn't a bad guy, she ıght as she draped a sheet over him. Despite his faults, and yone has a few, she reasoned, she did still love him. She ed he didn't keep the company he kept when out of her :, but all in all, he meant well. Things will work out.

he raised Johnny and Sasha from their slumber and got ı dressed and downstairs for breakfast. She then started ı on their usual 9:30 routine each morning, coloring books ont of the TV while watching Sesame Street on PBS, and, king quickly to make sure Jerry was still snoring peace- upstairs, called Nancy next door from the kitchen phone nstairs.

Did everything go okay yesterday when you got home?" cy asked immediately upon hearing Carly's voice.

Yes," Carly said confidently. "No problems."

You looked a little uneasy when you left," Nancy said. "I ld have had you call me last night. I spent all evening worry- bout you, you know."

That's very nice of you, Nancy, but you needn't have wor- " Carly assured her. "He really is just a big teddy bear under- h that grizzly suit he tries to show off for everyone."

You know him better than anyone, I guess," she said, not ding entirely convinced.

I guess I still owe you a story, don't I?" Carly said.

You don't owe me anything, dear," Nancy replied. "I'm just g a nosy neighbor, is all. As long as you're sure you are okay, ; all that matters."

Oh, no," Carly said. "I don't think you're being nosy. And I re- lo appreciate your concern and help this week. Really. I got an " she continued. "Jerry's working this weekend because of all ain, assuming it ever stops, anyway. If you don't already have ;, why don't you and I take the kids out for a picnic Saturday.

We'll let them wear themselves out while I fill you in on everything then."

"That sounds fun," Nancy said. "Randy is working this weekend, too. This is his busiest time of year with taxes coming up soon. Everyone always waits until the last minute. What time you got in mind?"

"How about ten? We can take them over to the chutes and ladders park in Burnsville," she suggested.

"Great! Mikey loves that place. We can take my van and all go together," Nancy offered. "Be ready at ten then?"

"Looking forward to it," Carly said.

At 1:30 p.m., Carly, Jerry, Johnny and Sasha were settled into a game of Mickey Mouse Yahtzee at the kitchen table after having an indoor picnic on the living room floor while it continued to rain outside. Johnny was getting a good idea of how to play the game properly. He couldn't decipher the meaning of the numbers that Jerry was writing on his score card, nor could he actually read the different selections yet, but he knew how to play the game and what his options were. He watched his Dad record his score intently after each roll, explaining this time that he wanted to use the two Goofy's and three Donald's for a full house. Sasha just liked throwing the dice and watching the different Disney character heads roll out of the cup and noisily onto the table. She didn't have a score card in front of her.

Play was interrupted for a moment when the phone rang. Jerry pushed back from the kitchen table and pulled the phone from the kitchen wall.

"Hello?"

"Um. Is, um…I think I have the wrong number. Sorry." The caller hung up.

Jerry put the phone back in its cradle on the wall.

"Wrong number," he said to Carly as he sat back down at the table. "Whose turn is it?"

In the back of his mind, he was remembering something Billy had once said. One of the reasons Billy had begun to suspect his wife had been cheating on him was the dramatic increase in calls that were apparently the wrong number, or dead air…at least when Billy answered. But that was only the first time it had happened to Jerry in as long as he could remember. He decided not to worry about it, but noted it just the same.

Chris felt disoriented and tried to collect his wits. It was difficult to think. Too much to think about. What day was it? Thursday, he informed himself with effort. And time was running out. He couldn't wait for Carly, for Friday night. Kimberly didn't look like she could afford to wait. Her fading had accelerated dramatically. She might have two or three days left, or he might already be too late. He needed to find Kimberly. It was time for her to know what she was up against.

He glanced at the clock beside his bed. The large red numbers read 1:30.

A.M.? P.M.?

The light wasn't right coming through the slats of his blinds, but any light at all told him it was p.m. The skies had remained dark from the storm which had seemed to stall over Minnesota the last few days and had only added to his initial confusion and fuzziness. He had to think. Calm down. Think. Think.

And what he thought of was Carly. She would help him think. Maybe they could all meet at 'X' yet this afternoon. Chris got out of bed and signed on to the Internet, but she wasn't there. He signed right back off and dialed up her home on the phone. A man answered.

"Um. Is, um…I think I have the wrong number. Sorry," he said and quickly hung up as if the receiver were burning his fingers.

"Damn," he said out loud to the phone. "Jerry must not have gone to work."

Chris picked the phone back up and dialed Kimberly's number. It rang…

…and rang.

…and rang.

…and rang.

Chris let it ring fifty-five times before slowly replacing the receiver in its cradle. All he could think was that he was too late. He knew she worked at home. Plus, it was storming out. He wouldn't have thought she'd be out running errands, this wasn't the day to do it, though it was certainly possible.

And he hadn't gotten the chance to ask Kimberly for her address in the dream. He looked up her name in the phone book. There were no Kimberly Stringer's listed, but he did find one K. Stringer, but not listed as an Eagan resident. Hoping maybe she was too new to the area to have made the phone book's last edition, he dialed information and asked for her number, which he already had, hoping to then try to "confirm" an address with the operator. The operator informed him that she was unlisted. Another dead end.

He called her number again, let it ring twenty times more before hanging up. Apparently, she didn't have, or had forgotten to turn on, an answering machine. He remembered trying all evening to call Benjamin's dad in Kansas, getting no answer for hours, only later to discover that he had been too late. An uneasy feeling of déjà vu infiltrated his mind and his stomach did a cartwheel.

At midnight Chris hung up the phone feeling frustrated and

bordering on desperation. Kimberly's number had been no answer all afternoon and evening. He had called every half hour, allowing twenty-five rings each call, but with no results. Carly hadn't been online all day, either. He signed on to the Internet service after each attempted call, to no avail. Time was being wasted. Time was running out.

He tried to ease his worry with reason. He had never actually called Kimberly or confirmed this number with her. It was possible that he had remembered it wrong from the dream or maybe she had even recited it wrong to him. It was possible she was out of town, or with a friend, or a parent. He knew nothing of her life. There were a hundred possible explanations. She was fading fast, but it had just started. She still had time. Not much, but some, he assured himself.

Chris heard the "beep, beep, beep" of a truck backing into his driveway. He had to abandon the phone and the computer and begin another night of delivery. At least the rain had finally stopped at some point during the evening, he noticed. He would try to get done early and then sit on Boardwalk Avenue and watch for Kimberly. If he didn't see her again in the morning, he would try calling again before bed. Then if there was still no answer, he would have to just go to sleep, hope that he wasn't too late, and get her address from her. He was running out of options. And Kimberly was running out of time.

29

At 12:00 noon Thursday, Kimberly stood at her front door grinning broadly as she watched the long white limousine pull up in front of her house. The chauffeur got out of the driver's door and walked slowly down its length in the steady rain under a black umbrella and opened the back door for his passenger. A sexy looking slender leg shot out first, hesitated, then another followed as Amanda Zwoyer made an overly dramatic exit from the exotic car. Kimberly was now bending over and laughing uncontrollably as she watched her friend swagger up the walkway under a large red umbrella, exaggerating the swing in her hips so much with each stride that she thought she might lose her balance on the three-inch spike heels of her red shoes. She was wearing a short black leather skirt under a bright red leather jacket, her shoulder length raven-black hair tied in a tight bun at the back of her head. Amanda was a thirty-nine-year-old devoted wife and mother of three teenagers, but she didn't look it in this outfit. She looked ready to party, to celebrate, which was just what the two of them had planned to do.

At 10:00 a.m., two hours earlier, Kimberly had called her best friend to tell her that she had finally written the words 'The End.' Her first novel was complete. Still a lot of work to do with second and third drafts, edits, consistency checks, but the story itself had a beginning, a middle, and an ending. The hard part was done.

Amanda, announcing that she would not take no for an answer, told Kimberly that a proper celebration was now in order.

"I'll pick you up at noon," she told her on the phone. "Dress up nice. We're going to do this right!"

Amanda was the illustrator Kimberly's professor's agent friend, had hired for her first series of books while she was still in college. Her name had since appeared in every one of Kimberly's books, right below her own on the title page, being credited for the illustrations in each. When Kimberly finished her college work and decided to pursue a writing career, she had chosen to move to the Minneapolis area so that collaboration with her new illustrator, Amanda, would be easier. The two had become very close friends over the years.

Kimberly had felt guilty at first, explaining that her next book wasn't going to have any pictures. She felt almost as though she were betraying her friend. But Amanda had smiled and replied with, "Someone's going to need to design your cover, no?"

Now Kimberly stood in her doorway, just out of the rain's reach, the first draft of her manuscript in her hands, waiting for Amanda to arrive so that she could be the first one to read it and come up with a cover design before sending it to the editors and her agent.

"Is that it?" Amanda asked as she reached the steps.

"This is it," Kimberly replied.

"I'm very anxious to read it," she said, "but that will be for a more sober time. Right now, we have a date with the town. You ready? You look nice."

"So do you," Kimberly said. "Better than nice. You look absolutely hot! And the limo is too much! You shouldn't have…"

"You only write your first novel once," Amanda interrupted. "I'm proud of you. You should be proud of you."

"You haven't even read it yet," Kimberly said blushing. "It might be totally trash."

"Don't even think it," Amanda said, shaking a long finger with bright red nail polish at her. "I have a feeling it is going to open up a whole new world for you. You might have to get used to this," she said, looking back at the limo and the chauffeur standing in the rain waiting for them.

"You think he would like to drive my beetle for me?" Kimberly said laughing. "I'll never be a limo girl."

"Tonight you will be," Amanda said. "You've earned it and we are going to have us a time. Put your book away. You've kept to yourself long enough. Today you're mine."

The afternoon's celebration consisted of a lunch at a very plush restaurant in Minnetonka overlooking a lake while sipping a couple of margaritas, followed by a three hour visit to a spa in Edina where they had a mud bath and received an herbal massage and rubdown while sipping champagne. Kimberly had never experienced anything like it before, didn't think she ever would again, but loved every minute of it.

After the spa experience, James drove Kimberly and Amanda to the Mall of America where Amanda had made an appointment at Glamour Shots. "For the back cover of your new book," Amanda told her. All in all, more pampering and attention in one afternoon than Kimberly had previously received in her whole life.

By 8:00 p.m. they were in downtown Minneapolis sipping on scotch at an Irish pub. Kimberly was not much of a drinker and was very glad they had a chauffeur to drive them home. At 9:30 they walked down the block to a magic show at the Orpheum Theatre where Kimberly assumed it was more than mere coincidence that the magician walked out into the audience and selected her to be his assistant for two of the illusions. She was a better illustrator than actress, Kimberly decided when Amanda tried to act surprised by the magician's random audience participant selection. But again, despite the embarrassment, Kimberly was having a ball.

"So," Amanda said as they walked out of the old theatre towards the waiting limousine, "can I plan a celebration or can I plan a celebration?"

"It was absolutely the best time I've ever had in my life," Kimberly confessed. "I just hope my book is worthy of what you spent tonight."

"Well, let me think here," Kimberly said, stopping and looking thoughtfully towards the dark sky, holding her chin with her right hand, her finger gently tapping the side of her mouth. "Fifty-six books times three thousand dollars per book for the illustrations...oh who cares. Math was never my strong suit. Let's just say you have already paid me back over the last six years several times over. Besides," she added, taking Kimberly's arm and walking again towards the limo, "I have no doubt that your book is going to be a big hit. And that many more will follow."

James saw Amanda wave to him and he climbed into the limo to drive over and pick them up at the corner.

"Oh look," Amanda said as they approached the corner. "It's one of those fortune tellers with the cards. What do you call them?"

"Tarot cards," Kimberly said.

"You should go see what she says," Amanda suggested, nudging her towards the old woman who was dressed just like a stereotypical gypsy out of a 'B' movie. "Maybe she can tell you when a man is going to come into your life. It shouldn't be long now that you are on the road to success."

"You don't believe that stuff, do you?" Kimberly asked with a giggle. "It's all a scam, you know. They just take your money and tell you what they think you want to hear."

"Come on," Amanda pushed. "It's my ten bucks. And who

knows. Maybe she'll tell you something about that guy you were telling me about that you met. You know, the paperboy," she laughed. "Maybe he's *the one*."

The gypsy woman was seated behind a card table with an oversized deck of cards stacked face down on the table. A handwritten sign hung from the side of the table offering one's future told for $10.00. There was an empty seat across from her in front of the folding table. Amanda literally pulled Kimberly to the table and dropped a ten-dollar bill on it. Kimberly gave in but felt silly as she sat down in the chair.

"My friend here is single and successful and would like to know when she's going to find herself a love life," Amanda said, stepping to the side of the table.

"A pretty girl like you has no man?" the woman said smiling. "I tell you it won't be long without the cards. But the cards tell you when and how many children you have. Sit. Sit," she said even though Kimberly was already sitting. "I tell you your future."

The old woman shuffled the deck and then placed them in front of Kimberly.

"You cut the cards," she instructed.

Kimberly picked up half the deck and placed it next to the other half. The old woman finished the cut. She then pulled the top cards off and made two rows of cards, three cards in each row, and then put a seventh card directly in the middle.

"The first card is the key card," she said as she reached for the center card. "This one will tell us if there is love in your future."

She turned over the key card and revealed a helmeted skeleton holding a sword. The word 'Death' was elaborately printed below the skeleton. The gypsy woman quickly gathered all the cards together and restacked them.

"That is not right," she said a little flustered. "I shuffle again."

"No, that's okay," Kimberly said, holding back a snicker as she began to stand. "I don't really need my future told."

"No, no. I just not shuffle enough," she said. "Lady pay for your future, cards will tell."

Kimberly knew she just didn't want to give the ten dollars back. She watched as the old gypsy woman reshuffled the cards. She noticed that the death card had never left the top of the deck with each shuffle. Then the old woman pretended to accidentally miss-shuffle, dropping three cards off the top onto the ground. She stooped over, softly cursing her old fingers, and replaced the cards back on top of the deck on the table. Both Amanda and Kimberly exchanged amused glances with each other as they both noticed that the gypsy woman had left the Death card on her lap, only half hidden by her colorful apron, the sword and helmet still visible peeking out from the edge. A magician, she certainly was not.

"Okay," said the gypsy woman. "Now you cut again. And this time I let you turn over the first card. They read your touch instead of my old hands. It work more true that way."

She put the cards in front of her and Kimberly sat back down again. She pulled off the top half placing it beside the bottom half. The gypsy put the bottom half on top and then dealt out the seven cards with one hand while keeping the other hand over her lap, trying to hide the oversized card laying there.

"Okay. Turn over center card, the key card in your future."

Kimberly turned over the card.

It was the same card. The Death card.

The gypsy woman stood up quickly, her eyes looking wild and in shock. She held a card in hand, the one that had been sitting in her lap, and looked at it. It was a picture of a mother holding a baby.

"This cannot be," she said shakily as she gathered in all the cards. "I am done. I close now. Here is your money back. I am sorry." She dropped the cards in her apron pocket, the ten-dollar bill back onto the table, and hurried off without looking back, leaving her table and chairs and a very stunned Kimberly still seated there.

James pulled up at the curb at that moment. Kimberly slowly stood, still trying to decide if her own eyes had deceived her. It had happened so fast. She had seen the Death card in the old woman's lap, and then it was on the table, a different card in her lap. And the gypsy woman had been shaken, too. That much was obvious.

Amanda saw the concern in Kimberly's face. She too had seen the Death card sitting in the fortune teller's lap, but that was just more proof that this stuff was all a big scam.

"She probably had more than one of those cards in the deck," she said. "Come on, hon. Where do you want to go next?"

"Home, I think," she answered.

"Hey. Don't you worry about that card baloney now. You know it's all just a scam."

"I know," Kimberly said. "But I'm getting tired. It's almost midnight and I get up early to run. I've missed the last couple days," she explained, "because of the rain. And after that lunch we had today, I shouldn't be skipping any more any too soon here. I've had a really wonderful evening. Thank you so much, Amanda," she added smiling at her friend, trying to forget about what she had just seen. It wasn't as though she believed in that stuff. Not something to worry about, she assured herself.

"Me, too," Amanda said. "We'll have to do it again when you publish your next book."

"We'll make it a ritual after each one. Only next time, I buy," she said. And then added, "But we'll skip the fortune teller next time."

"Deal," Amanda said with a laugh as they slid into the back of the limo. Then to the driver as he began to close the door, "Home, James."

"Very good, ma'am," he replied soberly.

"I always wanted to say that," Amanda said to Kimberly when the door was shut. The two friends laughed, the fortune teller all but forgotten, as they chatted giddily and nonstop during the ride home about the rest of the fun day they had shared.

30

Chris was having a tough time concentrating on his job. It wasn't as though he usually needed to do so, but tonight he seemed to find himself stopping in front of unfamiliar mailboxes and staring at them for a moment before realizing the one he wanted was the next one down. At least the rain had finally stopped. It was dry and warm out and Chris was slightly ahead of his usual schedule despite having to correct an occasional missed or wrong delivery.

As he approached the final neighborhood of his routes and the sky began to light up, he watched intently for Kimberly. He had no idea how or what he was going to say to her, if and when he found her, but he was already sure that he was not going to let her out of his sight again until this mess was over with. He wasn't sure that even telling her the truth would convince her that she needed his full-time protection, or, given the truth, that his protection would even help, but he decided that was the only way to go. If he found her this morning, if he wasn't already too late, he was going to lay all his cards on the table. It was time.

Chris pulled up to his last delivery, fifteen minutes earlier than usual, and sat in his idling van at the corner of Boardwalk Avenue and Pacific Avenue watching for Kimberly to arrive. It wasn't five minutes before he saw her orange figure round the corner a block away and head straight for him. She was still alive. He wasn't too late. He let out a heavy sigh of relief and realized he'd been holding his breath.

"Thank you," he said out loud, startling himself at the sound of his voice. He briefly wondered who the hell he was thanking. Certainly not the Priest.

Kimberly jogged right up to the driver's side of his van and, still jogging in place, pony-tail swishing back and forth behind her head, smiled and said to him through his open window, "If I didn't know better, I'd say it looks like you were waiting for me here."

Chris forced a smile. It wasn't as hard as he would have thought.

"Indeed I was," he finally replied with mixed emotions. So happy to see her, to be looking at her, to be talking to her. Yet so worried about her, about what he had to tell her. And still so unsure if she would even be alive in a few days. He had no idea what to say next. He was at a total loss for words, but he knew that the next few he spoke were going to be crucial if she was going to have any chance of survival.

"Any particular reason?" she asked with a smile when she could see he wasn't going to offer the explanation right away. "Or did you just miss me?" she added, still bouncing in place.

"Both," he heard himself say before he could stop himself. "I mean, I need to talk to you, seriously, um, about something." His smile waned as he looked into her deep, beautiful, questioning blue eyes.

She saw the concern in his face and stopped jogging in place. "This has to do with that dream of yours, doesn't it?" she asked as she caught her breath.

"Yes. I'm afraid there's more to it than I have told you," he said. "I mean," he stumbled over his thoughts, "I told you there was more to it already, but…um…time is…um…it won't wait until Monday," he finally said. "Are you free tonight?" he asked, knowing 'no' was not an option.

"What's the matter, Chris?" she asked without answering. "What's going on?"

"I wish I had an easy answer for you," he said, "but I don't. I have a lot to tell you. Carly said we could come to her place tonight, and I still have to confirm it with her. But I think I need to tell you about this even sooner than that. I don't think we can wait any longer."

"Tell me what?" Now concern replaced her smile.

"The rest of the story behind the dream," he said flatly.

"Okay," she said. "We can do that. Let me finish my run and go home and shower and stuff and I can meet you somewhere around ten, if you like."

"No!" Chris said too quickly. "I mean, we have to talk now. I'm sorry, but you'll understand after I explain. I would really rather we go to your place or mine right now. I don't want to tell you out here in the street."

Kimberly put on a half-smile. "Your place or mine?" she repeated. "Sounds like a come-on to me." Her smile then vanished and she added, "For some reason I get the feeling that it isn't, but that it would be better if it were."

"I wish," Chris admitted. Then, "Can I drive you home?"

She looked at him for a long few seconds before answering. He knew she was trying to decide if he was sincerely worried about her or if he himself might not be the threat. But, she thought, it wouldn't be the first time she had jumped into his van. She nodded okay and walked around to the passenger side. "Should I be worried?" she asked as she climbed in.

"Not yet," he told her honestly, now that he had her with him. He was going to drive very carefully. She'd be fine for now. He'd make sure of it. "Where to?"

It wasn't a long drive, just a mile away. Kimberly pointed the way as they went. Chris recognized her mailbox as she directed him into a driveway.

"Sunday only," he said.

"What was that?" Kimberly asked.

"Sunday only," he repeated. "You get the Sunday paper but not the rest of the week. This is the first street I deliver on one of my routes."

"You seem to know a lot about me," she said.

Not as much as I would like to, he thought. And of course, what he wanted to know more than anything, not even she could tell him…how she was supposedly going to be dying soon. "Not really," he said instead.

He parked his van in front of her garage and they both got out and headed towards the house. She brought a key out of her sweat pants pocket and opened the door.

"I guess you can come in," she half-heartedly offered.

"I tried calling you all day yesterday," he said. "But I never got an answer. I wanted to meet with you then, but had to wait to find you this morning since I didn't know where you lived. I don't mean to impose," he added, feeling guilty, "but this really is very important."

"I was out celebrating with a friend yesterday," she told him.

"Well at least you are okay," he said.

She raised an eyebrow as she turned to face him. "And why shouldn't I be?" she asked.

Chris looked at his feet. "It's a long story," he said.

"I have nothing better to do today," she said as she led him into the living room. "Would you like something to drink?"

This wasn't going well, he thought. He could sense a touch of antipathy in her voice, probably towards his insistence on changing her routine. But he figured that might only be a fraction of what she might be feeling towards him pretty soon.

"You don't happen to have any Mountain Dew, do you?" he asked.

"No. Would you like some orange juice?" she asked. "Or I have milk or coffee or water."

"Orange juice would be good. Thanks."

"It's in the fridge. Glasses are next to it. Help yourself. I'm going to go take a shower and get into some dry clothes."

Hundreds of people a year die in their own bathtubs. Chris hadn't solicited the thought. It just suddenly appeared in his mind. *They slip in the shower, bang their heads. People can drown in two inches of water.* "Be careful," he blurted out unintentionally.

She turned and stared at him. She looked like she was about to say something but then just turned away and walked down the hallway. Chris heard a door shut and went to the kitchen to find the glasses and the refrigerator. As he returned to the living room and sat on the couch in front of a coffee table, he heard the water from the shower turn on. He noticed he was holding his breath again and forced himself to exhale.

Fifteen minutes later, Kimberly returned to the living room, hair still damp, dressed in black jeans and a red plaid lumberjack shirt, and barefooted. Chris tried not to think about how good she looked.

"Okay," she said taking a seat opposite the coffee table from him. She leaned back, crossed her arms, then her legs, and said, "Start talkin'."

Lay the cards on the table, he thought. *She has a right to know.* "I have reason to believe," he said slowly, looking directly into her eyes as he spoke, "and I need you to also believe," *here goes nothing*! he thought as he paused briefly, "that your life is in danger."

It wasn't the reaction he expected. Kimberly tilted her head back and laughed. "I got to hand it to you," she said. "This is the most elaborate and imaginative scheme anyone has ever used to get me to invite them into my house."

Chris didn't say anything. He just sat there, looking disappointed. She noticed, as he hoped she would, and stopped laughing.

"You're serious, aren't you?" she asked, suddenly sober.

"I'm afraid so," he replied. He was content for now to just let her ask the questions.

"What do you mean my life is in danger? From who? How?"

"I don't know," he admitted. "But you are in my dream and everyone in my dream," he paused, not wanting to finish, but knew he had no choice. "Everyone in my dream has died."

"What, are you some kind of psychic?" she asked. Then suddenly she lifted a hand to her mouth, "Oh my God! The gypsy!"

"What gypsy?" Chris asked.

Kimberly told Chris about the old woman and the tarot cards from the previous night, and how she had practically run away when the Death card had mysteriously returned to the table from her lap. A year ago, Chris would have written the incident off as a scam gone wrong, or even a bad joke on the gypsy's part. But now it was just a very strong confirmation to Chris that time was short, that Kimberly was *supposed* to die.

But not if he could help it, he thought. The only problem was, he didn't know *if* he could.

"I don't believe it has to be true," he told her.

"Why do you think my life is in danger," she asked shakily.

Chris told her about the dream, Sherry, the fading, and about Benjamin, just as he had to her dreamland self. He felt helpless as he watched her eyes slowly get moist as he spoke. Her arms and legs were no longer crossed, her body slouched in a pose of resignation. At least she was believing him, he thought. That would help.

He didn't mention the Priest.

This insanely fantastic, not to mention unbelievable, story Chris unfolded for her was not something she would normally have believed, especially coming from someone she had only just met. But she kept remembering how she had guessed his name during their first encounter. That had been even more eerie than the gypsy woman's performance the previous evening. She didn't want to believe him. She never would have believed she could believe such a wild tale. But she did believe.

"So, there's no hope?" she asked when he had finally finished his story, tears now rolling silently and abundantly down her cheeks.

"Of course there's hope," he said quickly. "That's why I am…"

"No," she interrupted. "I even have a second opinion. The gypsy. She confirmed your diagnosis. I am going to die and come tornado or hurricane or maybe a meteor falling from the sky, it is apparently my destiny."

She was trying desperately to hold onto her composure. Chris stood to move to her, to comfort her, but she held up a hand to stop him.

"Don't," she said, anticipating his sympathy. "You should just go. Let me die, if I must, in peace," she said, obviously trying to be strong.

"I can't do that," Chris said, sitting back down. "I will not leave you until this is over. I have to try to help. You need someone with you. You can't beat this alone."

"But what can you possibly do?" she almost shouted. "You couldn't save your girlfriend, or that kid, or any of them! You have no idea what is going to happen! You have no idea what we need to beat! What makes you think you can change my fate?"

She buried her face in her hands and wept, no longer holding it back. This time Chris made it to her chair without her stopping him. He sat on the arm of the chair and placed a hand on her head, softly caressing her hair.

"Because I am here," he told her. "We may not know everything, but we know more than we're supposed to know. I am not going to leave you, Kim. I promise you," he said, then took a deep breath and made the promise he didn't even know himself if he could keep. He put a hand under her chin, gently lifted her tear-streaked face forcing her to look directly into his eyes. "I promise you," he repeated, "I am not going to let you die."

31

By 11 a.m., Kimberly had packed away the tears, as well as a small duffle bag with a weekend's worth of clothes and necessities in it. Chris had called into the distribution office of the Star Tribune from Kimberly's phone and left a message for his supervisor saying that he had acquired a fever from all the delivering in the rain the last few nights, and he regrettably needed someone to sub his routes for the next two or three days while he recovered. He said he would keep him up-to-date as to when he was well enough to resume his routes. He had estimated from the severity of Kimberly's fading last time he had seen her in his dream that it wouldn't take any longer than that to get past whatever was supposedly going to steal her away from this world. *If* they were going to get past it at all. Either way though, the time was near, of this he was sure.

"This is silly," Kimberly said, as she walked into the living room with her packed duffle bag where Chris waited on the couch.

"What? Coming to my place?" Chris asked.

After Kimberly had regained her composure from the initial shock of seeing her death lying somewhere around the corner, they had talked. One conclusion they had come to had been that her routine should be broken. Assuming that they were not supposed to know of the unsuspecting death, it would most likely occur during some routine event. Jogging was definitely out. Shopping and any driving at all, for that matter, were out. Chris would pick up anything she needed and run any errands. Chris would do all the cooking. No handling of knives. No running electrical appliances. They weren't going to take any chances. It was only for a few days, Chris assured her. Chris tried to convince her to take baths instead of showers, but she drew the line there. She liked her showers. Chris understood. The shower was his own personal sanctuary, after all. But he made her promise not to take one at least until he went out and bought a shower mat for the tub, making it harder to slip and fall.

"No," she said. "This whole thing is silly." She tried to smile. "Look at me." She dropped the duffle back at her side. "I'm a reasonable, sane, well-adjusted person running off to hide from an unreasonable death because of an insane dream someone I don't even know had and a card trick gone wrong by an old gypsy wannabe."

"I know it's all hard to believe," he said, "but you've got to trust me. You can't let your guard down. We don't know what is supposed to happen."

"I know, I know," she said, plopping down in the chair next to her bag. "And for some stupid reason I do believe you. I just don't believe the fact that I believe you," she said shaking her head. "And that's the other thing," she said looking up again. "We don't know what or when or how or anything. What makes you think your house isn't going to blow up or burn down? Someone could fall asleep at the wheel and drive into your living room as easily as mine."

"We talked about this already," Chris said, remaining patient. He knew her nerves were probably testing their threshold. "We want to change routine, lay low, and yes, hide."

"I know," she conceded again. "It's just all so…unreal."

"As much as I wish it weren't real," Chris said, "knowing that it is real is probably our best chance to get through this."

"Yes," she replied, giving in with a shaky sigh. "I know you're right. I guess we better go."

"Do you want to bring anything to work on?" Chris suggested. "Your writing or anything?"

"I wouldn't be able to concentrate," she admitted. "I hope you have plenty of food," she said sarcastically.

Chris smiled. Even with her world caving in all around her, she still had her sense of humor.

"I'll have to go shopping this afternoon," he said, "but I'll let you take an inventory and make a list."

"Deal." She stood up, grabbing her bag again. "I guess I'm ready." She looked around her living room, a long, slow look as though she were saying good-bye to her familiar setting. Then back to Chris who was also now standing. "Drive carefully, okay?"

"You can count on it," he assured her with a smile.

It was only a short ten-minute drive from her place to his, but he still felt a wave of relief as he pulled into his own garage and shut the door behind him, closing out the world.

"Make yourself at home," he told her as they entered into the kitchen from the garage door. "It's not much. You can have the bed, of course. The sheets are freshly washed. The bathroom is right next to it. I will be quite comfortable on the couch. It won't be the first time I've slept on it."

"Wow," she said, looking around as she walked through the kitchen and into his living room. "It's remarkably clean for a bachelor pad. I'm impressed."

"I clean to pass the time," Chris admitted with a blush. "It was never this clean before the accident. Cleaning helps me take my mind off the dream and stuff."

"What do you charge?" she asked. "I could use you at my place."

Chris chuckled. "You can throw your stuff in the room down the hall there. There's paper and pen in the kitchen for your shopping list. I need to get online and try to find Carly, the friend I told you about. We were supposed to meet her tonight at her place, but I'm thinking I might try to get her to come here instead, if she can."

Kimberly said okay, dropped the bag in his bedroom and headed into the kitchen to begin her task. Chris signed on to his Internet service. He hadn't been able to get in touch with Carly for almost two days. A lot had happened in that time. He breathed a sigh of relief when his computer crackled onto the on-ramp for the Super Highway, making its connection, and he saw her screen name on his buddy list waiting for him.

F8meNOT: Good morning, gorgeous
LorettaC: Hey there, handsome
F8meNOT: guess who I brought home with me today
LorettaC: really!? Kimberly?!
F8meNOT: yeah…been trying to get a hold of you, she's fading fast. I think this weekend will tell the tale…three days at the most
LorettaC: do you still want to meet tonight? I'd love to meet this woman that's stealing my e-lover away
F8meNOT: I would, yes, but I don't know if we should be out on the road…we're not taking any chances
LorettaC: I understand
F8meNOT: I've already told her everything…. it was tough

at first on her, but she is taking it pretty well now… was wondering if you wanted to come here maybe, she needs to know she's not alone in this…the more allies the better I think

LorettaC: I don't think I can, Chris…Jerry will have the car and I'd need a sitter

F8meNOT: how about tomorrow morning? I could pick you up…Kimberly should be fine for an hour here by herself

LorettaC: she's staying with you?

F8meNOT: yeah…wanted to keep an eye on her

LorettaC: taking the kids on a picnic tomorrow with neighbor

F8meNOT: okay…so best for you is tonight there then

LorettaC: probably, haven't heard that Jerry is going out yet, but most likely, but I don't want you to drive here if you think you shouldn't

F8meNOT: I don't know…feels trivial…even told her not to shower til I get a mat for the tub, maybe I'm being overly paranoid, but I know the time is very near…wish to hell I knew what it was we were trying to avoid

LorettaC: hey, maybe I can get my neighbor to watch the kids tonight and I can take a cab there…if you tried to come here and something DID happen, I would never be able to forgive myself…get back to me at 8, I should know what I can do by then

F8meNOT: too much trouble to go through for what would end up being an hour or two…let me talk to Kim, see what she says…if she wants to go out there tonight, I'll drive very carefully…we should be fine…

LorettaC: maybe we should just forget it and you can just keep me posted
F8meNOT: let's let it be her decision…it's her life at stake here…I'll talk to her, then look for you at 8… sound reasonable?
LorettaC: agreed…but I thought of something else just now, Chris
F8meNOT: ??
LorettaC: I was thinking of Benjamin…the tornado… by your staying with her, you are risking your own life too
F8meNOT: I thought of that too but got no choice, gotta do what I gotta do…I'll be okay
LorettaC: I sure hope so…wish I could help more
F8meNOT: you have been a big help, Carly, really! one more thing I should tell you though
LorettaC: what's that?
F8meNOT: no one is stealing your e-lover away
LorettaC: :-)
F8meNOT: xo
LorettaC: hopefully see you tonight…but if not, I understand…good luck there, Chris
F8meNOT: 8:00 then
LorettaC: be careful xoxo

Chris signed off the Internet and found Kimberly busily writing in the kitchen. He could tell she had quite a list going already and didn't appear to be done yet.

"Your house may be cleaner than most bachelor pads," she said as he walked in. "But your food stock is typical, if not worse."

"Keep in mind this should only be for a couple days, three at the most," he said, looking over her shoulder at the list.

"These are just the basics," she replied, still writing quickly. "I haven't even gotten to the good stuff yet."

Chris smiled. He couldn't help it.

"Hello?"

"Hey, baby. On my lunch break. Say, you know the poker game tonight? Billy's wife is really sick. I wanted to have it at our place tonight. Okay with you?"

"Um, yeah, sure. I guess so."

"You don't mind? We all gotta work tomorrow so I'm sure it won't go too late."

"Fine by me, I guess. Just keep it to a low roar. The kids will be sleeping. We're going to Chutes and Ladders with Nancy and her kids tomorrow since you have to work. Making a picnic of it."

"Okay. The guys will be over 'round six or so. You sure you don't mind?"

"No. It's okay. Thanks for checking though," Carly said, still in shock that he called to ask. "Bring home snacks if you want them for the game. I'm not sure we have much right now. I was planning on shopping Sunday."

"Will do. See ya at five-thirty or so," Jerry said.

"Love you," Carly said, but the line disconnected before she got it out.

Carly sat staring at the phone a minute before she could move. Maybe she'd been wrong about Jerry. Maybe he really had been playing poker since bowling season was over. But what was even more unbelievable was the fact that he called for permission. Maybe her efforts over the past week had really paid off. Maybe he wasn't as dense as he pretended to be. Maybe he knew what she was doing and was, in turn, doing his part. *Wouldn't that be wonderful*, she thought. *Almost too good to be true.*

"You fuckin' wimp," Billy said with a mouth full of tuna fish sandwich. "I knew you'd cave."

Jerry handed Billy back his cell phone. "You wouldn't understand," he told him, then got out of the truck and headed back to work.

"She got you whipped," Billy called after him.

"Fuck you," Jerry said without turning around.

32

Chris returned from the store, half an hour and sixty bucks later, almost in a panic. Kimberly had assured him she would be fine alone in his home while he went shopping. The store was only a couple of miles down the road, but he had practically run through the grocery store picking out the items on her list and with each passing minute felt worse and worse about leaving her alone. Not that he would have even considered taking her with him at this point, but there were far too many ways one could meet death. Picking up Carly was definitely out. If she was still alive when he got back, which he had to continually reassure himself she would be, he wasn't letting her out of his sight again.

He pulled into his garage and didn't even take the time to gather up the two grocery bags from the back seat before sprinting into the house. She was fine, sitting on the couch, playing solitaire on the coffee table with a deck of cards she had found.

"No groceries?" she asked as she saw him race into the room.

"They're still in the car," he said, now feeling silly for his panic attack.

"Need help bringing them in?" she asked.

"No. I can manage." He was breathing easier now. "Just wanted to check on you first. Shouldn't have left you alone."

"I'm fine, Chris. Really. I'm a big girl," she said with a smile. "I'll help you put the groceries away."

They got the food put away and Chris made some sloppy joe sandwiches for lunch, checking three times to make sure the stove was turned off when he was done. It was going to be a long weekend.

"You play Rummy?" she asked.

"I do."

"Penny a point?"

"You're on," Chris laughed. "How are your joes?"

Her mouth was full but she gave him the thumbs up sign while nodding and chewing and still never losing her smile. She even liked his sloppy joes. *Damn*, he thought as he watched her eat. *Why her?* And then, *There is no way on earth*, he vowed anew to himself, *that I'm going to let anything happen to this woman.*

"What?" she said as she swallowed. She could see in his face the battle going on inside his head. "You look like you have something on your mind."

Chris blushed. He hadn't realized he was so readable. "Oh. Nothing. I mean," he said thoughtfully, "I guess I was just thinking how life can be so unfair sometimes."

She put down her sandwich. She looked soberly at Chris and said, "Yeah, I was thinking about that while you were gone. I've been pretty lucky in life. Things just kinda fell into place for me. Was thinking maybe there's a price to be paid for such luck. You know? Maybe this is my price."

Chris shook his head and frowned. "No. No way. I don't believe in karma, prices to pay for the life you lead. That's all baloney. You don't owe anybody anything, and certainly not with your life." He put his own sandwich down and looked at her seriously. "I do strongly believe everyone has a gift, something they are good at. Everyone is special in some individual way. Some people find out what their specialty is in life, and some never do. But whether you do or don't, there is no price to pay."

"What's your specialty?" she asked.

He looked away. "I haven't found mine yet, I'm afraid."

"Maybe you have found it and just don't recognize it yet," she suggested. "Maybe your specialty is helping people, like me."

"I doubt it. I didn't help Benjamin. I didn't help Sherry." He looked back into her eyes. "But what I was really thinking a minute ago was, I'll be damned if I'm going to let anything happen to you."

Kimberly smiled softly, pushed a hand out to the center of the table, inviting one of his to hold it. He accepted her hand and felt her give his hand a firm, comforting squeeze.

"I believe you, Chris," she said softly. "I'm not so scared anymore. I do feel safer with you." Then added with a timid smile, "for some reason I can't really understand. But I do."

Chris smiled weakly. He was glad she was feeling stronger, that she was trusting him, that she had faith in him. But as he took her hand in his, he was suddenly more scared himself than he had ever been in his life. He was scared of the things he didn't know, all the questions still left unanswered. He was scared of the Priest. He was scared of letting her down.

"I won't let you down," he finally promised, despite his fears and doubts. "But enough about all that," he said, releasing her hand and adopting her infectious smile. "Finish up your lunch and prepare to part with your pennies."

While Kimberly and Chris were playing Rummy, Carly was trying to prepare an email for Chris. He wasn't online. She intended on telling him not to worry about whether to risk a drive out to her place since Jerry was going to be home. But so far all she had managed to type was 'Hi Chris.' A raging mix of conflicting emotions was swirling around in her mind, making it difficult to think.

She tried to reason with herself. She knew it was silly. She wasn't actually a part of all this, yet she still felt like she was being left behind. It was Chris' dream. It was Kimberly's life. Their lives, or deaths, will be changed forever at any moment, regardless of the outcome. She was just a friend, an acquaintance really. She had no stake in any of this. Her life should go on as it had, albeit maybe a bit more confused about the location of the borders of reality.

But still, if they couldn't come to her, she wanted to be at Chris' place, involved, seeing this through to the end. She wanted to tell Jerry she was going to spend the weekend with a friend, to help him and his friend through a crisis. But she knew he would never, ever, understand. Especially the 'him' part.

But then she also recognized the fact that she was feeling jealousy, and hated herself for it. She was married, had a family. Things had even improved in her marriage lately. She had no right to be jealous, but she was anyway and couldn't repress the feeling. She had no claim to Chris and she was feeling jealousy towards a woman who was presumably about to die. It was all so silly.

Okay, she resolved silently to herself with a deep breath. The jealousy thing she had to overcome. Chris was her friend. A very good friend. True, they had been a little intimate from time to time online, but that was where it had remained. She had never had any intention of letting it develop into anything more. At least she was pretty sure of that. So get over the jealousy factor.

Done.

Now as far as the other thing goes, Jerry was the problem. He would never understand. But damn if she didn't want to be there for her friend. Okay, so maybe not staying there the weekend, she'd probably only be a fifth wheel. But there was no reason why she shouldn't be able to take the car after the kids are put to bed and visit a friend in need. Well, if you don't count Jerry's not understanding as a reason, then there was no reason. He was going to be home with his friends, she wanted to go spend a little time with her own friends. And her mind was made up. That's what she was going to do.

She typed:

Hi Chris

Don't worry about trying to drive to me tonight, not even an option. Jerry is having the poker game at our place this week. But that means he won't be out with the car and he will be busy with his friends. So, if you get this email before we have talked, why don't you email me your address. I haven't yet figured out exactly what I am going to tell Jerry, but I am planning on being available tonight if you still want me to stop in. I'll still be online at 8 to confirm. I'll want to get the kids to bed about that time before I leave, so would probably be able to make it there around 9 or so. Let me know. Talk to you soon. Maybe see you tonight. Be real careful, okay?

Ever your friend, xo,
Carly

She clicked on the 'send' icon and watched the email disappear from her screen. Okay. She was going to use her own car and visit one of her own friends while Jerry played poker with his own friends tonight. It was very reasonable. Very simple. She had made up her mind about it. Plus, she had forgotten to ask earlier if Chris had tried talking to the Priest yet. She anxiously wanted to know how that had gone.

But what the hell was she going to tell Jerry? Certainly not the truth. At least not the whole truth and nothing but the truth. She wished to God she could, but she knew she couldn't. Not if she wanted to keep the peace. Not if she wanted to actually go. Maybe someday, if things continued to improve in her relationship with her own husband, maybe someday he could handle the truth. But not yet. She was still trying to process some of the truth herself.

At 7:00 p.m. Chris was in the hole $1.14 to Kimberly as they ate ham and cheese sandwiches while playing rummy at the kitchen table. Jerry was $48.50 in the hole already in his poker game as he cracked open yet another beer. Carly was sitting in the next room at her computer, looking for Chris, passing the time talking to her other friend, *LadyAvec2.* The kids were playing quietly upstairs in their room.

Shortly before his poker buddies had arrived, Carly had mentioned to Jerry that she was planning on going out for a little while, while he played cards. He had asked where. She said to see a friend. He had of course asked who. She gave up Julie's name again without hesitation. *The one with the cheating husband?* Yes, she could use a friend. *When will you be back?* Not sure, but not late. *What about the kids?* I'll put them to bed before I go and you'll be here should they get up but I'll tell them to stay in bed.

She could tell he wasn't fond of the idea, but he hadn't seemed able to come up with any valid objections. A few tense seconds passed before he finally shrugged, and said okay. The doorbell rang a moment later and the game had begun.

She had gotten the kids ready for bed early and told them to play in their room so as not to disturb Daddy's game, but it was also so they wouldn't have to hear the casually tossed out profanity floating through the living room archway every few seconds. Johnny got out the Spirograph. Sasha watched her big brother work while holding three crayons in her little hands with a blank poster board on the floor in front of her to doodle on.

Carly went back downstairs and picked up the phone in the kitchen to try calling Chris when she heard the chips bouncing on the table in the living room. The hard part was done, getting the idea past Jerry. Now she just needed Chris' address and she'd be on her way there in another hour or so. Just as she was beginning to dial his number, Jerry walked in to grab a round of beer out of the fridge. *Who ya calling*? he had asked. *Nancy next door*, she had quickly replied. *Confirming our picnic plans tomorrow.* She had hit the hang-up button on the hand-held phone and punched in her neighbor's number. She was confirming the picnic plans with Nancy on the other end of the line before Jerry had managed to return to the game with an arm full of Old Milwaukee bottles.

After making the unnecessary confirmation with Nancy, Carly hung up the phone and went to her computer, deciding to keep her communications to Chris less over-hearable. The noise from the living room was a little above the requested low roar stage. Jerry had seemed to take his time a bit gathering the beers out of the fridge as she was calling Nancy, revealing his natural jealous nature. He was certainly trying to believe her. She felt bad about lying to him about who her friend in need actually was, and what that need had actually been. But he just wasn't ready. She figured better safe than sorry.

Chris had not been online. She checked the status of her email to him. It had not yet been received. But she knew he would be online looking for her before too long. Instead, she had seen Julie on her buddy list and struck up the first conversation in two or three weeks with her friend. She had a lot to talk about. She briefed *LadyAvec2* with a short version of what was going on.

LadyAves2: so let me get this straight. my husband cheated on me and your husband thinks you are coming over to my place to console me tonight, but really you're going to see this guy who is dreaming of dying people and is currently trying to save the life of the girl he's sleeping with, who according to his dream, is supposed to die any day now of causes unknown???

LorettaC: well I don't think he's sleeping with her, but you got the rest right

LadyAvec2: and where do you fit in?

LorettaC: I am just a friend of the guy…Chris

LadyAvec2: A close friend?

LorettaC: well, maybe not as close as I would like, we've actually only met twice f2f... but yes, a good friend

LadyAvec2: ahhh…then enter me, the devastated friend. alas, always the excuse, never the mischief, that's me…so is Chris cute?

LorettaC: very ;-P

LadyAvec2: I lead such a boring life! :-o

LorettaC: I somehow doubt that…hee!…but I must admit, this is the most exciting thing that's happened in my life in longer than I can remember.

In the living room, Billy tactfully jabbed his elbow at Jerry who was sitting next to him at the poker table while Buzz raked in a healthy pot he had just won and Brad collected the cards to shuffle. Gary was flipping through the stations on the TV looking for ESPN. Billy raised an eyebrow and nodded through the archway at Carly sitting at the computer. Jerry naturally followed his gaze. Carly was sitting at the computer in the next room typing rapidly and laughing out loud while staring into her screen. Jerry frowned.

LorettaC: almost 8…gotta get the kids to bed…brb
LadyAvec2: I'll be here

Carly stood up, then, remembering the other day when she had been in the kitchen when Jerry had come home early, she sat back down and hit the minimize icon to hide the dialogue box containing her conversation with Julie. The box shrank to a little rectangle appearing on her menu bar at the bottom of her screen and she stood again to go put the kids into bed and turn out the light.

Billy tapped Jerry's elbow again as he watched her start up the stairs. Without saying a word, he nodded again towards the computer and pushed his chair away from the table. Jerry followed suit and they both stood and started walking towards the computer.

"Grab me one, too," Gary called from the TV.

"Get you own fuckin' beer," Billy said as they left the room.

"Where you going?" Buzz asked while stacking his winnings in their appropriate stacks.

"Go ahead and deal me in," Jerry said. "Be right back."

"Deal me in too," Gary said getting up. "Anyone else need a beer?"

Buzz and Brad shook their heads. Gary headed into the kitchen. Billy and Jerry stopped in front of the computer.

"Nothing there," Jerry half whispered.

"Down here," Billy said, reaching for the mouse. He moved

the arrow over the only rectangle at the bottom of the screen, labeled, *IM To: Lady…*, and clicked on a smaller icon on the rectangle. "I used to have AOL," he said. The dialogue box for Carly's conversation with Julie on sprang up on the screen.

They could only see the last few lines, Carly saying she was more excited than she had been in a long time and that she was going to go put the kids to bed. Billy aligned the pointer on the edge of the dialogue box, held the mouse button down, and dragged the dialogue box up making the area containing text larger. Now they could see an additional ten lines or so. They both read quickly.

"What's f2f?" Jerry asked.

"Face-to-face," Billy said soberly. "Do you need to see more?"

"How do I do that?" Jerry asked.

Billy reached for the mouse again, but stopped short at the sound of a door squeaking open. The sound had come from the computer, they realized, and they watched as a new screen name blinked into sight on the buddy list in the upper left corner of the screen.

"That's the one she was talking to before," Jerry said as he recognized the screen name that appeared, *F8meNOT*.

"That's not a flower," Billy teased.

Before Jerry had time to answer, the computer chimed a different noise, a quiet bell sound, and a new dialogue box suddenly appeared, laying over the old one Billy had enlarged.

F8meNOT: hey there, Sexy…so what's the story? make it to my place tonight?

"Uh-oh," Billy said.

"What the fuck is that?" Jerry asked.

"Someone else sending an instant message to your wife," Billy explained. "My guess is that it's the Chris dude."

"Well get rid of him!" Jerry quietly yelled.

Billy moved the pointer on the screen into the new dialogue box and clicked on the 'cancel' option. *F8meNOT's* IM screen disappeared. He heard movement upstairs and changed the remaining IM screen, the dialogue with *LadyAvec2,* back to its original size, then re-minimized it, placing it back where Carly had hidden it. Billy and Jerry scurried silently back into the living room, taking their seats just as Gary returned with a beer and Carly started down the stairs.

Billy tried not to meet Jerry's eyes. He picked up the cards in front of him that Brad had dealt and pretended to study them. Jerry's cards still lay in front of him, a scowl on his face as he watched Carly take her seat in front of the computer again.

"Five draw, jacks to open, trips to win," Brad announced as Buzz and Gary also picked up their cards.

Jerry picked up his cards, fanned them out automatically, and still looking over the top of his cards at Carly who was already typing fast, asked, "What's the game?"

"Pay attention man," Buzz said. "Jacks and trips. Throw out your ante. An' I go fifty," he said, tossing two more blue chips into the pot.

Jerry threw in two blue chips after Billy called the open and then finally looked at his cards for the first time. Three deuces. He added another blue chip. "Raise it a quarter," he said. But it was just a conditioned response to the cards he held. He wasn't thinking about his hand. He was still thinking about his wife. He was thinking about *F8meNOT*. He was thinking about Chris. Julie. Sexy. Cute. Know him better. He was thinking of so many things he couldn't think. He asked for two cards. Another deuce. Somebody was raising a bet. "And fifty," he heard himself absently say as he threw four more blue chips into the pot without taking his eyes off Carly.

"Put your cards down," Brad was saying. "We called you. Whatcha got?"

Jerry laid his cards face up on the table. He started raking in the pot, still not looking down.

"Whoa there, buddy," Buzz said, hand on Jerry's outstretched arm. "Four sixes beat four two's last time I checked. That's too bad, man. Fuckin' lose with four of a kind," he chuckled. "But them's the breaks."

Jerry withdrew his arm. Buzz raked in the pot. Jerry said nothing. Brad pushed the cards towards Billy to deal, looking quizzically at Jerry. Billy put a finger to his lips for Brad, signaling, *shhh.* Jerry watched Carly typing.

Chris pulled out his wallet and handed two dollars to Kimberly, covering his $1.93 in losses. "Keep the change," he said with a smile. "It's almost eight o'clock. Carly wanted me to get back to her about this time. I should probably go sign on and see if she's there."

"Okay," Kimberly said. "Got any good movies?"

"They're in the cabinet under the TV," Chris told her. "Take your pick. But be careful putting it in the DVD player."

"I'll make sure I don't electrocute myself," she said sarcastically.

Chris chuckled. "Sorry," he said. "I'm just paranoid. I know the DVD player won't kill you."

"Go talk to Carly," she smiled. "And I still say I'm fine with driving out there if you want. I know you'll drive safely. Either way is fine with me. Really."

"No," Chris said. "I would just as soon not go anywhere we don't have to at this point. It's not that important. Not worth the risk. But I'll see if she can come here. I know you'd like her. And she's had a lot of good ideas."

Chris headed to the computer, while Kimberly moved to the TV stand on the opposite side of the room and started hunting for a movie she hadn't seen before.

Chris signed on to his Internet service and was met with the familiar metallic announcement, "You've Got Mail!" He also noticed *LorettaC* on his buddy list. The mail could wait. He double clicked on Carly's screen name and wrote her an IM greeting.

F8meNOT: hey there, Sexy…so what's the story? make it to my place tonight?

Chris waited. No reply. Maybe she wasn't at her computer. He waited a moment longer. No response. As long as he was waiting, he clicked on the mailbox icon, expecting to see something from his mom in Seattle. He smiled as he noticed the only mail in his box was from *LorettaC*. He opened it and read it.

"Looks like she can come here," he called over his shoulder to Kimberly. He hit the 'respond' option and wrote his address on the blank email form that appeared on top of the old one. Then he wrote a description of the route she should take to find his home from hers and added that she could come on over as soon as she was ready. He'd leave the light on. And added that Kimberly looked forward to meeting her.

He signed back off line after sending the requested response and took a seat on the couch.

"Find anything you want to see there?" he asked Kimberly, who was now stretched out on the floor trying to read the titles of the bottom row of videos.

"Yeah," she said. "Several. Just a matter of which one."

She picked out *The Matrix*. She popped it into the player, pushed 'Play,' turned out the floor lamp next to the couch, and then jumped onto the couch next to Chris.

"I heard this one is weird," she said. "Right up our alley, eh?"

Chris smiled. "Yeah," he agreed with a chuckle. "Just what we need. More weird."

33

Carly came back downstairs from putting the kids to bed and returned to her computer and to *LadyAvec2*. She brought the dialogue box back up on her screen.

LorettaC: Hey…back
LadyAvec2: little ones down?
LorettaC: yep…'bout time for me to go, soon as Chris signs on so I can get his address
LadyAvec2: well be careful…let me know what happens
LorettaC: Oh I see I have some mail, maybe it is him,
LorettaC: yep, it's from him…I'll let you know. b'bye for now
LadyAves2: b'bye

Carly opened her new email from Chris. She figured he must have signed on and gotten hers while she was putting the kids to bed. She clicked on 'print' and the address and directions slid out of her printer. She then clicked on the 'respond' and shot him back a quick email letting him know she was on her way, in case he signed on again before she got there. She closed out her Internet service and grabbed her purse, dropping the printed directions into it. She turned and saw Jerry looking at her from the poker table in the living room. He didn't look very happy.

She figured he must be losing. He hated losing. She didn't want to talk to him if he was losing. She smiled and waved from next to the computer and headed for the door.

Carly climbed into the car, backed out, rolled down the window, and headed towards I-35W south. The cool breeze coming in the window felt wonderful. She felt wonderful. She felt free. She decided she needed to get out more. She needed more friends, more time for herself. She didn't even notice the car that pulled out from the curb in front of her house as she left. She didn't notice that it followed her onto the Interstate. She was enjoying this feeling of independence too much to notice that the same car remained in her rear-view mirror all the way to Eagan.

The minute Carly was out the door, Jerry tossed his cards on the table face down and pushed his chair back from the table. "Fold," he said, even though the betting hadn't even begun yet.

Billy had his keys out of his pocket before Jerry asked. "Check the gas. Make sure you don't run out," he said as he held them out for Jerry to grab.

"I'm just seein' where she's goin'," he said. "Thanks. I'll be back in a bit."

"Where you goin'? Brad asked. "Beer run already?"

"No, man," Billy answered for him. "Bitch run."

"Huh?"

"None of your business," Jerry snapped. "Just deal me out a while. I'll be back."

"No prob, man," Brad said, holding out his hands defensively. "Don't get your tail feathers all bent outta shape. You been like on edge all night. A drive'll do ya good."

"Shut the fuck up, Brad," Jerry said, as he walked out the front door.

"Shit, man," Brad said. "What got into him?"

"His wife is on her way to meet her lover right now," Billy said without emotion. "But you didn't hear it from me. Deal."

Chris' duplex was easy to find, even after dark. The house number was well lit under a bright porch light. She pulled into his driveway just after 8:30. She saw the drapes move as she got out of the car. She figured they were probably inside jumping at every sound. As she walked up the sidewalk, she decided that when her time comes, she didn't want to know when she was expected to die. Knowing something was supposed to happen without knowing what would be bad enough. Waiting for it to happen while not knowing when must be pure torture.

Chris opened the door as she approached.

"Hey, Carly," he said. "Saw you drive up. Glad you could make it."

He gave her a friendly hug in the doorway, and then invited her in.

Neither of them noticed the idling car sitting at the corner a few houses down without its headlights on.

Carly did like Kimberly. The three of them were talking like old friends in no time. They snacked on chips and dip while drinking apple juice. They talked about ways of being cautious while doing every day chores. They talked about the reality of the dreams, the odds against Chris meeting someone from them.

"Well maybe the Priest picked someone he knew you would meet," Carly suggested. "Maybe that was the idea."

"What Priest?" Kimberly asked.

"I hadn't told her about the Priest yet," Chris confessed.

"What Priest?" Kimberly repeated.

"I meant to ask you. Did you talk to him again yet?" Carly asked.

"WHAT PRIEST?!" Kimberly asked again, this time loud enough to make sure she would get an answer.

Chris sighed. "You know about the graveyard scene in my dream. I told you about that." He explained. "Well, I'm not the only one standing beside the grave in it. You see me, but you don't see the Priest and a group of six mourners, all standing on the other side of the grave. He's been in every dream I've had, but only recently, Carly and I came to the belief that in some way, he is just as real as you are."

"What do you mean he is just as real?" Kimberly asked. She was calm, but this new information seemed to have shaken her up a bit. She looked worried again for the first time since she had arrived at Chris' home.

"He told Chris he was 'the one whom he denied,'" Carly said, using her fingers in the air as quotation marks. "Chris was going to try to talk to him more next time he went back."

"Which I did," Chris added, looking at Carly. "He told me he doesn't take, he receives. He told me I was a fool because I denied his existence. He told me I would not defy him again." Chris looked at Kimberly. "And when I told him he couldn't have you, he told me he would. And then I woke up screaming at him."

"Wow," Carly said quietly.

"Who is he?" Kimberly asked.

"I don't know," Chris said. "Before this all happened to me, and actually up until only the last week or so, I denied the existence of anything like this. God. Satan. The Grim Reaper. Fate. Destiny. Angels. Father Time. Mother Nature. The Easter Bunny. Santa Claus." Chris tried on a weak smile. "I do believe in aliens from distant planets, so I guess he isn't an alien."

"You think it is God?" Kimberly asked.

"No," Chris said quickly. "No, I don't. I'm not counting anything out anymore. If there's one thing I've learned from all this, it's to keep an open mind. Anything is possible. But no. I don't believe it is God."

"Chris is an atheist," Carly told Kimberly.

"How about you?" Kimberly asked Carly.

"I believe in God," she said. "But I agree with Chris that this guy isn't Him."

"Do you think he is the one making all this happen?" Kimberly asked. "Is he the one that wants me to die?"

Nobody answered her. The three of them sat silently staring at the floor as though trying to read the answers off the wood-stained finish.

Carly looked up and broke the silence first. "He said he doesn't take. He receives. He is just waiting for Kimberly to die. He's not going to make it happen. That cancels out The Grim Reaper and Satan. They are both takers."

"And I think we can eliminate the Easter Bunny and Santa Claus," Kimberly added. "It's not their style."

"But this means," Chris said, finally looking up, "that he can see the future. If he is waiting for her to die, then he knows she is going to, or at least is supposed to," he corrected himself. "And that is something I just can't accept. That the future is already scripted and we are just playing out our roles. Despite all that has happened, I just can't believe that for a second."

"He also said," Carly said slowly, "that you would not defy

him again. Key word there being 'again.' How did you defy him before?"

"I don't know," Chris said. "I haven't saved anyone that I know of. I failed Sherry. I failed Benjamin. I didn't try to save any of the others."

"What about yourself?" Kimberly asked seriously. "Sherry died in an accident you were also in. You didn't die."

Carly and Chris both looked at Kimberly, then at each other. "Shit," Chris finally said. "*I'm* supposed to be dead. *That's* what this is all about."

"You think you defied the Priest by surviving?" Carly asked.

"I do," Chris suddenly said with surprising enthusiasm. Then he clued them in on what he was thinking. "And if I denied him by living, that means it *can* be done. That means Kimberly can, too! It means she *doesn't* have to die!"

"But he also said he *will* have me, you said," Kimberly reminded him.

"Okay," Carly interrupted. "Back to who this character is. Assuming God wouldn't waste his time with this, that leaves Angels and Fate, or Destiny, or whatever you want to call him."

"Does it really matter what name we give him?" Chris pointed out. "He's after Kim. That's all I need to know, to know that I have to stop him."

"It's not him you have to stop," Kimberly interjected again. "He said he receives. He is waiting for me. It's whatever is going to happen that brings me to him that we need to prevent."

"Which takes us right back to where we were," Chris said gloomily.

Jerry watched his wife jog up the steps to the house she drove to. He watched a man open the door and smile. He watched the two of them hug in the doorway. He watched his wife disappear into his house. Then he watched the door shut.

He sat in the idling car at the corner for a few minutes, trying to decide if he was going to go bust in the house and then bust in some heads. He remembered that was pretty much what Billy had done. Then he had spent the next four years in prison. Jerry didn't want to spend any time in prison. He wasn't going to let this guy, or Carly for that matter, get away with playing him for the fool. But he wasn't going to go to prison.

Jerry put the car in gear and drove past the duplex, memorizing everything he could about it, and headed back towards the Interstate. The forty-minute drive home did nothing to calm his building rage.

When he got back home, the card game had already been wrapped up early. The guys were all still hanging around. He knew Billy had probably filled them in and they were waiting to see if he was going to put on a show for them with his rage. He held Billy's car keys out to him and said nothing.

"Well?" Billy asked.

"I didn't check the gas," Jerry said. Then to the others, "Time to go."

"You were down $83.25," Brad said. "You…" Brad saw the red almost bursting through Jerry's eyes and made a quick u-turn. "But we'll worry about who gets what later. Thanks for havin' us over for the game, man." He headed straight for the door.

The others quickly followed. "Yeah. Thanks, man. And good luck with Carly," Gary added. But after receiving the same glaring look from Jerry that Brad had just earned with his comment, he wished he'd just kept his mouth shut. The four men were quickly outside and heading for their cars as though a fire alarm was sounding. No one said another word.

Jerry closed the door and returned to the living room where the poker table was still set up with neatly stacked poker chips and two decks of cards.

Two minutes later, the table no longer stood, having only two legs left to support it, and there were red, blue and white poker chips broken and scattered all over the room, as well as a hundred and four playing cards.

34

As much as she hated to leave, Carly knew she had to go. It was getting late. They were getting nowhere. Lots of fresh ideas, more new questions, but no answers. She thought Kimberly was holding up remarkably well for someone who was essentially waiting to find out how she was supposedly going to die in a matter of days, or even hours. She liked her a lot. If anyone was going to take Chris away from her, she thought, even if he wasn't actually hers to lose, she was glad it was Kimberly. Again, she silently scolded herself for even thinking of Chris as 'hers.' She had a husband. She had a family. And she had a friend. Maybe two if Kimberly survived this ordeal. End of story.

It was just after 11:00 p.m. Kimberly yawned again and Chris looked like he hadn't slept in weeks. The meeting had started with rapid fire chatter as they passed around their thoughts and beliefs, but had now become just an occasional pot shot at the side of the barn as their ideas began to run dry and the needed answers continued to elude them.

She still didn't want to go. Something was eating at her. Just a feeling, an instinct, something she couldn't define. She felt like something important was on the edge of her mind and she simply couldn't get a grip on what it was. But she couldn't stay. Her own life awaited her.

"Well," Carly said, standing slowly. "I should probably try to get home before the game ends and my husband starts to worry about where I am."

Chris and Kimberly were sitting at opposite ends of the couch, across the coffee table from Carly.

"It was nice meeting you, Kim," Carly continued, holding out a hand. "Try not to worry too much, if that's possible. I know you are in good hands with Chris. I'm sure everything will work out." Then to both of them, "Let me know if there's anything I can do. Really. Anything at all. You got my number, Chris. Good luck, Kim."

"It was nice meeting you too, Carly," Kimberly said, standing and taking Carly's hand. "And thanks. This whole thing is so hard to believe to begin with, but I do feel better knowing I have you and Chris watching my back."

Chris stood as Kimberly dropped Carly's hand and sat back down. "I'll walk you to your car," he offered.

"Thanks," Carly said. "Good night, Kim. Sorry I couldn't have been more help."

"Your being here and caring is a big help in itself," Kimberly said. "I'm sure I'll be seeing you again. Drive home safely."

"Thanks. I will," Carly said as she followed Chris towards the front door.

She *really* didn't want to go.

Chris opened the door for Carly and walked her out to her car. She fished her keys out of her jeans pocket and unlocked the door. She opened the door but didn't get right in. She looked at Chris standing next to her, worry in her eyes.

"I have a bad feeling in my gut," she said. "Be careful tonight, will you? Promise me?"

"What," Chris asked with a teasing smile. "Woman's intuition?"

"I didn't think you'd believe in something like that," Carly laughed timidly. "But yes, something like that. I can't explain it, but I feel like something very wrong is just around the corner."

"There's a lot of things I've never believed in," he told her. "But women have always been somewhat of a mystery to me. Woman's intuition would be just another part of the mystery," he joked. "I'll be careful, Carly," he then assured her more seriously. "I'm really glad you were able to make it tonight. Thanks for coming."

As often as she had reminded herself that she was married, she couldn't stop herself. He stood there looking at her with a gentleness she rarely, if ever, had seen in Jerry's eyes. She stepped away from the open car door and flung her arms around him, resting her head against his chest, and gave him a hard squeeze. She could hear his heart pumping, or was it hers? She wasn't sure. She could feel the warmth from his body, a body that felt so comfortable pressed against her own.

"I just don't want to lose you," she said softly, looking up into his eyes. His tired, caring, beautiful eyes.

"It's not me you have to worry about," he reminded her, returning her hug. God, she felt good. *A different time and a different place,* he thought again. "You aren't going to lose me," he said, returning her gaze.

She stepped up on her toes and kissed him. Not on the cheek as she had done twice before. Her lips found his and pressed against them, hard, passionately, and almost desperately. She floated a moment in his arms, relishing the tender touch of his lips against hers, soaking in the warmth and safety of his arms wrapped protectively around her, and then she parted her lips ever so slightly, her tongue pushing through, parting his lips and seeking the moist warmth of his tongue. Chris, against his policy on married women, could not resist the passion she let flow and returned the kiss, wantonly.

It was only a few seconds in her life, but seconds Carly thought she'd still remember for many, many years to come. She pulled back, reluctantly, softly giving his lips one final taste, one last loving, precious kiss and then stepped back beside her awaiting car door.

"I'm sorry," she said, a little embarrassed. "I shouldn't have…"

"It's okay," Chris interrupted. "It meant a lot to me. You are a very special friend. Had we met at a different time and a different place…well, who knows where we might have taken our friendship. Sometimes I wish we had. But we didn't. You have a family," he said softly. "As much as I would love to get to know you, Carly, *really* know you, I can't. But I am so glad to have you as my friend and confidant. I wouldn't have been able to get through all this without you, you know." Then he smiled genuinely at her, "Thanks for the kiss. You are truly special, Carly."

Carly smiled, a single tear clinging to the corner of her right eye. "Thanks," she said. "I better go. Be real careful, Chris. I'll see you again soon."

"You can count on it," Chris said. "And you be careful, too, love."

He closed her car door for her after she climbed in. She turned the key in the ignition, started the engine, gave him one more longing glance, and then turned to back out of the driveway.

What's the matter with you? she silently berated herself as she pulled out onto the street and steered towards the Interstate. *You are married with kids and trying to make it better, not worse. Damn you!*

As she pulled out onto the highway, working the car up to sixty miles per hour, she tried to readjust her mindset for arriving back to her world. Sleeping kids. A husband playing poker with his friends. Maybe they'd still be at it and she could just wave hello and go up to bed. Forget about the kiss, *But*

God, what a kiss it was! and wake up back in her normal life with her normal routine. Jerry would need breakfast before work. Picnic with Nancy and their collective five kids at ten. Dinner later with her family. Kids to bed. Sex with her husband. Sleep. She didn't have it so bad. Not as bad as Kimberly had it at any rate, she thought. Not to mention Chris and his living nightmare.

No, she tried to convince herself as she neared home, she didn't have it bad. Not exactly and entirely what she wanted, but things could be worse.

Chris came back inside after seeing Carly off and sat down at his end of the couch again.

"She's got the hots for you," Kimberly said.

"Who? Carly?" Chris asked innocently. "She's married."

"I can see it in the way she looks at you, my friend," Kimberly continued. "Married or not, she likes you."

"Well, I have a strict policy on married women," he told her. "Don't. It only causes heartache and pain. Sometimes even physical pain as well as mental."

"Sounds like you speak from experience," she said with a raised eyebrow.

"Not personally," he admitted, "but close enough. Let's just say I know better."

"A good policy. I'm not arguing with you there," she said, putting both hands in front of her as if pushing him back. "I was just wondering if you were aware of how she feels about you."

"Yeah," he said, her kiss still feeling warm on his lips. "I'm aware. A different time and a different place, who knows. But she's married. End of story."

Chris reached for the dishes and cheese dip on the coffee table in front of him. Kimberly stopped him.

"I'll get that," she said. "You look dead on your feet. You go ahead and lie down in your room."

"I thought you were going to take the bed," he said.

"I am. It looks big enough for the two of us. And you look like you need a good rest, better than a couch would offer. Besides," she added, noticing the stunned expression on his face, "you look far too tired to try anything. And if you did try anything, you *will* be sleeping on the couch, if you catch my drift?"

Chris couldn't help but laugh. A tired laugh, though it was. He knew the real reason was probably that she just didn't want to be alone. He couldn't blame her a bit. He let her pick up the dishes and transfer them to the kitchen while he went and laid down on half the bed.

Kimberly came into the room no more than two minutes later and Chris was already asleep, above the covers, still dressed, having removed only his shoes and socks. Kimberly stripped off her shirt and jeans, pulled her extra-large, orange U of I sweatshirt out of her bag and over her head and shoulders and laid down next to Chris.

For a few minutes, she watched him sleep. She tried to figure out what she was doing in bed next to this man she had only just met, who had come to her with a wild, unbelievable story about how she was going to die, of all things. Yet here she was, just a few days later, believing him, trusting him, sleeping next to him.

She had dreamed of the man that was going to sweep her off her feet someday, take her away on a romantic ride that would never end, make her smile and laugh and yearn for more. Looking at Chris sleeping now, though he may be her knight in not-so-shining armor, coming to save her, the damsel in distress, she knew Chris wasn't the man she had been dreaming of. She almost wished he were. He was certainly a good man, a caring man. But he was not her man.

She'd seen the way Carly looked at Chris. She'd seen the way Chris looked at Carly, even if he was denying it or unaware of it himself. Supposedly there was nothing there, but clearly, at least to her, there was definitely something there. She liked Carly a lot. She liked them both a lot. She almost told them at one point tonight what a good team she thought they made as they bounced ideas excitedly off each other, seemingly feeding off the other's input, but had decided not to ruffle any feathers. Carly was married. Chris didn't get involved with married women. End of story. Kimberly had to wonder how long that would last. She hoped it wouldn't get them into trouble down the road.

She quietly thanked him anyway for caring enough to try to help her, to try to save her from some unforeseen disaster, and kissed him lightly on the cheek. He wasn't the man she had been looking for, but she was ever so glad he was here, nonetheless. She believed his story. She was scared to death that everything he had told her was true and that her life was indeed in grave danger. But she felt safe lying next to him.

She wouldn't have thought it possible under all these weird and foreboding circumstances, the stress and fear swirling and churning inside her stomach, but once she closed her eyes, she too fell asleep very quickly.

35

Carly pulled into the garage shortly before midnight. Her plan of sliding in, waving and heading quickly up to bed was shot down before she had even turned into the driveway. The street in front of her house was empty. The three cars that had been there for the game when she had left were gone. Jerry would be inside, drunk, waiting for her. She got out of the car, closed the garage door, took a deep breath and braced herself as she walked into the house.

The den was empty. The lights were out in the family room where the game had been played. The house smelled of stale beer. Had he gone to bed? Carly turned out the light in the den, then the kitchen and went upstairs and looked into the kids' room. They were sleeping peacefully. She'd been home two minutes and the house was still quiet. About ninety seconds longer than she would have guessed.

She walked into her bedroom, trying to keep a nonchalant façade, bracing herself again for a wrath she didn't feel she deserved, but was sure she would receive. Okay, so maybe she did deserve a little, she thought. No way Jerry should know, of course, but she had kissed Chris. And not just a peck on the cheek. It had been a real kiss. A passionate, wonderful, loving kiss that she would never forget for as long as she lived. But it was still just a kiss. Nothing was going to come from it.

The bedroom was empty.

Where the hell was he?

Carly went back downstairs and started turning lights on again. When she got to the family room, she froze. The room was a wreck. The table lay on its side, two legs missing. Poker chips and playing cards and empty beer bottles were scattered all over the furniture and floor. The TV had a crack down the center of the glass screen. The lamp on the end table was broken, lying on its side. The room looked like a miniature tornado had swept through it.

At first, she thought that maybe there had been a misunderstanding during the game, followed by a fight to solve the disagreement. But then where was Jerry? The hospital? That didn't feel right. He wouldn't have gone, even if he had been the one taking the beating. But he was twice the size of the other guys that had been here. If there had been a real poker problem, he would have just kicked them out. If there had been a fight, he wouldn't be the one in the hospital.

And why would he have left the kids home alone sleeping in bed?

She would have preferred to have him waiting for her, question her, get angry with her, rather than this.

She checked the kitchen, the desk with her computer, the TV, the dresser upstairs, for a note of some kind. Nothing.

Nervously, she began picking up the mess in the living room. She folded the remaining two legs of the poker table and rolled it out of the way, leaning it against a wall. She grabbed a large trash bag and filled it with the bottles, poker chips, and cards, and set the bag in the garage. She righted the broken lamp.

A half hour passed and the room was at least cleared of the debris. The rug and couch were both beer stained and ruined, and the TV was still cracked. Still no sign of Jerry. She didn't want to go to bed and wait for him. She had no way of knowing when he would return and what mood he would return in. She turned out all the downstairs lights and made her way upstairs, deciding to sleep with her children.

She crawled into Johnny's bed and cuddled up next to her son. Johnny turned and instinctively hugged his mom without waking. She wasn't sure how long it took, it seemed like it took most of the night, but at some point, she finally fell asleep.

After Jerry trashed his living room, he went to the phone and dialed up Billy's cell phone. Billy answered on the first ring, a juke box playing loudly in the background.

"I figured you'd be calling," Billy said. "You want to talk about it?"

"Where you at?" Jerry asked.

"At the Black Cat. Just down the way from ya. You wanna come on over here, I'll buy you a beer."

"I know where it's at," Jerry said. "Come pick me up."

"The walk'll do ya good, man. Cool ya down a bit first," Billy said. "It's only five or six blocks. I'll be here."

Jerry hung up. He was still pissed as hell. He knew he'd still be pissed after the walk. He also knew that if Carly walked in the door right now, he'd probably break more than just her nose and he really didn't want to do that. But he was so goddamn pissed. He needed to think. He needed time to think before he saw her again. He wasn't going to let her, or Chris, get away with this, but he didn't want to act rashly. This situation was going to require some thought. He knew he had to do something about it, but he wanted to do it right. He needed to talk to somebody. Billy was waiting for him.

He didn't check on the kids. They were still asleep, he assumed.

Carly would be home soon. They'd be fine. He didn't lock the front door as he stormed out.

The ten-minute walk did clear his head a bit, but did nothing towards cooling his anger. He walked into the Black Cat and found Billy at a booth by himself with two fresh beers in front of him.

"What happened?" Billy asked, pointing to a beer.

Jerry sat across from him and told him what he'd seen.

"Sorry to hear it, man," Billy said without any real sympathy in his voice. "So whatcha gonna do about it?"

Jerry had thought about this on the walk over. He took a long drink of his beer, polishing off half the bottle in a single swig and looked Billy squarely in the eye. "Can you get me a gun?"

"Ah, man. You don't want to go that route," Billy said. "She ain't worth it. No woman is worth it."

"I'm not going to shoot anyone," Jerry assured him. "I just wanna scare the living piss out of him. Make damn sure he doesn't go near her again."

"I don't know, man. You been drinkin' all night," Billy said. "Guns and booze definitely don't mix."

"I'm not going over there tonight," Jerry said, although that had been the original plan as he walked to the bar. "I'm gonna talk to Carly first. Then I'm gonna go talk to the guy. Tomorrow," he added.

"You sure just talkin' is all you got in mind?" Billy asked.

"I'm not as stupid as you, ya dumb fuck," Jerry fired back. "I'm not gonna land myself in prison."

"Who you callin' a dumb fuck?" Billy said, taking offense. "I buy you a beer, offer you an ear and you come in here callin' me a dumb fuck? Hey, it ain't my woman screwin' around."

"No, yours is too fuckin' ugly. Remember?"

"You better shut the fuck up, Jer, if you know what's good for you. Leave the bitch alone. Just walk away, you want my advice."

"I don't want your fuckin' advice, man," Jerry said. "I want a fuckin' gun. I know you got some and you ain't supposed to own arms while on parole. You want, I can make a call or two and you'll have some explainin' to do. Might even go back to the pen."

"Fuck you, man," Billy yelled. "Yeah, sure. I got a clean piece you can have. And you go shoot the fucker up. See if I care if you land yourself in jail for the rest of your fuckin' life. I was tryin' to help your sorry ass. But what do I care."

Jerry swallowed down the rest of his beer and stood up. "Let's go then," he said.

Billy shoved back from the table hard, knocking his chair over, and started out the door. Jerry followed.

It was three a.m. when Billy dropped Jerry off in front of his house. Billy and Jerry had had several more beers at Billy's place before Jerry finally insisted on being taken home. Billy didn't know why the hell he cared, maybe because he liked Carly, maybe because he knew how Jerry felt having been there before, but he had hoped to get Jerry drunk enough to stay at his place for the night. It hadn't worked.

"Nothing tonight, right?" Billy called out to Jerry as he got out of the car in front of his home. "Just go to bed. Think about it, man. One night. Tomorrow you do what you want. Got it?"

"Yeah, yeah," Jerry slurred as he stumbled towards his door. "Tomorrow."

Jerry fumbled with his key for a few minutes at the front door before finally getting it unlocked. He dragged himself inside, went to the refrigerator, grabbed another bottle of beer and twisted off the cap. Then, gun still in hand, he staggered into the family room and sat on the couch in the dark and passed out without even taking a sip of the freshly opened beer. He let loose his grip on the full bottle, its contents foaming out onto the carpet next to the couch. The gun stayed firmly in the grip of his right hand.

36

Chris approached the gravesite apprehensively. Not that he had ever approached it any other way over the last seven months, but everything seemed to be spiraling out of control at the moment. Not that it was ever in *control, he just felt more helpless now than he ever had in his life. Kimberly had faded to a point last time that, had he not seen her just before going to sleep, he would have made it even odds as to whether or not she would be returning to his nightmare or would have already been replaced by a new dying guest tonight. But even if she did return, he knew it would be the last time he would meet her here.*

And then there was the Priest, or whatever, whoever, the hell he was. More than anything, Chris wanted to put an end to this madness. He was tired of playing spectator to this macabre being's game. He looked at the Priest as he came to a stop in front of the fresh hole and made a decision.

The coffin slowly opened and Chris held his breath. He didn't know how long he slept each day before this dream began. He had no sense of time here. It seemed as though he awoke directly from the dream every day, but always tired as if he'd slept even less than he had. Dreams, they say, only take seconds to play out an entire story and one has hundreds of dreams every night while sleeping. But as he had already determined, this wasn't really a dream. It seemed to have its own set of rules. It may consume most of his night, explaining why he never felt rested anymore, or maybe it just came to him before he awoke and drained the energy his sleep had just restored. But either way, ever since this nightmare had begun, he hadn't remembered a single other dream from his sleep. Only this one.

He hoped Kimberly was still here. He hoped she was still alive, that he hadn't lost her while he slept. Then suddenly he thought maybe he hoped she wasn't here. He'd wake up and find her next to him and know that she was safe. Maybe his bringing her to his place was all it took to change whatever was supposedly going to happen to her. Maybe her time was not…

His thoughts and wishful thinking immediately ceased. She was still there. A rock seemed to have lodged itself in his throat. He couldn't swallow his fear. She was even more faded than previously, though he wouldn't have thought that possible when he last saw her.

Nothing had been changed. She was still going to die.

Kimberly looked up at Chris with sad eyes that were almost white. He could barely make out the pattern in the soft fabric of the coffin beneath her head. He knew beyond a doubt that this was the last time he would see her here on the ominous mound. She would not be back tomorrow. He had to save her now or she was lost.

Looking away from Kimberly, up at the Priest, recalling the thought that Carly had earlier that evening about his own escape from death, he made up his mind.

He took a deep breath. "Let her live," he told the Priest, in a voice sounding more sure of itself than he felt. "Take me instead. I am the one you want. I am the one you have been after. Let her live and you can have me."

Kimberly shook her head. She couldn't see who Chris was speaking to, but she understood what he was saying, understood that her time was up. Yet she didn't want anyone to be sacrificing themselves for her. If her time was now then she would have to accept that. She couldn't live knowing someone had died in her place, for her, instead of her. "Chris, no!" she said, as the lid began to close just as soon as it had opened. "Don't. Not for me."

But Chris did not so much as look at her, let alone listen. His mind was made up. If he was living on borrowed time, then he would pay off his debt right here and now, for Kimberly. His life for hers. He was ready. He was willing. He was tired. He wanted this all to stop. Now.

The coffin lid shut, Chris kept his concentration on the tall, black robed figure in front of him, boldly awaiting his response.

"A valiant offer indeed, young man."

The voice was not the overpowering rumble of a voice that the Priest had played inside his head the last two visits. In fact, it sounded almost familiar, pleasant even, and hadn't seemed to come from the Priest at all.

Suddenly the half-sized mourner to the Priest's right slowly lifted his arms from his sides and pushed back the hood that had been covering his head and shadowing his face.

It was the face of William Shavver, the old man who had replaced Sherry in her coffin after she had died.

"But I don't think it works that way," William added.

"William?" Chris barely heard his own voice over his pounding heart.

But then it wasn't William. The lines and aged cracks in his face suddenly smoothed out, the hair on his head grew dark, his eyes changed from brown to blue and his cheeks appeared to sink in. Chris recognized Benjamin's young face in an instant. Benjamin, smiling his same energetic smile, his eyes gleaming brightly.

"It's okay, Chris. It doesn't hurt," he said sounding every bit the little boy he once was.

Chris stood, mouth agape, unable to comprehend what was happening, unable to think at all, as Benjamin's face dissolved and a new one appeared again.

The small mourner to the Priest's right now wore the face of Sherry.

"It's her time, Chris," Sherry said sympathetically. "You have to let her go."

Finally, Chris found his voice again. "Why can't I go instead?" he asked Sherry.

Sherry spoke softly and melodically. "You missed your time, Chris. You were supposed to come with me, after the accident. But you denied him. You got your wish. You control your own fate now."

"Who did I deny?" Chris asked Sherry.

But Sherry was no longer there. Barry "Trust Me" Johnson's face, the out-dated, greasy salesman had replaced her. "Death. The Grim Fucking Reaper," he said.

The face changed again. William was back. "Don't listen to him, Chris. His is an angry soul. He is the Angel that reunited me with my Annie."

"He is God," said the face of Gloria Bitterman, the suicide.

Martha's face, the old school teacher. "He is Fate, Chris. He is everyone's destiny. He is your destiny, too, but you have made him wait."

"Wait for what?" Chris managed to ask.

"For your soul," Sherry was back. "He is the collector of souls."

"Then let him to take my soul and leave Kimberly with hers," he offered again.

"Her time is now," Sherry said.

"Why is it her time?" Chris pleaded. "She is young, healthy, vibrant."

Martha, the teacher, returned. "We are all born with a time, Chris. Some have more time than others. It is nature's way. What we do with our time is up to us while we have it. But when our time comes, he comes for us."

"But why is it her time?" he repeated, not satisfied with the teacher's explanation.

Benjamin fielded his question this time. "Some people are born with deformities or defects you can see. Some you can't see. But he can see all. He knows when your time is here."

A new face, a woman's face, one Chris recognized but hadn't seen more than a night or two and whose name he couldn't remember, replaced Benjamin. "You are given a soul at birth, Chris. It is one of the miracles of birth. It is what makes each of us unique."

William again. Chris was having trouble keeping up with the changing faces. "It's nature's way, Chris. Can you imagine if everyone lived out their life to be a hundred? We'd use up the world."

Sherry returned. "Our soul, Chris, is energy. It is born in the brain, which operates the body, which is just a very complex organic machine. Not all the machines are made to last. They all have defects, some more noticeable than others. Some only he can see. No one is perfect. But our souls are pure energy, a life force that animates the machine, makes us who we are, makes us individuals different from each other. It's what makes each machine think differently, react differently even though they all operate basically the same way. The energy still exists when it goes home once our body, the machine, fails to run anymore. He collects our souls. He gives us a new home."

"But her body is not breaking down," Chris tried to reason, to understand, but this was too much, too fast, and from too many faces. "Mine didn't break down. My time supposedly came and went and I am still living! So can she!"

Another recognizable, but unnamed man's face appeared. "Nature's natural balance. Everyone is born with a time."

Sherry again. "You somehow slipped by your time. You have cheated your fate. You have cheated him of his only purpose, to collect the souls of those whose time has come."

Barry returned, and said with a snide snicker, "You pissed him off!"

"So that's why he's torturing me with this nightmare?" Chris asked.

"No." It was Gloria this time. "He did not come to you. The sight is yours."

"Your head injury from the accident, Chris," Sherry returned. At least she didn't seem to talk in riddles as much as the rest of them did. "Somehow you have tapped into your own soul. The energy doesn't hold the same boundaries as our consciousness does. It is not contained within ourselves. But we are not supposed to be consciously in touch with it. You are. From the accident."

"Lucky me," Chris said.

"ENOUGH!" thundered deep inside Chris' head. The Priest himself finally spoke. Sherry pulled her hood back over her head, her face disappearing into the shadows again.

"It is her time, Chris," he heard Sherry say. "Let her go."

"I can't do that," Chris said, responding to Sherry, but looking at the Priest.

"It is not your choice," the Priest said. "Her time is now. You cannot change her fate!"

37

Chris woke up feeling groggy and disoriented. The faces of all his dreamland guests and the information they had tried to give him were still racing through his head. Some of it made sense, but most of it was against everything he had ever believed in, or--more accurately--not believed in.

Chris rolled over, trying to gain his bearings. The large red numerals on the digital clock on his night stand next to the bed read 10:15.

A.M.? P.M.?

He remembered Carly leaving around eleven. That meant it was A.M. But that also meant he had slept almost eleven hours. Twice what he had managed in one block of time ever since he had started delivering his papers full time. Yet he still felt totally exhausted.

Then suddenly the Priest's final words hit home. *Her time is now. You cannot change her fate.*

Her time is now.

Her time is now.

Kimberly had said she was going to sleep on the other half of the bed. She wasn't there. Chris jumped off the bed.

"Kimberly?" he called out. He had slept too long. The Priest had held him in his sleep until it was too late. Panic swelled inside his stomach and exploded upward as he sprinted out of the room.

"In the kitchen," he heard her respond.

Chris ran into the kitchen. The smell of freshly cooked bacon filled the room. Kimberly was standing at the sink in front of the window cleaning the pan she had used. On the table was a plate full of bacon, a bowl of eggs, another plate with stacked toast, a bottle of orange juice and two empty glasses.

"I was just going to come in and wake you after cleaning up here," she said with a smile.

Her time is now.

What? She was going to choke to death on the bacon and eggs? Drown in the orange juice?

"You should probably close the curtains there," he said.

"Relax," she said, scrubbing the pan and dropping it into a sink full of suds. "Why don't you go get changed and I'll have breakfast ready by the time you get back."

Chris tried to relax. *Her time is now.* He walked over to the window and closed the curtains for her. Better safe than sorry.

"But it's a gorgeous day out," she protested playfully, but left them closed.

"You have to be extra careful today," Chris warned her seriously. "The dream was wild last night. I'll tell you about it over breakfast." Then finally feeling a bit more relaxed, he added, trying to smile, "Smells great by the way. Thank you very much."

"The least I could do. Now go hurry up before it starts getting cold," Kimberly said.

Chris turned and headed back to his room where he found some fresh clothes. He thought about a quick shower but didn't want to leave her alone for that long.

Her time is now.

He took off his old jeans that he had slept in and slipped into a fresh pair. Eleven hours of sleep. He couldn't believe it, but he had to pee like a race horse so he figured it must have been true.

As he stood in front of the toilet relieving himself, he heard the sirens off in the distance. He didn't pay them much attention. He shook, zipped up, took off his old shirt and grabbed the fresh one. It wasn't until he was sitting on the toilet lid fumbling with his socks that he realized the sirens were close, very close. Then as he heard the screech of tires out in the street in front of his home, the panic he had felt moments ago, that had just abated, returned tenfold.

The time is now.

"Shit!" he yelled at himself and ran once again towards the kitchen.

Carly woke up at nine, the sun shining in the window, Johnny was still sound asleep next to her, Sasha just beginning to stir in her crib across the room. Quietly she got up feeling a little stiff and with a headache sitting on the fringes of her brain right behind her eyes threatening to turn into a real boomer. She walked out into the hallway and slowly peeked around the corner into her room.

No Jerry.

At first, she felt relief, thinking his absence was a good thing, but inside she knew it could only be a bad sign. She walked past the room to the upstairs bathroom and found two *Advil* in the cabinet and took her robe off a hook. She swallowed them dry, slipped on the robe and headed for the stairs to complete her search for Jerry.

It didn't take long. She found him still sitting up on the couch, asleep or passed out, she wasn't sure which, his head hanging on his chin. Looking at the bottle of beer on its side at his feet, she assumed it was passed out. Anger replaced the nervousness she had felt descending the stairs.

"Well look what the cat dragged home," she said, loud enough to wake him from his stupor as she bent over to pick up the bottle at his feet.

He opened his eyes and glared at her. She knew she shouldn't, that she was treading on shaky ground, but she couldn't help feeling angry. Hands on her hips, as if she were getting ready to scold a child, thinking he had probably been acting like one last night, she asked, "So what the hell happened here last night?"

"It's not what happened here that matters," he said, standing up and facing her. "It's what *you* did last night that matters."

"You know what I did," she said. "I was helping a friend cope with a bad situation." Then she noticed what he held in his right hand and took a quick step backwards as he took a step towards her.

"And just how did you help this *friend*?" he asked, still moving towards her.

Carly couldn't speak, couldn't take her eyes off the gun he was holding nonchalantly, waving around a bit as he spoke now that he knew she had seen it.

"What was this *friend's* name again?" he asked. "Julie?"

"Where did you get that?" Carly asked, eyes still glued to the gun. She backed up another two steps.

"Or would her name be *Chris*?" He almost looked like he was enjoying this. "And might *she* really be a *he*?" He matched her steps slowly walking towards her.

"Yes," Carly said, unable to lie in the face of the gun, panic and fear making it even harder for her to think. "His name is Chris, but it's not what you are thinking." She never thought she'd have to use that line, but there it was. "And I *was* trying to help him out."

"Not what I think," Jerry huffed. "I saw you hugging him, you slut!" he then screamed. "I followed you to his home! It is *exactly* what I think!"

This wasn't going well. She knew there was no way it could. She had to get the gun away from him.

"Put down the gun," she tried feebly. "We can talk about this. It really isn't what you think. Really," she pleaded.

"I wasn't born yesterday, bitch!" he yelled back, spittle flying from his lips. "He's gonna pay for playing me the fool!"

She was now backed against the wall, his bloodshot eyes just inches away from her face. She could smell the stale beer on his breath as he yelled at her. She could run for the door, try to reach Nancy's house next door, call for help. But he'd grab her before she got two steps away. He'd beat her. He was probably about to do so anyway. She needed to get the gun from him. She had no choice.

Shooting out her arms, she directed one at his chest to push him away, the other swiping sideways to knock the gun from his hand. She caught him off guard, as she had hoped, but she didn't have the strength to get the job done. He grabbed the back of her head and pulled her towards him, yanking her hair so hard she screamed.

"Fucking bitch!" he yelled as he let go of her head and slapped her hard across the face. She could feel the gun in his hand at her waist and again tried to take it from him. A shot boomed out as her fingers squeezed for a grasp on it. Carly looked into her husband's angry and confused eyes. They appeared as shocked as her own were. Then she collapsed to the floor.

"Fucking bitch!" Jerry repeated as he watched his wife slump to the floor against the wall. "Goddamn you! Now look what you've done!"

Carly slid farther down, laid her head on the floor, arms over her stomach. Blood was rapidly changing the left sleeve and middle of her white robe to a bright red. She closed her eyes.

"SHIT!" Jerry screamed at her, watching her helplessly. "GODDAMN HIM! NOW HE'S SURE AS HELL GONNA FUCKING PAY!"

He left Carly where she lay and ran out the front door, still carrying the gun. Jumping into the car still parked out in the street, cursing everything and everyone he could think of, he started the car, jammed it into gear and peeled out, heading for the highway.

At about twenty after nine, Nancy had her kids dressed and eating breakfast, getting ready for a picnic. She had sandwiches made, chips were bagged and the cooler filled with ice. She was just dropping in the fruit drinks when she heard the bang. She'd never heard a gunshot before, but she'd heard a car backfire, and she instantly recognized the difference.

She ran for the front door and instinctively looked towards Carly's house. She didn't know what to do. Call the police? Run next door to see what it was? No. No need to get yourself shot, too, she decided and was about to turn for the phone to dial 911 when she saw Jerry shoot out of the house swearing madly. The front of his shirt was covered with blood. Nancy's heart skipped a few beats. She saw the gun he still held in his hand and thought her friend was surely dead.

As soon as Jerry had shut the door, before the engine even gunned, she was sprinting towards Carly's house. Jerry never saw her. He was already speeding down the street as she reached their yard.

She ran in the front door and stopped short as she saw Carly lying on the floor. Nancy had trained in first aid. It was a requirement to get a day care license in the state, though that was all she had done so far in acquiring her license as she had still not yet decided if it was something she was going to do. But she had never seen this much blood. And Carly wasn't moving.

She ran into the kitchen first and quickly dialed 911,

frantically instructing them to get an ambulance to their address as fast as possible. She had no idea where Jerry was headed and didn't even think to mention him. Carly was her only concern at the moment.

After hanging up, she returned to Carly in the den. There was so much blood. She needed to see where it was coming from and try to stop the bleeding.

"Carly," she forced out loudly, trying not to cry. "Can you hear me?"

To her surprise, Carly stirred, then opened her eyes.

"Oh, Carly!" Nancy said, the tears finally breaking through. "Where are you hurt?"

"I…don't…know," Carly managed to say, trying to lift her head and look at herself.

"Don't move," Nancy told her. "I have an ambulance coming. Where are you bleeding from?"

Carly began to sit up again despite Nancy's instruction. She looked at her bloodied robe, then at her arm. "Here," she said, pointing to her arm. Then with a feeble, exhausted laugh, she said, "He missed."

He hadn't exactly missed. Nancy worked Carly's robe off of her and found the source of the blood. The bullet had gone clean through the forearm.

Nancy ran back out to the kitchen and grabbed a dish towel and a garbage bag, the first things she saw that she could lay her hands on. She ran back out to Carly, tied the garbage bag tightly around her upper arm, and then wrapped the towel around the wound, balling up the loose ends and keeping it tight. "Hold this tight," she told her, placing Carly's good hand on the balled-up ends. "Can you?"

"Yeah," Carly said. "I think so."

Nancy ran into the bathroom and came back with a bigger

towel. She wrapped that one around the first one, pulling it as tight as she could. The blood seemed to be slowing. It had looked bad at first, but now knowing the source and seeing the damage, she knew it wasn't nearly as bad as she had first thought. Carly would be fine. As long as the damn ambulance would hurry the hell up.

"Someone's got to stop him," Carly suddenly said. "Jerry's gone after Chris."

"Oh shit!" Carly had never heard Nancy swear before. "Do you know where he lives? I'll call the police."

"Get me the phone. I'll talk to them," she said. "It's in the kitchen."

Nancy brought the phone in, dialed 911 for her and then handed it to Carly.

"This is Carly Brandt on North 46th. You have an ambulance on the way here?" she asked.

"Yes ma'am. It should be there in a few minutes."

"Well I won't be here," she surprised Nancy by saying. Send it or any closer that you have to Hickory Lane in Eagan. My husband is on his way there to shoot someone. Send the police, too. No, I don't know the exact address but they'll see him. You have to hurry. He has a gun."

Without waiting for an answer, Carly hung up the phone. "Come on," she said, obviously regaining her strength. "You're driving."

"Are you out of your mind?!" Nancy screamed in dismay. "You've been shot, Carly!"

"I'm fine. I fainted. If you won't drive me then give me your keys," Carly said as she stood up, determined to be on her way before the ambulance arrived. The EMT's would certainly forcibly restrain her and prevent her from going.

"Okay, okay," Nancy gave in. "I'll drive."

Charlotte, Carly's neighbor on the other side, was standing outside watching Carly's house. She too must have heard the shot or seen Jerry running out looking insane but hadn't been bold enough to investigate.

Nancy yelled out to her as she and Carly headed the opposite direction towards her car. "Charlotte! Round up my kids and Carly's, will ya? Take them to my place and watch them 'til we get back. It's an emergency!"

Charlotte just waved okay and quickly started across the yard, willing to help, but unwilling to ask what was going on. She must have seen Jerry leaving or she probably wouldn't have entered Carly's house.

Carly and Nancy jumped into Nancy's car and Nancy started up the engine, backed out of the driveway and, remembering Carly's quick chat with 911, asked, "Eagan?"

Carly nodded and, still pressing tightly on the knotted towels around her forearm, directed the way.

Jerry sped straight to the house he had followed Carly to the night before. His vision was blurred from his own tears for Carly. He hadn't meant to shoot her. Sure, he had thought about roughing her up a bit, but the gun was for Chris. And even then, he had had no intentions of shooting Chris. He had only wanted to scare the hell out of him. Make him sweat. Make him swear he'd never go near his wife again.

Now those plans had changed. Carly may very well be dead, and Chris was going to pay. Now, as he sped off the freeway into the quiet Eagan neighborhood, just a few blocks from Chris' home, he had every intention of shooting Chris. Now he had every intention of killing the wife-fucking bastard. Now he was *really* going to pay.

Jerry heard sirens nearing. He paid them no attention. He had a debt to pay and nothing was going to stop him. He pulled to a stop at the curb across the street, in front of Chris' house. He saw the kitchen curtains pull shut just as he was getting out of the car and began walking towards the house. The sirens drew closer. He knew they'd be on top of him at any minute.

"I see you, you fucker," he said to himself, looking at the shadow behind the curtain.

He'd never shot a gun before. He knew he'd only have the one chance. The sirens were very loud. He kneeled down in the middle of the yard. Slowly, he aimed the gun at the window. Tears poured from his eyes as he thought of Carly, of what this bastard had made him do to her. He wiped his eyes with one hand trying to make his vision clear, his aim precise. The sirens were here. He heard car doors opening and slamming shut. He didn't turn his head.

"Drop your weapon!"

Jerry heard the officer's call. He didn't move. He looked at the shadow in the window.

"Drop your fucking weapon now!" the officer yelled again.

Only seconds passed, but it felt like an eternity to Jerry. He knew if he did as the officer ordered, he would be immediately cuffed, arrested, thrown in jail, and would probably stay there for life for the murder of his wife. There's no way they would understand it was a mistake. And Chris, the wife-fucking bastard, would get away with it.

But he also knew in that same instant, without even looking around, what would happen if he pulled the trigger.

He had the bastard in his sights.

"I'm not going to fucking prison," he said softly to himself as he calmly steadied his hand. "You fucking bastard."

Jerry squeezed off three shots at the shadow in the kitchen

window as fast as he could before he heard, more than felt, an explosion behind him. He knew he was done. He knew what the explosion had been. He was surprised that he was feeling no pain. Jerry dropped his gun, laid down, closed his eyes, and had just enough time to hope he hadn't missed before he died from the eight gunshots that had just riddled his body.

Just as the shots were fired, Chris reached a confused Kimberly standing at the window. Just as he grabbed for her, putting himself between her and the window, hugging her tightly against his body, he felt twenty wasps sting him in the back in the same place at the same time. Then his head was suddenly pounding. He heard the explosion of a multitude of bullets all being fired at once, then a moment of silence.

The silence was immediately broken by Kimberly screaming. He looked at her. Blood covered half her face and ran down her neck. Her blood? His blood? He wasn't sure. She screamed again. A piercing scream that filled his throbbing head. Then he realized that was a good scream. A wonderful scream. Because he couldn't have screamed if he'd wanted to.

Chris collapsed to the floor, still holding Kimberly in a bear hug, dragging her to the floor with him. Everything wavered, turned a tint of red as his blood ran into his eyes, and then went dark.

Chris felt hands all over him, pushing him, probing him, hurting him. The pain was immense. He hurt everywhere. His head throbbed to the beat of his heart. He opened his eyes and saw two men in white working frantically beside him. He heard one of them ask him something, but he couldn't make out what the question was. Then over the shoulder of one of the men he saw Carly's face. Tear streaked and bloody, but a welcome sight.

"Carly," he managed to say, trying to reach out to her, but unable to move his arm which was strapped to some kind of stretcher. "Kimberly…is she…"

"Right here," Carly said as she moved a little to the right.

Chris saw Kimberly peek over Carly's shoulder. "I'm okay," she assured him.

Chris slowly rolled his eyes back towards Carly and a huge grin spread across his face. "I did it, Carly," he struggled to say. "I beat him…again."

Carly couldn't help but give him a smile in return, though it was accompanied by a flood of tears. "Yes," she said sniffling, "You did it, Chris."

"I did it," he said again out loud to himself. Now he could rest. Now he could finally get some real sleep. Still smiling, Chris closed his eyes. "I did it."

Epilogue

"How's the arm today?" Kimberly asked Carly.

"I think it's almost good as new," Carly told her new best friend. She pulled the arm out of the sling and shook it a little as if that proved it. "I probably won't be needing your services anymore, though I hope that doesn't mean you'll stop coming by."

Ever since Carly had gotten home from the hospital a few days after the fateful morning of the shooting, Kimberly, now Aunt Kim to Johnny and Sasha, had come to Carly's house to help with laundry, cooking, driving, shopping and keeping up with the kids. She actually moved in with Carly at first and stayed with her for a week until she was able to start managing most of it by herself. Lately Kimberly had just been coming by for a couple of hours a day to help with a few things that were still difficult to do one-handed.

"You can't get rid of me that easily," Kimberly said with a smile. "You gonna go see Chris today?"

"Yep. He gets to go home as soon as I get there," Carly said. "He asked me to drive him home."

"How do his parents feel about that?"

"They headed back to Seattle yesterday when the doctor said he was going home today," Carly told her.

"Bet he's excited to go home after two months of hospital food," Kimberly said.

"Why don't you come with me?" Carly offered.

"Okay. I can do that," she said. "But I can't stay long. I have an appointment this afternoon with my editor."

"Cool," Carly said. "Nancy said she'd watch the kids. Let me take them over and I'll be ready. I'll meet you in the parking lot."

Chris had been hit twice as Jerry took his last breath. The first shot had entered his back on the right, just missing his lung. The second had just missed his brain but had managed to fracture the left side of his skull. The third shot had been dug out of his front door, thirty feet to the left of the kitchen window.

It took three surgeries to get him out of the woods, one to remove the first bullet from his chest area, two more to repair the skull damage where he now had a steel plate replacing a small portion of it. And even then, he hadn't fully regained his consciousness until two and a half weeks after the surgeries. All in all, the doctor told him he had been very lucky.

His parents had flown in from Seattle the same evening that he had been brought to the emergency room. Kimberly had driven Carly down to visit him every day for a few hours until Carly started driving herself, shortly after he had become coherent again. Chris had told Carly while they were getting to know each other online that his parents knew nothing about the dreams or even about his new job. During the time that Chris was still recouping from the surgeries and was heavily sedated, Carly had the unenviable task of filling them in on most of what had been going on. She told them almost everything, tried to answer their endless questions, tried to assure them that he merely didn't want them worrying. There really was nothing they could have done to help. She never mentioned the Priest. And neither did Chris when his turn came to explain the past seven months to them.

The three of them, Chris, Carly and Kimberly, had largely avoided the subject of the dreams and even the events of the tragic day during their visits together at the hospital. They were just very glad it was all over. Now was a time of healing and of new beginnings.

Carly found Kimberly waiting at the front door of the hospital and the two of them headed up to the third floor that Chris had called home for the past two months. They found Chris in his room sitting in a wheelchair, still in a hospital gown, smiling broadly in anticipation of his release.

"Hi, Kim. Carly," he said cheerily as they walked in his open door. "I couldn't think of two more lovely chauffeurs to drive me home if I tried."

"Well, actually Carly is going to drive you home," Kimberly said. "I just stopped by to say hi. I have to go see my editor in a bit here."

"I had a dream about you," Chris said seriously, looking at Kimberly.

Kimberly's heart skipped a beat. "You did?" she asked hesitantly.

"Yeah," Chris said, readopting the smile he had when they walked in. "You were on some talk show doing an interview about your latest book."

"Oh god, you scared me for a second there," Kimberly said with exaggerated relief. "That wasn't funny." But the smile on her face told him she'd get over it rather quickly.

"As long as we're on the subject," Carly said, "how is your slumber land going these days?"

"Been sleeping like a baby," Chris said. "Haven't been to a graveyard ever since I got this metal plate put in my head. Should have thought of that months ago," he said with a snicker.

"Well, I for one am glad you didn't," Kimberly said.

"I don't know," Chris said. "If I hadn't insisted you come stay with me so I could watch over you, then you'd never have been put in harm's way to begin with. I just about got you killed."

"I disagree," Kimberly said. "Carly and I have been talking about this a bit. I think that Priest character had been playing with you, with all of us. He'd been manipulating us, leading up to that day for quite some time."

"I was showing her how I happened to find you on the Internet," Carly told him. "You know, how I put the word 'fate' in the profile search." She paused. "Seventy-six names appeared as people in the Twin Cities with the word 'fate' somewhere in their profile, including yours. Thirty-two of them were currently online. But when I had done it that first time, yours had been the only one offered."

"I think had you not found me," Kimberly continued, "had you not taken me to your place, had you never seen me in your dream, then some other fate would have befallen me like Benjamin or the others and you wouldn't have been there to save me." She leaned in and gave him a kiss on the forehead. Then she said seriously, locking her eyes to his, "You saved my life, Chris. I am convinced of that beyond the shadow of a doubt. I will be forever grateful."

"Well, you are quite welcome then," Chris said with a blush. "I'm just glad it's over."

"I second that," Carly said, raising her bandaged arm as best she could.

"Well, I better get going," Kimberly said. "And I'm sure you are anxious to be doing so, too. Just wanted to congratulate you on your release. I'll see you two later."

Carly and Chris both said good-bye as Kimberly turned and headed out the door for her appointment.

"So," Carly said, after Kimberly had left, "was I in that dream you had, too?"

Chris smiled. "You sure were," he said, rubbing the back of his neck. "You were standing behind me massaging this crick out of my neck."

Carly moved behind him and started massaging the place he had indicated just above his shoulders. “Like this?” she asked.

“Oh yeah,” Chris moaned. “You are a dream come true.”

Carly laughed, then leaned in and whispered into his ear from behind him, “So are you ready to bust outta here?”

“Sure am,” he said. “But I need to change out of this gown and into some real clothes and pack. Meet you in fifteen minutes at the elevator.”

Carly stopped massaging his neck and came around the wheelchair and faced him, hands on the arms of the chair, her nose inches from his. Softly, she said, “Actually, I was hoping to meet you at a different time.” Chris opened his mouth to ask when would be good for her, but she placed two fingers gently over his lips, stopping the question before it began, and continued softly, “and a different place.”

Chris smiled. “I think we can arrange that.”

Lightning Source UK Ltd.
Milton Keynes UK
UKHW022129070722
405551UK00009B/193/J

9 781977 239600